DEAR CLAUDIA
THANK
(handwritten inscription)

AMERICUS

A NOVEL

MICHAEL DATCHER

Third World Press Foundation
Chicago

Third World Press Foundation
Publishers since 1967
Chicago
© Copyright 2018 Third World Press Foundation

Printed in the United States of America
ISBN: 978-0-88378-405-1
Library of Congress number on file
22 21 20 19 18   6 5 4 3 2 1

Cover art by Francisco Letelier
Interior design by Denise Borel Billups

Advance Praise for AMERICUS

"In AMERICUS, Michael Datcher expertly captures the painful lyricism of sharing a bloodline. Asar and Set epitomize Yin-Yang—the oneness of opposing forces. The twin brothers are back-to-back and skin-to-skin. Yet, the bitterness of birthright, first chances, and missed patriarchal nods tear them apart while holding them together. Datcher explores the familial and human spectrum with eloquence, symmetry, and a glimmer of hope while we follow the Americus Family into hell's belly."

—JENOYNE ADAMS
National Bestselling author of
Resurrecting Mingus & Selah's Bed

"Michael Datcher's first novel triumphs as myth, history, social critique, and family story. AMERICUS simultaneously attracts and repels with the beauty and pain of a literary blues song. The poetry of his language and the strange familiarity of his characters will compel his readers to bear witness to the unraveling of a promising young African American family and the failure of the American promise. Living through the awful failure of personal and social love, readers cling to the hope of renewal. AMERICUS is an experience and revelation not to be missed."

—DAVID KILLORAN
Professor of English, Emeritus,
Loyola Marymount University

1

SATURDAY, JUNE 10, 1893
EAST ST. LOUIS, ILLINOIS

Set knew he could never disrespect his father, but his twin brother was fair game. Being born seven minutes behind Asar had taught Set the bad math of birth order. Taught him that it was wrong. He knew his life could've been different had his mother's egg not been divided by two. Had he kicked and wiggled enough to slide his head out first. Had Asar died in the womb. Set wished his brother no harm, usually. But sometimes slippery thoughts grew inside of him when he looked at the boy who had the same part running down the center of his scalp. The boy who always got to play the best part as the first-born son. Set tried to wrassle down an ugly thought as he stared at Asar standing next to their father. But the image in his mind was too slimy to be stopped. Too strong. Dead wrong.

At seven a.m. sharp, Keb handed the map scroll to Asar. Though Set knew well the familial protocol, he shut his eyes to protest the hand-off from father to first-born. Asar ignored Set's blind fit. Instead, he dropped to his knees as if he weren't wearing his Stern Brothers brown suit pants, with the matching vest and jacket. Using both palms, Asar unrolled the scroll across the manicured bluegrass lawn. The map was long as he was tall. His father's meticulous script was the only thing he recognized.

Asar knew this was no map of the circular backyard. No round fountain in the center. No Specialty Shed along the curving back wall of red rose bushes. And most obvious: no 33 round tombstones forming a circle.

Eyes wide as a Morgan Dollar, Asar looked up into his father's smiling hazel irises. His mother's frown went unnoticed as she gazed out at them from the kitchen window. Asar wanted to throw a roundhouse to Set's calf. Instead, he reached out and pinched hard his brother's thigh.

"Stop playing blind and get down here."

Set refused to flinch or open his eyes, but he did buckle down to his own brown-suited knees next to his big brother. Asar jabbed his index finger onto a perfectly drawn red X.

"Our presents are buried on Bloody Island."

2

Keb Americus had been burying his sons' birthday presents since they were five-years-old. It allowed him to combine his love of map-making and man-making. He inherited his own father's skill with maps, but was determined to shake the patriarch's crude child-rearing approach—and shake off its effects. A slow process: Keb still had the self-conscious look of a critical father's only child. Just beneath seamless skin was a puzzle face with pieces jammed to fit.

Keb had learned—from experience—that tough love without hugs, playful rides on knees and tender forehead kisses wasn't tough love, it was just tough. That's why it made Keb feel like such good daddy last week when the twin's big rusty butts tumbled into the library and asked to test his bucking bronco knees. A rambling ride that he enjoyed more than his boys.

Keb had long decided that the twin's 10th birthdays would officially start their rites of passage into manhood. His own father had always told him that ten was a number of perfection. When Keb's wife, Nutilda, went into labor on Sunday, June 10th, 1883, he knew there was going to be something special about his child. What Keb didn't know was that the specialness would come in twos. From the day baby-faced Dr. Nathaniel Mandrake handed the twins from exhausted wife to elated father, Keb Americus began plotting how to build his little boys into perfect men.

Asar and Set leaned down close to study the intricately detailed map of East St. Louis. Set traced his index finger along Bond Avenue until he reached 10th Street. His brother gave him a knowing nod. Home.

Keb dropped to one knee to address the twins. His almond-shaped eyes were moist.

"Which direction is west?"

Without raising their own almond-shaped eyes, both boys pointed towards the rose bush-lined back fence.

"How can you be sure?"

"Because the sun always comes up in the east, so west must be in the opposite direction," Set said.

"Good," Keb said, gently placing his hand on Set's cheek. "Remember, as long as you always know one of the four directions, you'll always know the others. Now run inside and get your gifts from last year and I'll send you off."

From the kitchen window, Nutilda used both hands to part the curtain of wavy black hair draping her buttermilk face. A face that embodied the agitated curiosity of the smart girl searching for interesting questions, while others were content with convenient answers. Nutilda watched the twins skip towards the house. When she met them at the kitchen door, Nutilda sucked the frown into her reckless eyeballs.

"Mama, Mama, Mama," they said, forcing a smile on her face.

"I know, Mama knows. Now run along like your father told you and get your compasses."

Indeed, Nutilda did know. Keb usually shared his plans with his wife—in infinite detail. Sometimes to get her opinion—rarely to get her approval. An approach that kept a fire under most discussions about rearing their sons.

Nutilda remained at the kitchen door surveying the circular backyard. The thick band of roses that caressed the 10-foot-high pine wooden fence was an extension of her wedding ring. All fragrance and passion and thorns. Downwind from the National Stock Yards that kept much of East St. Louis immersed in a potpourri of death, hundreds of red petals defended the backyard with airborne rose oil. The aromatic backyard helped with the throbbing headaches Nutilda had been suffering from since childhood. The 26 train lines criss-crossing the country's 2nd busiest transit system were not helping. Illinois Central Rail Road. St. Louis & Ohio Rail Road. Chicago & Alton Rail Road. Steel wheels rumbling on steel rails. Steel wheels braking and screeching on steel rails. A riot of train whistles screaming steam. When she first married Keb, Nutilda would sit on the edge of the Americus Fountain, feet in the water, eyes closed, and breathe in all the blooming red oil around her. With each inhalation, she liked to imagine the petals wafting closer and closer to her flaring nostrils. Brushing across her cookie dough cheeks. Lodging in her ears. Seducing the pain from her throbbing temples. Not the only seduction witnessed by those roses. Many an argument had been laid to rest atop a bed of plucked red petals.

Nutilda stormed out the kitchen's back door and stomped towards the Americus Fountain. The sienna tea gown hugging her waist flared out over her quick moving ankles. Keb was still crouched over the map, awaiting the twin's return.

Not every husband could have heard their wife's small bare feet high-stepping across a thick carpet of bluegrass, but Keb did. He expected it.

Nutilda Americus was the kind of woman who took things to the end of the line. The boys had yet to leave the property, so the end of the line had yet to be reached. Keb knew his wife would have to try one last time to change his mind.

Lips pursed like a short-tempered nun about to break a vow of silence, Nutilda stood over her husband and his goddamn map. Keb's eyes shifted from map to sienna tea gown with embroidered monarch butterflies on the flowing fringe. Peeking beneath the fringe: a small-boned, high-arched foot that could've belonged to a 12-year-old Cake Walk Champion. Keb knew each individual toe so intimately. Over a decade of placing them phalange by phalange into his mouth. His tongue knew the knuckle-hump of his wife's petite big-toe. His lips could calculate the angle of her curving pinkie-toe. Nutilda squatted face-to-face with Keb's half-lidded, hazel eyes and lump-of-coal nose. East St. Louis on the grass between them.

She leaned in. Her reckless eyeballs redirected to opposite corners like gentlemen prize fighters.

"Keb, you know this town better than I do."

Nutilda's hard whisper sent spittle onto the short lapels of his black silk sack suit.

"Bloody Island?" she continued. "You know what goes on there. You should be out here having this talk with yourself."

Keb leaned back. Examined Nutilda's Dakota Indian cheekbones. The buttermilk that covered them. The lips spitting on him: two fleshy wedges of pink grapefruit. And those carnival freak eyes. The opposite of crossed-eyes. If it were not for some dramatic flaw in such an alluring high-yellow face, Keb still wondered, at times, whether she would've agreed to marry a man with onyx skin. *Light is right* usually trumped colored money.

"Say something," she said.

"Nut, I've already said what I've planned to do and ..."

"These are my sons too and 10 is too young to be putting them in danger. You can't let them go across all those rail tracks, way out to Bloody Island."

"This will help them learn ..."

"Why don't you just trail behind them. Don't send my babies out there to have their little heads crushed under a train."

"Stop being ridiculous Nut."

"They *could die* out there."

"Who died?" Set said.

From the kitchen door, his big-boned, athletic body came bounding across the bluegrass. He yelled over his shoulder, "Asar, we have a new body coming in. Daddy don't start until we get back, okay?"

Nutilda stood, avoided the twin's faces, and marched back towards the kitchen. At the door, she spun around, giving flight to monarch butterflies on the dress' fringe. Reckless eyeballs found her husband. His eyes were cast down upon East St. Louis. Index finger imagining a course for his sons.

As Asar and Set nestled beside him on their knees, Keb avoided almond eyes. He didn't want them to see the emotion welling in his own pair. Keb had waited a decade to send the boys on this journey. He hoped they would return with the gift that would initiate them into young manhood—even if they didn't understand the gift—or what the gift bestowed.

3

Keb stood between his two sons on the 40 by 30 foot front porch. Locomotives in sight. Black plumes rose and followed cabooses like combustible kites. Trains rambled and whistled across the flat landscape, rumbling the wood boards beneath six black Oxford brogues.

Keb had a languid arm draped over each twin's suit jacket shoulder. A wooden sign hung above their heads from the eaves:

AMERICUS & SON FUNERAL HOME

The three could have been posing for an advertising photograph for their family business. Father in a Stern Brothers black silk sack-suit with silk-covered buttons, black vest, and an ascot tie around the high-collar white shirt. Formerly nappy hair, deeply greased, aggressively brushed and smoothed in opposite directions away from an inch-wide part running down the center of his head. The skin on his scalp was coal black. High cheekbones resting on an angular anvil face.

The twins in their matching, waist-level, brown linen suit jackets with four stylish pleats running the length of each breast. Casually opened to reveal a five-button brown vest, atop a crisp, high-collar white shirt. Black bow tie. Brown pants with three buttons positioned on the outside of each knee. Johnston & Murphy black Oxford brogues. Greased hair brushed and parted down the center, but wavier and running past their ears, courtesy of their half-Dakota mother. Shiny skin, black as their father.

Keb loved that his boys inherited his complexion and not their mother's buttermilk tone. During last summer's heat wave, as they all lay shirtless on their backs in the backyard, he had explained, "The more sunshine grows on your body, the more God trusts you with the power that makes food grow out the ground." Asar had raised his naked onyx arms to the sky and smiled.

Here, on the expansive porch, they were a picture of relaxed confidence. Gravitas. The kind of people you'd entrust with your dearly departed.

It was not just their natty attire that could sell a thousand caskets, it was the expression on their faces. Especially the twin's faces. An expression they had learned from close study of the man standing between them.

Their inherited almond-shaped, hazel eyes were half-lidded and serious as death. Their mother's grapefruit-wedge lips, suggesting a smirk. Chins up. Lump-of-coal noses and high foreheads cocked at an angle that could get a Negro man—or 10-year-old Negro boy—lynched on the other side of the Mississippi River. An explosive picture when fused to dark skin because it proclaimed, *I can do anything.*

This very home that Keb had grew up in doubled as a place of business. As a child, he had spent many hours on the same porch, peering west towards the Mississippi River. Coal-smelling smoke settling above the city like a horizontal veil. The airborne, fine coal-dust made spitting a necessary part of inhaling.

As a 12-year-old, Keb stood alone on the porch that he now shared with his sons and watched the construction of the mighty Eads Bridge. It was his after school ritual. He'd climb the Americus & Son steps and stop on the porch to see if he could notice any change in the bridge from the day before. Witnessing its gradual growth made the bridge seem alive. Like his pet lizard, Booker, whose tail his father forced him to chop off with a meat cleaver.

Without explaining why.

Lizards can teach without words.

The tail grew back. Segment by segment. Similar to steel slowly growing across the Mississippi. Connecting St. Louis to the land where St. Louis shed its skin. And blood.

Years later, Keb shared the same experience with his twins, standing on the porch watching the Free Bridge, three miles north of the Eads, complete its middle passage.

Now, the 6 foot 5 mortician looked down to his left and right; he examined the parts running the center of his sons' tender scalps. He wanted to say, "Be careful," but didn't because he'd already trained them to do so. He turned his head south to the Free Bridge, and said, "If you can't locate and return with your gifts by 6 p.m., you forfeit them."

Keb removed his arms from the twin's shoulders and walked into Americus & Son; the twins turned to each other, smiling hard.

Set snatched the telescope sticking out his back pocket and swung it up to his squinting eye with dramatic flair. He moved like an underage, ambitious, shipmate. One who thought he was ready to lead, but blamed his superiors for not being ready to follow. After a pregnant pause that only a real pirate would know to use, Set tromboned the telescope tube to its full 28 inches. Through the watercolor gray-sky, he began to survey the rail yards that dominated the waterfront. He enunciated the initials on the side of boxcars.

"P. A. R. R. ... B. & O. R. R. ... N. Y. C. & ST. L. R. R."

Set shifted his sights north until the National Stock Yards came into view. Through the cylinder, the livestock pens looked like neat rows of matches on the 656-acre stock yards. He couldn't see the thousands of sheep, pigs, and cows waiting to be killed.

"ARMOUR & COMPANY."

On a four-story brick building, long as a 100-yard foot race, the name was written in block letters the size of shot-gun houses. Set had heard his father speak with Grandpa Nema about the meatpacking company—and the men who worked there: men who killed for a living.

That must be the best job in the whole wide world, Set thought.

He had never witnessed the killing of a large animal. His family always got the bodies after they were already dead and boring. Set wanted to see the look in a sheep's big eyes when the animal knew it was just about to get it. Place his hands in the gooey redness.

Experience the feeling of blood when it was still warm.

"Let's go north up 10th Street then west on St. Clair until we reach the riverfront," Set said. He squashed the telescope between his open palms.

"That's not the fastest way," Asar said, irritation in the quick steps he took towards his little brother. Asar carried himself like a boy who'd been baby-sitting since he'd been five-years-old, but wanted someone to baby-sit him. Asar awkwardly embraced premature responsibilities because his father told him he was good at being responsible.

"I'm not gonna risk forfeiting my gift messing around with you," Asar continued. "I've got the map so are you coming with me on the fastest way or ..."

"We have all day, let's go exploring and have some fun," Set said. He began to spin in a circle with his brown jacketed-arms extended. Asar, map scroll tucked under arm, stared at the spinning top until he came to a stop.

"We'll get enough exploring as we hunt for our presents. Anyways, you know Daddy wants us to be careful."

"It's not Daddy's birthday, it's ours. And don't tell me what Daddy wants. What do you want?"

"To be careful."

Set swung his left leg like he was kicking a pebble off the porch.

"Do you wanna have fun or not?"

In the split-second of Asar's indecision, Set pulled the Morgan Dollar from his vest pocket.

"Flip."

"Let's use mine."

Asar pulled his silver dollar from his vest pocket. "Call it."

Asar flipped his dollar high into the air beyond the porch stairs.

"Heads," Set said.

The boys hopped down three steps at a time, before becoming human hot air balloons over the last dozen wooden rectangles. The dollar bounced and rolled. The twins followed.

In a scrambling crawl, they raced towards the coin.

"Heads!" Set yelled.

He jumped to his feet, and pulled his brother up after him. "Let's have some fun."

The mirror images in brown took off running north up 10th Street with wind racing through the inch-wide parts cooling their scalps.

I   I   I

The rail-scarred industrial city was still cranking awake. And cranky. The twins were accustomed to attracting cranky Yugoslav, Hungarian, Pole, and Czech hard looks when they were out in public with their father. He'd always taught them to stare back.

"These gibberish-talking bohunks come to our country and treat us like they're the Americans and we're the foreigners. Stare back like you were born here," Keb would tell them.

They approached another ogling Yugoslav. He was wearing too big, heavy-cotton blue coveralls cuffed widely over his boots. He passed them in the opposite direction looking down his cauliflower nose at the brown-suited Negro boys with dirty knees and dusty jacket elbows. And the uppity little nigglets cocked their heads and stared back.

The ritual continued up 10th Street past the library and St. Mary's Hospital. The twins turned it into a game. They would return the hard looks then quick-draw their telescopes to squinting eyes and intone, "Peek-A-Boooo."

Emphasis on the "Boooo."

The Americus Boys, bursting into laughter, would take off running until their next stare-down.

As the twins approached St. Clair, Set turned to his brother.

"We should stop by Bogdan's store and see if he wants to come with us."

"That's why you wanted to go way up to St. Clair Ave. You … ."

"No it wasn't! The idea just popped in my big brain just now," Set said.

"Why you always wanna hang out with Boggy Doggy, anyway?"

"I don't *always* wanna hang out with Bogdan. It's only when I wanna hang with someone who's not a Mr. Scare D. Cat like you."

"Yeah, right. It's like you got a crush on ol Boggy Bow Wow. I thought you were supposed to be sweet on that Alllllllset girl," Asar said.

"I can't help it if Auset is sweet on me, and you're just bringing her up—again—because you're mad that she ain't sweet on you. Now, we're gonna go see Bogdan because we've already flipped for it, and "heads" decided we're gonna go have some fun. And here's some more heads for you," Set said, as he slapped the back of Asar's skull. He started running up 10th towards St. Clair with Asar giving chase.

I   I   I

Bogdan Dabrowski's family owned a meat market on St. Clair near the Polish part of town, downwind from the St. Louis National Stock Yards. Sometimes the twin's father would take them there to buy the Kielbasa sausages that they loved so much. Last year, they stopped at Dabrowski & Son Meats for the first time because neatly packed Blutwurst and Kielbasa sausages hung from the picture window in a perfectly straight line. When they had walked into the market, Keb was immediately struck by two things: the cleanliness and the boy about the twin's age standing behind the meat-filled glass counter in a spotless white smock—with a pencil behind his ear.

"How can I help you fine sirs?" he'd said, in the confident voice of one of those street kids who worked as carnival hawkers. Keb chuckled. The twins had looked at each other and broke out into broad grins.

But the boy butcher had the biggest smile in the room. And the most hair. His oiled, jet black, mane was combed straight back, hanging an inch above his shoulders. His pale face made the blood flowing beneath his dimpled cheeks look like faintly applied rouge. This all framed by a smile that made customers feel good about spending their hard-earned money with Dabrowski & Son Meats.

On their initial visit, when the twins and their father had approached the counter, they could see the 2 by 2 foot wooden crate Bogdan was standing on.

"You're probably the son in Dabrowski & Son, but you handle yourself like you're the Dabrowski in Dabrowski & Son," Keb had said with a tinge of sadness in his voice. Bogdan handled himself like an obedient son. A son who knew his loving father had already created his life-map without his input.

"Thank you, sir, but that job is already taken by a man who won't be quick to give it up. Now, what'll it be, sir? We've got the biggest steaks for the smallest price on St. Clair, and sausages so good you'll float on air, and whatever you fancy, we'll weigh it on a scale that's fair!"

"How'd you learn to talk like that?" Set blurted out.

"By needing the good business of fine sirs like yourself. Now, what'll it be, something from the hog or something from the heifer?" After leaving the market with their six pounds of Kielbasa, though they had only planned on buying three, Set had looked up to Keb and said, "Daddy, we should always buy our sausage from that place."

"You might be on to something, son."

I I I

Asar finally caught up to Set at the corner of 10th and St. Clair, then returned the slap to the back of his head—and tried to sneak in a second one.

"Okay, okay, okay, we're Even Steven, Even Steven, cut it out," Set said. The twins turned right on St. Clair. They stopped jostling. Stopped walking.

The hard dirt street was filled with scores and scores of grim men. A human cattle drive. Many carrying brown paper bags. Some talked in gibberish among themselves. Others walked alone in silence. Eyes straight ahead. Almost all walking westward. A direction that the sullen faces among them seemed to resent.

A B & O train rumbled by, parting the men to opposite sides of the street.

The twins shifted to the sidewalk and scampered the two blocks into Dabrowski & Son.

"Hi, Mr. Dabrowski!" Set shouted.

"What this, stick em up? Even with dirt elbow and knee, you two look sharp, sharp. You going to cut me to pieces with those vests and take all my sausages?" Sacha Dabrowski said in his bass voice. He started walking from behind the glass meat counter. His left leg was almost two inches shorter than his right one, so his body hiccupped towards the twins.

"Can Bogdan come treasure hunting with us today?" Set asked.

"Well, if there treasure to be found, why you not ask me to join you? I can out treasure hunt my son any day!"

When Mr. Dabrowski leaned his 6'2" body down to shake their hands, Set could see the tear-drop blood-stain on the white smock's left breast. The only blemish on a garment that covered Sacha Dabrowski from neck to knees.

"Mr. Dabrowski, no grown-ups allowed! It's our birthday and … ."

"Hi, Set!" Bogdan yelped, coming out of the door behind the counter. He was wearing a smaller version of his father's white smock, except his was blood free.

"Son, Americus twins have birthday today, but their extra year doesn't give them wisdom to know that Sacha Dabrowski find treasure with eyes closed."

"It's your birthday right now? Hi, Asar. Is there going to be babka cake like we had on my nameday?"

"No, something better," Set said. "Daddy always buries our birthday presents in the backyard and gives us a map so we can go find them like pirates. But this morning, we unrolled the map and it said our presents are buried on Bloody Island!"

Set grabbed the map from under Asar's arm, dropped to his knees and unrolled the hemp scroll across the floor. A June bug crawled across the Eads Bridge; Set scooped up the green beetle and slid it in his pocket.

"Right here where this red "X" is. We want you to come with us and help find our treasure."

"Papa, Papa, can I go, can I go? I'll come right back and do all my chores quick and on the double, and I promise to be good for a whole month straight. Please let me go, Papa, please."

Mr. Dabrowski looked down at the map. At the blood red X. His playful grin faded.

"Mr. Americus come with you?"

"No, sir. Daddy said that we're young men now and that's why he's letting us go by ourselves," Asar said.

"We are young men and so is Bogdan. Please let him go, Mr. Dabrowski," Set said, looking up from the map into Mr. Dabrowski's stern face.

"Bloody Island no place for boys. Even big boys who young men. I'm disappointed your father let you go there alone. Not right. Place not safe for some grown men."

The severe tone of Mr. Dabrowski's voice made Set slowly roll up the map and stand next to his brother. Set pocketed his left hand and squeezed the writhing, crunchy June bug between his thumb and forefinger, until he could feel the wetness ooze over his thumbnail.

"Mr. Dabrowski, my father knows what he's doing," Asar said in his grown up voice. "If it wasn't safe enough for us, he wouldn't allow us to go and I don't think he'd like hearing you talk like you know what's better for us than him."

"That may be true young man, but Bloody Island too dangerous for my son. He can't go."

Bogdan dropped his head. Mr. Dabrowski turned around and hiccupped towards the door behind the meat counter. Set pinched his nose and stuck out his tongue at Bogdan's father. He tapped his friend's hand. Bogdan looked up. Set mouthed, "Next year." Bogdan nodded and dropped his head again. Mr. Dabrowski returned from the backroom and stood in front of Set and Asar. He opened his nicked and cut long fingers to reveal two silver dollars.

"Happy birthday boys."

"Thank you Mr. Dabrowski!" the twins shouted in unison.

He gave them the silver coins, then placed a hand on each of their shoulders.

"Be careful."

I   I   I

The twins left Dabrowski & Son Meats feeling like bonafide young pirate men. They had stood their ground—and added silver to their birthday booty. As they started walking west on St. Clair, they joined the throng of slaughterhouse men crowding the street on their way to work.

"It's stinky," Set said.

"Stinky inky," Asar corrected.

The grayish-brown-tinted air was scented with a mixture of sooty coal, hide-less cows, bone bits, big gobs of fat, leftover sheep meat and pig intestines. Asar fought the urge to cover his mouth and nose. He glared at Set when his little brother moved his hand mouth-ward. If the ogling immigrants could take the smell of death, so could they.

As the boys approached the entrance of the Stock Yards on the corner of 1st Street & St. Clair, men seemed to be streaming in from every direction. And not just the gibberish speakers. Many of the men spoke good English. A few were even Negroes. Whatever their language or color, almost all of them headed under the same arched gate with the arched lettering that Set looked up and read aloud:

"St. Louis National Stock Yards." Asar looked up too.

"I wonder why it's not called East St. Louis National Stock Yards?" Set said.

"You know how Daddy always says no one who lives here owns anything—but us. I betchu the owner lives across the river," Asar said.

"Make money here, spend it over there."

Set started walking under the gate. Asar grabbed his arm.

"What?"

"You don't work here," Asar said.

"I'm a pirate explorer. Explorers can go anywhere. Come on. We already flipped and my heads said fun."

"What if someone stops us?"

"We'll tell em Daddy forgot something at home."

"I'm not gonna tell a lie Set."

"I'll tell it."

Set grabbed his brother by the wrist and pulled him through the arched gate, joining the crush of men. They all walked towards the bleating sheep. Towards stinky inky death.

Pens that looked liked matchsticks through Set's telescope were really filled with thousands of mooing cows, snorting pigs, and wonderfully vulnerable bleating sheep. The sheep stood out to Set because they seemed to bleat with more urgency and frequency.

The animals were separated by type, and fenced into crowded wooden pens 25-yards wide and 50-yards long. Flat wooden elevated walkways ran the length of each pen. A man in a dark suit and derby stood on a distant rail looking over a pen of cows.

The mixture of hundreds of animal sounds unsettled Asar. It reminded him of being in the Christ Our Savior nursery. In the basement of the church, where the nursery was located, infant babies would start to cry, setting off a spectacular crying contest.

It was still early in the yards. Workers entering through the main gate walked straight towards the huge building with "ARMOUR & COMPANY" across the top. The outdoor pens were mostly unmanned.

"I guess it doesn't take too many men to watch over sheep, since they've got their own big ol eyes," Set said.

Asar was quiet. Tense.

"Maybe we should pet one?" Set said, smiling. Asar's body jerked towards his brother.

"No, Set."

"You are more scare-dee than these stinky inky sheep and they're about to get kilt," Set said, drawing his forefinger across his throat. "No one's even watching us."

"If you climb that fence I swear-to-God I will sock you right in the bee-hind."

"I'm not gonna climb it Mr. Scare D. Cat. I'm just gonna stick my hand though and pet one."

Before Asar could come up with a good reply, Set stuck his whole left arm into the pen, and began doing his sheep call.

"Sh-ee-ee-ee-peee, sh-ee-ee-ee-peee, sh-ee-ee-ee-peee."

Asar looked quickly left, right, then behind himself. To his relief, a young sheep about five feet from the fence, stayed there.

"These sheep don't speak English, stupid. And you don't know which of those gibberish languages they understand," Asar said.

Set ignored his brother. He stuck his other arm through, wiggled his fingers, and added his best imitation of a Polish accent.

"Sh-ee-ee-ee-peee … skeee, sh-ee-ee-ee-peee-skeee, sh-ee-ee-ee- peee … skeee."

The lamb looked right at Set and bleated. Bleated again, then started to cautiously move towards him. Set poured on the Polish.

" Skeeeeee…"

A horrified Asar began looking around to see if anyone was watching.

"Cut it out, Set."

"Sh-ee-ee-ee-peee … skeeeeee."

The baby Polish sheep again bleated and came within petting distance. Set lunged forward, grabbed the startled lamb by the throat with both hands, and squeezed as hard as he could. The sheep bucked but Set snatched him closer until the sheep's wild eyes were inches from his own. In one quick motion, Set released his left hand just long enough to forcefully jab his left forefinger through the soft flesh adjacent to the lamb's eye, and yanked the bulging oval right out of its socket. The bleating, hysterical sheep, broke free of Set's grip and wildly zig-zagged like a puffy bronco, big eyeball flopping from its optical cord. A crazed stare on a string. Set's eyes grew large too.

"Sh-ee-ee-ee-peee … skeeeeee."

The bleating bronco started a bleating contest among the other sheep. This collective animal wail reverberated inside Asar's skull as he stared at Set who was staring at the traumatized ewe. Asar watched Set's excitement at creating chaos. And pain. Again. In these moments, Asar felt a kind of fear. He wasn't afraid of his brother; Asar was afraid that he and his brother were only twins on the outside.

Asar dropped the map scroll, balled his fist, and threw a haymaker that connected with the back of Set's skull.

"Owww," Set said. Still shaken, Asar grabbed his brother by both shoulders and shook him hard.

"Stop, being a doo-doo brain."

"He's gonna die anyway. I just wanted to see his eyes get big."

"We're getting out of here."

Asar picked up the map with one hand and started pulling his little brother by the wrist with the other.

"He won't even need that eye."

"Dookie brain!"

"Who you boys here to see?"

Distracted by each other, the twins hadn't seen him coming.

The boys turned to see a man in brown cotton coveralls, who was as tall as their father and just as black. His two bottom center teeth were missing. An absence that gave his words a whirring sound.

"Our daddy," Set quickly lied.

"Who yo daddy?"

"Mr. Jones."

Asar's head swiveled back and forth between the two.

"Work inside?"

"Yessir, I think so."

"Got something for him?" the man whirred, looking at the scroll under Asar's arm.

"Yessir," Set lied.

"I know Jonesy," he said through his gap-tooth smile. "Just follow me."

He put both of his long arms around each boy's shoulder. Asar shot his death-look at Set. Set pretended not to see it. The three of them walked in silence towards the huge building with the shotgun house-sized letters across the top.

"Armour & Company," Set mouthed.

The friendly man walked the twins inside and up to the top floor.

"Yo daddy is right down there in the back," he said, pointing down the long walkway.

He was talking loud to be heard over the terrified lowing, snorting, and bleating of hundreds of animals. Their anxious appeals reverberating off the white corridor walls. Set started walking down the long corridor. Asar was still. Transfixed by the bleating. It seemed louder on the top floor. More urgent. So human.

"Daddy's waiting, Asar," Set snapped.

He was afraid that his Scare D. Cat brother would crack and confess. Set stepped over and snatched the map scroll from beneath Asar's arm, then turned to walk away. Asar slowly followed his brother down the corridor.

The gap-toothed man stared at Jonesy's peculiar boys. He hollered out, "Be careful."

The dying was so loud, neither twin heard him.

I I I

Armour & Company had a top/down production approach. The nervous cows, sheep and pigs were rustled from the outdoor pens into the main building and prodded up the 12-foot-wide wooden ramps with side-rails, to the top floor. From this fourth floor, they worked their way down to slabs of meat, hooves, and bone bits by the time they reached the first floor. A series of macabre demotions. Asar and Set walked across the fourth floor corridor towards the doorway where the loudest clatter was coming from. Once they exited the passageway, the sound level exploded. They found themselves standing in a room three-times the size of their house and backyard. They both looked skyward. The 50-foot ceilings gave the space an open-air-market feeling. Except there was no bartering, no negotiating, no options for these lives-turned-products. No sky or breeze to help release the humid, sticky, stench of death.

The twins continued walking. But slower now. More careful. On their right, they came upon a deep-cut, rectangular room with hundreds of sheep. It was like walking past a warehouse-sized boxcar with the door slid wide open.

Asar's body stiffened as soon as the boxcar room came fully into view.

The eyes.

Asar was stopped by a pair of eyes that reminded him of his brother. When Daddy would fetch the leather razor strap from the bathroom to whup Set in the kitchen, Set's eyes would detonate and ricochet around the room. His wild gaze usually found the door leading to the backyard— even though he knew the outdoor gate was locked. Insulted by Set's refusal to obey his call for punishment, Daddy would catch him, then call Asar out to the backyard. Asar hated when his father made him watch Set's frequent punishments. True enough, Set usually deserved a whuppin for being such a dookie brain, but it hurt Asar to serve as witness. He loved his big-headed brother.

"Let this be a lesson for both of you," Keb would say, before stepping Set out of his pants. He'd hold Set by the wrist and let the flying strap teach. Set would do the Whuppin Dance: A high-stepping circle, like a boy holding onto a merry-go-round bar that was spinning too fast for him to jump on. Set's high-stepping circle was often a half-step too slow to escape Keb's stinging leather. As he danced and screamed, Set's wild eyes would be locked on his twin brother, pantomiming, "Save me!"

The slaughter-house boxcar had a funnel that narrowed to a point where only one sheep could stand. That sheep, twenty-feet from Asar, had his wild eyes locked on him. Behind that sheep, were two, then five, then a panicked huddled mass. A soft-padded insurrection turned civil war. Ewe banging against sheep banging against lamb. A collective Whupin Dance. With a lot more at stake. Where the kitchen door wasn't an escape route, but a vulgar destination. The point sheep, with little wiggle room, bucked up and down. An unbroken bull in a chute. His soft neck at a forty-five-degree angle, eyes pantomiming a message that Asar was an expert at decoding.

"Save me!"

The killer of sheep, a pale, black-haired man in denim coveralls with no shirt underneath, slid down the metal brace that held the head in place. The body bucked on. His fingers, thick and long as Sunday morning Kielbasas, patted the soft wool just above the eyes. It's gonna be alright. The knife in the left hand was pulled straight across the neck.

The eyes.

The eyes bulged, trying to escape the head. Asar turned and whispered in his brother's ear.

"He's a lefty like you."

4

In silence, Asar and Set Americus walked west down 1st Street towards the riverfront. Set hated when Asar tried to act all grown up just because he was seven minutes older. Asar hated when Set insisted on being a dookie brain because he knew better. So the twins in brown Stern Brothers suits, with dirt on their knees and elbows, wore their mad faces. Asar on the far right side of the street, Set on the far left.

They walked past the Terminal Railroad Association yards. Hundreds of boxcars carrying goods from all over the country lined the side-by-side rails. Locomotive pews. Twenty-six pairs of tracks meeting at the train church. New York big-cat Jay Gould getting an offering from every boxcar because he owned the riverfront track on both sides of the Mississippi.

Set could have easily read the names on the boxcars with his naked eye, but he snatched out his telescope because that's what explorers do. The sooty air was dirtier near the riverfront. He could feel the fine grit on his tongue. Set wiped the lens of his Semeticolo special and lodged it to his squinting eye. He mouthed the letters and words to himself: C.B.Q. R.R., Vandalia R.R., C.P. & ST. L. R.R., Illinois Central R.R.

Asar looked at the boxcars with his naked eye. He wondered if any big-eyed sheep were inside. He could still smell the stench in his nostrils. Asar wiped his nose on his suit jacket sleeve. Soot-laced snot left a faint track on the brown fabric. Asar glanced over at Set and tried to see inside his head, tried to understand why he acted the way he did sometimes. Set's dookie brain behavior made Asar feel very far from his twin, even when he was just across the street. Like kiddie railroad police on parallel patrol, the boys stopped at each corner—Summit Ave., College Ave., Ohio Ave.—to peer down the short dirt lanes that all ended in dead ends at Cahokia Creek. Saloons lined both sides of each street. Stale beer wafted on the breeze towards them. Men, dressed in last night's clothes, left a bar, crossed the street and entered another. That's what drew the boys' attention. It seemed to be a game. Dozens of men criss-crossed each other, exchanging bars. Some were arm-in-arm with women who wore last night's clothes too.

At the corner of First and State, Asar dropped to one knee and unrolled his hemp scroll. Set wished he had been carrying the map.

He crossed the narrow street over to his brother, kneeled beside him.

"Let's be twins again," Set said.

"Okay."

Set formed a pyramid by joining his two index fingers as the sides, and below, the tips of his thumbs touched to form the base. Asar formed the same pyramid with his own index fingers and thumbs. Asar slid his horizontal pyramid into his brother's upright pyramid to seal the truce.

"I think we should take State until it crosses the Chicago & Alton line," Asar said, illustrating the route with his finger. "Then follow those tracks all the way down to the waterfront."

"Since we have all day, I think it would be more fun to just follow Cahokia Creek down to the river and walk back up Wiggins. But we can go your way if you let me choose the route on the way back home," Set said.

"Let's just find our presents first, then flip for who gets to choose the way home."

"Flip now for the way there," Set said. He stood up and reached for his silver dollar.

"No, Set, your way's too long ... okay, okay. You can lead us on the way back home."

"That means I get to carry the map, right? The lead explorer can't find the way home without the map."

"You make me sick."

Asar smacked his little brother's neck and ran off laughing down State Street, with his laughing mirror image gaining fast.

I I I

It was almost a mile southeast down the C & A line to the waterfront. From State Street to the Mississippi River, the Chicago & Alton line cut a sickle through the damp, marshy landscape. Asar walked along the outside of the tracks. Set walked and jumped and skipped inside the parallel rails. In mid-stride, Set hopped on a single rail with his arms spread wide for balance and lunged into a teetering full sprint until he fell off. He walked back to his brother counting the railroad spikes to measure his distance.

"Thirty-four!"

"If you bust your head open, your present is mine," Asar said, hiding his concern with bombast.

"Deal, but if I get 50 spikes your present is mine."

"Fifty's nothing. I could do 50 running backwards. Do a hundred and we've got a deal."

"Okay," Set said. He leapt back on the rail, scampering like an impatient tight-rope walker.

"Set, nooo. No deal, no deal!"

Too late. Set teetered down the rail at full speed. Asar watched his brother fall sideways in a mud of his own choosing.

Asar smiled.

He loved these times most with his twin. When they were out of the sight of the man whose eye Set tried so hard to attract. Asar knew his little brother's need to be their father's favorite brought out the worst in Set's competitive nature. Set wanted to be the only child in a family of twins. A desire that tightened Asar's stomach muscles when he thought too long about it.

That's why Asar loved when they were alone. The other Set came out. The little brother who wanted to spin for his big brother. Asar's gaze became the light Set wanted. Athough Asar would have preferred the direct light from his father's eyes, the reflected light from his father's favorite made him feel warm inside too.

"Forty-five!" Set said, running back between the rails.

"We didn't shake on it. You know the rules."

"Let's race then. You take one rail, I'll run the other. Whoever gets the farthest wins both presents," Set said.

"I don't want to see you go crying back to Daddy."

"Sure, Mr. Fraid D. Chicken. You're the biggest yardbird in the all of East St. Louis. It's good we left the slaughterhouse cause any second those bohunks would've been sizing up your chicken neck."

"Like this."

Asar reached for Set, grabbed him by the neck with both hands, and brought him to the ground. Still choking, he straddled Set's chest. The way he'd done since before they could read maps. Set's wild-bronco bucking couldn't dislodge him.

"What do my subjects call me?" Asar said. Set tightened his lips and bucked harder. "What do my subjects call me?"

Asar went for the emergency weapon: The double-sided tickle.

"His Highness-Big Brother Asar-My Personal Master-and Ruler of the Whole World-Including Our Bedroom," Set screamed, in a writhing fit.

"Now kiss my pinkie," Asar commanded, still tickling. Set obeyed The Ruler of the Whole World.

Asar jumped off his little brother, barely escaping a wild left hook. Still running, he hopped on a rail and tight-roped down the C & A like a circus veteran. Set leapt to his feet and shimmied along the opposite rail and shouted, "The King's gotta chicken neck!" As he teetered down the track, Set snuck quick glances over at Asar. He loved spending time with his big brother when Asar was smiling all big and having fun. He wished Asar would always act this way. Like a Kid Treasure Hunter and not like a Kid Daddy Imitator. Set felt himself beginning to fall to his left. Just before hitting ground his peripheral vision caught Asar tipping over too, knocked off balance by the size of his smile.

❚ ❚ ❚

The C & A line split into 10 parallel tributaries at the riverfront, allowing for maximum cargo movement. Perpendicular to the river, the lines were packed with boxcars. Set pulled out his telescope. Along the coal-smoked coast, a sea of men loaded and unloaded wooden crates. Many of the crates were destined for the Wiggins Ferry which came and went across the river morning and night. Asar squatted down and unrolled the map.

"Look how big the Eads Bridge looks from down here," Set said, looking up into the bridge's massive steel underpinnings.

Asar ignored his brother and examined their father's finely detailed map.

"We need to walk north up the shore till we get to the end of the Chicago-Peoria & St. Louis line. It's the last line in the city limits."

"The bridge looks a lot bigger than it does from our porch. I'd bet a whole dollar that some of these men working on the tracks right now were the same ones who built it up," Set said. He returned his spyglass to his back pocket and squatted next to his brother.

"The X is 120 paces in a straight line from the end of the track," Asar said.

"What do you think it is?"

"I hope it's a replacement brain for your dookie brain. Let's go," Asar said. He rolled the map and stood up.

"My brain's bigger than your little mustard seed brain."

"Is not."

"Is too."

"Is not."

"You think you're so smart," Set said, rising from his crouch.

"Smart enough to be born first."

"Shut up or you'll be the first one to die Mr. Mustard M. Mind."

"Just follow me little brother ... but stay seven minutes behind."

Asar quickly stood and broke into sprint up the shore.

"I hate you!" Set said, running after him.

"Seven minutes."

The twins stood in their muddy brown suits at the end of the Chicago-Peoria & St. Louis line. Asar returned his compass to his pocket, then argued about who would take the 120 paces south by southwest and who would stand at the track and keep the pacer in a straight line. They decided to flip for it. Set looked at cargo-laden Wiggins Ferry boats keeping commerce in motion up and down the Mississippi. His body did a slight involuntary shudder. He thought of the porch-reprimands his father gave them when Daddy felt they were being unappreciative of their lifestyle.

▮ ▮ ▮

"Four decades ago, you two could have *been cargo* on one of those Wiggins Ferries running down the Mississippi," he'd say.

During what the twins privately mocked as "Big Speech Time", their father had told them the history of how the state line muddled in the river between slave-state Missouri and free-state Illinois. The boundary didn't run down the center of the Mississippi; it "curved and arched towards bondage and emancipation," he'd explained. At the far north end near the McKinley Bridge, the state line was only 400 feet from the Illinois shore. The boundary then snaked south through the river until it was 700 feet from the Missouri shore, near downtown St. Louis, and snaked back within 400 feet from East St. Louis just south of the Eads Bridge.

The murky boundary helped create Bloody Island. A clump of land in the middle of the Mississippi that received its name, Daddy had said, because "murk and mayhem are blood relatives." The 1/4 mile by 1 mile island was a popular dueling ground in the early part of the century. "Duelists, some not that much older than you two, would row out to the island and settle scores with pistols from ten paces. A duel between Missouri's first senator, Thomas Hart Benton and his rival Charles Lucas left Lucas dead."

The Army Corps of Engineers, under the command of lieutenant Robert E. Lee, began a dike in 1837 that slowly attached the island that they were now standing on to East St. Louis. "When it officially became the city's 4th Ward, the island brought the blood with it," Daddy had explained.

I I I

"Heads," Set said, turning away from the Wiggins Ferry.

Asar's silver dollar flipped into the sooty sky and fell at Set's feet. Heads it was and Set stood at attention at the end of the C.P. & ST. L. rail. Asar had his compass back in his hand; it was the only gift that Set didn't also have. Anymore. Last year, the day after the twin's 9th birthday, Set had dropped it at school, while being a big show-off in front of the Jenkins brothers. The glass cracked, but the compass seemed to still work fine. With Asar right behind him, Set rushed home, tracked down his father in the kitchen and asked how long it would take to fix. Keb held the compass in his baseball- mitt-palm. Examined the Y-shaped crack in the glass. Looked at Set. Turned it over. Again, looked at the cracked cover. He handed it back to Set.

"Place it on the floor."

"Hunh?"

"Boy, don't *hunh* me. I said place it on the floor."

Set looked at Asar, then squatted down and placed the compass on the floor.

Keb's thick, black heel stomped the compass so hard that Asar heard a piece of glass ricochet off the stove.

"If you don't respect the gifts I give, how can you expect me to respect them?" Keb said.

I I I

"If you start going crooked, I'll scream stop. Be sure to take the same size steps and count out loud so you don't lose count," Asar said, looking down at his compass.

"Stop trying to sound like Daddy. Besides, I know what I'm doing anyway."

"And don't start digging till I get there."

Growing serious, Set placed his arms to his side. Chin up. Eyes forward. He looked like a boy soldier in a muddy brown suit.

"ONE ... two ... THREE ... four ... ."

With minefield care, Set measured his steps, south by southwest, across Bloody Island towards the Mississippi. To irritate his brother, Set loudly enunciated one step then whispered the next. He didn't let himself get distracted by the throng of men unloading rail cars a few hundred yards to his left, nor by the black-smoke-blowing ferry sweeping north towards the Merchants Bridge, nor by his brother's critical eye on his back.

"Eighteen ... NINETEEN ... twenty ... TWENTY-ONE ..."

Even at ten, Set Americus had to know how to be focused on more than one thing at at time. This was the best way to get his old-fashioned daddy's attention off the first-born son. When Set would see their father standing, talking alone with Asar off in the corner of the living room, behind a pine tree near the back gate, in the library, on the front porch, Set wondered hard what his father was passing along. What father-to-firstborn wisdom? What information about the Columbian Exposition? Which razor worked best?

Asar's seven-minute lead could only be overcome by being the twin who did twice as much, twice as fast, and twice as better. Why does it even matter who was born first? he often thought. That's so stupid. What if Asar had been born first with arms or legs like Jimmy Ray Blacksmith? He wouldn't even be able to flip his coin, or carry the map, or walk 120 paces to get our birthday presents.

"FORTY-NINE ... fifty ... FIFTY-ONE ... ."

Asar doesn't even like to get the bodies ready, he thought. General Chicken L. Jackson uses the gloves whenever Daddy makes him help with the cutting. That's why Set was sure that he was the favorite although Daddy tried to play everything Even Steven.

Set often stood in front of the circular mirror in the bathroom and quietly read his own lips, "Everybody knows that I'm the Son in Americus & Son cause the only thing that Asar is good at is being born first—and acting like Daddy."

"Stop! You're getting crooked," Asar yelled through his megaphone hands.

Set stopped on his SEVENTY-THIRD step. His arms froze in walking position. Like Lot's wife, he had to look back. He slowly turned his neck to see his brother in the distance. At around step 68, he had started to slightly veer right.

"Walk back in your footprints until I tell you to stop," Asar shouted.

"I know how to do it."

"Don't lose your count."

"If you'd shut your monkey mouth, I'd be able to concentrate on my figures."

"If it wasn't for my monkey mouth telling your monkey brain to stop making your monkey feet go crooked, we'd be digging up Bloody Island till Christmas. Now turn around and stay straight this time or I'm going to take over."

"You ain't taking over nothin." Set turned around and faced Asar.

"Seventy-two ... SEVENTY-ONE ... seventy ... SIXTY-NINE ... sixty-eight."

"Stop! Okay, now turn around and stay straight this time."

"Sixty-eight ... SIXTY-NINE ... seventy ... ."

When Set whispered "hundred and twenty," he snatched the hand-shovel from his back pocket, dropped to his knees, and started quickly digging into the damp river bank.

"You're supposed to be waiting for me!"

Pumping the rolled map like a baton, Asar sprinted towards Set.

Set glanced over his shoulder at his huffing and puffing brother and started digging and flinging dirt faster. In mid-stride, Asar dropped the map and pulled the garden tool out of his back pocket.

"You better wait Set!"

At full speed, Asar barreled his left shoulder into Set and knocked him off the hole. Asar got in a couple of digs before Set threw his body next to him and they dug side-by-side, knee-to-knee.

"Scoot over some Asar, I was here first."

"Just dig."

The identical twins, in muddy brown suits, fixed their energy on the Bloody Island soil. They dug with the passion that only 10-year-old boys can muster when digging for buried treasure.

For other boys, make-believe ended with a hole in the ground. But Asar knew they had a father who wanted their make-believe to be real. Their dreams to be possible. He knew buried treasure was beneath their fast moving shovels, because their father said it was so.

Daddy always buried the presents deep, so Asar knew they'd have to work hard for them. Just as he had worked hard, as the first-born, to be a good example for Set. As Asar dug, he thought of the times his father had pulled him aside and repeated his odd mantra, "Love your brother by being like me in his presence." Asar always felt a little sad when he heard the phrase because it made him feel like his father's mind was on Set—again. And made him feel like he wanted to do something very bad to Set for being his father's favorite. But Asar usually just shook his head hard when those thoughts came up. Hoping that if he just kept working hard on being like his father, his father would be capable of loving the first-born like his favorite-born. And right now, being like father meant working hard on digging hard for the treasure Asar knew they would find. Over the years, he'd learned that hard work wasn't so bad when you knew it would pay off in the end.

After the Semeticolo telescopes, on their fifth birthday, their second gifts were two shiny silver dollars wrapped in a black velvet cloth inside a deeply buried square pine box. The X had been right at the entrance of the Specialty Shed. Their father said they could do anything they wanted with the silver dollars—except spend them. His way of teaching them the value of holding on to money.

The next year, the twins unearthed two gold watches outside the kitchen window. The only disappointing gifts came for their eighth birthday, when they opened a pine box near one of the circular unmarked grave-markers to find two copies of the Egyptian Book of the Dead. Even the dead-curious Set asked his father, "Daddy, how can a book be a present? We have books all over the house and at school."

"If you want to know the end, start at the beginning," Keb said, and walked away. The disappointed boys looked at each other and said at the exact same time, "You want mine?"

Last year, at nine, the boys dusted off a dirty pine box to find two compasses placed in silver casings. Set walked back in the house and shrieked, "The kitchen is due west of the library!"

I   I   I

The twins dug the Mississippi bank until their arms began to tire.

The hole was over two feet deep.

"Are you sure you didn't miscount on your steps," Asar said. He put down his hand-shovel.

"You're not the only one who knows how to count," Set said. He kept digging.

"I know the X is right here. Daddy just buried the box deeper this time."

"You count good like you walk straight. I'm going back to the tracks and count it off myself."

"Go ahead. I hope you count yourself right into the river and drown," Set said, still digging.

Ignoring his little brother, Asar stood up, brushed his knees off and started walking back towards the C.P. & ST. L. rail.

"Asar!"

Asar knew the scream of discovery. He rushed back to his brother's side and started helping to remove the dirt from around the pine box.

The boys' father carved their gift boxes with the same care that he hand-carved Americus & Son coffins. Like the coffins, each gift box was designed with the contents in mind. The pine box for the matching spyglasses was 4 by 24 inches. The lid had an engraved eye, an Utchat, that their father had told them was an Egyptian symbol for looking within. "A boy has to ask someone to answer his questions, a man looks inside himself and begins to question," he'd said, as he stood over them while they opened the spyglass gift box. Outside their father's earshot, they joked about the "Riddle Talk" he often used when passing down life lessons.

The pine box now resting in front of them, here on the bank of Bloody Island, was 4 by 16 inches. The length of the box was covered with a carving they recognized from their own home. It looked like a stick figure of a man with his legs together, and arms stretched out to his sides, with no eyes, mouth or nose. It was an ankh. There was a giant one sticking out of the center of the Americus Fountain.

"I should get to open it because I'm the one who found it," Set said. He reached for the box.

"Touch it and I swear I'll bite off the finger that reaches the box first. Now, get your dollar out so we can do it right. You flip, I'll call it."

Set pulled the Morgan Dollar from his vest pocket, kissed it, and from his knees, flipped the coin high into the air.

"Heads," Asar said.

The coin landed right next to Set's black Oxford brogues.

"Tails! My dollar is undefeated today."

He kissed it and put it back in his vest pocket. Set squatted over the hole, lifted the box, and placed it on the ground. Like a gloating carnival magician, he hovered his palms along the length of the treasure.

"What do you think it is, Asar?"

"Will you stop messing around and open the box!"

"When you win the flip, you can decide how to open the gifts."

"You make me sick."

"Maybe it's two pirate flags rolled up?"

Set hovered his hand along the box again. Extra slow to further irritate Asar.

"Maybe Daddy found out what a big chicken you are, so he gave you some chicken guts—and gave me the look on your face," Set said.

"Set!"

"Okay, okay, okay."

Set unlatched the solid gold clasp. He leaned towards the box and peeked under the lid like it was a bed blanket.

"Stop playing!"

Set pulled the lid completely open. Lying atop the red crushed velvet lining was a miniature sword, with a shining steel, slightly curved, eight-inch blade. Three-inches wide and double-edged, the blade was attached to five-inch sold gold handle. Inset in the center of the handle, a single ruby, the size of marble.

The twins looked at each other. Set picked up the large knife and felt around the box.

"It's heavy," he said.

Asar looked back down into the hole. He picked up his hand spade and poked around. Nothing. Set stood up and took a few sweeping, swashbuckling swings. Asar stayed on his knees and looked at his brother. Glanced back down into the hole. At his brother.

"Where's the other sword, Set?"

"How should I know? All I know is this one is mine, because I found it when you had already given up and started walking back to the tracks."

"There's only room for one knife, so it's not like he forgot one," Asar said.

Set continued to behead imaginary pirates.

"Do you think he wanted us to flip for it," Asar said.

"No, I think he wanted whoever found it first to have it, and whoever didn't find it first to stop being a big baby and wait till next year."

Asar's feelings were hurt. He always tried so hard to be a good big brother like his father wanted. Standing up for Set, protecting him, constantly sharing. And here Set was being selfish—again.

"There have always been two gifts, Set."

Knife clutched by his side, Set turned to his brother and snapped,

"We're on Bloody Island, maybe he wants us to duel for it; find your weapon, I've got mine."

Asar stared Set down. He wanted to go smack him upside his head. He took three deep breaths to help calm his rising emotions. His father had taught him this technique because, "When you act on emotion, emotion acts on you." Asar took another breath.

"Let's go Set, I need to talk to Daddy." Asar rose to his feet and brushed off his knees.

"I'm not ready to go and we have a deal. You were in charge on the way here, I'm in charge on the way home, and I say we go do some exploring. It's our birthday, Asar, and you're not going to ruin it by acting like Fred E. Frown. Here, you can hold my sword for a while." Set extended the handle to Asar.

"I don't want to hold the knife, stupid. If there aren't two, I don't want it at all. And you shouldn't want it either. We're brothers and it's our birthday, and look at how you're acting. It's not even your knife, it's our knife, if I wanted it."

"I found it. It's my sword, so it doesn't matter if you want it or not. What does matter is that it's my turn to be in charge, and we're going exploring, so follow me, Frederick E. Frown."

Set snatched the rolled up map from the ground and started walking back towards the tracks, decapitating imaginary pirates along the way.

The first-born glanced down into the empty hole. Something was wrong. His father had never before forgotten one of their gifts. Does Daddy really want us to fight over a gift on our birthday? Asar thought. He looked up at sword-swinging Set. Back down at the empty hole. Asar hated when he couldn't figure things out, couldn't make things right in his head. He hard-pinched the skin on the side of his neck. For almost a full minute. He bent at the waist to pick up the hand-carved sword case. He ran his hand along the soft velvet, searching for an extra compartment. Nothing. The first-born let the empty box fall from his hands into the earth from which it came.

5

SATURDAY, JULY 2, 1927
EAST ST. LOUIS, ILLINOIS

Auset had to shame Asar into coming to his own son's 10th birthday party. From the open French Doors, Asar's hazel eyes scanned the dining room. Their almond-shaped squint stopped on the Westminister Chimes grandfather clock against the far wall. Two-twenty-five. He was glad he was late.

Next to the six-foot walnut time-piece, Miss Beaudreaux, his son's new Creole school teacher, wearing a Louise Brooks' helmet-bob and curtain bangs, was clearly trying to make a good impression on Auset. But the cream flapper frock and black Mary Janes—with the diamante trim—were working against her.

Asar's downcast eyes shifted to the lion's paw feet grounding the Regency dining table. At the head sat 10-year-old Heru Americus. Asar's only child. And the only child at his own birthday party.

Chocolate cake in front of him. Untouched. Unsweetened face. Shaped into oval coal by East St. Louis and his father. An appropriate shape to compliment the almond-shaped eyes bulging out of his sockets. When Heru looked in mirrors, he saw a black frog face with anvil irises.

At Heru's upper forehead was a reverse widow's peak: a widow's cave. The peach-fuzz hairline receded into an inverted "U" from forehead to crown. It gave his soft face the look of a bald black pubis. From Asar's French Door point-of-view, it was a face too soft for a pirate. Too soft for an adventurer. Too soft for an Americus son. His son. Asar wanted Heru to be muddy, be different. Be different from the little boy sitting at the dining room table. Different from the embodiment of fatherhood failure. "I didn't protect him," Asar said aloud to himself. He stared at his son and shook his head. Memories oozed down Asar's thick neck and shoulders, past his now deep-breathing chest. "I should've been there." These memories had the capacity to shift Asar's deep love for his son into feelings he knew were wrong. Feelings that Asar had long struggled to change were becoming feelings that were changing him.

▮ ▮ ▮

When Heru's dark-brown eyes couldn't see who was staring, he could *feel* the staring. Heru wondered if everyone knew when they were being stared at. When he asked his mother Auset this question, instead of directly answering, she kneeled down and said, "When people stare they're just seeing something unique in you, something so special that they have a hard time looking away." Heru remembered her smiling in that big way that made him focus on the mole in her right dimple.

Well, Heru didn't feel special when eyes spit on his face. At least that's what stares felt like. Like someone's eyeballs hacked up green-loogey-snot from deep inside their sockets, and spit it across the room onto his face. The stares made Heru feel slimy, green and sticky.

He wanted to know if other people had the same magic power to detect loogey stares. If not, the magic power was all his. That would make him special.

Heru quickly turned his head towards the direction of the French Doors. He caught his father's green-loogey-snot stare. Or it caught him. Again. Heru felt that slimy, green feeling slide down his widow's cave, over his forehead, covering his pretty onyx face. Past his narrow neck and shoulders, into his lap, running down his brown short-pants, intermixing with the pee pee splashing on his brown shoes and pooling on the floor. As each party guest's turning head alerted another, Heru could barely catch all the stares that were coming his way. He stopped trying. He focused on the warm liquid passing over his calves and the eyes across the room that caused the pee pee to flow.

Heru's father had a way of looking at him that made him magically shrink into a tiny, tiny, boy who somehow could release a secret scream so big and loud that people way over the river in St. Louis could hear.

Asar let his eyes fall from Heru's face to the puddle of urine forming beneath his son's chair. The same location that party guests were shifting their eyes. Heru's mother was so deep into her conversation with Miss Beaudreaux that she didn't notice something was wrong. It was Grandma Nutilda's reckless eyeballs that saw what needed to be seen. Nutilda grabbed Auset's hand and with a nod motioned for her daughter-in-law to turn around. Auset abruptly turned to see her baby sitting in a pool of piss. His almond eyes wide as anvils watching Asar stomp towards him.

"Asar!" Auset yelled from across the room. Heads swiveled towards her soft copper-penny-face. Then back towards Asar. Then to Heru because his storming father was right upon him now. Heru fought the urge to slide off the pissy chair and run towards the sound of his mother's panicked voice. With his large eyes locked on his father, Heru willed his effeminate, fragile body to sit still as the black porcelain vase in the sitting room.

The party guests became still too. Silent. Their taut bodies and heads turned. Curious.

Asar was standing so close to the side of Heru's chair that pee pee encircled his shiny black brogues. He bent his long torso at the waist until the wavy salt-and-pepper hair, that Big Grandpa Nema complained was too long for a 44-year-old man, brushed across Heru's forehead.

Auset hurried in their direction with both palms extended forward.

Heru stiffened but continued to look up through his father's hair into Asar's grave marker face. He noticed how wrinkles framed puffy bags under the hazel eyes.

"Boys stand when they piss," Asar hissed, spittle flying into Heru's wide-eyed face. Heru started to shake so hard that he instinctively grabbed the edge of the dining room table.

"Stand your narrow ass up."

Heru wanted to obey his father, but his trembling spaghetti legs wouldn't let him.

"Boy, what did I tell you?"

Asar's mind was moving through a tunnel. All he could see ahead were quick flashes of his son sleeping summer nights atop his bare chest. Burrowing through his chest the first time he watched Heru's lips form, "Da-dee." Now looks led to disappointments. Asar had done this. He was the father. Heru was his fault. Like breath, the flesh could hold guilt for only so long. Before exhaling and igniting combustible air.

"Asar please," Auset said. She had walked right next to him.

Heru felt himself holding his breath. He couldn't make his legs obey his father. Asar's sausage-like right-hand fingers shot towards his only son's neck and snatched Heru's pissy body straight up out the seat. Tiny dangling feet kicked over the chair. Asar slammed him down back on his pissy shoes, but Heru's spindly legs wouldn't hold. Father held son up by the throat. The party guests were held by the throat too.

Auset reached and grabbed Asar's left wrist. Husband pulled away from wife and pushed the flat of his palm into her chest, sending Auset sprawling backwards onto the floor. Her ruffled dress billowed like a russet parachute.

Heru's big anvil eyes were bigger than the scary owl eyes that spied on him in his dreams.

"Boy, I tell you to do something, goddamnit, you best well do it. Now stand your ... ."

Asar could hear himself cursing at Heru—something he promised Auset he wouldn't do again. He felt the invectives forming in his mouth. He knew how they would sound and hurt when they crossed his lips. Asar didn't want to hurt his son. But he did. Because he needed to hurt his son. He needed to punish Heru's wrongness. And punish himself for fathering an Americus who could be so wrong.

"Stand your sissy-ass here till I tell you to move."

Heru could tell that his frog-eyes were extra-wide by how the air in the room seemed to prick all around his exposed whites. He released tears to roam free between his father's fingers, which were still around his neck.

Heru was not crying on purpose. Because boys don't cry.

His father had taught him that.

"Clean it up," Asar said, releasing Heru's neck. The boy's knees betrayed him. Heru's birthday brown knee-pants plopped right down into his own piss. And he was relieved to be there.

"Don't make me tell you again," Asar said

Confused, Heru looked up at his father. Raised his empty palms. "Use those pissy pants. They're already soiled."

"But ..."

"Take them off."

In a panic, Heru's eyes shot around the room catching stares. I can't take off my pants in front of all these people, he screamed inside his head. He couldn't let them see. He looked back at his father and wanted to say, "Why are you doing this, Daddy?" But his trembling mouth couldn't form that many words.

"Please, Daddy."

"Now."

Heru's head swiveled around the room again. Then it dropped. He inched the knee-pants down his legs. He scrunched them into a towel and crawled around the dining table's lion's paw feet absorbing pee pee.

"It's soaked through, use your underpants."

Heru froze there on his sticky, smelly hands and knees.

"Don't make me repeat myself, boy."

Heru began to cry harder. But he was not going to let anyone see his wrong.

"I can't, Daddy."

Then Heru felt his body lift straight off the ground. He was flying. An image flashed in his mind of stories he'd heard about boyhood Uncle Set and his boyhood father jumping off the front porch stairs. He'd often smiled at those stories, but he'd replace Uncle Set and fly next to his boyhood father. Imagine that his father could play with him that way too.

The flash-image passed and Heru was back on the floor. His ripped white underpants above him in his father's bear claw. Heru's own black orchid palms shrouding shame.

Father and son disappearing into absence. Heru glanced up to see his father looking right through him.

6

Heru wouldn't get out of bed. It had been almost a week. Said he was sick and he was. Though no fever was present. No cold sweats. No shakes. Just the fatigue that comes from carrying heavy shame.

Heru blinked open his eyes and, through the dark, focused on the white ceiling above his bed. The sticky humidity didn't help. When he dosed off during the day or at night, he often would see those birthday party eyes watching him in his sleep. His skill for catching stares had developed into catching stares in his dreams.

He doubted whether other people had this dream-talent. He would have seen tiredness in their eyes. Catching stares in your sleep can wear you out.

7

Heru got out of his sick bed on the seventh day. He rolled out to his feet, arched his back, stretched his hands to the ceiling. Brought them back down to his sides.

Heru didn't know what to do next.

He was hungry, but he didn't want to risk going downstairs until he was sure his father was done with his breakfast. Asar hadn't come up to visit his son, let alone speak to Heru, since the Bed Rest Protest, as Asar called it.

Asar forbade Auset from bringing Heru food to his room.

"You know that boy isn't sick. If he's going to eat, he's going to have to come down to the dinner table and that's that. We've already let this game go on too damn long. The boy is spoilt as it is."

Auset just nodded and started thinking about how she was going to sneak up food to her baby.

Grandma Nut usually made just enough grits, eggs, and bacon to feed everyone a single serving in case the whole family showed up. But since all six rarely showed up during the same time, Heru almost always got to have seconds.

"That narrow behind boy eat like he got a tape worm," Grandma Nut liked to say to Auset, then chuckle aloud like it wasn't the 1000th time she'd said it.

"He's just greedy and needy," Auset would say.

On Saturdays, everyone usually finished eating by 7:30 a.m. and it was now approaching 9 a.m. Standing next to his bed in his white night shirt, Heru stretched his hands to the sky again and thought about how much longer he should wait. By the time his arms returned to his side, the thought of cheesy eggs and bacon had given him an answer.

He cracked the door. Peeked. Tip-toed down the hall, past Booker T. Washington's face on the wall to his right. Heru paused at the top of the stairs and listened. Nothing. In that silence, a plan formed: rush to the kitchen stove where leftovers are kept, quickly fill a plate with cheesy eggs and bacon—and a biscuit if there's time—and some grits—then rush back up to the bedroom.

Sliding his hand down the curving rail, Heru scampered down the stairs with his socked-feet barely grazing the edge of each pine stair. He turned into the kitchen and saw a plate of cheesy eggs and bacon in the hand of Uncle Set standing at the stove. Heru froze. Uncle Set smiled. Asar, who was sitting at the small wooden table by the window, spoke first.

"Hunger chased that sickness hunh, boy?"

"Yessir," Heru mumbled, without looking over to his father. Heru curled his fingers in a nervous clinch. He wanted to immediately turn around, run back upstairs and put the covers over his head, but he didn't know if his father would reach out that long, magic arm to snatch him by the back of the neck.

Uncle Set walked past Heru and sat back down across from Asar. Taking the last two pieces of bacon with him. Heru stood very still. And very small. His eyes dropped from the stingy stove to his white socks. He could hear his father and his uncle eating to his left. They ignored him with purpose. These twins eating in the comfortable silence of a long married husband and wife. Uncle Set, in his black trousers and white undershirt, was not wearing his eye patch. That was for customers.

The hole in his uncle's head never bothered Heru, because it had always been there. Standing there in the kitchen, Heru snuck a glance at Uncle Set. The place where his bulging anvil eyes often landed. They were safe there. Maybe because lack attracts lack.

"Bring me that saucer off the counter, Heru," Uncle Set said.

With his head still down, Heru walked across the pine wood kitchen floor and grabbed the white porcelain dish. He walked back towards the table. The small plate extended before him in both of his open palms. He stopped in front of his uncle. Set looked up at his nephew. Then, from his own plate, placed two pieces of bacon on the saucer.

"Now, pull up a chair, son, so you can stop standing there looking like you have absolutely no sense," Set said.

At the word "son," Asar looked up from his plate at Set but didn't speak. Heru placed the saucer down on the crowded round table then turned to retrieve the straight back chair next to the sink. He sat down his slight frame and carefully picked up a strip of bacon as if it were a stick of dynamite. The crunchy pork between his molars sounded to Heru like little explosions in the quiet kitchen. He chewed with his head so bowed, he could've been praying to a Pig God.

Shoulda waited longer, shoulda waited longer, Heru repeatedly thought.

The three of them sat eating with their heads down. No words. To slow his heart rate, Heru focused on the sound of dead pork dying again. On an impulse, he looked up. Clustered around the dart board-sized table, their two long bodies seemed even longer than usual. Especially his father's long arms and fingers close enough to grab a son's neck in an instant.

But it was their faces that most struck Heru's bulging eyes. Their broad, garlic bulb noses, identical in width and fleshiness. Pronounced cheekbones looked like walnuts lodged beneath their skin. His father's skillet-black scalp visible in the inch-wide part running down the middle of his wavy, salt-and-pepper hair. Uncle Set's pale bald skull. Three half-lidded, hazel eyes. One hole in a face. Heru had an urge to stick his thumb in it.

"Boy, you staring at me like a first-timer," Set said, looking up at Heru.

Asar looked at Heru too. Heru dropped his eyes back into his plate.

"Maybe he's trying to look inside and see what part of the brain controls pee pee."

Heru's head was so low, he could've licked the plate in front of him. He imagined himself as the smallest, thinnest boy in the whole world. Thin as a penny. Penny Boy. Able to crawl under porcelain and lie on his back. Safe from stares that his own skin couldn't protect him from. Penny Boy. Able to roll faster than the B & O Line when it was running late.

8

When Set walked into Mabel's Kitchen at 6 p.m. sharp, he didn't expect to see Nephthys' long legs anchoring a body that was still slender at 46. Her many winning attributes didn't include promptness. He quickly scanned the room anyway. Nope. He smiled and sat down at one of the three unoccupied tables. The smell of chicken, re-used hot lard and warm bodies in close proximity made Mabel's seem cozy and cramped as usual.

Set was often struck by things that remained the same. There had been so much unwanted change in his life that he craved sameness. Longed for the constant. It soothed him. Like the feeling he got while sipping steaming gumbo rue straight from the bowl. That thick rue, heavy on okra juice, oysters, thyme and garlic, was one of the reasons people came to Mabel's. It wasn't for the rickety circular tables that leaned no matter how many spare pieces of wood customers placed under the legs. They weren't coming for the semi-sucked penny candy that was stuck beneath the table. Stuck until unlodged by unfortunate fingers trying to pull the table closer.

"Been waiting long?" Nephthys said with that gap in her smile the width of a coffin nail. A gap wide enough to suck away the irritation Set felt at her predictable lateness. She was the kind of woman who stopped to count the number of petals in a marigold. Even if petal calculations made her later. Nephthys found genuine joy in the specific, because people often categorically judged her. She loved Set, because he knew she was more than her suspect categories. Nephthys loved herself for the same reason.

"Not long as usual."

"Long enough to miss me?" she said, plopping her leggy long frame down in the chair. She could feel the stares quickly move in their direction. Nephthys Nelson was used to stares.

When her father Crefflowe Nelson walked towards the entrance of the school holding the hand of his, then, 11-year-old daughter, it was hard not to stare. The railroad spike-thin girl was a hair shorter than her 5-foot-7-inch father and two shades lighter than the pie-crust-colored

Alabama-native. Nephthys had inherited her mother's height and skin tone.

Set liked staring at Nephthys, even though he once bloodied a drunk bohunk's nose for staring too long in Aunt Kate's Honky Tonk. Her green eyes, like her smile, were all big and open on her buttermilk face. Those eyes often carried a hint of moisture. A suggestion of emotion. A palpable kindness. As if she were seeing a newborn baby for the first time each day. That's what intrigued Set so. And made him envious. How did she do it? Keep those kind eyes in East St. Louis?

"Nephthys, I asked you down here to run something by you."

"Can a girl order some chicken before you tell her you're about to quit her?"

She looked around for Old Mabel to take her order.

"I was wondering if you'd like to come live with me over at Americus?"

"As the family maid?"

Set slid the gold band across the rickety tabletop.

9

No matter what Big Grandpa Nema said, Heru liked his new Auntie Nephthys. It wasn't just because her eyes smiled at him like he was the most perfect boy in all of East St. Louis. It wasn't just that she made him fetch her purse, when no one was looking, so she could slip him butterscotch candy. It wasn't just because each morning she held his frog-eyed face in her long fingers and kissed his forehead like he was human butterscotch. These things made Heru's insides feel as warm as the stove after Mama baked bread. But what made Heru really like Auntie Nephthys was how she used magic to make Uncle Set act different.

Peering between the stair railing's polished wooden poles, Heru watched them nestling close on the sitting room couch. Uncle Set's muscular body softly leaning into Aunt Nephthys. Her pale slender arm resting over his shoulder like Uncle Set was her little brother. Only a person who knew magic could make big strong Uncle Set seem like a little brother. Only a person who knew magic could craft a smile on a face that was usually stuck on stern. A smile noticeable even from the second floor railing.

Sometimes, even when Aunt Nephthys wasn't around, Heru would see a little smile on Uncle Set's face. For no reason at all. Just walking out to the Specialty Shed or working on a body downstairs with Grandpa Keb. Even a froggy-eyed boy could see that it took magic to change someone like Uncle Set. And Auntie Neph had that magic.

Heru watched the magician turn to face Uncle Set, slowly placing her slender fingers on both sides of his cheeks. She cupped him, handled him, like his skull was one of those China bowls Mama carefully brought down from the cabinet to set the dinner table.

Aunt Nephthys' nose was so close to Uncle Set's nose that Heru wanted to close his own eyes—he knew she was going to kiss him. But she didn't. She just held Uncle Set's China cheeks. Stared into his lone eye. Into the hole in his face. Then stared some more. Longer than it would take Heru to run up and down the curving staircase three times. Longer and softer than anyone had ever stared at Heru. Heru wanted her to stop. Turn away. Even kiss him. Anything. But she wouldn't. He could have ran up and down the staircase again. Aunt Nephthys kept looking all soft like that. Her magic drawing a smile on Uncle Set's lips.

Kneeling behind the railing, Heru closed his eyes, so he could see better. Imagine better. In the dark. Similar to how he could see things so clearly when he dreamed at night. How he could see all the kids at school gathering around him, pushing and shoving trying to be the one to sit next to him when he ate his lunch. In the dark of his sleep, Heru could see so clear because his eyes weren't all froggy. They were as tiny and perfect as two black eyed peas.

Heru squeezed his eyes real tight to imagine someone looking at him the way Aunt Nephthys looked at Uncle Set. Squeezed real tight so he could see a nose just inches from his own. Feel the faint breeze of fluttering eyelashes. He squeezed tight enough to see soft magician eyes resting on his face, like they had nothing else to do. No hummingbird to watch. No clock to check. Soft eyes that only had time to look at Heru Americus.

10

Set wanted his other eye. Wished for it. Right then with his wife so close to him. Looking at him in that way that she did. Set rarely spent time on regret because regretting wouldn't bring it back. But during times like these, when Nephthys made him feel warm and whole, he wanted to be whole for her.

"I've been thinking on getting one of those glass eyes."

"I liked you when I met you and you had one eye then. Switch up now and you're liable to make me change my mind. Don't mess up your good thing, baby."

Nephthys leaned and placed her kumquat lips on the hole in Set's face.

"People been staring at me since Asar and I were little so it don't make me no never mind. When I don't feel like no staring I know how to get the point across right quick. When we're out though baby I watch the stares shift from me to you. People wondering what a pretty woman like you doing with me."

Nephthys placed her mouth towards his right ear. "What I'm doing is acting real grown."

Set leaned back.

"Neph, I don't want people looking at you wrong cause I look wrong. If putting a marble up there will help I think... ."

"Don't you get it, baby? I want whatever is coming your way. I want to feel what you feel, know what you know. It makes me understand you more, feel you more, want you more. What these nosey people out there don't know, and what you still somehow don't know, is that the more they look and stare, the more they make me feel closer to the man who I'm always trying to be closer to. The more they look, the more I want to give all myself to my husband. The more they try to get all up in our business, the more grown I want to act with Set Americus. So stop worrying about those silly people. Next time you catch one of them staring, smile and say, "Thank you," and if you don't, I will because they just making my good thing better."

Set tried to crinkle his brow to stop from smiling. That was the thing about Neph: she didn't want anything from him but for him to be himself. And that made Set want to give her everything. He leaned towards her ear.

"Let's go take a walk down Broadway."

"Right now?"

Set grabbed his wife's right hand and brought Nephthys to her feet. He grabbed her other hand. Their connected hands creating a human suspension bridge between them. They held gaze across the expanse. When they finally walked past the staircase towards the front door, they didn't see their nephew gazing at them. Wondering would someone ever look at him the way Auntie Neph looked at Uncle Set.

11

SATURDAY, JUNE 10, 1893
EAST ST. LOUIS, ILLINOIS

Set and Asar walked in silence along the waterfront. As he was quick to do, Set changed his mind after consulting the map again; he wanted to take Spring Avenue home instead of Wiggins.

"Because it's summer and we're going back towards the direction we came from, so we should take Spring Avenue because spring is back before summer," he said.

Spring Avenue was hidden among the parallel tracks of the Wabash R.R. and the C.P. & ST. L. R.R. Just before both lines came to an end at the Mississippi, they collectively split into 16 separate rails to maximize riverfront loading. When the 16 rails were full of box cars, as they usually were, it was easy to walk right past the narrow Spring Avenue—unless it was your destination. And it was a destination for many.

The one block dirt street was only as broad as a very wide sidewalk. On each side of the street, wooden shacks were crowded together. Some had wooden, hand painted signs above their narrow doors: The Happy River, Bucket O' Blood, Uncle John's Pleasure Palace, The Monkey Cage, Aunt Kate's Honky Tonk, The Lucky Hand. Other establishments didn't need signs. They had human advertisements: a young girl sitting gap-legged in a backwards turned wooden chair, polishing her nails while offering a sneak preview of what lay inside The Cat's Meow.

Set stopped at the top of five wooden steps that led from the upper river shore to the beginning of Spring Avenue. Asar was directly behind him on the third step.

"What are you waiting on Set?"

Set was waiting for his senses to settle down and take in the sight before him. It was as if he had climbed some stairs that offered a view to a crowded school hallway with the sky for a ceiling. Except the students bustling past each other were all grown-ups. Some men were in their Sunday-going-to-meeting clothes. Others in coveralls. Several had coffee cups, but Set could tell it wasn't coffee that was splashing as they stumbled past each other. They bumped and moved between the shacks on both sides of the dirt street.

Asar's index finger poked his brother in the side.

"Get moving," Asar said. He took a step around Set, then stopped. The two birthday boys in the muddy-kneed, brown suits stood side- by-side with their eyes wide as the parts running down the center of their wavy hair. They had been around plenty of crowds of grown-ups before: carnivals, funerals, the Saturday market. Usually, they were bored out of their minds. But this narrow street on Bloody Island was unlike anything they'd ever seen. It seemed like someone had gone knocking on doors from all over the different parts of town. Polocks and Russians, and Czechs, and made-up Negro women in bright purple, red, orange, and green dresses, all so close to each other. Sack suit and coverall wearing Negro men standing dangerously close to made-up white women in bright yellow, blue and red dresses—with their knees showing.

It was this closeness that immediately caught Set's eye. He was so compelled by the different colored bodies rubbing together right in the street that he couldn't tear his eyes away to check his brother's response.

Asar was disturbed.

He had heard his father talk many times about how hard the bohunks were on East St. Louis Negroes. And how many Negroes carried guns and knives to protect themselves. Daddy often said, "Negro and white are the ingredients in dynamite."

Asar's discomfort wasn't enough to avert his eyes or grab his little brother and get them out of there. He was glued to the top of the wooden step by something that he was too young to have a name for. It was how the women looked at the men and the men looked at the women. How the women pressed their whole bodies into the men to whisper in their ears. How the men's eyes stared down into the women's bosoms and how the women seemed to like it. Seemed to invite it by laughing and bending forward.

Something caught Set's eye to his left along the storefronts. He crouched down and pulled out his Semeticolo telescope. Through the blurry, magnified bodies passing in front of him, he captured brief glimpses of a girl sitting in a backwards turned chair. She can't be older than Sarah, the bible study teacher, he thought. The usher board gave Sarah a birthday cake after class last month when she made 17. The

Negro girl in the chair was alabaster-complexioned like Sarah. Through the passing bodies, Set could see that she was painting her finger nails. Turtle green. A white-haired white man in a white suit was standing to the side talking to her. She was smiling. But she never looked him in the face; she just kept polishing her nails. The same color as the dress that she had hiked up to her pale open thighs. Set moved down from her nails and locked in on the pubic hairs visible between the straight back chair's slots. Into his field of view, Set saw a wrinkled white hand slide between the chair's wooden slots, past thighs.

Asar felt Set touch his hand. He hadn't even seen Set crouch down.

"Look, Asar."

Set held the telescope in the same position for his brother to look through.

"The girl in the green dress."

In the tubular field of view, Asar saw the white-suited-man whisper into the green-dress-girl's ear. She stood up from the chair, grabbed his hand and turned to enter The Cat's Meow.

"What's happening," Set said. He snatched the telescope back to his own eye before Asar could respond.

Set saw the old man resist her pull and lean towards her ear. They both turned from the Cat Meow's entrance and started walking towards the narrow alley between the two wooden shack storefronts.

"They're going in the alley. Let's go see," Set said, bolting forward.

"No, Set!"

Too late. Asar's little brother was zigging, squeezing, zagging, and pushing past the waists of adults too focused on pleasure to pay him more than a curious downward glance.

Asar ran after Set into the crush of people. With so many big bodies moving in every direction, Asar was swept towards The Happy River, then Bucket O' Blood, then Uncle John's Pleasure Palace. He quickly lost sight of Set. Asar didn't want to scream out his name and bring any more attention to either one of them. He kept pushing towards the alley.

Asar saw the back of Set's head. He was peeking around a building into the eight-foot-wide alley. Set didn't even flinch when Asar rushed up to him and grabbed his elbow. Set snatched away and continued his furtive lean around the building. Asar moved next to his brother and leaned too.

All along one side of the alley, women were bent at the waist with their dresses raised up and resting on their lower backs. Their hands outstretched wide against the alley's brick wall, as if they were collectively trying to keep it from falling. Behind each of them, men in suits, men in ragged work pants dropped around their ankles, men in coveralls, held the women by the waist as they humped their grunting bodies into them. Some of the women moaned with their heads twisted around to see the face of the men who moved inside of them. Others were silent with their heads down to the ground.

Some men looked at the women on both sides of them as they pumped into the women in front of them.

Set was mesmerized. Asar was appalled, but he couldn't pull himself away. Near the far end of the alley, the old man in the white suit had his pants down around his ankles. He was bent at the waist with his hands on the wall in front of him. Behind him, the alabaster girl gathered her green dress in one hand, as the other held him awkwardly by the waist. She pumped her naked pelvis against his wrinkled pale ass. Grizzled moans echoed throughout the alley each time her body smacked into his. She looked disgusted.

Asar backed out of the alley and rested his back on the building. After a few seconds, he snatched Set away from the alley by the wrist.

"Ain't no Mr. Scare D. Cats in heaven," Set kept repeating, as Asar dragged him through the crowd.

12

Keb stood at the kitchen window watching his wife sitting on the edge of the Americus Fountain. Sienna tea gown hiked up over her creamy knees. Embroidered monarch butterflies resting on her knee caps. Feet in the water.

Nutilda held a palm full of red rose petals in her right hand. Her left hand chose one of the petals and extended it into the fountain's waterfall.

Release.

But no release yet for her pounding head. She watched the red blur rush down below the water's surface, then quickly resurface, joining dozens of petals that danced around her calves.

Keb could never discern whether these post-fight trips to the Americus Fountain were about helping Nut to relax or about helping Nut to make Keb feel guilty. A visual reminder about what a woman must do to survive the terrible rule of Keb the Terrible.

He suspected it was probably a little of both—and a lot of Nut's attraction to dramatics—especially when the twins were involved.

Nut did most things like a runaway train on wet tracks. As the daughter of a former slave who became a sharecropper then a store owner, holding back anything meant not reaching your potential.

Nut's approach to loving transformed the various offices of the couple's work/live mortuary into spontaneous bedrooms throughout the day. It was the offspring of such intensity that became Nut's most ardent passion. Keb drew the boys to him to keep some of his wife's love for himself. She often sat in the fountain, barefoot and frustrated, thinking of how to work with Keb—and around him.

"Nut, the twins are home," Keb yelled from kitchen window.

Hand-in-hand Keb and Nut reached the doorway leading to the front porch. Set, muddy knees matching his brown jacket elbows, ran towards his mother brandishing the bejeweled sword like the pirate he was.

"Look, Mama!"

He beheaded an invisible pirate. Nut stepped forward.

"Yes, baby, I don't think a pirate has ever had such a fine sword as that one right there."

Nutilda's eyes quickly shifted to her first-born. He stood near the steps. The rolled scroll lying near his muddy black Oxford brogues. His almond-shaped eyes beaded on the back of Set's head.

"Mama doesn't get to see her oldest pirate swing his sword?" she asked Asar.

Asar shot his death-look at his father who was still standing in the doorway, studying how Set handled the sword.

"Boy, do you hear me talking to you?"

"Yes, ma'am," Asar said.

"Well, show, Mama."

Asar started walking towards his brother.

"Give me the sword Set."

Set ignored him and continued slashing and jabbing imaginary pirates all over the large porch.

"Set."

"Get your own."

"Where's your birthday sword, Asar?" Nut said.

"There was only one sword in the box, Mama."

"Did you keep digging like your daddy taught you?"

"There was only one, Mama."

Nut looked at her husband. Keb met her quizzical stare. With a roundhouse swing, Set slay another pirate. Asar stood silent, staring at his father.

"You boys take those brogues off and go inside and get cleaned up. Leave those dirty clothes outside the back door and boy quit swinging that thing before you hurt somebody and make me hurt you," Nutilda said.

I   I   I

Once the twins were out of earshot, Nutilda faced Keb but did not speak. At just over five foot, she usually had to look up to her 6'5" husband, but, in times like these, she did the looking down. Even if her reckless eyeballs did so from opposite corners of her face.

He had gone too far. Again. He treated her sons like damn laboratory mice. Always putting them through stupid tests. Putting them in harm's way, so they could learn how to be men before their time.

Her refrain to Keb for years: "God'll bring manhood on them when God's good and ready."

The problem with the man in front of her was that he wanted *to be God*—like his own daddy. Nut leaned in close.

"You told me you were getting them knives, Keb."

"Don't start."

"You know what a knife is, and you know that ain't no damn knife. If it was a knife, Set wouldn't have been sword fighting, and practicing a way to get his narrow ass thrown in jail once you done rushed him up into manhood."

"He'll grow into it and ... ."

"And I suppose I should be happy you only buried one sword for my sons to get tossed in jail behind or lynched? It's both the boys birthday, and you only got Set a gift?"

"Keep your voice down woman," Keb said, leaning in so their bodies were only a couple of inches apart. "I didn't select the gift for Set, he received the gift by being the one to find it. Asar was presented with the same opportunity and did not do what he had to do to come home with a present."

"*Do what he had to do?* Was he supposed to knock down his brother to get a birthday present when he thought his own was there too? You didn't even tell me there was only one gift."

"The true measure of a man is how he responds to the unexpected."

Keb took a step past her towards the house. Nut grabbed his wrist.

"Don't try to proverb-me-off like we're done talking. You know I hate when you do that. As I was saying, men are not 10-years-old."

"They won't be ten-years-old next year or forever."

Nutilda released Keb's wrist but kept her reckless eyeballs focused on her husband. She took a breath.

"You keep putting my sons in danger and I swear to you Keb Americus, my sons and I won't be here *forever* either."

She turned, marched down the 33 Americus & Son stairs. When she reached the bottom, Keb yelled out to her, "Where are you going?"

"Keep your voice down man," she mocked. "I'm going to buy my son a birthday present."

I I I

Nema slammed his office door hard enough for his son to hear. A man shouldn't just let his wife talk to him any such a way. Especially no man reared under Nema Americus. If he'd told Keb once he'd told em a thousand times, "When a woman's mouth stops respectin ya, her heart gone stop next. Then what? Ya gotta knock her down to make her act right again. And once ya hit ya wife, I don't care what ya do, things won't be the same again. That's why ya gotta stop the foolishness before it gets a good head of steam." But he couldn't tell Keb nothin. Seemed like Keb would rather nap in a crowded grave than listen to Nema Americus' good and free advice bout woman folk.

Nema walked back to his large pine desk that his own hands had made. It was the first piece of furniture in the house that he built from the ground up. After months of sleeping on the ground, then the floor, Keb's five-year-old back was sore enough that he started sobbing when Nema told him the plan to build the desk first—not the bed.

"Boy, don't ya know ya always finish ya work before ya go to sleep?"

No, Keb didn't know, but he would learn that belief system by seeing it put into action throughout his childhood. Keb wouldn't have minded so much if the saying hadn't included the fine print: "Boy, don't ya know ya always finish ya work before ya play with ya boy—or talk to ya boy—or hug ya boy?"

Nema and his only child slept on the floor for another two days until Nema finished his second piece of furniture: a sturdy wooden bed and headboard for Keb. And two days later, a sturdy wooden bed and headboard for himself. But on many nights, the desk over which Nema now stood, was also the bed he fell asleep on. Nema would have slept on that bed every night, if it would've assured he'd have something of value to pass down to Keb. He wanted to give his son everything—and train him to keep it—and pass it down one day to his own kids. When Keb was little, every once in awhile, Nema would wake out of his sleep just smiling. A sign that he had been dreaming about Keb again. Sometimes, he couldn't even remember the actual dream, but the *feeling* let him know that his little man had stepped behind his eyelids. On those early mornings, Nema would step into Keb's room and stand over his sleeping son. Listen to his breathing in the dark. Waiting for his eyes to fully adjust to the dark so he could see the rising and falling of Keb's chest. A physical reminder that the flesh of his flesh was alive. Keb wanted so much to teach his son everything, so he could stay alive in a world that was death on Negroes. Stay alive and thrive. But Nema knew the dangers that a thriving Negro faced. First hand. He knew he had to prepare Keb better than he'd been prepared himself.

Nema rested his rough palms on the cool pine desk surface and looked out the bay window. The window offered a view up Bond Avenue. Just below, European immigrants shared the sidewalks with the grandchildren of Europeans immigrants—the prior looking down their noses at recently arrived versions of themselves. The few Negroes who walked beneath Nema's window gave him the chance to look down on his own. Nema loved hard and expected much. When Negroes couldn't make bricks or bread from straw, couldn't get the white boot off their black necks, Nema blamed the black necks. He was a Race Man who believed that the Negro could do anything he set his mind to—as he had. When Negroes fell short of his good example, Nema's hard love turned harsh disappointment. The sight of an unsuccessful Negro broke his heart so much that he'd rather not see Negroes at all. Mercifully, most stayed up beyond 14th Street. Nema rarely dealt directly with colored clients or worked to prepare their bodies. Keb handled dead Negroes. Nema saved his expert hands for preparing the occasional white bodies. The ones who discreetly stopped by his mortician's table on their way to Jesus. After the Civil War, the Negroes who had the good sense to leave Mississippi, Alabama, and Georgia headed north towards Chicago.

Some stopped in East St. Louis along the way.

By Nema's recollection of the last five years of the 80s, Negroes had begun to settle along Bond Avenue up around 26th Street. He just shook his head when he saw these rag tag families arriving with their stitched clothes and mush-mouth talk. Their too-loud laughs when there was absolutely nothing funny about being poor and Negro. Sitting at his desk, he sneered when they appeared through the bay window, which looked out on the corner of Bond and 10th Street. One Sunday, Nema pounded on the window at a disheveled man and woman passing by, "Don't come this far down Bond till ya can represent The Race better!"

I I I

Nema loved how the heavy desk felt beneath his palms. The smooth surety. Steadfastness. The desk comforted him because it reminded Nema of himself: It was solid. He could spend hours leaning on it, looking out the window, watching Bond Avenue come alive.

The glimmer of the brass knuckles brought Nema out of his head. Nema knew it was the same man, even though he couldn't see his face.

How many Negroes polished their brass knuckles?

The month before Nema had watched those same polished knuckles crush into the temple of a gray-haired white gentleman, in a dark blue suit, knocking him flat on his back. In broad daylight. The robber had reached down, and snatched the wallet out of the man's suit jacket, and ran back up Bond Avenue. Broad daylight. The bold violence of the attack turned the witnesses on the sidewalk into statues. No one even chased him.

Nema saw the new victim-in-waiting. Someone's white grandfather who had done well for himself and wanted the world to know. Nema scurried over to the window knocked hard on the thick glass but the white-haired dandy was preoccupied with removing and refolding the red handkerchief in his cream suit jacket. Nema grabbed from his desk the gold-plated scalpel, which doubled as his letter opener, and rushed out his office towards the front door. From the top of the Americus & Son steps, Nema saw the old dandy crash against the ground face first. Heard the sick echo of brittle bones cracking.

"Hey! … Stop! … My God" rose from the sidewalk, but the bandit's menacing whirl—and flashing brass knuckles—stopped the advancing would-be helpers. The tan sack suit-wearing robber dropped to a knee, keeping his eyes on the semi-circle of witnesses. He rolled the unconscious white-haired man on his back. Reached inside the dandy's now dirty cream jacket and palmed the wallet.

"Ya black sumbitch," Nema shouted at the caramel robber who was three shades lighter than him.

The robber didn't even look up. He was busy pulling off the diamond pinkie ring. By the time Nema reached the bottom of the steps, the bandit was a tan blur moving up Bond Avenue. Nema flashed his anger towards the band of white witnesses.

"Ya shoulda jumped on that nigger!"

13

Set and Asar sat at the small wooden table in their bedroom playing chess. Grandpa Nema had carved the board and chess pieces from a single tree stump in the backyard. Their 7th birthday gift from their grandfather. Then their grandfather forced them to learn the game by making them play an hour a day, for a whole year. Under his tutelage. No wonder they hated chess at first. But their feelings thawed when the harsh Illinois winter came. Too cold to play outside, they found themselves sacrificing pawns and capturing rooks on the battlefield in the center of their bedroom.

"Will you move Molasses R. Matthews?" Set shouted across the board.

"Why do you think Daddy did it?"

"If you ask me about my present one more time I'll spit in your eye. Let's just finish the game. And how should I know anyway? You should just go ask him yourself. Now move or I'm quitting."

"He's always buried one for me and one for you. It's almost like he wanted us to fight over a stupid sword. Check," Asar said.

"Maybe he wanted to find out who was the most like him."

Set looked up from the board at his brother in the matching white undershirt.

"What does that mean?" Asar said

"You know what Daddy always says, 'A man always finds a way.'"

"First, you aren't a man, second you're not even the oldest and third, without me keeping you on a straight line, you wouldn't of never found our present."

"A man always finds away."

"And a woman always saves the day," Nutilda said.

She walked through the door with one arm behind her back.

"Who's winning?"

"I would be if Molasses R. Matthews would move faster so I could hurry up and capture his men and trap his king," Set said.

"The only way you'll capture my men is the same way you captured our sword: by being a big fat cheater."

"I'm not a cheater, you big fat loser."

"Cut it out boys or Mama's gonna give you both a big fat whuppin."

"Cheater!"

"Loser!"

"What did I say?" Nutilda said.

The boys dropped their eyes back to the chess board. "Both of you close your eyes.... Okay, open up."

The boys blinked open to find their mother's right fist hovering over the chess board between them.

"Asar tap my hand."

Set's hand shot up first towards Nutilda's fist, but she snatched it away just in time.

"Boy is your name Asar?"

"I was just playing Mama."

"Now, *Asar* tap my hand," she said, glaring at Set.

As soon as Asar touched his mother's hand, her fist transformed into an open palm holding a skeleton key.

"Happy birthday. baby."

Asar took the key and gave it the once over.

"In the hallway," she said.

Asar took off towards the door, followed closely by his little brother. He turned the corner to find a 2 by 4 foot wooden box resting against the hallway wall. At the box's center, a bronze latch clasped it shut. Asar quickly inserted the key and opened the lid.

Inside lay a steel sword that King Arthur himself could've been proud of. The shining 30-inch double-edge blade was attached to a eight-inch bronze handle.

"How come he got a real sword, Mama?" Set protested from over Asar's shoulder.

"Yours is real too, baby. It's just different type of sword."

Asar rested his palms on both knees staring into the box but not speaking.

"I don't want no baby sword. Take mine back Mama and get me one like Asar's."

Nutilda ignored her youngest son and placed her hand on her oldest son's shoulder.

"Do you like your birthday present, baby?"

Asar turned his head around to face his mother. He ran his middle finger down the center of his exposed scalp, crown-to-forehead, the way he did when he was thinking.

"Did Daddy like it?"

Caught too much off guard to lie, she hesitated.

"Your father hasn't seen it."

Asar slowly nodded his head.

"You think he saw Set's present when he picked it out and buried it?"

"Boy, don't you sass me. Now, that's a perfectly nice sword. The biggest and best one all around these parts. If you don't want it I'll... ."

"I'll take it, Mama!" Set said.

"Be quiet. If you don't want your present, Asar, I'll take it back and you just won't have one this year. So what you wanna do?"

Asar ran his fingers along his scalp.

"Mama, I'm 10 now. I know the difference between a make-up present and a birthday present."

Asar closed the heavy wooden lid, making the make-up sword disappear. He stood and walked back into his bedroom and sat in front of the chess board.

Set blurted, "Mama, every pirate has a back-up sword in case the first one gets stuck in somebody."

"Set, don't make me choke you in front of Jesus."

Nutilda bent down, picked up make-up box and started stalking down the hall towards the staircase. When she reached the stairs, she heard Asar scream out, "Checkmate cheater!"

▮ ▮ ▮

Keb wasn't in the basement. Nutilda left the box by an empty casket and headed back upstairs. She found her husband in the upstairs bathroom washing his face in the early evening. Always a tell-tell sign. She quietly leaned against the frame of the door and watched her husband bend his naked muscular, upper-body over the wash basin. From behind, the inch-wide part running down his scalp looked like a calm, dark river running through his brushed hair. His waist, as small as a big-boned woman's. His broad back, a side of beef ribs with scratches across it.

When Keb was sweating on top of her, she loved feeling her palms sliding in circles across his back's sinewy ripples. Until his bucking forced her to dig in. She kept her short nails filed almost to a point. When she first thought about doing it, she hesitated, because she knew people would look at her peculiar-like. But she figured, her reckless eyeballs brought the same looks anyway, so she went right ahead and equipped her petite hands with something to use on her husband.

During relations with Keb, Nutilda's spontaneous explosions of profanity often brought her tightly-controlled husband to a place she wished he spent more time. She loved to bear hug his shuddering body as he released into her. As he let go of familial expectations. Let go of restrictive traditions and outdated obligations. In those moments, she had the unrestrained Keb. And contrary to her father-in-law's opinion, an unrestrained Keb was a happier Keb. Nutilda saw it as her wifely duty to carve a happy face on Keb's back that made its way to his cheeks and eyes.

In the small oval mirror, Keb dragged the tan towel down his clean-shaven coal face then saw his wife's reflection leaning behind him in the door frame. Their eyes met in the mirror.

Working in her father's store, it was Keb's heavy-lidded hazel eyes that had first caught her opposite-of-crossed-eyes. They caressed her face. Weren't repulsed by the eyeballs shoved to outside corners.

"Who you staring at?" Nut said to Keb's mirror reflection.

"The wife who wants to be the husband and the mother who wants to be the father."

"Nooo, I'm the mother who carried her babies to term and the wife who deserves to have some say-so on how they're being raised." Keb slowly turned from the mirror to face his wife. He grabbed the thick bristle brush off the sink and, starting at his center part, he brushed down the left side of his head, then the right. Down the left.

Down the right.

"Let's not do what we do and look up—again—and see we've wasted two months of not getting along. I don't want this to follow us on our trip. Let's be smarter this time. You just need to trust my judgment, Nutilda."

"No, *you* need to trust your judgment, Keb. Your good judgment led you to choose a smart, capable wife, now keep trusting that good judgment and let your smart, capable wife help you raise some smart, capable sons."

14

Coal powered the engine car, but it was pure electricity that ripped through the packed coach. Like the Americus Clan, most of the passengers were on their way to the World's Columbian Exposition in Chicago. Blurry trees and grazing fields and cows and fences and farm houses hurtled past through the train's windows. Keb watched the well-dressed Negroes as they watched the Illinois landscape speed by as fast the 19th Century.

Not yet three full decades removed from slavery and here they were riding in a locomotive car. Keb smiled. There was a palpable sense of pride, even though their Jim Crow coach was over-crowded. Church hats and Sunday suit clothes were the weapon of choice to ward off the dingy feeling of being forced to ride in the segregated car. Some of us are more educated than the people we aren't allowed to sit next to, Keb thought.

But there were no audible complaints about Jim Crow or the sticky humidity or the sticky racism or the White Man. All the talk was of the White City. Many had seen the white buildings sketched in passed-around copies of *Harper's Weekly, Atlantic Monthly, Frank Leslie's Illustrated Weekly,* and *Scribners.* The magazines detailed the palace-like structures' ability to hold thousands.

The twins were more interested in the Ferris Wheel.

Since it was now August, Set looked at the whole trip as a summer-long extension of their 10th birthdays. Summer would be over when school started in September, and, a few months later, 1893 would be over too. That's why Set wanted this to be the best summer ever; as twins, it was their first summer in the double-digits. He liked to write their new age in the dirt, on paper, on a dusty window: 10.

They were officially big boys now.

As Daddy had let them birthday-present-hunt alone on Bloody Island, Set hoped their father would let them do more big boy-stuff at the fair all by themselves.

Asar glanced at Nut. This fair is a better make-up present than a big sword, he thought.

"Daddy, when we get to the tip-top of the Ferris Wheel, will we be able to catch a bird right out of the sky?" Set said to Keb.

"I suppose you could son, but it wouldn't be wise to do a lot of jumping around that high in the air."

"Daddy, I wouldn't slip and if I did I'd just pull Asar down with me so he could break my fall," he said, elbowing Asar in the side.

Asar elbowed his brother back.

"The only thing I'd break is your arm if you tried to grab me." Asar grabbed and twisted Set's arm.

"Owwww."

"Boys, cut it out or the only people who'll be riding the Ferris Wheel will be me and your Daddy sending birds down to go poop on your heads."

"Uuuuuhhhh," the twins said in unison.

"That's right, so you better be good cause your mama knows birds in high places. Don't believe me, ask your father about the time I sent some pigeons to go deal with your grandfather."

"For real, Daddy?" Set said.

"Play it safe boys and just be good," Keb said.

Keb closed his eyes. He wanted to *feel* the passengers excitement as the train rambled north across the Southern Illinois landscape towards Chicago. The Southern Negroes, who had transferred at East St. Louis, were heading towards a destination that held promise for them since the end of slavery. Chicago held the promise of getting a job that didn't cost in dignity. A job where a man could make enough money to feel like a man—even when he had his clothes on. Enough money to provide for his family. In many families, the Negro women did the providing. Chicago's promise knew no gender.

Keb had followed the story in the papers about Chicago beating out New York, Washington, D.C. and St. Louis for the right to host the fair celebrating the 400th Anniversary of Columbus' arrival to the Americas. But Chicago was only the host for what was really a national coming-out party. A celebration for a young country that wanted to put the rest of the world on alert.

President Harrison appointed the National Board of Commissioners that was charged with putting the country's best foot forward. "Which meant making sure no nigger toes were showing," Keb joked when he read the *St. Louis Post Dispatch* story to Nut. Although America's 10 million Negroes represented one-eighth of the population, the 208-member, all-male National Board didn't include one Negro. An agitated Keb complained to his wife, "Next to the Indians, there isn't anyone more American than Negroes. No one values life more than a man who lives in skin that can be the death of him. No one understands liberty more than a man who has been shackled. No one believes in the pursuit of happiness more than a man who has been pursued, hunted, like a wild boar! Hell, all Negroes should just drop all these slave surnames and start calling themselves Americus. It worked for my daddy. Booker T. Americus. Frederick Americus. Sojourner Americus. If Vespucci turns over in his grave, won't be our fault—we didn't bury him. With all we've done for this country, you'd think President Harrison would include one Negro man, one Americus man around the table!" Nut had just stared at her husband.

"I wish you'd get this upset by the absence of any women, by any name, at the table." It was Keb's turn to stare at his spouse.

Like many well-to-do Negroes, Keb wanted to have the Race's contributions to America duly noted and show the world, and their fellow Americans, the progress the Race had made since Emancipation. The World Columbian Exposition was the perfect opportunity.

Since the fair had begun on May 1, 1893, and was running until October 30th, Keb expected there would be time for millions of people to visit the fair from all 44 States and from abroad. He also knew there would be historians, philosophers, scientists, artists, ministers, intellectuals and other opinion makers who could get out the good word about Negroes inspirational up-from-slavery story.

These opinion makers would be participating in hundreds of congresses and parliaments: The World Parliament on Religions, Congress on Labor, Congress on Medicine, Congress of Representative Women, Congress on Africa. When word of these congresses, the intellectual aspect of the Columbian Exposition, emerged in 1889, Keb began reaching out to a loose network of Negro America's Race Men to discuss the best way to represent the Race. From New York to Chicago to Washington, D.C. to Cleveland to East St. Louis, the strategy seemed obvious: These Negro ministers, doctors, morticians, dentists and academics should secure as many speaker spots in the thousands of individual sessions occurring daily inside the fair ground's elaborate white buildings.

After one late-night strategy meeting in the mortuary's Upper Room with East St. Louis' small band of Race Men, Keb told Nutilda in bed, "A man should narrate his own psalm, that way nothing gets lost in the translation."

Excluded from the meeting, Nutilda replied, "What gets lost when a man narrates a woman's psalm?" Then she rolled over.

"I'm getting right tired of hearing you bring up women whenever I talk to you about what I'm trying to do for the Negro."

With her back still turned, Nut said, "Aren't Negro women, Negroes too?"

Keb could scarcely believe he was finally heading to the Exposition with his family. Nutilda would see why he had to do things his way. America would realize what good company it's been keeping in the presence of its darker brothers. The jubilant Negroes on this train would have a much needed reminder that our people are capable of being loved and respected, Keb thought. Colored American Day at the World Columbian Exposition would see to it.

"Asar, ask your mother if she knows how many Colored people will have spoken once the fair is over," Keb said.

"I know Daddy," Set said.

"I know too Daddy."

Like their father, the twins were wearing identical black sack suits, over white shirts, with black ascot ties. Too hot for vests.

"I know you two know, but we want to make sure Mama is up to speed."

"How many Mama?" Asar said.

Nutilda glanced at her husband

"Almost 6000. Now, Set ask your daddy how many of the speakers are women and …"

"Nutilda."

"Ask him how many speakers are women, and when he tells you he doesn't know, ask him why he doesn't seem to have the answer about The Race when the question is about women-folk like your mother. Then close out the questioning Asar by asking your father if women are *really* part of The Race or just a spare rib lying around the kitchen?"

Nutilda winked her left eyelid over a reckless eyeball.

Their father's irritated smirk told the twins that Question & Answer time was officially over.

The 11-hour, stop-filled trip ended when the locomotive pulled into the Chicago train depot just after 9 p.m. A late August sun had set, but not the humidity. The Jim Crow car's Colored American Day excitement had turned into nodding heads and gap-mouthed snoring. Keb eyed his sons. Asar and Set slept leaning on each other with their heads touching. They looked like Siamese twins joined at their parted-scalps. His wife slept on his shoulder.

Keb loved his family most when they were asleep. Quiet. Nothing coming out of their mouths that he had to challenge or correct. No portal for conflict. He was in the profession of death. The ultimate conflict. The last thing he needed was conflict with his family and that's exactly what he had every day. Maybe his father was right. Maybe he did give Nutilda and the boys too much room to question and challenge. But Keb didn't know of a better way to train his family to think for themselves, even when those thoughts were at odds with his own. What he did know was that his father's do-what-I-say–or-the-strap-I-shall-lay method didn't work. Keb was still unlearning those lessons as a 32-year-old husband and father.

"We're here, baby," Keb whispered to Nutilda. He kissed her on the forehead.

"Sons."

❚ ❚ ❚

The Americus Family stood outside the Dearborn Corridor home of Rev. Dr. J.F. Thomas. The deep-voiced, barrel-chested minister with the round, peach cobbler-crust face was the leader of Olivet Baptist, Chicago's oldest and most influential Negro church. During one of the early Race Men strategy sessions, he insisted "Mr. Americus, you and your family must stay at my home when you come up for the Columbian Exposition."

Keb found Rev. John Francis Thomas' insistence odd because they had bumped heads at so many of the strategy meetings. Rev. Thomas, like many others, was insulted by the National Board of Commissioners offer of a single Negro program to celebrate the amazing achievements of Colored Americans during a 6-month fair. "One day? One day? We helped build this country!" he had bellowed at Keb during the raucous meeting in the Olivet Baptist basement. Keb also was offended by the offer of a single day but, like Frederick Douglass, he thought it would be foolish to pass up the opportunity to showcase The Race. Unconvinced by Keb's argument, Reverend Thomas was even encouraging his 2000 parishioners to boycott tomorrow's Colored American Day.

The large double doors opened.

"Mr. Americus you should have warned me that your family was this attractive. I would have reached a little deeper in my closet and grabbed that Easter suit. Come on in."

After getting the family settled into the guest room, Keb met Rev. Thomas in the sitting room and they walked to his oak-paneled study. The cherry-oak desk in the middle of the room was wide as a hauling wagon. It reminded Keb of his father's desk. It said: stability. Importance. The men sat across from each other on matching tan Queen Anne chairs.

"Mr. Americus did you bring your Cake Walk shoes for tomorrow," Rev. Thomas joked.

"Yes, Reverend and I shined them with watermelon seeds."

"Well, I suppose if you run short on your seeds, some our fine Cheyenne District Negroes can spit some on stage from the audience."

Keb understood Rev. Thomas position—and his uncomfortable humor. He knew Thomas, like many of the country's small but influential Negro elite, viewed the fair as the ideal place to celebrate the Silver Anniversary of Emancipation. The perfect time and place to showcase the intellectual, social, educational and economic victories that The Race had achieved in the face of extraordinary obstacles. An opportunity to show that Colored people had transitioned from disenfranchised slaves to blood brothers in the American Family. Keb agreed, but he figured the one day offered would be their best bet, so he supported it.

"Rev. Thomas, I'm sure Mr. Douglass has put together a program that, like his own life, will proudly represent The Race. Besides, the Sage of Anacosta has done so much Race work that even if he does decide to pluck a banjo with a watermelon rind, we should find it in our hearts to forgive him."

"Well, Mr. Americus, if Douglass pulled a trick like that I don't even think the Sweet Savior Jesus could handle it. You know how much is at stake. You know the terrible way our kind has been represented. I'm a Christian minister … with a doctorate of divinity… living in a Christian nation … and I can't even pray to my savior in a white church. How do you think that makes me feel … about my Lord? Have mercy. And why? Because even white men of the cloth think we are just above the blackest monkey in the jungle. This fair is a major opportunity to change some of those perceptions, so I am not willing to rest my hopes of a wooly headed *sage* who doesn't have the good sense to see what an obvious mistake this blasted Colored American Day is. Good night, sir," Rev. Thomas said, then rose and walked stiffly to the study door.

I I I

The next morning, Friday, August 25, 1893—"the real Good Friday," Keb had joked to Nut—the Americus Family arose before dawn to get ready to go see Colored people shine. The official Colored American Day program at Festival Hall didn't begin until 2 p.m., but everyone wanted to get an early start so they could also explore the massive fairgrounds. There was a lot to see.

The Frederick Law Olmsted-designed grounds amazed Keb. "An architectural marvel," he had told Nut after returning in May from the Olivet Baptist strategy/shouting session. Two years earlier in Chicago, Keb was in the crowd at the June 1891 fair ground-breaking. He had his doubts whether the marshy landscape along the south shore of Lake Michigan and Stoney Island Avenue could be transformed into a series of lagoons, canals and enormous columned white buildings that the much publicized plan called for. It was a huge undertaking. Just to build the canals, it eventually took 537,000 cubic yards of soil and filler. A fact Keb memorized to later quiz his sons about.

Their rented buggy turned onto Stoney Island Avenue. Keb asked his boys where they wanted to go first. The twins simultaneously shouted, "the Ferris Wheel!" On the eastern horizon, the rising sun was shooting rays through the Egyptian-influenced, Greek-inspired white columns. Morning light glancing off white domes. The twins were stilled.

The Americus Family rode north up Stoney Island Avenue in silence.

During his bi-monthly strategy session trips to Chicago, Keb had seen the magnificent buildings gradually rise above the marshland. However, he had not seen the White City undressed at sunrise. No cranes. No pulleys. No scaffolding. As they rolled the avenue's last mile towards the World's Columbian Exposition entrance, Keb didn't resist the emotion rising up through his tight throat. He didn't try to wipe away the tears. Even when he felt his wife's reckless eyeball peripheral stare. And his sons stealth glances. Keb Americus was going to let beauty move him for a change. Witnesses be damned.

The twin's 50-yard sprint to the wooden swinging gate had been called a dead heat by the Negro man in the dark blue uniform and cloth cap guarding the Ferris Wheel. Set immediately pulled his silver dollar from his breast pocket, flipped it high into air, and yelled for Asar to call it.

"Tails."

"Heads. I'm going to be the first Negro to ride the Ferris Wheel on Colored American Day!"

As the Americus Family stood around waiting for the 265-foot wheel to open, they talked to the guard.

"I bet you get to go up there all the time and go around and around and around," Asar said.

The guard chuckled.

"Funny thing is, I ain't been up on this here wheel one time."

"No, sir!" Set said.

"Well, son, I couldn't guard the wheel if I was riding it."

"But how about when you're not guarding it, when you come back with your family, and you're not at work and you're like everybody else who's just coming out to the fair. Don't they let you ride it when... ."

"Set, will you let that nice man have some peace."

"It's okay, ma'am," he said. "Young man don't ask questions, young man won't learn nothing. Besides, people don't talk to me much once this here wheel gets to spinning. Tell you the truth, they don't talk to me much at all. I disappear in this big wagon-wheel's shadow... but they don't know I cast a shadow too."

When the Ferris Wheel opened Set and Asar led their family into the first car. It looked like a street car hanging from a giant wheel. The long line of people snaking behind the Americus Family began to load, hanging street car by hanging street car, into the gigantic wheel's 1440 seats. Each new filled car lurched the Americus Family closer to the heavens.

The White City was impressive from the ground, but seeing the landscape from the top of the Ferris Wheel was enough to make a 10-year-old boy never want to come down.

Being in the sky with her twins, and the man who helped give them their good looks, was a kind of heaven for Nutilda Americus. Keb glanced over at his beautiful wife lost in her own thoughts.

One hand holding a tan hat, big as barrel cover. He loved seeing her in the high neck, soft caramel dress as opposed to the simple, canvas-bag looking dresses that she wore around the house—and at times to church just to give those old hens something to gossip about.

Keb glanced in the opposite direction and tried to locate Festival Hall. He purposely had avoided learning anything about the program. He wanted to experience everything anew. The way his sons seemed to. He loved their exuberance, their rambunctious reminder that life was to be lived. That was their greatest gift to him. Even if he couldn't manage to open the gift in his own life too often.

15

When Keb saw the boys hurrying through throngs of people towards Festival Hall, he instinctively pulled the silver watch from his vest pocket. Eleven fifty-seven a.m. He had told them they could go explore awhile by themselves, but that they had to be back by noon. These boys don't know anything but cutting things close, Keb thought. That's why he still had to think for them. Although the Colored American Day program didn't start until 2 p.m., the well-dressed crowd was already amassing and looking up at the impressive 2,500 seat building: a massive rectangular edifice with four white columns stretching from floor to the hulking roof—where the Stars and Stripes waved in the much appreciated Lake Michigan breeze.

"You boys are cutting it awfully close."

"Dang, Daddy! You told us we had till noon and I told Asar to check his watch and... ."

Before Set could get another word out, Keb had leaned down, grabbed the back of Set's neck, and snatched him so close that their foreheads were almost touching.

"Boy, dang, sound too much like damn, and I know you aren't cussing your father are you?" Keb whispered with a menace that made Asar take a step back from them. He had seen his very calm father do this before. One moment being the caring Daddy who would do anything for his family and the next moment filled with an intense rage that didn't seem to match the situation. A process that made Asar sometimes feel very tiny butterflies in the pit of his stomach when his father was around. Even when Daddy was smiling, Asar didn't always trust those smiles—or his father. Asar never had a good sense of what exactlty would unleash the spontaneous acts of intensity, so his strategy was just to focus on making his Daddy proud. Watching Set now and over the years, Asar knew his little brother had no strategy, no filter for dealing with their father. He tended to say whatever *dang* thing popped into his head. And suffered for it.

"No, sir," Set said.

"I can't hear you, boy. Speak up and look me in the eye when you talk to me."

"No, sir, I'm not cussing you, father."

"Good because I would hate to beat the cussing out of you in front of all these fine and respectable people gathered here for such a special occasion. Now, wouldn't it be a shame twenty years from now when your own children ask you what you remembered most about Colored American Day and you have to say, 'Well, I guess what I remember most is your grandpa beating the cussing out of me within ear shot of Frederick Douglass.' Now wouldn't that be a dang shame?"

"Yes, sir, it would be a shame," Set said.

"Wouldn't that be a shame, Asar?"

"Shame, shame, shame," Asar said.

"Now, stand your narrow ass right here next to me, and don't say a *dang* word until your mother gets back."

Much to Keb's chagrin, Nutilda had insisted on going to make an introduction to Ida B. Wells. It wasn't that Keb disliked the anti-lynching activist. In fact, he respected the work that she was doing on behalf of The Race. Dangerous work that should have been done by a man. No man with the same gumption showed up to get the work done, so a strong woman had to do man's work, Keb thought. He glanced down at Silent Set by his side. Set kept his eyes southbound. What Keb didn't like was how Miss Wells openly defied Mr. Douglass by attacking Colored American Day. Sure, one day isn't enough to even begin to display Negroes' great accomplishments since Emancipation, but it was a start. And under the steady hand of Mr. Douglass, it certainly was going to be a start of note. Miss Wells calling this grand occasion an insult to The Race, *in the papers no less,* was in all actuality an insult to Mr. Douglass. It was one thing to say those things in private, but to be all out in the street about it was just too much. The very thought incensed Keb. That man has poured himself out for our people, Keb thought. Mr. Douglass' book about his life and times had proved it. Just because Miss Wells was a good woman didn't give her the right to defy the Sage of Anacosta.

"Daddy...Daddy," Asar carefully said. Keb was lost in his thoughts.

"Yes, son?"

"Where did Mama go?"

"Your mother's over there in that crowd of people," he said.

Keb pointed to a cluster of mainly Negroes about a 100 yards to the left of Festival Hall.

"She'll be back shortly."

"What's Mama doing over there?" Set said. "Did I give you permission to speak yet?"

"No, sir."

"Say something else and watch me smack your cussing mouth into next week. You hear me, boy?"

Set knew a trick question when he heard one. He wasn't about to say another word. He just vigorously shook his head up and down.

I   I   I

Nutilda stood at the fringe of the crowd. Fringe was safer. Especially when in new places, dealing with new people who weren't accustomed to her old eyes. It seemed like once she forgot that each eyeball had retreated to its respective outside corner, she would encounter someone she'd never seen. Their first impression, their facial reaction, would remind Nutilda Americus that she had, "the ugliest pretty face I've ever seen," as one conflicted suitor once said. It was a conflict that made Nut try to draw attention from her flawed face to her full breasts. She would have preferred to captivate with her quick moving brain, but she found that with men, her active mind usually worked against her.

Nutilda's reckless eyeballs also complicated her relationship with some women. With her jet black hair reaching down to lower back, Dakota cheekbones and buttermilk skin, select women seemed relieved that her eyeballs had scampered to opposite corners. At least, that's the feeling that Nut got. Especially the women at church. Unlike men who rarely brought up the obvious, many women relished drawing attention to her unfortunate eyes. Some would bat their own lashes—relentlessly. Others would pretend as if some invisible fleck had landed directly on their pupil, and after successfully trying to rub it out, they'd *have to ask* Nut did she, "See anything stuck in my eye?"

At first, Nut thought she was being overly sensitive. Maybe it was a coincidence that things happened to fly into the eyes of women when she was around. Bad luck of the iris. She certainly had enough bad luck to pass around.

As Nut moved beyond puberty, and her grown-womaness settled on her body, the more mean-spirited some of the women became. Comments began to change from, "Is anything stuck in my eye?" to "What's wrong with your eyes?" to "Is it catchy?" When fed up, she'd say, "No, but I wished women folk sticking together was catchy."

So around groups of unfamiliar women, like the crowd of about 100 around Miss Ida B. Wells, Nutilda Americus tended to drift towards the fringe—and did so on Colored American Day—wearing a wide-brimmed tan hat tilted south.

Wells was a respectful 100 yards east of the Festival Hall entrance, explaining why Negroes should not support the activities that would be starting in a couple of hours. The eyes looking out from Miss Wells' soft-brown face had the gleam of a very curious girl. She was wearing a brown cotton dress with ruffles that covered her small, gesticulating wrists.

"Today, as we gather in the warm and continuing afterglow of our Emancipation's Silver Jubilee, we have much to be proud of. I could stand here behind this podium, in middle of this field, and list the accomplishments achieved in the face of the most un-Christian-like opposition. I've done that before, but that's not what's called for this afternoon.

On this Friday afternoon, the only accomplishment that I need to mention is that our Race has proven itself to be the most American of Americans. In this land of the free, no one has longed for and loved freedom more then us. No group of people has suffered as much to taste freedom. To touch it. But now that we have it, all we ask is that we be a permanent part of the American Family. It is an unacceptable insult to separate us from the rest of the family at this Great Fair designed to show the world America's wondrous achievements. Achievements that all Americans have made manifest through our collective hard work and faith in God."

The almost exclusively female audience nodded their heads and interspersed a few respectable, "Amens."

"There's no need for a Colored American Day, just like there is no need for a White American Day. This important and obvious point could have been made early in the planning stages if Negroes had been allowed to sit on the National Board of Commissioners, sit at the decision-making table along with other Americans but—as evidenced by the late-coming crumb known as Colored American Day—that was not the case. It would've also been appropriate for women folk to be on that same Board, because we know that women would've had the good sense to include all Americans in the American Family. Why? Because we know something about keeping a family together, don't we?"

Bursting into applause, the women turned to look at each other, offering knowing nods. Yet, they were careful not to be too exuberant, as if too much passion would somehow make fraudulent the long gloves, heavy dresses, and church hats they wore on a humid August day.

"In fact, the only day that needs to be celebrated is the day when there is only one America. That day is today. And quiet as it's kept, it's been that day since the Emancipation Proclamation was signed into law. We've simply come too far to go back to a time when Colored folk are treated differently from any other American.

Now, please step forward if you haven't yet received a copy of our pamphlet, *Why the Colored American is Not in the Columbian World's Exposition*, which further lays out our positions and complaints about this token gesture from the fair's all-white, all-male leadership."

Under her tan, broad-brimmed church hat, with a magnolia pinned on the left side, Nut looked around and saw that most women already had their pamphlet. She wanted to receive a copy from Miss Wells herself. The crowd rushed around the lectern. Nutilda could tell that they were as excited as she was to meet Ida B. Wells. In a Negro leadership dominated by Race Men, Miss Wells was one of very few nationally recognized Race Women.

In order to get to Miss Wells, Nut would have to move from fringe to center. Risking the stares of women who weren't accustomed to reckless eyeballs.

Nutilda had read several of Wells' articles denouncing lynching as a tool of intimidation. She was horrified and intrigued by the graphic accounts. What Nutilda loved most about Ida B. Wells was that she was strong and womanly. Nut had heard people, including Keb, criticize Miss Wells for "trying to be a man" but just listening and watching her you could see that she loved being herself, loved being a woman too much to try to be a man. Loved being a woman enough to know that a woman doesn't have to act like a man to be strong. Loved being a woman enough to know that she had the same right to speak for the Race as any man did.

Especially about that evil that has taken away many a woman's man.

A mental image from one of Miss Wells' articles flashed in Nut's mind: Negro hanging from a poplar tree, private parts shoved in his mouth. A fire rising beneath him. Surrounded by smiling white men. Sunday, after church clothes. The curious wives. The watching children.

"I see Mr. Douglass' own writing is in the pamphlet, but he's the one in charge of Colored American Day?"

The questioning woman was flipping through a pamphlet with her bright purple gloves. Earlier, Nut had to look around the woman's lavender hat when they both were on the fringe of the crowd. They had now both moved within a rope's length of Miss Wells.

"Yes, that's correct. We came to a different conclusion about the best way to fry this fish. Presented with the undeniable truth of the issues raised in the pamphlet, and the attention it was drawing, the all-white, all-male, National Board of Commissioners felt they had to offer us something. Let me say here, Mr. Douglass and I agreed that Colored American Day was not what we hoped to gain by presenting our complaints to the commissioners. Our hope all along was to be in a position to help present a more complete image of America, one that included the contributions of Negroes.

Mr. Douglass and I disagreed on how to respond to the crumb offered. He felt it was impossible to pass over an opportunity to present the Race in our best light, even if only for one afternoon. My perspective is simple: If a mother only feeds her child crumbs, she'll never have the nourishment and strength to be the woman the good Lord intended her to be. So yes, although Mr. Douglass was not only a contributor, but actually one of the architects of *Why the Colored American is Not in the Columbian World's Exposition,* he is inside the luxurious Festival Hall and I'm outside in this open field with the smarter—more attractive people."

Miss Wells laughed in her infectious way. A laugh that made the woman in the lavender relax enough to co-sign her compliment.

"We are looking mighty blessed this afternoon aren't we," the woman said, as she glanced around at the women huddled near Miss Wells. The smiling women nodded and chuckled as they acknowledged each other. Nutilda looked down beneath her wide- brimmed hat.

Nut was paralyzed by a spontaneous jolt of anxiety. She hated when she acted this way. She knew how to be confident and assertive, but sometimes her mind and body just wouldn't go along. At least this time she knew why: In order to get her pamphlet signed, she was going to have to make eye contact with Ida B. Wells. Reckless Eyeball Contact.

It wasn't like she didn't understand this reality when she first stood on the edge of the crowd, but now she was so close. And being so close to someone whose approval she wanted made Nut feel like the little girl who wanted friendship from the teasing girls who called her Itty Bitty Crazy Eyes.

The purple-gloved woman shook Miss Wells' hand and moved aside giving Nutilda Americus a chance to be judged by an honest to goodness Race Woman.

"Yes, hello, thank you Miss Wells for, um, being so great," Nut said.

She was embarrassed by her shaking hand as it received the pamphlet from Miss Wells' own fingers.

"I'm honored for everything you've done, I mean, you're honored, and you should be honored for everything ... I had a question, I ... why do they cut the men's private parts off?"

Miss Wells had such a warm smile on her face that Nutilda smiled back.

"You know my name, but I haven't had the pleasure of yours."

She bent to peek under Nut's wide-brimmed hat and looked Nut directly in the eye.

"Mrs. Nutilda Americus."

"Mrs. Americus that very question has bothered me for the longest time. Interviewing these horrified families who had to bury their loved ones, in that condition, my sweet Jesus, they could hardly speak on it, but ..."

"I could hardly ask you about it myself, it's so ... wrong."

"Un-Christian-like is what it is and mighty unbecoming in a Christian country. I don't know how these folks can step into a church without throwing themselves on the altar. I ..."

"Or how could they step into a thunder storm knowing lightning is a witness."

"Yes, they should be scared of a good rain. Now, as far as I can tell, the lynchers defile our men's privates because ... well you know how men place a lot of importance on that type of thing, if you know what I mean. That's one of the ways a man feel good about himself. Make a man feel powerful. They kind of measure their manliness by it. And manliness ain't nothing but a kind of power. White men running round the South with all the power over the laws, power over the jobs, power over the money, power over the land, power over the sea.

When they brought our people across those waters, they wanted to send a message: you may have that thing hanging down there, but I've got the real power ... enough power to cut your power off and stick it in your mouth."

Nut blushed and lowered her reckless eyeballs.

"I know, Mrs. Americus. But there ain't no civilized way to talk about uncivilized behavior. That's what the lynchers want us to do though. They want us to be shame-faced and not talk about it. Be too embarrassed to speak on what they do because they know there's power in naming the devil's work. When you name the devil's work, it's the devil who's shame-faced, not the victim. When we see the devil's work and don't name it aloud, we become the devil too."

Nutilda walked towards the men in her life. She liked being able to see them when they couldn't see her. Set was standing next to his father, looking glum and surprisingly silent. It seems he's been talking since he was born, she thought. Unlike most babies, Set didn't need no prodding from Dr. Mandrake to test those lungs. The lower half of his body was still in the womb when he started yelling for attention.

Asar didn't cry at all. When Dr. Mandrake adjusted his round eye glasses to smack his little bottom, Asar fiercely wiggled his little body and opened his mouth. Then closed it without a peep.

Nut saw Asar standing a few feet from his father and brother, watching what seemed to be all the Negroes on the fairground approaching from every direction. Unlike Keb, Nut didn't like her family best when they were quiet. She liked to listen to her men talk. Although she often disagreed with Keb's methods, she loved to watch her husband interact with their sons.

She still remembered the mix of wonder and pride that instantly spread across his face when Dr. Mandrake handed Set to him. A son for each arm. He began to talk to the boys as if they could understand exactly what he was saying. Keb began training the twins for manhood, making them in his own image, before they could open their eyes. Before they could see her.

I   I   I

"How are my treasures?" Nut said, walking up to the trio, clutching her pamphlet.

"Buried," Asar said.

He nodded towards his brother.

Set smirked like his father. Keb looked down to see if those lips were about to open. Set thought better of it and the Americus Family started making their way towards the four white columns of Festival Hall.

"Daddy, why are so many white people going in," Asar said.

Both Keb and the black-suited white man with the handlebar-mustache, walking next to him, looked down at Asar.

"Son, Colored American Day isn't only for Colored people," Keb said.

He spoke quickly and quietly, intending to end the conversation.

They climbed the white steps.

"Then why didn't they call it Colored and White American Day," Asar said.

Nutilda and Set looked at Keb.

"The day is about celebrating Colored people and you don't have to be Colored to celebrate Colored people, do you?" Keb said.

"I guess not, but why does there have to be a special day for white people to be nice to Negroes? Why can't they be nice to us all the time?" Asar said.

"There are whites who are nice to Negroes and support our causes, many of whom will be joining us today in Festival Hall. Now, that's enough."

▮ ▮ ▮

The boys were growing restless. They were sitting side-by-side between their parents. Nut sat next to Asar, and Set sat in jail next to his father. Set was especially fitful. He literally hadn't said a single word in over three hours. Not one peep. The strain was starting to show. Set was pretending to be a man with no teeth, by drawing in his upper and lower lips deep into his mouth. Worse, he had bid his toothless man to mutely sing along with the Fisk Jubilee Singers. The Fisk ensemble was on stage moaning a praise song for the wonderful things that God has done, called "My Lord, He Done-Done."

Set was silently gumming the lyrics with real passion; his wide-parted scalp swaying back and forth caught Asar's attention.

Asar glanced quickly to his father who was caught up in the emotion of the old slave spiritual. Asar gave a secret poke to Set's side who turned to look at him. Asar slowly shook his head and mouthed, "Don't do it."

Set ignored his brother. His eyes grew wider, the movements of his silent, gummed-up mouth grew more dramatic, forceful. A soulful, geriatric mime in the body of a ten-year-old boy. He started rhythmically moving his black-suited shoulders side-to-side, then rolled them forward-to-back, then side-to-side. When Set let his eyes close, Asar knew his little brother was really playing with fire—on Colored American Day—sitting next to their father.

The Jubilee Singers abruptly changed the song's tempo to a foot stomping revival pace:

My Lawwwd
He done-done!

uh-My Lawwwd
He done-done!

Set picked up his own pace. His sucked-in, mime lips imitated the singers, his shoulders and head keeping time. Eyes still closed. The choir increased the tempo again, stomping and clapping faster:

My Lawwwd
He done-done!
uh-My Lawwwd
He done-done!

The raw emotion of gospel truth caused the Negro man in the brown suit sitting right in front of Asar to thrust his open palm to the sky and shout, "Yes, Lawd."

An elderly Negro woman in a broad white hat, directly in front of the shouter, turned and glared at him. Nutilda, and other people seated nearby, nodded their heads and smiled. The Jubilee Singers torched on. Another man towards the front shouted, "Sing it, sing it." Someone else, "Whose Lord?"

Asar shot a glance at Set who was now sitting up on the edge of his seat. Both feet tapping in time. Set's whole body was rollicking and gyrating—and from his quick moving mouth, just the hint of sound. Asar leaned towards his brother's left ear. That's when he first noticed the lima bean-shaped white spot. It was inside the ear, just above Set's dark earlobe.

Asar was sure there was no spot on his own ear because after he cleaned his ears he usually used the mirror to do a wax check.

Their first physical difference.

Studying the spot made Asar hesitate before saying, "I know you can hear me Set, you better not do it."

As if Asar had screamed, "Fire," into his ear, Set leapt to his feet and started clapping and singing in his gummed-style. Mocking an imagined, toothless old man. With a slight change in the lyrics:

My Lawwwd
He gum-gum!
Uh-My Lawwwd
He gum-gum!

The white-suited, white man with a red carnation in his lapel, looked over his shoulder and smiled at Set. For a split-second, Nutilda thought that her youngest had simply been moved by the spirit. "He'll never sing again" was the weird thought that Asar had when he saw his father's beefy baseball-mitt-fingers reach up and clutch around Set's straining neck. Keb yanked him down to his seat, but didn't release his neck. Father and son's foreheads touched. The carnation-wearing man turned his head back towards the stage.

"You hate your father don't you?" Keb hissed. His tightened neck-grip hidden by their close proximity. Set could not breathe. Or look away from the fury in his Keb's half-lidded hazel scowl. A very real terror widened Set's eyes. Widened his mouth. No sound. An involuntary mime. No air. Set began to kick his legs.

"Say it!" a Negro man in a brown derby down front exhorted the singers.

"You want Daddy locked up for killing his flesh and blood in front of a room of witnesses, don't you?" Set writhed and kicked harder for oxygen. Eyes big as a scared sheep's eyes.

My Lawwwd
He done-done!
uh-My Lawwwd
He done-done!

When Nutilda was really scared, she became really calm. Almost sedate. At their wedding, Nut's father–in–law misinterpreted her fear-induced, pre-nuptial calm for disinterest—which made him distrust her motives.

Nutilda leaned across Asar who was cowering away from Keb's intensity. She began to rub circles into her husband's knee. While rubbing, she calmly, evenly, rhythmically repeated in Keb's ear, "Set is your favorite, Set is your favorite, Set is your favorite … ."

He done-done!
He done-done!
He done-done!
He done done what he said he'd dooooo!

The Jubilee Singers ended with a long held note, the crowd jumped to its feet and clapped feverishly. Keb released his favorite. Set's wide-eyed, breath-gushing wail was sucked into the roaring applause. Nut clutched Set's terrified body to her bosom. His chest was heaving. Breath caught, he began crying and kicking his feet. Nut, Asar and Set snuck evil-eyed stares at Mr. Boog E. Man as he stood applauding the Fisk Jubilee Singers.

After the standing ovation, Keb sat down and didn't say another word to his family during the rest of the program. He refused to even look at them. His 6'5" foot frame sat erect. His heavy-lidded gaze focused on Atlanta University student Paul Lawrence Dunbar. Keb was impressed with the lanky young man's confidence and booming voice as he read "Sympathy" from his poetry collection *Oak and Ivy*:

… I know why the caged bird beats his wing
Till its blood is red on the cruel bars;
For he must fly back to his perch and cling
When he fain would be on the bough a-swing;
And a pain still throbs in the old, old scars
And they pulse again with a keener sting—
I know why he beats his wing!

Keb sat stoically through Desseria Plato's rendition of "Lieti Signor." He clapped politely for Hallie Q. Brown's impassioned recitation of "The Black Regiment," about Negro valor under fire during the Civil War.

Keb wanted to be more engaged in the program, but he was distracted. It was hard to focus when he was this mad at his family. If were not for Mr. Douglass' upcoming keynote, Keb would've left early.

Father was right, Keb thought. He had given Nutilda too much say so in the twin's rearing. Set had openly defied him. Had tried to embarrass him, not only in public, but at the single most important event for the Negro since Emancipation. A chance to show the whole world how far we've come and his own son was acting like a damn monkey. Like his father had said, he'd been too light on the strap.

"That strap taught ya the discipline that helped ya become the big-time man ya think ya are today," Nema would often start, heading into what Keb called Proverb Mode.

"When the son strays too far from the teachins of the father, the journey home brings him cross the path of the lion."

Against his father's wishes, Keb had married the woman who was encouraging his sons to defy him.

The seat next to Keb was empty because Set, who was still sobbing, was in Nutilda's lap, snuggling against her bosom like a nursing baby. Asar was leaning deeply into his mother's side. Nutilda had her arm around his shoulder.

She, too, was distracted. Nut could barely pay attention to the slender and intense violinist with wavy-hair, Joseph Douglass, who was the prelude to his grandfather's closing address. She kept staring at Keb. Studying him with her reckless eyeball peripheral vision. The prominent forehead. The walnut-sized cheekbones. The humongous hands. She wished he would turn and look her directly in the eyes. She would like to stare into those half-lidded hazel eyes now. Examine them. Make *sure* she knew the man in front of her. She wasn't feeling so sure right now.

Keb didn't have to turn to know his wife was staring. He could feel the heat of her judgment. The way it warmed the blood in his cheeks. Keb wanted to turn and order her to "Stop looking at me!" But he would not give her the satisfaction. She wanted him to look into those reckless eyeballs and feel guilty for disciplining his own son. What did a woman know about raising a boy into a man? A boy into a leader of men?

Keb was relieved, instead of excited, to see Frederick Douglass rise from his seat next to Harriet Beecher Stowe's sister, Isabella. The Sage of Anacosta limped across the stage with the help of his bamboo walking stick. The limp, the stuffed girth, and the white mane sobered Keb. His lion was far into winter.

The program had been long. His family irritating. Keb was ready to go home.

Douglass stood at the podium, four buttons of his long brown suit jacket bowing out, exposing what seven decades of Negro life can do to the body. In silence, he allowed his eyes to methodically move throughout the multiracial audience. Across the front row. Then a broad arc through the distant seats. Then back towards the front. His extended silence made the gathering uneasy. People in the audience began to look around. Heads turned from side-to-side. Some in the front sat up in their seats and turned fully around.

Had there ever been assembled such an audience? Keb thought, taking his own survey of the room. Accomplished, well-dressed Negroes, sitting side-by-side with accomplished, well-dressed whites. All gathered to celebrate The Race that the Supreme Court decided had no rights a white man was bound to respect.

"Our presence … here … in such numbers … is a vindication … of our wisdom and our good nature," Douglass started.

His deep baritone rising and falling, pausing, inserting verbal commas into his oratorical rhythm.

"I am glad we have cheerfully embraced this occasion, to show by our spirit, song, speech, and enthusiasm that we are neither ashamed of our cause, nor our company."

The audience broke into hearty applause.

"It is known to many of you, that there is a division of opinion among intelligent Colored citizens, as to the wisdom of accepting a Colored people's day, at the Fair. The division, has been caused in part, by the slender recognition we have received, from the management of the Exposition."

What Keb wanted was some recognition from his wife about the skill at which he had been raising his sons. Preparing them for a homeland that treats them like foreigners because of their skin. A homeland where bohunk foreigners are treated with more respect than Negro Americans. Isn't American Negro skin American skin? I was born here, he thought.

"That we are outside the World's Fair, is only consistent, with the fact, that we are excluded from every respectable calling, from workshops, manufacturing, and from the means of learning trades. It is consistent, with the fact, that we are outside of the church, and largely outside of the state."

Keb looked at Douglass standing before him and shook his head. How did Nut think a man rose to this stature. By having a mother cuddle and hold him? A Colored man can only rise in this country by showing the white man that he can stand on his own two feet, tall enough to look right in his eyes.

"The people who held slaves, are still the ruling class in the South. When you are told, that the life of the Negro, is held dog cheap in that section of the country, the slave system tells you why it is so. Negro whipping, Negro cheating, Negro killing, is consistent, with Southern Ideas inherited from the system of slavery."

No hug or tears or pleas for mercy will save them if confronted with noose and fire and knives and guns, Keb thought.

"We fought for this country. We ask that we be treated, as well, as those who fought against our country. Instead, we hear nowadays, of a frightful problem called a Negro Problem. The Negro Problem, is a Southern device, to mislead and deceive. There is in fact no such problem. The real problem, has been given a false name. It is called Negro for a purpose. It has substituted Negro, for Nation, because the one is despised and hated, and the other is loved and honored. The true problem, is a national problem. The problem is whether the American people have honesty enough, loyalty enough, honor enough, patriotism enough, to live up to their own constitution."

16

SATURDAY, JULY 9, 1927
EAST ST. LOUIS, ILLINOIS

Heru was in the backyard sitting on the Americus Fountain, feet dangling in the water, like Grandma Nutilda often did. His head popped up when he heard his Aunt Nephthys' high-pitched hyena laugh as she walked past the side gate. It sounded like she had hundreds of tiny smiles shooting up through her throat. Heru loved to hear those smiles coming even though Big Grandpa Nema made those smiles sound ugly when he called Auntie Neph "loud and uncouth." Sometimes right to her face. But Auntie Neph wouldn't pay him no never mind. One day in the kitchen, after Big Grandpa Nema told her, "A grown woman shouldn't be so goddamn loud," she just threw that long neck back and released those smiles right in the space over Big Grandpa Nema's head. Then wrapped her skinny porcelain arms around him and squeezed tight.

"You are about the most ornery man in all of East St. Louis and that's saying something. I'mma go find you a girlfriend," she said then kissed him on the cheek and released some more smiles from her throat.

Heru didn't hear Uncle Set, which wasn't unusual when his uncle was with Auntie Neph. She had a way of making all the light focus on her. But Uncle Set didn't seem to mind.

Heru pulled his feet from the water and swung his legs around so he was sitting on the fountain ledge facing Ta Neter. He felt a fondness for the private cemetery. Uncle Set had taught him how to count by holding his hand and guiding him in a wide circle around the 33 silver dollar shaped tombstones. The grave markers were tall as then 2-year-old Heru. As they passed each stone, Uncle Set would place Heru's hand on it and say, "One." Making Heru repeat. "Two… three … four … ."

Before Heru turned three, he could count to "Thirty-three."

Heru hopped off the fountain ledge. He walked across the bluegrass to the grave stone that Uncle Set used to always start their counting lessons because it was the oldest. The grave of Big Grandpa Nema's wife. The wife whose name he never knew because Big Grandpa forbade anyone to speak of her.

Heru ran his hand across the top of the smooth circular surface.

"One."

He moved on to the next.

"Two."

It was when he got to number 29 that he saw Uncle Set staring at him from the kitchen window.

Heru stood there by the grave marker, watched his Uncle disappear from the window and exit the kitchen door heading in his direction. From a distance, Uncle Set's big, bald head seemed like the moon had snuck out in the day and landed atop his fully buttoned black shirt. Being more "presentable," as Big Grandpa Nema would say, was another thing that had become different about his Uncle Set since he and Aunt Neph jumped the broom right there in the backyard.

Heru could see Uncle Set's privates bouncing in his black trousers to the rhythm of his long-legged gait.

"What you doing, boy?"

"Just counting."

"I guess ain't nothing wrong with a little practice, but you way beyond counting to 33. Then again, I suppose a smart boy gonna always stay up on his early lessons, less they leave him. What number you on?"

"Twenty-nine."

Uncle and nephew stepped over to the next marker. Then became still.

The week before Grandpa Nema had personally and privately chiseled his name into the headstone that had he had long reserved for himself.

Set tried to think of any signs that Grandpa Nema was especially down in the mouth. Last night, he'd said, "My back is actin like it don't like me none." But whenever Grandpa Nema grew tired of complaining about people, he'd start in on his back. Or his knees. Or how his ears could barely hear a goddamn thing. That was just his way, so putting his name of his grave marker number 30 was probably nothing.

But it was just hard to tell with Grandpa Nema. Set had heard enough stories from grieving wives and sons and sisters and daughters about how their loved ones seemed to know. How death had taken up residence in their face. Casting shadows on tombstones.

Set felt Heru staring questions up at him.

"Don't tell me now boy you done forgot your lessons that fast? You know what come after twenty-nine."

Heru looked back at the giant silver dollar sticking out the earth.

"Thirty...Nema Americus."

Grandpa Nema had always made Set feel like the first-born son.

Treated him like an heir.

"Is Big Grandpa Nema dying?"

"Your Big Grandpa is too mean to die. He's not done yelling at you to pick up your feet when you walk through the house and yelling at me for not yelling at you first."

"Why's his name on the tombstone then? It wasn't there before." Heru grazed his fingers again across the chiseled letters.

"You know how your Big Grandpa is. Cant' sit still for too long. That's what happens when you been working hard, been busy, your whole life. You work even when you don't have to work anymore. Hard to be still. No one was probably around for him to yell at, so he shuffled those old knees out here and put his name on it."

Heru had been around enough grown-ups to know that they sometimes told stories. Heru Americus wasn't raised to call grown folks liars, but now that he was becoming a big boy, he had his own mind. Enough of it anyway to decide when he thought someone was telling him a story and not the truth.

"Uncle Set?"

Set reached out and placed his big right palm on Heru's frail left shoulder.

"Yes, son?"

"Is that really what you believe?"

Set looked into eyes wide enough for him to dive in head first.

"Yes, son, that's what I really believe," Set lied.

He brought his nephew close and hugged him tight. Heru could feel the length of his uncle's privates pressed on his shoulder. It reminded him of carrying the nets full of catfish over his shoulder as he walked home from Cahokia Creek with Uncle Set.

Set unwrapped his arms from his nephew and took a step towards the house.

"Let's head inside, son, and see if we can get Big Grandpa Nema to yell at us."

"Uncle Set?"

Set looked back over his shoulder. Heru dropped his head.

"I never seen privates before."

The whispered declaration was also a painful question.

Heru's head was bowed so deeply that Set's thick index finger could barely fit in the space between his nephew's chin and upper sternum. Set tried to gently lift the boney chin. Shame resisted. With steady pressure, the index finger finally forced his chin up. Heru looked into his uncle's glistening eye. Set looked inside himself.

"Okay, son."

Set released his nephew's chin and wrapped his heavy arm around Heru's shoulder. They headed towards the Specialty Shed. Red paint still covered the rough hewn wood on the outside. Set called it the Devil's Workshop because his mind got idle, calm, when he worked in there.

When they got inside, Set slid the two barn door-like panels close enough so no one could see inside from the house windows, but not all the way closed, to avoid creating suspicion. The doors were rarely shut because the Specialty Shed was often used as an overflow room. Heat and humidity could raise the stench of death from the blood-stained floor boards.

Set led his nephew towards the shed's back corner. Four saws of descending size hung from four nails on the wall. Dust particles did a slow jig in the cylinder of sunlight shooting down through the wagon wheel-sized window five feet above the saws. As they stood before each other, the dusty beam of light shot between uncle and nephew. A porous barrier.

Heru's head was bowed deep again. Set extended his long arm, across light, onto his only nephew's shoulder. Gently patted three times. Reassuringly. With his free hand, Set freed himself from his trousers. His heavy dark phallus hung in the sunlight. An overstuffed bratwurst hanging in the window at Dabrowski & Son Meats. Cooked to a crisp.

Careful not to make eye contact, Heru raised his head just high enough to see it—which made his lips part a little. He was startled and intrigued by the size of it. And the color. He had always imagined it would be the same pale color as Uncle Set's moon head.

Set had planned to just look away until Heru got his peek, gather himself and look casual walking out of the shed. But Set could not glance away. He couldn't stop watching his nephew watch what he'd been missing.

There would be no son for Heru Americus.

The thought crossed Set's mind as he saw Heru's tiny hand reaching through sun light towards his phallus. Reason enough to let his nephew touch him. Feel him. Run the tips of his fingers down the thick vein along the side of the shaft. Know him. Even when he felt himself hardening beneath those tiny fingers, he did not pull away. Heru deserved at least this.

Set watched Heru cautiously bring the other small hand up towards his now erect penis. It was tilting up as if stretching towards the source of the sunbeam. Bathed in light.

Heru leaned his face closer. He wanted to see better as his fingertips followed the turns that the smaller veins made along the side of phallus. His frog eyes examining the uncircumcised foreskin. Using his left thumb and forefinger, Heru gently pulled back the black skin, fully unsheathing the penis head. It looked like the smoothed head of a railroad spike. But rounder. On his tippy-toes, Heru looked down into the two holes atop the spike. Set stood tall looking down on the top of his nephew's head. He could see that Heru's hair was thinning on his crown. Heru's reverse widow's peak already extended deep up his scalp like a dull arrowhead eliminating hair along the way.

The two holes reminded Heru of picture books he had seen with whales spouting water out of blow holes. He wondered if invisible little bursts of air were shooting out of Uncle Set's holes. Still holding the foreskin with his fingers, Heru turned his face sideways and rested his cheek over the blow holes. Uncle Set chuckled. No air. But there were eyes. Heru's sideways head allowed him to see parted lips too. They belonged to Auntie Nephthys. She was standing at the almost closed barn door. How long had she been there? Watching.

Maybe Uncle Set's holes were suction holes not blow holes, because Heru's cheek seemed stuck there. Much like his froggy eyes were stuck on Auntie Nephthys' squinting pair. Like she was trying to really see what she was really seeing: Her husband's 45 degree-angled phallus near her nephew's mouth. Both awash in a broad beam of sunlight. As yellow as her flaring sun dress.

Heru was stuck. Cheek frozen on Uncle Set's penis like last winter when his tongue got stuck to the corner lamp post. His stare stuck on the barn door. Set whipped his head around to see what Heru was looking at. Now Set's eyes were stuck too. Frozen on a look that he had seen so many times on the faces of dirty, gibberish speaking bohunks who crossed the street rather than walk next to him. But it was a look he was now seeing for the first time on a woman who had showed him he was capable of love: A look of disgust.

Instinctively, Set knew the very next action he took was going to determine whether Nephthys was still going to be in his life or not. Whether that action was the movement of his lips and the utterance that followed, or the blinking of his eyelid and the water that followed. Indecision had him. He couldn't act with his wife looking at him like that. Those lips that had just been at his ear, had now twisted surly like a Bloody Island bohunk broke at the bar. Her eyes: green slits. Her jaw: molars squeezed tight as a vise over at Blacksmith McGee's.

Set could feel his body start to shake a little. The subtle shaking was the only movement he was able to manage.

It was Nephthys who had to make the major move. Two steps through the door into the Specialty Shed. Then another. From the quickly unbuttoned top of her yellow sundress, she freed her right breast. Squeezed the peeled potato-sized gland near the base so her nipple aimed towards Set's white skull. Then she reached down and hiked up her dress. She rarely wore undergarments in the summer. Her naked pubis spoke before her lips did.

"I can feed him and fuck you at same time and that's not enough?"

She froze like that. Only her words moved now. As echo in the new space, the new distance between husband and wife.

Heru's bulging eyes had now discovered two new body parts. Like his father and uncle before him, Heru Americus had become a treasure hunter. His pupils digging into Aunt Nephthys' briar patch of wispy blond pubic hair. He had overhead adults talking just enough to know that he came from such a place. And that he would never be able to help create a person who came from such a place.

Heru watched Aunt Nephthys unfreeze first. She released her dress' yellow hem as if it were a pained sigh. Slowly covered her bosom. Heru didn't see Uncle Set move next. He felt him. The massive open palm slapped down on Heru's cheek, knocking him from hard penis to hard floor. Set's violent show of remorse did not move Nephthys in Set's direction. It pushed her away. He watched his wife's back as she stumbled out the almost closed door.

Frustration roiled through Set. An urge to run competed with an impulse to fall to the floor. He abruptly turned around. His single eye landed on Heru. Set stalked towards his nephew. Heru was lying very still on his back. Stood over him. He hated Heru right then. He had tried to help his sissy-ass and look what had happened. Set could feel his own abdomen tighten. His breaths quicken.

Heru's stare-catching eyes saw the black bottom of Uncle Set's heavy boot rise over his bleeding brow. His frog eyes bulged. The boot slammed down next to his left ear. Heru's mouth was now wide too. No breath. No words.

17

Nephthys kicked off her shoes onto the bluegrass before walking out the side gate. She headed up Bond Avenue. In bare feet, Neph was a sliver under six feet, but looked taller because of her crane- like, buttermilk neck—and her penchant for keeping her chin up. The yellow dress' flaring skirt ruffled in the breeze. Nephthys' long- armed gangly stride made her look both adolescent and regal. As she long-stepped rhythmically along, men with cocked bowlers and women with cocked noses, shifted their eyes towards the two- legged giraffe striding in their direction up busy Bond Avenue.

Striding is what Nephthys did when she was troubled. Like she was now. She had always known there was some power in movement. She'd seen it in the rocking arms of women as they quieted screaming babies. Her own soul had been quieted many times, standing along the shore of the Cahokia River, watching water move by.

Nephthys strode on. She didn't need to turn to read the names painted on the store front windows. She had walked past them many times. Troubled. Businesses that she had been in many times. After closing. Cigar smoke and counter tops. Grandfathers and their grandsons. Men in her mouth.

During the day, she smiled and laughed right on through her past, but during the late night something seemed to change. At times, Nephthys would be so troubled by midnight memories that she would climb out of her marriage bed. She would do this even though Set loved her. For who she was and for what she had been. She wondered if he was haunted too by those days. If memories followed him into night. The creeping details looking for an entrance into the mind. Her details were many and relentless. Chewing tobacco breath and armpit hair and penny candy and piss and chest air and beer breath and semen and blood. Nephthys had arrived at Aunt Kate's long before Set. For the parts he was not a part of, she told him about. Filled him in on her details. Everything she could remember. These were the only times these memories saw the light.

Nephthys always confessed during the daylight hours, when he could see her face. Her eyes. Leaning over the small breakfast table at Mabel's Kitchen. Sitting face-to-face in the park. Facing each other on the rim of the Americus Fountain. Even when Set sternly said, "That's enough baby, that's enough." But enough would not be when he decided. Enough would be when he knew the truth about her—and the truth about himself for wanting someone like her.

Only then, when she had decided it was enough, she would stop and look into his one eye. Waiting for some sign, some hint of his real feelings towards the ugliest part of her. Sometimes they would sit across from each other for minutes. Nephthys staring. Set letting her. Sometimes he would reach out and take her long skinny fingers and stroke them.

"I know who you are—and that you—is who I love."

Yet, Set's affirmations weren't enough. Weren't enough to stop Nephthys from leaving her marriage bed to walk Bond Avenue. To walk past her past.

Now, I've got something else to forget, she thought, as she walked past Taylor's Barbershop.

"Set spends more time with Heru than Asar does," Nephthys said aloud.

They're always going off alone doing things together. Set creating maps for them to go pirate exploring around the damn city. Fishing at Cahokia Creek. You'd think Set would let the boy's father take him fishing now and again. There's no telling what they've been doing, she thought.

Nephthys had always thought it was sweet that Set and Heru shared a special bond. She knew he was trying to fill holes. Nephthys loved when Set's heart showed through. It made her look at her husband with soft eyes.

As she walked by Ladron's Hardware, she thought of where her mouth had been. She slowed to a stop in front of Jimmy's Furniture Store. The bile of memory sliding from gray matter to the back of the throat. She had to stop. Nephthys leaned forward and spit on the sidewalk. Her eyes began to water there in front of the furniture store. She glanced over. Saw her reflection before the eyes of others. White customers looked through her translucent image on glass. As they had looked through her on sidewalks and on street cars. But not in backrooms. There, they saw Nephthys. Because she made them. Giving herself so fully over to pleasure that it was impossible for them to take their eyes off her open body. It was in those moments that her green eyes caught their intense stares. Their recognition. Their acknowledgement that there was something of value inside her.

These are the thoughts that Nephthys told herself when she lay in bed next to her husband trying to make peace with her past. Sometimes the thoughts made her feel better, but usually she had to get out of bed and walk the sidewalks of East St. Louis and confront memory at the street level. The storefront level. Looking though plate glass for a glimpse of self-forgiveness. She usually found a self-reflection.

Nephthys turned around. She needed to talk to somone.

I I I

Nephthys approached the stone walkway of Nutilda's House of Roots and Herbs. Who else could she talk about what could not be told?

She paused outside the door. Through the lightly-frosted glass, she could see the frosted outline of Miss Nutilda facing the far wall of mason jars.

With her opposite of crossed-eyes, Nutilda looked at the wall of herbs with her extreme peripheral vision.

She stretched up her five-foot frame and took a jar down. She unscrewed the lid and raised the jar to her nose. St. John's Wort. Pulled her nose out. Raised her head to the wood beamed ceiling. Brought the herb jar to her bosom.

Nutilda couldn't even count the number of people who had come through her door. Wheezing. Pus spilling from sores. Shame-faced men with infections they couldn't go to a respectable doctor with. Troubled women with constant womanly flow. Children with the gout.

Nutilda knew she was rarely the first choice. She was usually visited only after all other remedies had failed. The last hope. When people were too broken for their pride to stand in the way of seeking out a crazy-eyed Negro woman for help. She tried not to take it personal, but she did.

Nutilda looked at the jar squeezed against her bosom then back up at the wall of herbs.

"Why didn't any of you work?" she said aloud.

An herb could betray. She was a witness. Nutilda had taken pride in showing the power of the earth through herbs, but when she needed the earth most, when she needed roots to stand up for her and her Set, these roots let her down.

Betrayed her. Betrayed her family.

The vibrating gong rescued Nutilda from the past. The second to last thing she did before officially opening Nutilda's House of Roots & Herbs was rig a mallet above the door to strike a plate-sized gong each time someone entered or exited. A vibrating welcome and goodbye. Nutilda turned and saw Nephthys standing in the doorway. She didn't want to like her daughter-in-law because once a whore, always a whore. But Nutilda was fond of Nephthys. She made Set smile. Not for too long. But the smiles were big and open and full of life.

"Miss Nutilda… ."

Nutilda quickly turned to face Nephthys. "What happened?"

Nutilda recognized the fear in Nephthys voice. "Is Set okay?"

The glass mason jar of herbs slipped from Nut's hand and smashed on the floor. She took a couple of quick steps over the broken glass and roots towards her daughter-in-law. Then Nut abruptly stopped when she saw Nephthys raise the hem of her yellow dress waist high.

"Isn't this enough Miss Nutilda? I thought this was going to be enough. Why didn't you tell me that this wasn't enough Miss Nutilda?"

Nephthys released the dress' hem; it fell to the floor again. Nephthys' slouching body and mind fell too even though she was still on her feet. Nutilda dashed to her.

"What's wrong with Set?"

Nephthys had collapsed onto her haunches. Nut grabbed Nephthys by the shoulders and began to violently shake her.

"What did you do to him?"

Nephthys slowly twisted free and pushed off her much smaller mother-in-law, who slid on her bottom across the pine floor. Nut knew her baby boy was dead. Dead before she could truly make things right between them. Gone before she could keep her promise. Nut began to weep. Nepththys' dam broke too. Both women sat convulsing on the floor, blinking at each other through tears. Nephthys brought herself to her knees and crawled towards her mother-in-law. She had to tell her, because she had to tell someone who loved Set as much as she did. She needed help carrying this pain. Nephthys wrapped her long buttermilk arms around her mother-in-law and placed her full lips at Nutilda's ear. Before she could speak, the gong rang.

Both women turned to see Set standing in the doorway.

"Get your lying mouth away from my mother's ear," Set said, stomping towards them.

Nutilda's open mouth stare was stuck on her dead-son walking.

In the room where she couldn't keep her promise.

Set stomped to a stop in front of his mother and wife. He towered above the women. His one eye glaring at Nephthys.

"What did this lying whore tell you Mama?" Set demanded.

Nutilda's quick-shifting emotions tangled her tongue. She was sad and relieved and confused and excited and afraid. Something was wrong with the way Set was talking and acting. When Nut opened her mouth, the sticky words tripped and tumbled out, sounding like she had a mouth full of salt water taffy.

This new language was not enough to make Nephthys take her eyes off her husband glowering down at her. Fear had silenced her sobs. Set was frighteningly close. Threatening.

"You were right, Mama, once a whore, always a whore. With my own eye in the Specialty Shed, I saw her raise her dress and show Heru her nakedness."

Nutilda turned her head to Nephthys. A look of disbelief, turned revulsion, turned anger. Nutilda's reckless eyeballs shifting like her fluid emotions. She had been through enough seeing her son suffer because of a problem she couldn't fix, she wasn't going to allow her only grandson to suffer because of a problem that she could fix.

"Why would you do a thing like that?" Nut demanded.

Nephthys' eyes shifted from Set to Miss Nutilda, before moving back to Set, who was still scowling down at her. Nephthys was silenced under their collective condemnation.

"You trying to mess up that child more than he already is?"

Nephthys couldn't answer because Nut's filed-to-a-point finger nails were scratching down her nose and lips. The release of warm fluid, a blood-pact between mother, son, grandson and whore.

Nephthys didn't even raise her hands to cover her face. She let her mother-in-law have her way. She wanted one of those filed- to-a-point nails to catch and lodge inside the soft flesh next to her eyeball. Rip it out. Along with the wrong it had witnesed. Yes, the eyes would have to go. If only they had been closed when she had walked into the Specialty Shed. If only she had been playing the Blind Game that she liked to play with Heru. The game where they took turns closing their eyes, took turns being blind, and searched the room while the other stood perfectly still. If she would have been the Blind Person, Heru and Set would have heard her coming. They could have stopped doing wrong before she witnessed wrong.

"Rip them out," Nephthys heard herself calmly say. Or were those words thoughts in her her head?

"Rip them out."

Yes, that was her voice. Nephthys was speaking what she was thinking. Miss Nutilda was not thinking, just acting with frenzied viciousness. A clawing, wide-eyed, feral cat atop Nephthys. There was no plan, no approach, no methodology to her manic blood- letting. Just desire. For nail depth. For blood. She had to get more blood to flow; it would serve as a salve.

"Mother that's enough," Set said, reaching down and snatching his frenetic mother off his calm bloody wife.

"Rip them out."

18

Set leaned down and picked up Nephthys' long limp body. Like a woman lying on elevated railroad road tracks, her head and feet dangled over Set's rigid forearms. Her pale face was a sloppy railyard of scratches. Misshapen tracks converged on Nephthys nose and chin, down her cheeks, beneath her eyes. He quickly turned his body sideways and ducked beneath the small back doorway that led to Americus & Son. That's when he realized that Nephthys' wary eyes were locked on his face.

He was grateful that no one else was around to see him carrying his bloody-faced wife up the curving staircase. But he was sure someone was listening. Had heard. One of the many problems associated with living at home as a grown man.

Set laid Nephthys on their perpetually unmade bed. He rushed to the bathroom and returned with a hot damp cloth soaked in aloe vera. Still standing, he gently placed the steaming white rag on his wife's face like a burial cloth. With both palms, Set softly pressed the fabric into her cheeks and held it there. He wiped her face clean. Set rushed back to the bathroom, returned with a new steaming cloth and repeated the ritual. The blood had made the scratches look worse than they were. Nephthys' constant stare made him feel worse.

Her hard glare followed Set as he sat down on the edge of the bed. Slit eyes dared him to turn his back. He didn't. He just sat on the bed looking at the giant oak outside the window. Feeling his wife's judgment. Wondering how to begin.

"You called me a whore," Nephthys said, with an uneasy calm.

Only her lips moved. With enough conviction to turn Set's gaze to her.

"You called me a whore, Set."

It hit Set harder the second time because he was studying her eyes when the words left the mouth he loved. Set wanted to kiss those lips and make this whole thing go away before Neph thought about doing something crazy—like leaving him. He felt a panic begin to rise. He felt vulnerable, so he attacked.

"You brought that on yourself. You ..."

"Don't, Set. I saw you."

"You don't know what you saw because it was dark. I'm sure what I saw because you were standing by the door, lit enough to put on your show. Showing that boy your privates like you just all of the sudden lost your damn mind. And that's what I saw bright as day. I don't know what the hell you saw. But I know you can't bring that old stuff up in Americus & Son. You're not a whore, but if you act like one that's what I'm going to call you, because that's what any woman needs to be called who raises her dress and shows her nakedness to a 10-year-old child. That's wrong Nephthys. And that's not who you are anymore. Now, we're gonna cut out this craziness and get back to the way things are supposed to be. Okay?"

"I saw you, Set."

19

Heru. Nutilda leapt to her feet. She hurried out the front door of Nutilda's House of Roots & Herbs. Nut pushed through the side gate. The sight of the slightly-opened barn-like door made Nut race her bare feet across the cool bluegrass lawn.

When she arrived at the portal, her body stopped. From the wagon-wheel window, a beam of sunlight sprayed across Heru's nakedness. His stick legs trembled under the strain of balancing on his toes. Humidity pumped sun-lit sweat down his forehead. Mouth opened wide enough to swallow a pregnant cherry from its stem. His child neck expanded and contracted with each emotional breath. Black bird-cage chest heaving. Between his legs, a sweaty black nub. Where is Auset? Nut thought. She started gingerly towards Heru.

He balanced and shook and sweated. Grandma Nutilda approached her grandson like she knew he was broken. Growing up as Crazy Eyed Nutilda, she intimately understood a child's fragility. She still remembered what is was like to be young and wrong. Remembered the Normal Eyed Girls at school who told her, "No boy is gonna want to be with a heifer with broken eyes."

Looking at her grandson trembling in sunlight, Nut knew another break might make broken, unfixable. Like Set. She took a breath and tippy-toed towards Heru with the caution of a breaking point expert.

Nut recognized the statue in Heru. She understood how statues were made. The building materials: active adult fingers, still children's bodies, secrets and silence. The chipping and chiseling tools that define and destroy.

Nutilda came to a stop and lowered herself down from her tippy-toes. She stood directly in front of Heru. Face-to-face. Crazy eyes to frog eyes. The six inches between them wasn't close enough for her to reach him. For the broken, distance is relative. Dependent upon how far they've caved. The amount of shame. The depth of the problem they can't solve.

Nut didn't know what to do. Touch? Adult hands had been Heru's enemy. Speak? Experience had taught her that a whole lot of talking could make things worse. Run and find Auset? Nut didn't want to risk leaving her grandson alone long enough to find his mother. These wives my sons chose ain't good for nothing but lying on their backs, she thought. Auset should be here dealing with this not me. This is a job for the mama, not the grandmama.

But Auset was not there. Heru was her grandson and her grandson was hurting. She had to do something.

My Lorrrrd he done done
My lorrrrd he done done
My Lorrrrd he done done
He done done what he'd said
he'd dooo.

She whispered the song like a meditative dirge. Much slower than how they sung it at church, where she'd sometimes change the words to "she done done." She knew a God so good at multi-tasking had to be part woman. Nut sweetened the hymn into a soothing chant.

My Lorrrrd … he done done/ … my lorrrrd he done done
my Lorrrrd he done done/ … He done done… what he'd said he'd dooo.

She imagined that each gentle lyric was a tiny hand of God gracing Heru's naked body with a healing caress. Doing what God said she'd do.

20

SATURDAY, AUGUST 26, 1893
EAST ST. LOUIS, ILLINOIS

After not speaking to his family the entire train ride from Chicago's Columbian Exposition back to East St. Louis, the first words Keb said when the hired carriage pulled up in front of Americus & Son were to Set.

"Run up stairs get my strap and meet me in the backyard."

Set quickly looked to Nutilda. She just nodded her head. Set slumped down out the buggy and made a lonely trek up the front porch's 33 stairs.

When Set got to the bathroom, he went straight to the mirror. On the ride from the train station, Asar had whispered, "What's that white spot in your ear? I don't have one." As Asar spoke, Set had tried to seem unconcerned, but he'd felt his throat tighten.

In the bathroom mirror, Set turned his face profile and cocked his neck until he could almost see inside of his ear. Set crooked his neck a little more. "Oh no," he said aloud. He placed his narrow black forefinger in his ear and rubbed hard, then checked again. The white, lima bean-shaped spot did not disappear. He knew it wouldn't. Just like the white spot near his privates would not rub away no matter how hard he rubbed.

"Don't keep me waiting boy!" he heard his father shout.

Set pulled the leather razor strap from the bronze bar to the right of the sink. He rolled up his black pant leg and swung the strap hard against his calf. He looked at himself in the mirror.

"We're ten now. No more crying. No more Whuppin Dance." He rolled his pant leg down.

When Set exited the kitchen door leading out to the backyard, he started twirling the razor strap over his head like a lasso. Asar saw him and felt a rush of fear for Set's safety; he was going too far. Standing next to Asar by the fountain, Keb glared at his lasso-twirling favorite striding towards him. He glared to keep the amused smile that was threatening to emerge.

Keb had already removed his jacket, tie and shirt. His white undershirt fit snuggly over his muscled black chest. Set knew that his father's shirt being off was a bad sign, but he continued twirling the lasso strap to let his father know he wasn't afraid of no whuppin.

Set stopped twirling right in front of his father and placed the strap at Keb's feet. Asar took a giant step back. Set stood erect looking up into the face that would one day be his own. Keb was amused. He found it difficult to stay mad at the son he wished had been born first. The wild son who brought him worry and pride in equal measure. Keb was amazed at the broadness of the shoulders that Set held back in defiance. His thick, black neck. 5'7"and stout. Ten going on grown man, Keb thought. He fought the urge to place a proud hand on Set's big-boned shoulder. Instead, Keb squatted down, while never breaking eye contact with Set, and picked up the razor strap. Arms at his side, chest thrust forward, Set's whole body stiffened. He had earned the right not to have to drop his trousers.

"Roll your pant legs up." Set obeyed.

Keb raised the strap, reached behind him and handed it to Asar.

"Strike your brother ten times about the legs. If you don't do so with all your strength, I will strike you 10 times about your legs with all my strength."

Set's eyes shifted wildly to his brother, who was staring at the strap in his hand.

"I wouldn't hit you," Set convincingly lied to Asar. Keb took a step back.

Asar became a still photograph. Framed by his father.

"Why are … don't make me … I can't father."

Asar dropped the strap. Set let the hint of a smile escape.

"Pick up the strap or it will be the last thing you'll ever not pick up."

Asar turned to face Keb.

"Please, Father."

"Boy, don't make me tell you again."

Asar turned back to Set. He bent and picked up the strap.

"I'm sorry, Set."

"Don't be sorry, be my brother!"

Asar raised the leather razor strap above his head and paused the way his father sometimes did when whuppin them. The thick strap hung heavy. Set braced himself by grinding his molars. With all his might, Asar swept the stinging strap across Set's naked left calf.

"Coward!" Set yelled.

"One," Asar responded. Keb looked on.

Asar returned the strap high above his head. Swung with all his might.

"Coward!"

"Two." Again.

"Coward!"

"Three."

After the tenth strike, Asar turned to face his father and raised the strap again and brought hard against his own right cheek.

"One," Asar said.

Then quick and harder against his own left cheek, drawing a trickle of blood.

"Two," Asar said.

"That's enough," Keb said, reaching for the strap.

Asar took off running towards the rose-lined back wall, fiercely whipping the lash across his cheek.

"Three...four...five... ."

"Stop it Asar!" Set said. He took off after his brother but Asar, still striking himself, kept zig-zagging to escape Set. Keb hesitated then ran after them.

Asar was on "nine" when Set finally tackled him among the grave markers. He wrestled him to the ground and took away the strap. Keb stopped a few feet away. Breathing hard. Trying to control his emotions by scrunching his toes in his shoes.

Set straddled Asar's heaving chest, watching blood trickle from matching worm-sized welts on Asar's cheeks. He cupped his twin brother's face to slow the flow of blood. It oozed between all ten fingers. One finger for each of the ten years they had shared as one. Set brought up his ten bloody fingers and smeared his own cheeks, then returned them to his twin's swollen skin. Asar cut his eyes towards his father's tense face.

"Ten."

21

The twin's bedroom had matching beds pushed against opposite walls of the room. With their father's yardstick, they had divided their sleeping quarters exactly down the middle.

Dead center, a two-by-two foot square table was hammered into the floor. Completely covering the surface of the table was a heavy, wooden chess board hand-carved by their Grandpa Nema.

On this night following Razor Strap Day, the boys lay on their backs in Asar's bed. After Nut had finished treating Asar's cheek with tea tree oil, and placed bandages on both sides of his face, Set closed the bedroom door and climbed right into bed with his big brother.

They had been lying there for hours, looking up into the darkness, listening to the pitch of their mother's voice rise the way it did when she was really angry. A portion of their parents' large master bedroom was directly above the twin's room.

The only words they could make out clearly were their mother's. "His face" and "lessons" and "your way." Their father's bass, muffled responses were indecipherable. Usually, Set liked to hear their parents argue. Those were the few times that Set felt like he had any real advantage in the household. Any break from his father's relentless teaching and training. If Mama and Daddy were fighting, they couldn't be paying as much attention to him and his brother. A victory for the small people in the house. When he heard his parents argue, it reminded him that the big people, who made the rules to rule the little people, couldn't even rule themselves.

This argument was different though. Set didn't receive any enjoyment from it. His mother's high-pitched voice just reminded him of how scared he was earlier in the day. It was the first time he really understood that if something happened to his twin brother, he'd be all alone.

Keb did not like to ignore his wife. Nut had earned enough respect to merit his attention even when they disagreed. He already felt terrible about Asar's face. *I shouldn't have made Asar strike Set,* he'd already thought by the time Asar had reached "three." It had all been a big mistake, but Keb didn't feel like he could confess to Nut; she'd really start questioning his man-making stategies. He decided to just stop talking. The problem: Silent Treatment made Nut work harder to provoke him. Yet, silence was his best bet—better to ignore Nut than risk knocking her down.

"What wisdom did the strap pass down, O, great teacher?" Nut yelled. She was screaming at the back of Keb's head. He had just sat down at the plate-sized, three-legged table he used for reading. Keb cracked open his worn copy of Narrative of the Life of Frederick Douglass.

"That's your damn problem," she hollered.

Nut bent at the waist to project her voice directly towards the back of Keb's right earlobe.

"You look in books, consult the elders, put your finger in the wind and everything else, but listen to me, the person who knew enough to carry those boys nine months, and bring them into the world healthy."

Keb turned a page. He wasn't reading. Just trying to stay busy. Nutilda moved to his left. Positioned her neck at an angle to line up her right eyeball to his ear, while her left eyeball locked on the far wall. She yelled at his profile.

"I'd like to hear what Mr. Douglass has to say about you treating your sons like slaves. That's it isn't it Keb? You just wanna be in charge over somebody. Passin down da lessons and layin on da strap, yes, suh. Keb da Ova-see-yah. Dat title fit you mighty fine, yes, suh."

Nut's wild eyes were wide, watery and all askew. Keb ignored the spittle flying against his ear and cheek.

"It's da Ova-see-yah's job to make da slaves whup da slaves. Dat's how he keeps them in line. You ain't nothin but da Ova-see-yah Keb. As much as you try to deny it, your crazy daddy is still da Massa at dis here Amer-eee-cus Plan-eee-tay-shun. You ain't nothin but a hired hand in da destruction of your own sons. Nothin but a Ova-see-yah. And I thought I married a man who was tryin to make somethin of hisself. If you gonna run slaves, Keb, at least be da Massa."

Abruptly, Keb turned to face his wife's reckless eyeballs. He raised his big hand up and flipped another page.

❚ ❚ ❚

"I'm going to sleep," Set said. He turned on his side away from his brother.

Asar was still lying on his back. He reached up and felt the bandage on his right cheek, then left cheek. The swelling was already going down. He looked to the ceiling. The abrupt silence upstairs made him think about what his parents were now doing. Asar put on his imaginary magic eyes and saw Daddy sitting at his reading table. He couldn't quite make out where his Mama was at. Just somewhere close to Daddy. Funny. Whenever he put on his magic eyes, he could never see Mama's whole face. Only crazy eyes. Almost like her eyes going every-which-a-way got real big and blocked out the rest of her face. No nose. No lips. No ears.

Asar's magic eyes jumped inside his brother's black ear. He looked at the white spot that he saw yesterday at Colored American Day. He thought, How come I don't have one?

"Where'd that ear spot come from," Asar said, up into the darkness. Asar knew Set was pretending to be sleep because of his fake-snore. Asar also knew that even when Set got caught, he wouldn't admit he was caught, whether it was caught play-sleeping or lying.

Set was a relentless pretender.

"Is it the cooties?" Asar said, then scooted away to provoke Set.

"It's not the cooties!" Set shouted.

His back was still turned. "Can I touch it then?"

Asar reached for his brother's ear.

Set flipped to face his mirror reflection.

"I swear, if you do, I'll grab your finger and break it right in two."

"Why don't I have one in my ear?"

Set turned his back to Asar and pulled the blanket up over his head. From a muffled voice beneath the covers, Asar heard Set say, "It's not the only one."

22

"**A**re you gonna show me or not?" Asar said.

They were in the bathroom getting ready for church the next morning. Set's other cooties were on his left inner thigh. Just below his private parts. A navy bean-sized white spot he had found the night before they all left for the Chicago fair. A spot that had sent him on a frantic search across the map of his body. But he hadn't thought to look in his ear. Until Asar saw what he saw.

When Set thought there was only one spot, he had stood in the tub, held his privates to the side, soaped up the spot and tried to wash it off. Even though it didn't seem like the kind of spot you could wash away.

That night before they'd left for the fair, Set had a dream that he'd gone to sleep and awoken to find the navy bean had become a lima bean. Like the one now in his ear. In the dream, he was on the toilet staring at the spot to see if he could catch it growing. The spot only seemed to grow when he wasn't looking. But soon as he'd take a long blink, he'd reopen his eyes, and the spot would be a little bigger. But very still. Like the lima bean knew it was being watched and played dead the way he'd seen the ugly possums do in the backyard. The bean would just sit on his thigh, right by his privates, and look ugly and white. And dead. Set knew better. He knew it was alive—and growing.

"If you're not going to show it, tell me, so I can go back in the room and finish getting dressed," Asar blurted.

With his back still to Asar, Set stretched out the band of his underpants. He placed his bare left foot up on the edge of the tub. He moved his privates to the side and waved Asar over.

23

"**I**'m disappearing."

It was the watery-eyed look of anguish on Set's face that made Nutilda know something was very wrong.

Nut had been sitting on the rim of the Americus Fountain when Nema brought the boys back from their post-church ice cream trip. It was rare that she got a headache after love making. Her head felt like a thick church bell, with an angry bell-ringer inside. Placing her feet in the cool pool and watching the water cascade down always made her feel better.

"Pull your shoes and socks off and hop up here with Mama."

Nutilda Americus watched her youngest son slowly bend down and take off his black left shoe. A pause. Then the right. It was as if her son was an old geezer in a 10-year-old body. A pause. The right sock. Then left. He began to slowly roll up his black right pant leg. Before he could get to the left. Nutilda had spun her legs out the water, and jumped off the rim of the Americus Fountain. She drew her son close. Squeezed him tight, long after she could feel his tears running down her arms.

I I I

Nut and Set sat side-by-side on the rim of the Americus Fountain. With Set's pants rolled up to his knees and Nut's white cotton dress pushed up over hers, Mama and her baby dangled their feet into the water. The fountain pool was filled with dozens of floating rose petals. Set watched how the red rafts near his mother's feet rested calmly, barely moving atop the water. The pirate rafts that had ventured too close to the waterfall and been taken under had completely different shapes. Their sides had rolled up like little map scrolls. Some sank because everyone knows a pirate map can't float unless you put it in a bottle.

Set looked up from the water and into the fist full of rose petals his mother held out-stretched over the pool.

"Release the rafts so the men can swim ashore," Set said.

"Aye, Aye, Captain … but what about the waterfall due North?" "The men who can't make it don't deserve to call themselves Pirates of the Americus. Release the rafts!"

"Aye, Aye, Captain."

Set watched the petals drop through the sky. The waterfall capsized almost all of the blood red rafts. Set kept his eye on one petal that fluttered to a safe landing just far enough from danger. The raft rocked but never went over or under. He pointed it out to his mother and said, "That's the raft the captain is on."

"Aye, Aye, Captain!"

Mother and son watched the captain's raft float securely to the shore near their dangling feet.

Once the captain was safe, Set raised his gaze from the water up to the reckless eyeballs of his mother who was sitting to his left. She seemed to be looking back to the house and over his shoulder at the same time.

"Look in my ear, Mama," Set said.

He leaned his head toward his mother. Nutilda gently placed one hand on the back of his skull, the other on his chin, and brought his ear close for inspection. She cocked her head slightly to line up her right eye.

Nut was not only disturbed by the lima bean-sized spot just outside her son's inner ear canal, but by the fact that she had not seen it before. She gently inserted her pinkie finger and tried to rub away the spot that she knew could not be rubbed away.

Nut's hands slid around to Set's cheeks and turned his face towards hers.

"How long has this been here, baby?"

Set could see right through his mother's attempt to look and sound calm. He could see and hear her fear—which made him more scared.

"A long, I don't know, I..."

"How long, baby?"

"I don't know Mama. Asar saw it at the fair and told me, but I don't know how long it's been there."

"But how long do you think it's been there, baby?"

The rising pitch of his mother's voice made his own pitch rise. "It could've been there since forever."

He started to cry. Nut hugged him close.

"It's going be okay. It's just a spot baby, it's just one little ol spot." Set snatched away. Snot smeared above his lip.

"It's not the only one!"

His intensity stunned Nut into inaction. I wasn't often that she was answerless when it came to her twins.

Nut thought about the first time she saw him. He was crying then too. Loud. Dr. Mandrake didn't even get a chance to smack his big bottom.

Set raised his head from his mother's chest and spoke between heaving breaths.

"The other white spot ... is by my privates ... I know they're growing ... I don't wanna disappear ... I don't wanna look different from Asar ... I don't wanna stop being twins."

Nut smiled. She reached up and placed her arm around her boy and brought his ear down to her mouth. She puckered her lips and placed them as far inside his ear as possible. Then she softly kissed his whiteness.

"You could never stop being Asar's twin, and you're not disappearing, baby. I'm gonna hold onto you so tight that if you disappear I'd have to disappear too—and best believe, Mama ain't going nowhere—and neither are you."

"You gonna fix it, Mama?"

He stepped back so he could look his mother directly in the face.

He wiped his tears.

"That's right, Mama's gonna fix it."

"You promise?"

"Mama promises."

Set's expression grew hopeful, then intensely serious. "Cross your heart and hope to die?"

Nutilda had a lot of confidence in her knowledge of roots and herbs, but she hesitated. She knew the power of words. Nut's hesitation made Set drop his head.

With her forefinger, Nutilda Americus raised her baby boy's chin. With the same finger, she drew one slash across her heart, then another slash down her heart.

"And hope to die."

24

SATURDAY, JULY 9, 1927
EAST ST. LOUIS, ILLINOIS

"**N**ephthys, you're trying to make it seem like I did something wrong with Heru, my own nephew, my own flesh and flood, when all I was doing was showing him what he doesn't have," Set said.

Nephthys was still lying on the bed next to him.

"Heru's getting to that age where wants to understand. He'd never seen a penis before, so he asked me to show him mine. I did because he's my nephew. But you know what? He didn't ask you to show him your privates. You just went ahead and volunteered. He's a 10-year-old boy, Neph, who's already been through so much. And the last thing he needs is his Auntie showing him what little boys should not see."

Nephthys stared at Set's mouth, but her eyes had travelled up into her forehead. Searching the Specialty Shed in her mind. Squinting a little, trying to get a better look. Trying to see again what she saw. What she believed she saw: wrong illumined in sunlight. Set's manhood sticking up like the flag pole in front of Lincoln High. Heru's open mouth at the top of the flag pole. Head cocked to the side. Eyes locked on hers. She didn't just see what was happening, she felt what was happening. And it felt wrong. And Nephthys was an expert on what felt wrong.

Neph looked up at Set staring down at her like she was wrong. Set was right, it can be dark in the back of the Specialty Shed. But not that dark. The light was shining on them through the upper window. And she saw what she saw.

"If he just wanted to see it, why was his mouth on it Set? Ain't no eyes on the lips."

"Neph I don't know. I wasn't even looking down there. I was just trying to stay turned away and…"

"Why was it hard like that Set? Like … when you're with me." Set felt his eye quickly blink twice. When he was caught off guard, his eyelashes felt like heavy vulture wings, double-blinking on his face. He hadn't even thought about why his penis was hard under his nephew's touch. Nor did he want to think about it, let alone try to explain it to his wife. His mouth couldn't move, but his eyelid moved twice again.

"I don't know, Neph."

"I don't know is not good enough, Set. You want me to believe this story, but when I ask you questions, you tell me you don't know. If you don't know Set, how am I supposed to know? Know if I should believe my eyes or believe you? Know if I should trust my husband or trust myself. Know if I should leave or stay? I can't be with a man who'd do that to their blood-kin. I don't know is not good enough, Set."

"You just gonna quit me Neph?"

"Make me understand how his mouth got there, Set."

"Like I don't got no *say so* in whether you stay or go."

It wasn't just Set's rising voice or the way he turned on the bed to square his body with hers that scared Nephthys. It was Set's twisted lips spitting say so. The way those two words had mouths too. Words that said *remember who gives you permission to live.* Like he had ownership over her breath.

Nephthys became conscious of how close Set's body was to her body. She was holding her breath.

Permission.

"You gonna hit me now?" Nephthys said.

The intensity of Neph's question made Set glance down at his hands. His fists were balled. Seeing the fingers that so often caressed his wife's face curled into weapons made him abruptly stand up off the bed. He took a step away from Nephthys.

"Just make me believe you. Why was it hard? Why was it by his mouth, if Heru just wanted to see it? Why, Set? Tell me, baby. Tell me that's not what you want. Tell me that's not what you need. Tell me I'm enough for you. Make me believe I'm enough for you, baby." Still shaken by the fists he was looking down at, Set couldn't seem   to bring his eyes up to meet his wife's pleading gaze. Nor open his mouth to explain erections and intentions.

"Please, Set."

25

All Nutilda's singing did was make her cry more. She gingerly picked up her rigor mortis grandson by his string-bean waist and carried him upstairs to his bedroom. When she laid Heru down on the bed. She stood over him. Uncertain.

Before her failure to save Heru's Uncle Set, when his own boyhood jumped the track, Nutilda had prided herself on having an answer. A certainty. For family, the herb shop, the bedroom. It seemed like the tiny people in her brain would yank on the long ropes that ran though her and her body would just jerk into action. When a problem arrived, Nut just seemed to know what to do and how to do it. And was certain that when she did it, it was the best way to handle the problem. Even if that solution turned out to be wrong, at the time, she was certain it was right.

Now the people in her brain cracked under pressure; they got caught between ropes. Gently pulling one rope, then changing their mind and pulling another. Even after making a decision that seemed to be working out, Nut would change course right in the middle.

One part of her wanted to yell for Auset and another part of her wanted to yell for Keb. She just wanted help. Wanted someone else to make the decisions. Someone else to deal with the consequences when things went wrong. She looked down at Heru's wide open eyes: The Frog-Eyed Grandson of Crazy-Eyed Nutilda. What scared Nut most was that she was probably the best person to help Heru. Nutilda who was certain of nothing.

Gently, Nutilda climbed in bed and lay behind her grandson. She studied the back of Heru's head. His skull was small as a black coconut. His bony neck: three side-by-side-by-side railroad spikes, covered in black skin. Her eyes travelled down Heru's narrow back to a waist that should have been on a seven-year-old girl, not a ten-year-old boy.

Lying behind her stiff, naked grandson she wished Auset was better. Nobody liked to talk about it, but Auset hadn't really been right since That Mess. Giving birth under those conditions had been too much. Afterwards, it was like she was living in a world where the air was three times as dense. Her body and mind just moved slower now. But Nut blamed her anyway. Heru is Auset's fragile child. A good mother of a fragile child don't have time to be fragile, she thought.

Nut inched her body a little closer to her grandson. His back was to her. She carefully placed her arm over his body. She placed her cheek against his back, brought her languid forearm to his stomach and hugged him. She closed her eyes and squeezed him a little tighter.

"What are you doing?"

Nut did not have to open her eyes to recognize the fear and accusation in Auset's voice. But she opened them anyway. In time to see her daughter-in-law taking the last step towards the bed. She had the wild look of a copper-colored, cornered raccoon. Auset pushed Nut's arm off Heru and picked up her son's naked body.

"Why's he naked like this? What did you do to him?"

Not something else, Auset thought. She simply couldn't take one more thing happening to her baby. She was just too tired. Tired of being up late anguishing over Heru's future. Asar complained about her lethargy, but what did he expect? What kind of life was her baby going to have with no privates? Who was going to love someone like him? How would he survive the rejection that was sure to come?

I   I   I

"Look at him. What did you do? Asar, Asar!"

The panic in Auset's rising voice brought a series of quick moving feet pounding up the wooden stairs. Asar rushed through the door first and stood in front of Auset. She was still clutching Heru to her chest.

"What's happening?" Set said. Keb hurried in right behind him.

Asar's eyes met Nutilda's as she began to sit up in the bed. Nutilda's eyes quickly dropped. Asar looked again at Auset.

"What..."

"Your mother did something to our son. Look at his eyes. Look at how big his eyes are, look how stiff he is."

Asar circled around and raised Heru's chin off Auset's chest.

"Here, give him to me."

"No!"

His wife spun from Asar and squeezed Heru tighter.

Grandpa Nema shuffled through the door, out of breath from climbing the stairs.

"Goddamnit, now, what's all this yellin and runnin and carryin on in my damn house."

From behind Nema's back, Nephthys appeared in the doorway. "Ask Set."

26

"Ask Set" made everyone in Heru's bedroom turn and look at Nephthys. Then Set.

Set let his head swivel around the room. He met his Grandpa Nema's searching stare. His sister-in-law Auset's wild-eyed maternal judgment. His mother Nutilda's concerned curiosity. His father Keb's raised brow. He turned completely around to stare down his wife Nephthys. He saved his last pin-point glare for his brother Asar.

The eyes in the room followed his. Set's hard stare dared Asar to say something.

"I know I was letting you spend too much time with Heru," Asar started. "If you were more like Dad, you'd know something about commitment and instead of running away when things don't go your way, you'd have your own damn son by now, so you wouldn't have to play father to my son. Now what did you do to Heru?"

"I didn't run away. I chose to leave, because it was time to live under my own roof, make my own mistakes, be my own man. Asar, you're supposed to be a grown man and you've never not lived under your Daddy's roof. You're still living out your little First-born Rights, still trying to be good enough for Dad, perfect enough for Dad, so when your own son turns out imperfect, you aren't even capable of loving him."

"What you know about love could fit in that hole in your face you fucking traitor. You ran out on me, on this whole family … ."

"And I came back in time to save your Scared D. Cat ass, save your wife who was my girl first, and save the son who you don't want because he came up short of perfection. You weren't there to protect Heru when he needed you most. Don't get mad at me because I've tried to do the job that you won't—as usual. You always talking about truth this, and truth that, except when you have to truthfully accept some responsibility. Well, here's some truth for you: I blame you for all this. And so does Dad. Don't you, Dad?"

Set turned his head towards Keb to get his reply. But Keb grew stiff when placed between his two boys.

"Don't bring him into this!" Auset shrieked at Set, then looked at

Asar. It seemed she had spent so much of their marriage trying to get Asar to open up, to express his emotions, to stop being like a younger version of Keb. No such luck. But just the prospect of Keb's opinion of him brought emotions from Asar that she wished she—or their son—could elicit. A reminder of who her husband was really married to.

"Don't you, Dad?" Set insisted, looking still at Keb.

Not wanting to look at Asar, Keb kept his eyes focused on Set. His rambunctious baby boy turned divisive grown man. Set had been at the center many of the family's difficulties. Conflicts. Arguments.

Keb took a step towards Set and placed his right hand on Set's left shoulder.

"Son, the old ones say, 'A man quick to point a finger had a hand in the dirty deed.'"

Asar took a hard step towards Set.

"Did you do anything to my son?"

"Stop trying to act like you care, because you don't. You wished you had a son who wasn't damaged, wasn't missing something. A son who was whole and complete. Perfect like you. Well, that's not what you've got. You gotta son like me. A son with holes in him. Holes you can see. Other holes you just know are there because you can feel the ugly coming out of them. It's hard to keep ugly inside, Asar. Hard to drink the shame of your father and not piss it out through your eyes. When you got so much ugly squeezed inside you, ain't hardly no more room for you. Least not the real you. So that real you, up and leaves. Departs. And what's left behind is something like me. Something like that boy over there. That's why he comes to me when your shame gets too thick for him. Even at his age, he can see that I'm stuck like this. Forever. And he's starting to figure out that he's stuck too. That ugly is going to be his life. Forever. Figuring out that kind of future at 10 will stun a boy into a statue. So don't stand here and accuse me of harming my nephew. I was doing what you should've been doing. Loving him when he needed it most. A son ain't no buried gift you dig up then throw away, because it's not the birthday present you wanted. You ..."

Set didn't see the punch, because it was an uppercut. Arcing up from down low, out of his field of view. Asar's mallet-head fist slamming up under the boney point of Set's chin. The force lifted Set up on his tippy-toes, Jack-in-the-Box-ed his skull up and back, snapping shut his open mouth on his tongue. A bloody parting gift from Set's bitten tongue sprayed Asar's face and Keb's shoulder— then the back of Set's skull fell straight back and hit the hard pine floor. Auset screamed, clutched Heru, and quickly stepped away towards the bed. Just in time to get out of the way of Asar's long body diving atop Set. He landed four vicious right hands on his unconscious little brother's only eye, before Keb could push Asar off. Asar rolled onto his back. Leading with her nails, Nephthys, lunged towards Asar and dragged her fingers down his face. She was aiming for his eyes. Asar's heavy palm smashed across Nephthys cheek and knocked her over.

"Cut out this damn foolishness in my house!" Grandpa Nema shouted, but no one was listening. Nephthys again lunged for Asar.

"I said cut it out Goddamnit!"

It was the succession of booming shotgun blasts—and the sound of falling glass downstairs—that quieted the room. Grandpa Nema calmly turned and shuffled towards the window. About 20 armed white men were leisurely walking up Bond Ave. Some held their shotguns skyward, intermittently firing off rounds. Others rested their barrels on their shoulders as they laughed and slapped each other's backs. The three men at the front seemed to be starting a chant but Grandpa Nema couldn't make it out. He cracked the window and leaned his ear close:

"Hap-py-Ann-i-ver-sary-Nig-gers ... Hap-py-Ann-i-ver-sary- Nig-gers ... Hap-py-Ann-i-ver-sary ..."

27

A sar and Set stood side-by-side on the porch. Neither made an effort to kick the shattered glass from under their feet. Most of the glass was in the living room where the rest of the Americus Family sat around in complete silence. It couldn't be happening again. Set looked over his shoulder through the broken window. Auset was huddled next to Nephthys on the Chaise lounge. Nephthys' head rested on her sister-in-law's shoulder. Auset looked up, met Set's eye, and looked away.

She always looked away now.

You don't have to be that way, he thought. He turned back to face the Eads Bridge.

"If they'll shoot a window out today, and it's over a week after the 10th anniversary of That Mess, it'll be an eye tomorrow. They're just looking for a reason to get something started," Set said to Asar. Asar kept his eyes straightway on the Eads Bridge.

"We'll stand post here with the family. If they come back we'll assess the situation," Asar said.

"What if it's nighttime? Hard to assess what you can't see."

"They didn't wait for nightfall last time. If this is more than just some drunk out-a-work bohunks mad at uppity Negroes, we'll know it soon enough," Asar said.

"We gonna give them time to go recruit around the bars?" Asar turned his head towards Set.

"Last time, I was away from my wife. I … if something happens this time, I'm going to be here."

"But that's just it, something doesn't have to happen. We run up the road here to see if they're around. If they've had their little fun and crawled their stinky-inky asses back under a bar stool somewhere, good, we'll come back home and play-wait-and-see, but if they're still milling around, trying to get something started, we need to get on the exchange and let people know. Thing is, we need to have more information than we got right now, and we ain't gonna get much information standing still on this porch, watching the Eads Bridge stand still."

"We can get on the exchange right now," Asar said.

"What we gonna tell them: 'We saw some drunk bohunks in the street carrying guns so grab what you can and run for the Free Bridge?' We'll have these scary Negroes spooked like sheep in a crowded pen with death in their nostrils. We gotta know more first. So I'm gonna go Asar. I'd prefer to have someone watch my back, but I've watched my own back long enough to know how to do it myself."

"I can't Set."

"You won't."

"If something were to happen here while we're gone, I wouldn't … I can't."

"You won't and that's just like you to make the wrong decision, when we can only afford to make the right one. To think, when you should act."

Set stepped forward and walked down the steps with the barrel of his Winchester pointing towards the earth. Asar wanted to say, "Be careful." But he didn't.

He said, "Wait."

▮ ▮ ▮

"Stop worrying about it and let em stare. If the bohunks can walk down the middle of the street with their rifles, we can at least walk down the damn sidewalk with ours."

The brothers walked up Bond Avenue returning stares like their father had taught them to do when they were kids. Across the street, a tall man wearing a brown derby stopped walking and turned to stare. Still striding, Set turn his torso and glared back until the man got so uncomfortable that he went along on his way.

"Let's go on down to Bloody Island and see if they're trying to round up some good ol boys from the bars."

"Is that where we want to be if they're trying to get something started?" Asar said.

"That's where we want to be if we want to know if something is about to get started, so we can get a plan. Didn't I used to call you Peter A. Plan?"

"We should get back and check on the house."

"Dad and Grandpa Nema haven't forgotten how to pull triggers in the last 20 minutes and aren't going to forget in the two hours that it'll take to rush there and back to see what the hell is going on," Set said.

"If we go, let's check on the house before we head down there."

"All that's gonna do is make Auset worry more, same as it will make my wife worry more. Begging us not to go, crying and carrying on, making things harder than they already are. That's not what we need right now. This has gotta be done and we're the ones to do it."

"We're gonna walk through Bloody Island with our Winchesters out like this?" Asar said.

"No we're not, because luckily one of us is thinking for both of us."

Set smiled his big smile as he pulled the tight roll of folded white butcher-paper from his overalls. The big smile that helped to make him the favorite. The smile that was hard to say "no" to because it came with such surety. The same smile that said, "Trust me, I'll make everything alright."

"Two hours, Set, and that's it."

I   I   I

They walked the streets with their butcher-paper Winchesters tucked under their arms, like they'd just bought enough sausage for a multi-death funeral reception.

The Bloody Island streets were filled with men holding glasses and flasks in their hands and clutching women by the elbow. To Asar's eyes, the crush of the bohunk-filled streets seemed more dense than usual. More ominous. But to Set, it seemed about the same. Drunk bohunks trying to stumble away from their lives, but, instead, stumbling into each other.

Directly in front of them was a tall man, pale as Set, wearing a black derby too small for his honeydew melon head. He was stumbling. He bumped hard into a burly man in front of him. The pale man's black derby stumbled forward off his head, as the burly man shot a mean elbow into the pit of his stomach. The mixture of dark beer, bile, and peanuts that spewed from the drunk's mouth sprayed the backs of necks, earlobes and collars. The burly man turned and pounced on him with such an aggressive frenzy that the victim's congested, nasally scream was immediately silenced by the knees and fists to his open mouth. He beat him in silence. The viciousness of the attack comforted Set, because a Bloody Island feeding on itself was less likely to be feeding on Negroes.

"Let's walk through and check a few bars," Set said. "We've got 15 minutes, Set."

"Well, let's go use em."

I   I   I

Standing men squeezed beside each other along the wooden bar inside The Cow's Teat. Octagon card tables filled the square main room. Poker. The men who weren't holding cards close to their chests were standing around watching men who held cards close to their chests. A thirty-ish woman, the color of a peeled potato in a tan dress, looked up from the lap-seat of her poker playing friend and made eye contact with Set. She didn't smile as good business practice should have dictated. On Bloody Island, most of the women at least tolerated Negroes—until their money ran out. In place of her professional smile were widening eyes. Nervous but controlled. A master of deciphering stares, Set knew that she wasn't just responding to the faded one-eyed Negro before her. It must have been something in his facial expression. Or maybe she had seen butcher-wrapped Winchesters before.

Set and Asar walked over to the bar. Towering above the standing men waiting to order their drinks, Set bellowed, "Two whiskeys."

A man in a black bowler, with a mustache thick as a Fuller Brush, stood directly in front of Set. He looked over his shoulder at Set but said nothing. The man next to him also looked over shoulder then slowly looked away. The twins were the only Negroes in the place.

Set smiled at Asar who was standing next to him, holding his dangling metal sausage by his side.

"Way these folks looking at us, must've been awhile since they let some real men up in here," Set said loudly. Asar cringed. But he knew that was his brother's way. To be the aggressor. The instigator. "Whoever lands the first punch usually wins the fight," Set liked to say.

Asar had seen him employ the strategy many times. Whether the punch was with a fist. A word. Or a bullet. Set had explained that the first blow not only served as the perfect way to mask fear, but it also immediately commanded the respect of the enemy. Made him think. "You get these bohunks thinking and you got them right where you want them," he'd chuckle.

The Fuller Brush Mustache Man turned completely around to face Set. He sipped on his beer, leaving foam on his bristles.

"I hear tell this is around the time of some big anniversary for you Negroes?" he said loud and boozy.

"Is that what you heard?" Set replied, looking hard at him.

"Being that July 2nd was my birthday and I've been celebrating for a straight week, I want to raise a glass to thank the Good Lord that I made it another year and change," the man said, smiling hard. "So it's like a double anniversary: my life and buncha nigra deaths. Now I hope you ain't one of those particular nigras who gets they britches all bunched up in they ass cause a man say nigra when he raise a toast. Don't mean no harm by it. Just a word, just a word. Take that word bohunk that nigras use to talk about my kind. Now, that word there don't bother me one bit. I am a bohunk. And proud to be one. Anyway, I'm raising a toast to you and your kind, not a shotgun or a lynching rope, so nigras like yourself should be happy."

"We'll, I don't know about most nigras, but I sholl is happy. You wanna …"

"Now, that's the kind of man I can get along with," he said, giving Set's beefy shoulder two quick affirming slaps.

"You wanna know when this nigra is most happy?" "Yes, boy, tell me, tell me."

"I'm most happy when I'm looking into the wide eyes of a bohunk, and I'm bringing my knife across his throat. Something about how that surprise turns to fear and that fear turns to piss and blood and shit on the bar room floor. Don't you just love when shit happens?" Set said smiling. He handed his butcher-wrapped Winchester to Asar.

Asar had the look of an exasperated parent. He shook his head one firm time signaling, "No."

But it was much too late for "No." Set was already intoxicated by the slow growing fear developing beneath the bowler in front of him. A fear that transferred power to Set, light to Set, the way pulling a string transferred power and light to a bulb. And the heat that came from the light, ran through Set. He was warmed by the fear he could create in others. Especially bohunks who were accustomed to creating fear in cowered Negroes.

"How'd you plan to celebrate this anniversary of Negroes being killed?" Set said.

The man's wide eyes hiccupped twice. As if he were trying to speak through his eyelids and the words got stuck in his throat.

"Some shooting? Some cutting? I understand that a knife can be a mighty fun thing. That's why I carry this around," Set said, pulling his bejeweled knife from the compartment on his overall's left leg.

"You'd be surprised how this thing move right on through bone. Cutting tendon like slicing an inch-worm in half."

Back when he was working at the slaughterhouse, Set would give his knife a good cleaning soon as he got back to his room. Loosening bone bits and tendon specks from a ruby-encrusted handle takes the kind attention to detail that can distract the mind from other concerns. The shine he got on the blade came courtesy of a concoction he made of saddle soap, lemon juice, and a tablespoon of lye. It turned the wide steel blade into a mirror.

Set held this mirror in front of the Fuller Brush Mustache Man. From beneath his bowler, the man saw his doughy nose reflected. He wanted to turn his head to see if anyone else was paying attention to this big nigra with a big knife in his hands. But he couldn't cut his eyes away from his nose's reflection. Almost clear as a mirror.

"Heavy though. You wanna hold it? … Reach up for it."

After years of people peering through the hole in his head, Set peered inside the pores of the man and stared at the swirl of indecision and fear. Examined how moisture molecules began to curve and form across those pores, creating a translucent veil across his face. Set wanted to calm him. Give him confidence to reach up for the knife. Or at least think about it long enough to flinch. To lunge. To jump.

"Feeling froggy?" Set said.

Set gently placed the flat side of the blade on the man's nose as if preparing to knight it. Paralyzed by the cool blade's touch, the barfly could not even make himself lean back away from the contact. Afraid that even the slightest shift in weight would cost him his sense of smell.

"Thing about you bohunks is that your courage always comes in numbers. When you gotta deal with a Negro face-to-face, man-to-man, that courage shrinks like a snail on salt lick."

The Fuller Brush Mustache Man's fear had grabbed hold of each eyelid and pulled them wide. Hoping to see help coming through his peripheral vision.

"Not so easy when you have to look the nigra right in the eye, is it?"

The man's lips parted, but no words came out. "Especially when he's gotta knife on your nose."

Set slid the flat cool blade south and subtly increased pressure on the tip of the man's nose, creating an indention with the point large enough to hold a tear drop.

"You got time for a little story, birthday boy? When I was really a *boy*, I walked into a shop and on the counter they had a whole jar of Negro fingers, toes and ears. Nigger souvenirs. Must have been stacked

20 high: pinkie toes atop ears, ears atop thumbs, thumbs atop big toes. Made me wonder, what it would feel like to take something like that from a man."

Set turned the knife until the blade's fine edge left a thin red horizontal line across the doughy nose tip.

"Would the part of him left, still be a whole man? Ninety-percent man? What is the cost of a lost thumb? Five percent? An ear? A nose? Privates? Can you put a price on never being whole again?"

Before the man could answer or blink or breathe, Set had his massive right hand clutched over the Fuller Brush Mustache and open mouth; Set's slaughter house left hand slit almost a half-inch off the tip of his nose. A muffled damp scream. Blood spurted from the nose, oozing between Set's clamped fingers. Set jerked his massive knee up into the man's groin. He crumbled to the floor like a drunk.

"Let's go to a bar where men know how to handle their liquor," Set loudly said.

Asar slid the sausage beneath Set's arm as they moved towards the door.

Once outside again on the crowded street, Asar grabbed Set by the arm and swung him around.

"We're supposed to be here to see if there's something to this anniversary mob, and you're in there trying to create a mob. You didn't have to cut that man. It's not the time for that type of …"

"Listen to how you sound. That same man would cut your ears off and stick em in some jar, rather than drink from the same cup as you. With all the cutting they've done on Negro bodies, I'm just trying to catch up, and balance the scales."

"Well, you can balance them without me because I'm going back home to be with my wife and son, which is where I should have stayed in the first place instead of running around with your crazy ass watching you cut off people's noses because you can."

Asar turned around and started walking down the street. Set walked behind and began to loud-talk Asar.

"You're just hiding behind your wife and kid … you're the same Mr. Scare D. Cat that you've always been."

Asar kept squeezing and pushing through the drunk revelers. Set kept shouting behind him.

"You're the one who should be cutting bohunk noses off instead of complaining about me. But that's just like you to let someone else be the man of the house ... to do the man's job that you should be doing ... what's gonna happen when ain't no man around to handle your business?"

Asar knew that Set was just trying to get his goat. He kept walking. "It takes courage for a Negro to live on this earth ... and ain't no cowards in heaven, so I hope you gotta Plan B."

Ignoring Set, Asar plowed ahead away from the bars until he approached the wooded-area. Again.

On the rare occasion that he ventured over to Bloody Island since That Mess, Asar usually found himself taking a route that had him revisiting this place. It called to him. As if there was a possibility of returning and rearranging the past. A mystical chance for a do-over. In that place where he lay on his stomach like a worm, and watched what happened to Dr. Mandrake.

"Remember that spot?"

Asar didn't stop in his tracks; instead, "Remember that spot?" broke his stride. Took him out of the forceful pace he was using to move across the marshy woodland back to his wife. Slowed him.

How could Asar not remember this spot? The dense pack of trees which looked like a forest squeezed into a baseball diamond. It was the kind of place a man could disappear from East St. Louis without ever leaving.

Disappear. That's what Asar had done over the years among these trees in front of him. Lying down on the cool ground. Invisible for thirty minutes as he thought about what he could have done differently. Should have done. How lives could have been different if he would've acted more decisively. More courageously.

Asar paused at the perimeter of the miniature forest. Laid down his Winchester.

"I thought you were supposed to rushing home Mr. Johnny C. Lately?" Set hollered.

Asar didn't so much as ignore Set, he simply couldn't fully comprehend him because of the chatter in his head. The self- inflected finger pointing was louder than Set could ever be.

Asar walked right into the area that he wished he didn't know so well.

Set stopped and stood 10 feet directly behind his squatting brother. He could tell Asar was remembering. The Totem of Remembrance was nestled inside the wooded-area. Regretting. It's good for him, Set thought. He looked down at the part running through the middle of Asar's wavy, ear-length, salt-and-pepper hair. He's never even had a hair style that wasn't his father's. Not enough courage to be his own man. Never lived outside his father's house. Never had a job that wasn't given to him by his father. Never had a wife that wasn't his brother's girl first.

"Being the first-born cancels out all that?"

Asar could hear that Set had said something. Again. But Asar was so deep in the well-hole of memory that Set's voice became distant background.

Set's hand on Asar's shoulder brought him back. Asar had no idea how long he'd been squatting there but long enough for Set to actually touch him. That was the thing about Set: Even when he was mad, he was there for you in times of trouble. Like he had been there for the family when the bohunks first came around shooting up Negroes' homes. Like he'd been there for my pregnant wife, Asar thought. There for my son. When I wasn't. It's time to move out of the past, he thought. I have to let all this go and get on with my life. Do right by my son. It's not his fault. That boy is flesh of my flesh. Set's right; I've been letting Heru's condition get in the way of me loving his goodness. My boy's smart as a whip. He's tough in his own little way. And my little man has the softest heart, Asar thought. I need to love him better and I know I can. Asar smiled to himself. Again, Set had challenged him, loved him in his inimitable way. Asar didn't always like Set's methods, but he never questioned his twin brother's love and commitment to him and the family. The truth: I could learn a lot about love—and truth—from Set Americus, he thought.

Asar's knees creaked as he slowly raised from his squatting position. Set's long right arm reached around from behind to hug Asar's stomach. Asar smiled. Set squeezed tight. Asar felt a surge of warmth. Blood flowed over the bejeweled knife slicing across his Adam's Apple.

Handiwork of a lefty.

28

Set stood behind Asar hugging and holding up his brother. The blood gushed from Asar's throat, down the front of his shirt, flowed across Set's trembling fingers. The blood was warm. That's what made it real. Familiar. Natural. Okay. Death made new life possible. The slaughterhouse had taught him that. Shedding blood fed daughters. Cutting throats, nourished sons. Bloodletting allowed families to thrive. Prosperity, respect, and love to flourish. Americus & Son was proof. Death was for the best.

"This is for the best," Set said aloud.

Still holding Asar, Set looked over his shoulder and slowly began to step back towards the center of the woods. Set wouldn't let himself look at his brother's face. Asar's dragging heels carved a winding tributary in the moist earth. Set gently laid him down alongside a fallen tree. He went back and retrieved the Winchesters. Leaned them against a pine. He sat on the log and tried not to look down at what was best. Instead, he studied the bark mantis on a tree two feet directly in front of him. How it tried to disappear by being completely still. And brown. Playing dead. And Colored. What gave the bark mantis away was the eye watching it. An eye with an acute sense of color gradation. An eye able to see that the slightly discolored spot on the tree was a lie. Was alive. Set shot his long left arm out and smashed the imposter spot with his palm. Bark mantis became bark. It disappeared better when it was dead.

Set brought his left hand close to his face. He looked on his palm for a trace of the bark mantis even though he knew he wouldn't be able to see it: Asar's blood was still smeared across his hand. And wrist and forearm and memory. To keep from looking down, Set had to close his eyes. He felt his toes scrunch up inside his boots. That's when Set began an insistent—and necessary—back and forth rocking on the log.

"This is for the best ... this is for the best ... this is for the best ... this is ..."

29

1893

"**A**bsolutely not."

This was Keb's answer when Nutilda first asked him about opening a roots and herb store next to Americus & Son.

"Why not?"

She was lying on her back next to her husband. She had figured this longshot request should be made in the place where she held the most power. At least in Keb's eyes.

"Because you already have two jobs: being a co-father to our sons and the occasional wife to me," Keb joked. He was trying keep the mood light.

Smiling, Nut turned on her side to face her husband.

"It wouldn't take any time away from my co-fathering, and it would make me so intensely happy that I'd want to spread that extra intensity all over you."

"I don't know if I could handle any more of your happiness and …"

"I already have a nice-sized garden, and we never even use the spare bedroom facing Bond. It would be easy to turn it into … ."

"Nutilda."

"You know Daddy would have wanted me to have it."

"Now, Nutilda, that's not right. Just stop."

"Don't you?"

"Your father doesn't have anything to do with this."

"Except that he knew more about roots than just about anybody…"

"Nut …"

"Let me finish, let me finish. And he would've loved to see his daughter have a little shop of her own. I could pay for my own supplies with the money Daddy left me. And if you thought it took too much time away from you and the twins, I'd close the shop faster than your *stingy* Daddy's change purse."

"Absolutely not."

Keb was still lying on his back looking up into the beamed bedroom ceiling. At the time, the boys had just turned seven, and Keb felt that they were too young for their mother to be playing businessman. Even if it was in a business that she knew an awful lot about. The former Nutilda Bravefoot was certainly her father's daughter. She loved to tell Keb how, "Daddy became a root man when he ran off from the Ragland Farm and was taken in by Dakotas." *How many times have I heard that? Keb chuckled to himself.* It still didn't mean that Nut could do anything that a man could do. Nor should she. Besides, how would it look for the wife of Keb Americus to be running a business, interacting with strange men? She did talk to male customers in the funeral home but that was different because it was under his watchful eye.

"Is that you speaking or does your Daddy just sneak into your mouth when I'm not looking," she said.

Keb turned on his side and glared at his wife. He hated that Nutilda brought up his father every time the husband had a different point of view than the wife. In all of her smart talk, she wasn't smart enough to understand that for the two to become one, she had to trust him enough to listen, Keb thought. Hadn't he been smart enough to grow Americus & Son to a point his own father couldn't have imagined? Hadn't he provided a comfortable life for her and the sons she bore him? Hadn't he been smart enough to become a man of influence even though his kind was hated by those he sought to influence? After all these years, didn't she realize that he knew what he was doing?

"I don't need my father to tell me that you already have enough to do," Keb said.

Nutilda turned on her side to face him again.

"I don't need you to tell me about my life. I'm living it Keb, not you. Since you're such a *big man,* you should be able to look down and see my need to create something, to build something for me. Like when you stand back and see what your hands have done. I want to stand back and lift my chin up too about what I can do. You and the boys bring me a lot of happiness Keb, but everyone needs to build something for themselves. Even a woman Keb, even a woman. I gave birth to our boys, but it seem like you took over all the creating. You the builder now. I need something else to birth Keb. I need something else that I can stand back and say, 'Look at what I've done.' Don't deny me that. Don't deny me what you want for yourself, what you already have for yourself."

❙ ❙ ❙

Nutilda's House of Roots & Herbs opened for business on January 1st 1890. Nut had spent almost a whole year getting ready. She wanted to do things right. She cleared out the large guest room herself. Breaking down the bed and carrying it out to the storage room in the basement. She turned the dresser on its side, dragged it on a blue blanket across the pine floors and gently slid in down the stairs. Nut chose the colors and painted the room herself. The bright yellow for the walls and green for the trim. Sky blue for the ceiling. White for the sky's billowy clouds. She wanted a business home for her herbs that felt as alive as their original home.

Nut put up the sturdy wooden pine shelves that climbed from just above the floor, stopping a foot from the ceiling. She bought each one of the scores of large mason jars. On rectangular strips of tan leather, using a hot stencil, Nut burned the names of roots and herbs with such care that sneaking up on her, one would have thought she was painting on canvas: yerba sante, tulasi, noni, lavender, black cohosh, echinacea, comfrey, hawthorn, saw palmetto, chasteberry, ginseng, barberry, horse tail, golden seal, eucalyptus, konjac, ginger, white willow, St. John's wort, valerian, sage, cat's claw, dandelion, cinchona, garlic, yohimbe, burdock, peppermint, milk thistle, arnica, neem, and scores of others. Nut glued on the labels and, on every jar top, she poked seven tiny holes in a circle. She bought four ladders, attached rubber wheels on the bottom and rollers on the top, so the ladders could slide along broom handle-sized rails that she constructed across the upper rim of each wall.

The only thing that Nutilda Americus couldn't do in creating Nutilda's House of Roots & Herbs was cut the door into the wall that would be the store entrance—not that she didn't try.

"How hard can it be to cut a rectangle into the wall," she said aloud with ax in hand. An enraged Keb made her stop and let him do it (but she installed the gong and mallet above the door to announce customers). She let him also build the cobblestone walkway that led to Bond Avenue.

The last thing she did was put up signs. The four by two foot wooden sign that hung over the door said:

NUTILDA'S HOUSE
OF ROOTS & HERBS

The one by one foot wooden sign that was nailed on the outside wall, next to the door:

VISIT US NOW
SO YOU CAN VISIT NEXT DOOR
MUCH, MUCH LATER.

30

O nly Set would think he was fading away, because he had a couple of spots on his body. Nut was amused by how strongly he felt things. It made Set seem like her son too and not just Keb's. That's why, with a tinge of guilt, Nutilda loved Set just a little bit more than Asar. Now, she had never said those words to anyone. Not even Keb. She scarcely let herself think those words. It felt wrong to love one child more than another—even if it was just a little bit more.

"It's all Set's fault," she would say smiling to herself. "If he didn't have so much darn gumption. If he didn't throw himself so wildly into everything. If he wasn't such a geechee rascal. If it wasn't all so adorable, I wouldn't be feeling guilty about loving my own."

After all, it wasn't like she didn't love Asar. Nut would've stepped out in front of a speeding Chicago & Alton train to save his life. That's her first-born. Such a good-hearted boy. Already strong- minded and responsible. Already so much like his father. That was part of the problem. Nut felt Keb already had him. Had already made Asar in his own image. She needed to see herself in a son too. Set was her best bet. Her only bet.

Hours after closing on the day Set revealed his disappearing act, Nut sat Dakota-style in the center of Nutilda's House of Roots & Herbs' pine floor. A few inches in front of her bent knees she had placed a pencil and a piece of yellow stationary paper. Then she closed her eyes, took slow deep breaths of herbal-scented oxygen and waited. Sometimes this was the process which allowed her to come up with remedies for difficult cases.

Most of her patients, as Nut called her customers, were easy. If Nut could read the red in their eyes, ache in their gait, and hear the phlegm in their rough coughs, she walked to her wall of herbs and gathered a mixture of elderberry, golden seal, feverfew and echinacea.

More than two months ago, Mr. Johnson's wife brought him in with a golf ball-sized goiter on his neck. He was having pain in his kidneys and chest palpitations. Nut asked him how long he had the lump and the symptoms, as she ran her tiny index finger lightly across the raised skin.

"Does it hurt when it's touched?"

Nutilda asked about what types of foods he liked and if he'd ever seen anyone else in his family with a goiter. She asked Mrs. Johnson if she'd noticed her husband sleeping more restlessly at night. Unconsciously, Mrs. Johnson reached for her man's hand.

"Since it come on him, Mr. Johnson toss and turn at night. He sweat so much that his night shirt be wet straight through," Mrs. Johnson said.

Nut took a step back and slowly looked around the wall full of herbs. For Mr. Johnson's heart, she pulled down jars of foxglove, hawthorn, and horsetail. For the kidney's the horsetail would help as well; she added dandelion. To help Mr. Johnson sleep better, she made a mixture of kava and valerian. However, the goiter stumped her.

"I'll need a little time to think about the best combination to treat the goiter, Mr. Johnson. Could you come back tomorrow around the same time?"

After the shop closed that night, Nutilda sat on the floor Dakota- style. A pencil and a piece of paper inches from her crossed legs. She closed her eyes and began to inhale and exhale deeply, focusing on the breath entering and exiting her rising and falling abdomen. While breathing, she pictured Mr. Johnson standing in the center of the store, an ankh and uas staff passing back and forth through his goiter. Her own imagined body sitting Dakota-style, her reckless eyeballs scanning the room. Individual jars began to rise off the shelves. They floated towards Mr. Johnson and attached themselves to the ankh and uas staff. The goiter grew smaller with each jar that disappeared into it. When the jars stopped arriving, Nut faced the opposite direction and repeated the process.

Nutilda opened her real eyes and wrote down the flying herbs: comfrey, evening primrose, neem, and thunder god vine.

The levitating jar-approach to herbal healing didn't always work. Sometimes Nutilda would sit Dakota-style for over an hour and not a single herb would fly. No matter how deeply she breathed. No matter how many times she changed directions.

As Nut sat on the floor the day that her baby said he was fading away, she hoped herbs would fly. She inhaled and exhaled deeply. She imagined Set standing in the center of the room. Her reckless eyeballs went into action. Reckless mind's eye seemed to scan every single jar of herbs in the room.

Nothing.

Not one jar of herbs floated towards her son. Not even an upsy/ downsy, as she called it when a jar slowly lifted straight up off a shelf only to slowly return.

Usually, Nut would have her answers within an hour, and rarely more than two hours. On this day, she meditated deep into the predawn morning. Having nodded off, she was jolted by a knock at the back door. Keb had come to retrieve his wife and not one root had flown.

31

A little uncertain, Nutilda walked towards the twin's bedroom door. She had decided on a potent blend of noni, marigold, aloe vera, elderberry and tea tree oil. She felt pretty darn sure that the mixture would work. When she felt pretty darn sure about the mixtures that she gave patients, they usually worked pretty darn good. She just wished flying herbs had confirmed her work. This was not simply a patient. It was her baby, who she promised to heal. Promised and crossed her heart—and hoped to die.

Nut silently stood in the doorway and watched Set sitting across the chess board from Asar. Set's body leaned forward, elbow planted on the table, chin resting in his palm.

Asar's intense wheels turned without the squeak of gesture. He leaned back, balancing his chair on two legs. Both hands clasped behind his center-parted, wavy head of black hair. Although she could not see his face, Nut knew his crooked smile was on display. He was the better player.

"Study long, study wrong," she heard Asar say.

"Shut up, Mr. Smart T. Pants, so I can concentrate."

"Or is that part of your top secret strategy. Bore me to sleep, sneak some pieces and wake me up with a 'Check mate!'"

"Shut your big mouth up or I'm gonna sneak my rook up your bugger nose!"

"Ohh, I'm *so scared.*"

"You're gonna be *so sorry.*"

"Slowpoke, how you gonna find time to make somebody so sorry, when you spend all your time getting your butt kicked in chess?"

"Mr. Bugger N. Nose!"

"Spot Boy!"

Set lunged forward, taking down kings and queens, and threw a wild roundhouse. Already leaning back on the two legs of his chair, Asar missed a black eye by falling straight back and crashing with the chair onto the floor. Set rushed around the chess board and pounced on him.

"That's enough boys," Nut said, surprising her twins.

"He started it, Mama!" Set said. He got one more shot into the ribs.

"Set get off him!"

Set climbed off Asar who was still holding his ribs.

"Spotty!"

Nut's presence helped Set fight the urge to kick Asar while he was down.

"Come over here, boy," she said.

Set gave Asar his death-look and then slowly walked towards his mother. When he arrived, she flicked her middle finger hard against his forehead.

"Owww!"

"Hit your brother again like that and I'm going to punch you in the ribs, youhearme?"

Before Set could answer she thumped him on the forehead again.

"Owww. Mama, okay-okaaay."

Nut grabbed Set by the wrist and led her baby boy down the hall to the bathroom. She closed the door behind them.

"Mama's gonna help you baby, but you need to do exactly as I say."

"Yes, ma'am."

Nutilda pulled a coffee cup-sized jar from the hemp satchel she was carrying over her shoulder.

"Pull your trousers down."

Set scrunched up his face. He wasn't a little boy any more. He and Asar were both big for their age. At 5'7", he and Asar were the biggest 5th graders in their classroom.

"I can do it myself, Mama."

"Boy, it's a little too late to be getting shy around Mama since she's been washing your rusty behind before you could wash it yourself. Now, drop your pants."

"Awww, Mama."

"Set, do you want me to make the spots go away or not?"

Set dropped his head then slowly began to unloosen his belt. Nut showed him the respect of turning away. When she turned back around, Set had his head bowed and stood there with pants and underwear around his ankles. Now, she was the one who was a little uncomfortable. Looking at her baby boy, Nutilda realized that she hadn't seen him naked in a couple of years. He was definitely his father's son. She now wished she would have let him put the cream on himself.

"Pull your thing to the side, son." Set couldn't even look up.

As Set, thankfully, concealed his hand-me-down privates, Nut pulled a cotton ball from the hemp bag and dipped it in the grainy, brownish-green cream. She kneeled down.

"Apply it like this on your thigh and inside your ear ... no, inside both ears—just to make sure—every morning when you wake up and at night before you go to sleep."

She didn't look him in the eye. Set was silent. Head turned away.

"And every time you have to go to the bathroom to pee ... Are you listening to me, boy? Now, if you can't pay attention and can't remember, Mama can go into the bathroom with you."

That comment got Set's attention. His face swiveled immediately down to his mother's reckless eyeballs.

"Morning-night-pee, got it, Mama."

"Alright then, let Mama know, cause you know Mama can't read minds, only lips. Now, pull your trousers up, and I'll leave the jar and some cotton balls here on the sink. You decide where you want to keep it."

She stood up and glanced away. He pulled up his trousers.

"Mama loves you, and this whole thing is gonna be gone before you know it."

Set dropped his eyes down. He wasn't so sure. He slowly looked up and met her smile.

"Really, Mama? Are the spots really gonna go away?"

"Is fatback greasy?"

"Yes, ma'am."

"We'll, sure as fatback's greasy these ol spots gonna disappear in time. Now, I ain't saying when or how fast, but Mama knows these spots don't have a chance. And Mama needs you to know that too, baby. These spots are good as gone."

"Promise, Mama?"

Hope rounded his question.

"Promise."

"Cross your heart and hope to die?"

With the confidence of the Pope Leo XIII, Nutilda used her index finger to cross herself.

32

Spying on Set and his mother, Asar wondered how his eyeball looked from the other side of the bathroom's skeleton keyhole. Did it look as big as it felt? Like a blinking black grape? Like a marble-sized buckshot about to blast from his socket?

As quietly as he had kneeled down, Asar stood up and walked down the stairs to the front porch.

His mother complained about the trains: the noise, the black smoke, the rumbling earth. But Asar loved to feel the wooden porch vibrating beneath his feet when the trains rumbled past. Just like he loved to feel his heart race when he imagined jumping a train and riding way out to California—all by himself. See some real live cowboys.

Maybe, if I was gone long enough, he thought, they'd miss me enough to make me feel like l was the favorite.

Asar didn't really understand. He tried his best to be responsible like Daddy had taught him, but when Set was bad, Daddy—and Mama—loved him more. When I'm bad, he thought, I just get in trouble. Where's the fun in being the first-born if I can't even get away with stuff? Set was born second, but everybody in the house seemed to forget except me, Asar thought, as he often did when feeling unchosen.

It was during these times that Asar would come out to the front porch and watch the trains carry people off to far away places.

"Son, ya spend as much time standin on this porch as this here swing," Nema said.

He was sitting on the four-person swing to the far right, behind Asar. He was dressed in his black undertaker suit, although he had no one to take under.

"Hi, Grandpa."

"Don't hi me, son, tell me what's on ya mind so tough ya can't hear an ol man sittin right behind ya. If I'da been a rattlesnake, you'd be dead."

"Yessir."

"Man should always know when somebody comin up em. Hell, when I was ya age, I could see and *smell* a man comin from round the corner, up the street—with my back to em. So, boy, tell me what's a youngin like you thinkin so hard on?"

"Nothing, Pa-Pa."

"Boy, don't make me reach up and slap the black off ya neck. Now, do what I say and tell me what's on ya mind, and bring ya little narrow ass over here and sit next to ya Pa-Pa when ya telling me."

"Yessir," Asar said.

Asar walked to the far end of the porch to join his grandfather on the swing. In silence, first-born sat next to foundation, rocking away the space between their generations. They both kept their eyes straight ahead on the Eads Bridge as they talked.

"Well, son?"

"What do I have to do to be capable of love?"

"Boy, you soundin more like ya Daddy every day and I'm not sure that's a good thing. Can you even spell capable?"

"C-A- ... ."

"Shut up, Mr. Smart T. Pants. Isn't that what you let Set call you? I know ya parents don't like to hear me say it, but anybody can see they favor that wild lil brutha of yours. I can see it and as much time as ya spend on this damn porch lookin out yonda, I know ya can feel it. It ain't right. I talked to ya father and that mother of yours and all they got to say is, 'We love our boys both the same.'" Like everybody in this house death, dumb and blind. Including you. Well, the proof is a-rockin on this porch right now. God hears me, it ain't right. Ya the first-born."

"It don't seem like that most times."

"Now, it ain't all ya parents fault."

"How you mean, Grandpa?" Asar said, turning to his grandfather.

"Why ya think they favor Set so much?"

"I don't know, Pa-Pa."

Nema looked hard at his grandson.

"Ya know well enough. Ya ain't no dummy, boy. Think on it now." Asar rocked in silence for a few moments.

"Because Set is more like Mama?"

"No, lil fool. Cause Set got some gumption. That boy got more backbone than a catfish. That Set will go out and do what he gonna do, damn the consequences from ya Mama, ya Daddy or me."

"Alotta times he's just being bad, Pa-Pa. I tried that but I just get in trouble."

"Ya get in trouble cause when ya bad, ya don't go all the way out, son. That damn Set get into somethin so deep, ya half-way hate to whup him cause the boy got so much heart. I mean he know a whuppin is comin, so he gonna squeeze the most fun out of whatever devilment he got himself into. It kinda make ya smile a little, even though ya be mad at em. The little sucka makes ya respect em. Like the time he asked that Auset girl, 'Can I have some?' That girl's Daddy, pullin her like a rag doll, came by here so mad, I thought he was gonna swing on ya Daddy. When ya Daddy called Set to the porch for an accountin of the particulars, I know ya recall what he said cause ya nosey butt was right there in the doorway. Now, how did Set explain that 'Can I have some' mannishness to ya father and that girl's father, what Set say?"

"A closed mouth don't get fed."

"That's right, he quoted ya Daddy's sayin right back to em and he didn't sound one bit sorry or scared, and he sholl didn't look one-bit shame-faced."

"But he sure was crying hard when Daddy put that razor strap on him," Asar said.

"But that's what I'm tryin to tell ya, son. Set knew he was wrong when he got fresh with that man's daughter. He knew he was in trouble soon as he heard the tone of ya Daddy's voice callin him on that porch. He knew that a whuppin was comin as soon as that Auset girl and her Daddy left. But his bad ass still stood there with a face as straight as the B & O Line, looked ya Daddy right in the eye, right in front of that girl's Daddy and said, 'Daddy, you always told me, A closed mouth don't get fed, so I asked Auset for some.' Ya Daddy's grin slipped out before he could catch it. Set caught the girl's Daddy so off guard that I'll be damned if he didn't crack a quick little smile too. I know ya saw ya mama. She had to leave the porch to stop from laughin. Now, I didn't think it was cute at all. If he woulda been my boy, he woulda got the cane right then and there, and on the double, in front of everybody. Ya grandpa would've drawn some blood, yessir. But I ain't ya parents. Ya gotta deal with the ones ya got. They tolerate Set's foolishness cause the boy acts a fool at full gallop. And there go ya answer son. If ya want ya damn fool parents to show ya more favor, go all out. Good or bad. Ya got the good part down. So when ya do wrong, be wrong and strong."

33

Set walked up 10th Street, heading towards St. Clair. He was kinda glad that Asar was stuck talking to Grandpa Nema on the porch. Those talks could last forever once Grandpa got going, so Set went to pick up sausages by himself over at Dabrowski & Son Meats.

He needed to talk alone with Bogdan.

Unlike Set's Mr. Smart T. Pants brother, Bogdan had a way of listening real good. It made you feel better even if he didn't have a good answer to your problem. But usually, Bogdan did have an answer. Working around so many adults, in his father's market, made it seem like there was a grown man's brain inside Bogdan's small body. Set could tell that sometimes Bogdan wished for a boy's brain—and a boy's life.

"Hey, Bogdan."

"Set!"

"You looking more lost in your head than Asar when he leaves home without his compass. Boy has no sense of direction; good thing he has me."

"Seems like the customers are lost too."

"Slow again?"

"More like not busy all the time. Still got to work though." Bogdan's right hand shooed a fly off his white smock.

"Where's Mr. Dabrowski?"

"In the back room, sick again. I missed school Wednesday, Thursday *and Friday.*"

"What happens when both of you get sick at the same time?"

"I don't get sick."

"Maybe you will one day."

"What, are you hoping I get sick?"

"No, I'm just saying sometimes—*things happen.*"

Bogdan heard the catch in Set's voice. He knew something was wrong with his friend. He looked him in the eye waiting for Set to continue.

"I'm disappearing."

"Hunh?"

"Look over here in my ear."

Bogdan leaned over and put his eyes so close to Set's ear, that Bogdan's pale nose almost touched Set's onyx cheek. He peered inside and examined the white spot. It resembled spots that developed when bleach splashed on his black clothes during laundry time.

"How'd it get in there?"

"I don't know. Asar just saw it when we were at the Chicago fair."

"It's not too big. I would've never noticed if you hadn't told me to look in there. I don't see why you're all …"

"It's not the only one."

"In the other ear?"

"On my thigh and it's bigger too. I think that one's growing and if that one's growing, maybe the one you're looking at now is growing too."

"What did your folks say?"

"You know how my Mama has the roots and herbs shop? She said she would fix it. She crossed her heart and hoped to die."

"For real?"

"Yep and she made me this spot remover cream that I've been putting on both spots, but either it's taking a while to work or its not working yet."

"Maybe you've just got to put on a double portion, like I do with bleach when I get a lot blood on my smock."

"You think that could be it?"

"If your Mama crossed her heart and hoped to die, she must know the spot remover is gonna work. Now, turn your head straight again. I wanna stick my finger in and touch it. Is it catchy?"

"I don't think so. I've put my own fingers all over both spots and it hasn't spread to those fingers. But I don't want to risk you getting it. No touching."

"Can't be that risky if I'm already the same color."

"Step back Mr. Curious B. Risky," Set said, moving away from Bogdan.

"Even if it does spread, wouldn't it be fun if we could be the same color? We could kinda be twins like you and Asar. We could be the same!"

"No, it wouldn't be fun and, no, we wouldn't be the same." "Sure it would. You'd be as white as me!"

"But I'd still be a Negro, Bogdan."

"But people wouldn't have to know. I sure wouldn't tell. It could be our secret."

"I don't want to pretend to be who I'm not."

"It wouldn't be pretending if you turned white."

"But I'd be Negro on the inside."

"On the inside? People are blood red on the inside."

"I know, I know … "

"Then what are you saying?"

"I'm saying, when you're born in America and other Americans—born here or not—treat you bad just cause you're walking around with Negro skin, you end up getting poked a lot until … "

"I'm white and I've never poked you and never will."

"But what if something changes when we grow up and …"

"Set Americus, there isn't that much change in the whole wide world."

"Okay, okay, not every white pokes cause there's people like you and your Papa. But the thing is, a white can always tell that I'm a Negro, but I can't always tell if they're the type of white American who pokes Negro Americans. And sometimes, it's a lot worse than pokes. Daddy says, because the white man is American on sight, it's his right to kill Negroes on sight—without getting in trouble with the law. Daddy says, that's what makes the white man the only real American: he makes the law so it can work for him, at least when it comes to hurting Negroes. So Bogdan, I have to keep my guard up when I'm walking down the street eating candy or whistling or standing still or just breathing. I can't breathe. When you have to keep your guard up just to breathe, Bogdan, it can change something on the inside of you. Something that can't be fixed just by changing what's on the outside of you."

❙   ❙   ❙

Set stood naked in the bathroom, still thinking about his conversation with Bogdan earlier that day. If I turned white, would I still really be a Negro? he thought. What if only half of me turned white? Would the bohunks treat me better half the time? He planted his left foot on the pine floor. What if a bohunk had black spots on him and turned black on the outside? Would he still be white? Mr. Arellano is from Mexico and he's dark as Daddy. If spots turned him white, would he still be black or still be Mexican or would it turn him into an American? Maybe that's it. I'm not turning white, I'm becoming a real American. Set balanced his right foot on the lip of the bathtub and bent down for a closer look at the

American spot on his inner thigh.

"It's getting bigger."

It was only a couple days before November. The year was almost over. Set had hoped that the white spots would be gone before the start of 1894, maybe even by Christmas—the best Christmas present in the whole wide world. But in the two months that he'd been using Mama's grainy greenish-brown cream, which he optimistically named The Mighty Spot Remover, the spots weren't shrinking.

They both were growing. Especially the thigh spot.

The ear spot, not so much. Since it was harder to see, it was easier not to think about. He just rubbed the cream in his ear and hoped for the best. But the lima bean on his thigh had grown into a baby onion. A baby onion with ambition.

As Bogdan had suggested, Set Americus had begun spreading on a double portion of The Mighty Spot Remover. Lately, he'd been applying the cream, not with the cotton balls that his mother gave him, but with the combined nails of his index and middle fingers on his left hand. His longest nails. He thought if he could get the cream on the underside of the skin's white spot, The Mighty Spot Remover would have a better chance of working. Attacking the enemy from both sides. The Problem: Set didn't know how deep to scrape to reach the underside.

For extra depth, he had decided to file his index and middle fingernails to a rounded point, like tiny shovels, similar to how his Mama filed all of hers. Since it was only two fingers, it didn't count as girly.

The recent repeated digging had created a continually fresh scab that never had time to heal before the next day's digging. Set slipped his pointy index nail under the cracking scab. He gave it a little lift and watched it spring up like a spider web.

The perimeter of the scab consisted of a white band. A wedding ring that held no promise of fidelity. A sore with roaming eyes. Set closed his own. In the dark canvass behind his eyelids, he saw the white perimeter with little tiny teeth eating outward across his black thigh. Spreading downward towards his knee. Then out of his ear. He saw the itty bitty teeth nibbling away at his black lobe until an entirely white ear hung from his black face. He had to get himself ready for this possibility. He kept his eyes closed and imagined watching as the sheet of whiteness swept up the base of his scrotum. His foot still on the bathtub rim, Set scooped The Mighty Spot Remover with his two filed fingers. He applied the cream, scratching and scraping towards the underside. Thinking about how Asar had called him Spot Boy. Thinking about the whole family calling him Spot Boy behind his back. Bogdan too. Thinking about stangers staring at him. Pointing. Calling him Spot Boy to his face. Set scratched and scraped towards the underside. Mental images flashed of the baby onion-sized spot spreading across his whole leg. He wondered how far people would go if the spots kept going, kept spreading. Would they point and call him Half-White Boy? Half-Black Boy? Who would want to be friends with Half-White Boy? Even Bogdan who wanted me to be All-White, Set thought. What girl would want to be sweet on Half-Black Boy? Set thought about Auset, the girl he was sweet on. Would she look at me different? Would her sweetness sour? Of course it would. Set scraped faster.

Deeper. Blood covered his thigh. His hands.

"Auset's sweetness will sour."

After he cleaned up the blood and put The Mighty Spot Remover away, Set pulled up his black trousers. Put on his white shirt. Buttoned. Black vest. Buttoned. Black jacket. Buttoned. Checked himself in the mirror. He was looking and feeling tightly buttoned, tightly wound. Tight. Taut. He studied his face. His onyx skin stretched across his cheekbones. Set felt agitated. Energized. An energy that he wanted to release. Unleash. Hurl.

"I wanna see somebody hurting," he said into the mirror. "I'm glad there's a funeral today."

Set left the bathroom and walked down the hallway to the top of the staircase. People were already arriving. A somber man with a St. Bernard whisky face. Dressed in black from his shoes to his top hat. The puffy-eyed woman with puffy cheeks. Black dress. Set looked down on them as they streamed in the reception entrance. That was one of the many strange things about having a funeral home in your home. A bunch of sad people were always coming to your house. Bringing their regrets about what they didn't do when their dearly departed were alive.

Set had been sitting through funerals since before he knew it wasn't church. Americus & Son was the dead choice of Negro East St. Louis. The city was hard on Colored folk and good for business. Set got a good look at the dead business up close.

Over the years, Set had sat on the same wooden bench in the back watching the proceedings for heaven hopefuls. Grandpa Nema had told him he designed the Americus & Son funeral sanctuary so he could keep an eye on what was happening. The circular room had 33 slightly curved pews. They were organized into 11 concentric rows, with the three, three-foot pews making the smallest circle nearest the casket. Like ripples caused by a heavy tear-drop dropped into a pond, the circumference of the rows expanded as they moved outwards and up on the gently sloping floor. The first three pews formed a center circle with a nine foot aisle between each pew. This center circle was reserved for the immediate family. The successive pews were three feet longer than the previous. Inset in the very center circle, a pine sarcophagus stand designed as a nine-foot golden lion with the back hollowed out to place the casket. Grandpa Nema always seemed especially proud of the job he did intricately carving the arcing whiskers around the roaring mouth.

Still standing at the top of the stairs, Set watched a black-clad, teenage woman walk alone through the wide double-doors. He thought of one of the many stories that his family had told him about studying mourning Negroes. How Saffron, Mr. Plafton's 19-year- old girlfriend, showed-out in the middle of his funeral. Keb said that Saffron Jenkins stood unsteadily on those skinny, long yellow legs of hers and began a punch-drunk stagger down the aisle towards the the center circle where the casket lay. As she stumbled along, Saffron shrieked a slurred chant, "Not my Daddy ... not my Daddy." Grandpa Nema had called it "a spectacle." Mostly because Saffron's black dress had no intention of reaching her knees and her bosom had no intention of going without air. This was before Grandpa Nema began to hire the boys from the Normal School to serve as ushers. With Grandpa Nema behind the pulpit and next to the casket-holding-lion, there was no one to stop the spectacle from playing itself out.

The mourners, not inthe know, assumed Saffron was Mr. Plafton's grief-stricken daughter. Negroes were accustomed to seeing their kind wail for lost loved ones. A few even said, "That's awright, now that's awright." But one look at Penny Plafton's broken face, evil-eyeing Saffron Jenkins, could have told anyone in the audience that Saturday morning that Saffron Jenkins wasn't no daughter of hers. Even in death, Mr. Plafton had opened a door for his widow to be embarrassed one more time.

Grandpa Nema said that at about the 5th row, Saffron had steadied herself by palming the pew back. She removed her black hat with her other hand, raised it skyward and started a slurred dirge.

"Ain't gone let no-bod-ee turn me a-round, turn me a-round/ Ain't gone let no-bod-ee turn me a-round."

As the mourning audience began to pick up the tune, disgust erupted on Mrs. Plafton's face.

"Ain't gone let no-bod-ee turn me a-round, turn me a-round/ Ain't gone let no-bod-ee turn me a-round."

Saffron kicked off her chartreuse, heel-less mules and again started staggering towards the casket with her very own choir music.

Grandpa Nema figured to leave the pulpit and rush to her would just make matters worse.

"There sholl was no tellin what a woman hurtin like that would do," he'd later say.

When Saffron reached the circle of pews reserved for the immediate family, she stood right in front Mrs. Plafton. Mrs. Plafton slowly gathered her tired body and rose to meet her eye-to-eye. The wife and other woman stood there, inches apart, tears streaming down both of their cheeks. A casket-holding-lion as the backdrop. Both high-yellow and skinny. The original version and the new model. The crowd continued to sing.

"Ain't gone let no-bod-ee turn me a-round, turn me a-round/ Ain't gone let no-bod-ee turn me a-round."

Saffron finally spoke between tears.

"That man loved you so much, he hated himself for being with me. But I loved him so much, I loved you just because he did."

Mrs. Plafton managed a smile as she clasped both of Saffron's hands. Squeezed them tight. Elizabeth Plafton spoke with a dignified reserve that matched her posture.

"When you violate love—love violates you. You've violated my marriage and now life is going to violate you. You'll always be some man's mistress, some man's secret. Once you're a secret, young lady, shame will soon come—or in your triffling case—shame will always be."

"Ain't gone let no-bod-ee turn me a-round, turn me a-round/Ain't gone let no-bod-ee turn me a-round."

Grandpa Nema told Set that barefoot Saffron Jenkins turned around and stumbled back up the aisle, returning stares and singing a little softer.

❙ ❙ ❙

Set watched the last mourning stragglers arrive through the reception entrance. He started heading down the curving staircase, because he didn't want his father to come looking for him—which happened a few weeks ago. An experience he didn't want to repeat. When Set came into the sanctuary, his mother and twin brother were already sitting on the Americus Pew in the 11th row. Soon as he turned the corner, his mother's reckless eyeballs were already slit in his direction. He tried to sit next to Asar.

"Over here," Nut said. She pointed to the space next to her.Soon as he sat, Nut flicked his right ear with her middle finger. She leaned her mouth towards the same ear.

"Be late again."

Keb was already walking down the aisle towards the small pulpit next to the Lion Stand. Even if Asar couldn't, Set could already see himself making that same trip from Americus Pew to pulpit. When he'd be the one in charge of services. Just like his grandfather and now his father. When no one was around, Grandpa Nema would pull him aside and tell him, "Boy, keep ya eyes open and make sure ya take in everything that happens when ya over there in service, you hear me?"

It's only obvious that Grandpa Nema sees me one day walking down that same aisle too, Set thought.

I I I

After the funeral, Elder Charles Bundy's stomach tightened beneath his brown pin-striped suit when he saw Nema walking towards him and his son Le Roy. He never cared much for Keb's ol man. Elder Bundy thought that Nema must really hate Negroes the way he talked so bad about The Race. Sounding as bad of some of those Mississippi crackers; it's ridiculous, he'd thought often. Last month, Elder Bundy finally just came out and asked Keb about it after church.

"What did Negroes do to your father to make him talk the way he does?"

"It's what he thinks Negroes don't do. He sees all the challenges facing us, so he feels that every Negro should share his passion for upliftment. When people fall short, his disappointment comes across as disdain."

"That's no excuse, Keb. I get disappointed in us too, but that doesn't give me a right to talk about hard working Negroes in a way befitting a Ku Klux Klanner. Your father knows the white man cuts a Negro's legs off then blame him for not being able to walk. Won't allow a Negro to even apply for the job then call the Negro lazy for not applying for the job. Lynch Negroes then label Negroes violent when we decide to defend ourselves. Your father should be more disappointed in white Americans' lack of patriotism for treating their fellow countrymen with such unpatriotic disdain."

"Should my father deal with his disappointment better? Of course. Will a man that set in his ways change now? Probably not. But you know as well as I do that my father has helped set up quite a few Negroes in business, mostly from your church. He wouldn't even let them give the money back. So don't get all sore at him Charles. Besides, he likes you."

"Afternoon, Elder Bundy."

"Afternoon, Mr. Americus."

"I tell ya, we put the salt back into the earth today, yessir, yessir."

"Speak on it, because Jethro Jamison was very kind to my family as soon as we arrived. His letter of introduction was like a key to the city."

"Well, he sholl took a likin to ya. Took a shinin to ya lil man here too. Can't tell ya how many times ya both popped up when we'd get to conversatin."

"I appreciate you telling me that, Mr. Americus."

"Nothin to appreciate, just the simple fact. Ya doin somethin right cause Jethro wadn't the only one spittin ya name in my ear. Lotta folk from that church ya'll go to talk real good about ya. Hell, ya bout my son's age and ya already an elder."

Despite the conversation's positive tone, Elder Bundy still had his guard up. Le Roy, wearing a smaller version of his father's brown pin-striped suit, had his guard up too. Le Roy had seen Mr. Americus jump mean in mid-conversation.

"Hey, Lee-roy!" Asar said. He left his brother behind and ran up to his friend.

"Hey, Asar."

Le Roy's hay color and chubby-cheeked softness standing next to Asar's onyx-skinned athletic body made the friends look like physical opposites.

"You wanna go play chess?" Asar said. Though he really wanted to go play pirates, but he knew that Grandpa Nema would say, "Not in those clothes you ain't."

"Can I, Daddy?" Le Roy asked.

"Long as you put that king in check and make that queen cry."

"Don't get ya hopes up; I taught that boy the game myself," Nema said.

As the boys started to run towards the house, they sped past Set.

"Where you going so fast with Roy-Lee?" Set said.

"To make Queen Bundy cry," Asar said, over his shoulder.

"If you believe that Ready-Go, you must be ready-to-go back to first grade," Le Roy, hollered back.

Set didn't care much for Le Roy because, like Asar, he was a know-it-all. That's why Set was so happy last year to see Le Roy's class work on triple-chinned Miss Smarney's desk. Mr. Know I.T. All didn't even know his letters right. Some of the "d"s and "p"s and "q"s were all backward like a little dummy would write them. Right in front of Miss Smarney,

Set snatched Le Roy's paper off her desk, raised it over his head with both hands in front of the whole class, and started sing-songing, "Lee-Roy Bunn-dy-iss baccck-ward/Lee-Roy Bunn-dy-iss bacck-ward."

Asar didn't have to turn his head around to see the blood rushing to Le Roy's cashew-colored face. Whenever he was mad or embarrassed, he turned as red as the bohunk boys in town. Miss Smarney alphabetically sat the students so Asar Americus had been sitting directly in front of Le Roy Bundy since the first grade (at first Set sat in front of Le Roy, but after a month of bickering and round-house punches, Miss Mayweather, their first grade teacher, switched Asar and Set and it's been that way ever since).

"Set Americus bring that here this instant!" Miss Smarney had shouted.

She was almost six feet tall with a kangaroo-shaped body. Two scraggly hairs jutted from her brown jowly chin, a voice deep enough to sing bass in the choir, and her black hair in a tight bun, Miss Smarney was not to be played with.

"Lee-Roy Bunn-dy-iss baccck-ward ..." Set sang and added a booty-twisting dance. The classroom burst into nervous giggles. Miss Smarney swept a hard stare across the room. The students caught their laughter. Set sang and danced on.

"Stop it!" Asar screamed from Row One, Seat One.

From Seat Three, Le Roy's locked-jawed jutted towards Set. Enraged by the youngest Americus' defiance, Miss Smarney jumped from behind her large desk and approached him with a 12-inch wooden ruler in-hand.

"You don't take things from my desk."

"Okay-okay-okay," Set said.

The ruler cowered him out of his song and dance. He extended Le Roy's paper towards her. When Miss Smarney was about to take it, he snatched it back and shimmied around the perimeter of the room holding Le Roy's paper high over his head. His classmates craned their necks as he danced by them.

"Lee-Roy Bunn-dy-iss bacck-ward/Lee-Roy Bunn-dy-iss bacck- ward."

Le Roy's red face and locked jaw followed the routine around the room.

"I will not chase you; you come here right now Set!" Miss Smarny's bass voice echoed around the room.

"Lee-Roy Bunn-dy-iss bacck-ward/Lee-Roy Bunn-dy-iss bacck- ward."

Asar jumped out of his seat and ran down the middle aisle. He dived pass Sarah James' shoulder and tackled Set in the back on the room. Set went down crumbling Le Roy's paper in his fist.

Even in protective fetal position, while being punched in the side by his big brother, the class could hear Set's muffled, "Lee-Roy ... back-ward."

From that day, Set always called Backward Le Roy Bundy, "Roy-Lee." Le Roy started calling Set, "Ready-Go."

▎ ▎ ▎

"I've got winners, Roy-Lee," Set said, walking into the twin's bedroom.

"Well, you should be talking to me," Asar said. "I'm gonna be the one winning."

Asar rarely beat Le Roy.

"You two Mr. Numb R. Skulls will probably knock the kings on the floor and lose them before you checkmate them, so I'll have no one to beat," Set said.

While moving his bishop to bishop level 4, Le Roy said, "Only one you can beat is your meat."

Asar burst into laughter, which made Roy-Lee look up and break from his deadpan into a serious case of the giggles. Set glared back and forth between the two thinking, That wasn't even funny. He watched the chessmen make eye contact again, unleashing more game interrupting giggles. Set hated their little inside jokes. He hated Roy-Lee's reddening face for acting like he was Asar's twin. He hated Asar's black face for letting Roy-Lee get away with it.

▎ ▎ ▎

From across the lawn, Keb saw his father bow slightly to Elder Bundy and amble towards the Americus Fountain. Elder Charles Bundy shook his head and smiled. He saw his friend with the inch- wide part coming in his direction. Could any father and son be more different? Charles thought.

Sure, they both were black as the night was long, tall as a maypole, and favored clothes dark as their profession. But Keb had such a respect for human beings. Seemed like working around the dead made him appreciate the living an awful lot, Elder Bundy thought. Keb didn't have to talk much because those slanted hazel eyes spoke for him. Listened too. He focused on you so hard, you'd swear there were earlobes hanging out his pupils. Make you feel like what you have to say is important.

On the other hand, that fool Daddy of his is the master of making you feel about as high as the dust under a pregnant rattlesnake. Elder Bundy didn't see how anyone could be a friend of Nema Americus. Even a friendly man like Jethro Jamison.

"Yes indeed, the Americus in Americus & Son was in rare form this morning," Elder Bundy said.

"I guess that's how it goes when you put your best friend in the ground. Wait until people see how I act out when I put you under," Keb said.

"The way you work, you're going to meet Jesus long before I do, but I'll be sure to act a fool for you."

"It won't be a far stretch. I've seen how that Holy Spirit makes you act behind that pulpit," Keb said. He leaned close to his best friend and lowered his voice.

"And I've also seen what happens when that communion wine gets good to you."

"You a fool, Keb," Elder Bundy chuckled. He threw his arm over Keb's shoulder.

"Stop me when I start lying," Keb said.

Nut stood in the kitchen watching the good times that a funeral can become. She loved when Elder Bundy was around because he made Keb laugh. Made Keb take off that stiff yoke that his crazy father had tossed over his shoulders since birth. Nema didn't like to see anybody having a good time, Nut thought. As if having a good time meant you weren't serious about life. Weren't serious about The Race. That's some empty-headed thinking. She smiled watching the big smile on her husband's face.

"How's the Old Man taking Mr. Jamison's passing," Elder Bundy said.

"You heard him today. Still ornery as a coyote with splinter up his ass. Which is a good sign for him, even though it's a bad sign for those of us who have to be around him. But it's gonna take a month of Sundays to see how he handles it. You saw how many times Jamison was here when you came by the house after church. That man was Daddy's only friend."

"Thank God he's got you."

"I'm his son, not his friend. Under these house rules, you can't be both."

"Keb, that's the dumbest rule I ever heard."

"I'm not the one who made it."

"Yeah, but maybe you should be the one to change it."

35

Nut watched Set through the kitchen window. On the day before Christmas, he sat on the snow-covered fountain looking like it was the day before death. She wondered if the spots were shrinking too slowly. Set hadn't let her see the spot on his thigh since she gave him the first jar of what he'd been calling The Mighty Spot Remover. A name that made Nut smile; it showed his confidence in her.

Nut grabbed her gray overcoat off the hook near the door and stepped out into the lightly swirling snow. She was sure Set heard the door close, but he didn't look up. His head was down and his cap had its own cap of snow.

"Merry Christmas," Nut said.

She sat next to him on the fountain rim. Set didn't speak.

"How's The Mighty Spot Remover working?" Nut said, smiling.

Set's head dropped. When he looked back up, his almond-shaped eyes were like sneering lips. Then, in that dramatic way of his, Set grabbed the front of his heavy black coat with both large hands, snatched it open, sending buttons flying. He wasn't wearing a shirt beneath. Over his left areola was a silver dollar-sized white spot.

"You promised."

36

Set knew 1894 would come and his spots would still be there. And he was right. The New Year had come and the spots had grown and new ones had emerged. The more they grew, the more the spots seemed like sores to Set. They didn't hurt to touch, but they hurt on sight. A relentless ache that throbbed no matter how hard he shut his eyes.

The spots were Americus Adventurers too: on his left calf, on his left shoulder, over his right areola, and most distressing on the back of this left hand, in the space between his thumb and index finger. It was the first spot that didn't have the decency to stay hidden in an ear or behind some clothes. If Set kept his left thumb pressed against the side of his left index finger, only half the sore was visible. But usually he just kept that left hand shoved in his pocket. No easy thing when you do your school work left-handed. At home, Set began to practice writing right-handed.

Just two weeks ago, Set, Asar, Tommy the Bully (sometimes confused with Toothless Tommy, because Tommy the Bully was the reason Toothless Tommy became Toothless Tommy) and a group of boys were walking out of school together when Set started talking with his hands.

"What's that," Tommy the Bully said, pointing at Set's gesticulating hand.

"I spilled some paint," Set said.

He shoved his hand deep inside his brown, wool overcoat pocket.

Looked away.

"I saw it when you raised your hand today. Didn't look like no paint then, didn't look like no paint before you hid it in your pocket. Let me see it again."

"I told you it was paint. Don't you know what paint looks like?"

"Look like the cooties to me. Is it catchy?" Tommy the Bully teased.

"Very catchy!"

Before "catchy" had finished echoing in the chilly January air, Set had drawn his fist out his pocket and caught Tommy the Bully square on the nose with a loud "crack." The punch had such force that Tommy the Bully fell straight back and his head landed on the frozen hard dirt road with another "crack." Set spun around looking at the group of stunned boys, a group that included Asar. His left hand was throbbing, but he didn't let on.

"Who else wants to see the catchy paint on my hand!"

Looking down at Tommy the Bully, who wasn't moving, made the boys step back. Their startled faces made Set feel strong. Powerful. He was especially struck by the look on Asar's face. The way his mouth was open. How big and sheepy his eyes were: He had made his big brother afraid of him. Set liked the feeling that creating fear gave him.

He carried that feeling with him as he stormed home. Alone.

Asar was a silent witness to it all.

When Tommy the Bully was falling straight back, Asar had been ready to pounce on him, tag-team style, as their father had always taught them: When you fight one Americus, you fight all the Americuses. But Set had turned on him like he was one of the other boys and not the twin brother who'd fought by his side all their lives. As they lay on their backs in Set's bed that night, Asar told Set that he would sock the next boy he saw pointing at his hand or whispering about his hand or even looking at his hand. Set turned to his brother and said, "What if it was Roy-Lee?" "I'd tell him to stop it right now."

"That's what I thought. Don't do no fighting or *telling to stop right now* for me. Mr. I. Cooties Handman can handle things himself."

The whispered classroom verdict handed down the next day: "Only someone with cooties would try so hard to hide it … and it's catchy too."

A verdict driven by evidence shoved in pants. The most intensely watched pocketed hand in the history of the East St. Louis' Lincoln School—and not the least touched. In fact, Tommy the Bully's nose was the first student body part to officially touch the Cooties Fist.

Set told himself he liked his own space, so it wasn't such a bad thing that no one wanted to touch him. At least, at first.

When Set and Asar met up with the group of boys they normally walked home from to school with (minus Tommy the Bully), each boy from a distance was quick to shoot a furtive glance down towards Set's left hand pocket, as he now only gestured with his right. In class, when Set quickly raised his right hand to answer questions before his Mr. Know I.T. All brother and his brother's Mr. Know I.T. All fake twin Roy-Lee, 26 pair of eyes shifted to see if Set slipped and raised the Cooties Hand. At the lunch hour, the boys could scarcely eat their own food for trying to see if Set would eat his peanut butter & jelly sandwich with the Cooties Hand. No such luck because not only did Set unpack his lunch with his right hand, he also was an excellent right-handed peanut butter & jelly sandwich eater.

The challenge: spots were appearing faster than Set could devise strategies to hide them. Nut was frantically altering The Mighty Spot

Remover. She tripled the tea tree oil then doubled the elderberry. Added echinacea. Removed noni. Reincoporated noni. Doubled marigold. Removed noni. Each week, she nervously gave Set a new batch of The Mighty Spot Remover even though the prior batch probably didn't have enough time to show its worth and each week Set nervously applied the new batch to his coal black body. Each week giver and receiver hoping for a different result and each week getting a result that they each didn't want. Each new spot coloring a wall growing between mother and son.

In March, the first white spot appeared on Set's face. It began as a faded black bean, an inch across from his left nostril. By the start of April, it was lima bean—and it had a navy bean right beneath it. Unlike the white spots now growing out onto both his earlobes, which could be hidden by pulling big hats low, there was no hat big enough to hide spots on the front of his face. Set bathed his face in The Mighty Spot Remover. By mid-May, there were beans sprouting all over Set's face: three butter beans on his left cheek, cannellini bean on his upper lip, two attached lima beans on his chin and navy bean on the tip of his nose.

People stared.

Each new encounter was a bad encounter. It was like he never got a chance to really recover, because each time he encountered someone who had never seen Mr. Spot T. Boy his face started a conversation without saying a word. The response of the gawkers was also nonverbal. No words are needed to express revulsion and pity. This repetitive conversation day-after-day had a way of eroding something day-by-day inside of Set. His changing exterior was changing something deep within him. He wasn't exactly sure what the change was. He experienced it more as a feeling. A desire. He was developing a passion to hurt people.

Set had stopped going to school in late April, because he kept getting in fights with starers who just couldn't help themselves. The family, not sure how to best help Set, tried to act as if absolutely nothing had changed.

"Set I need you to run down to Dabrowski's and pick up some Kielbasa," Keb said. He said these words as if he wasn't aware that Set hadn't left the house in the month of May.

"Can't you wait until Asar comes back with Mama?"

"Boy, I'm hungry now and I've got a taste for a Dabrowski Kielbasa—and I want it now."

Set knew his father was trying to help. Set hadn't seen Bogdan in over two months, and he needed to talk to his friend. He was tired of feeling ashamed. Set was also tired of being in the house; it was driving him crazy.

Mostly, he was tired of letting the starers win. Set was embarrassed that he let other people stop him from going outside. It made him feel weak.

"How many do you want, Daddy?"

"Get two apiece for me and you."

Keb slid a Morgan dollar in Set's spot covered hand.

The sight of the silver coin in his diseased hand made Set's heart start to race. He started upstairs to get his cloth cap but stopped mid-way.

"No hats, no hiding," he said aloud.

Set walked down the Americus & Son steps with his cap-free head up. East St. Louis was in bloom. May opened the eyes of Brown-Eyed Susans. The edge of sidewalks were shrouded in Queen Anne's Lace. Roses opened for the sun as Set walked down 10th Street. He stopped to smell the rose bush tumbling over a white picket fence. Set closed his eyes as the velvety petals brushed across his cheek; he inhaled deeply. Felt his chest expand. He exhaled slow and long, releasing tension from being cooped up in the house for almost a month. A petal brushed his mouth as Set allowed a subtle smile form across his lips. He raised his face from the fragrant bush. Opened his eyes. The little black boy staring up at Set did so with the openness that only 4-year-olds can muster. The open stare of boy turning onto 10th Street and encountering a giant black beetle climbing out of a rose. A black beetle with a spotted human face.

"Look, Mama!" the boy said, extending his index finger towards Set.

There was no need for a pointing finger. Set could see that the mother was already staring. Her face's mixture of revulsion and pity reminded Set of how people looked at Deformed Danny Schroeder's mangled limbs and missing fingers. Reminded Set of how he looked at Deformed Danny. *Is that how I look to people?* The thought stunned him into a reflective stupor. Evaporated his temporary confidence.

The woman quickly looked away and reached down to grab her son's hand. The boy snatched away his pointing finger.

"What's wrong with his face, Mama?"

"Boy, give me your hand and let's go."

The boy evaded his mother, rushed right in front of Set, and pointed again.

"What's wrong with your face?"

"I … I don't know. My… mother."

"God, I'm sorry, I'm sorry," the mother said, grabbing the boy's index finger and dragging him past Set.

"She promised."

37

East St. Louis June humidity, and predawn moonlight shining through the open French windows, made their bodies glisten.

"I'm not changing my mind, Nut," Keb said.

"It's not about changing your mind, it's about having some faith in me, Keb. Some faith that I know what I'm doing with the child that I carried. Some ... "

"You always bring up carrying our children as if that gives you more insight than me."

"Some faith in *my* tradition. You and your nutty father always talking about tradition. Well, I came from one too, and I'm tired of you trying to belittle it."

"Why do you keep bringing up my father whenever ... ."

"Daddy worked with the same herbs that I use. They work, they heal, Keb. And when my own son ... "

"Our son."

"And now that our own son needs some healing, you want to take him to the white man, who you know don't care nothing about him. At least take him to Dr. Mandrake."

"Dr. Mandrake is a good doctor, but this is a special circumstance. Let's see what Dr. Gentry can do."

Keb turned on his side and faced his wife. He placed his hands gently on her cheeks.

In the room below, Set turned on his side to stare at the full moon through the open window.

"Baby, listen, what doesn't make sense is forcing what's not working. That's not belittling your healing tradition. I helped you build that store. I recommend it to people all over town. I supported your efforts with Set. It's time to try ... ."

"I just need ... "

"Stop making this about you because it's not. It's about our son. What you've tried has not worked, baby. It hasn't. Not only have the blemishes not disappeared, the initial ones have grown and new ones have appeared—on his face, Nut. On his face."

"I just need a little more time to figure out the right blend."

"Tell that to Set."

"You make me sick!" Nut said, throwing herself over onto her back.

"Our son's the one who's sick. He's sick and tired of getting his hopes up with each of your new concoctions only to be disappointed again. It's been 10 months, Nut. 10 months."

"I know how long it's been."

"Look at how the blemishes are affecting him. The one on his hand has turned him into the One Armed Man. He rarely pulls it out of his pocket even when he's at home—and we know what's there. And his ... his face, Nut. He doesn't want to go outside. Think about what he must be feeling, because you know he's not going to tell us how he really feels. His attitude speaks for him. He's so hurt and disappointed Nut. So sullen. I barely recognize ... I ... our baby boy, Nut, our baby boy, I barely recognize him. He's so angry. I know you see it because much of it is directed at you."

Nut quickly flipped on her side to face Keb.

"What did he say?"

"He doesn't have to say anything Nut. It's obvious. He's hurt. He's disappointed. And he's started to blame you for not being able to fix him. It's just not a good situation. We tried your way, for everyone's sake, let's try my way."

Nut slowly turned over on her back.

In the room below, Set slowly turned over on his back.

I I I

Set climbed down the three steps of the Americus Carriage then froze on the sidewalk. Keb almost bumped into him.

"Go, boy."

Set ignored his father. Keb stepped around him, "Boy, what's wrong with ... "

The sight that stopped Keb's words was the same sight that stopped Set in front of the carriage steps. A Negro man was walking down the sidewalk towards them wearing a tan sack suit. His entire chin and lower lip were faded into a pale whiteness. His protruding forehead was black as Keb's, except for a molar-sized white spot above his left brow. The whole right side of his face was a sloppy, melted-chess board of black and white splotches. His broad nose was perfectly black, but the outer lining of this right nostril was a faded white circle. As the man walked right past father and son, Set was staring so hard that the man turned to look down at him.

"Mind your manners, if you were taught any," the man spat on the sidewalk, then looked over at Keb.

As the man passed, Set's head slowly followed him. Watching his own future. The future of Spot Boy: Spot Man. Set felt his father's hand on his shoulder. Keb drew him close and hugged Set. As Keb hugged, Set angled his body so he could see the fading man continue walking down the sidewalk. Embracing father and son stood there watching Set's future until the man faded away in the distance.

In silence, Keb, and his fading favorite, started walking down the street towards the cobble approach to Dr. Gentry's corner office. Set took a step up the walkway before Keb's grabbed his wrist.

"This way, son."

They walked around the back to the hardened dirt path that led to Dr. Gentry's back door. Keb raised his fist to knock, then hesitated. Set looked up towards his father, but Keb said nothing. Keb had never entered a business establishment through the back door.

Many of the businesses in East St. Louis, if they even served Coloreds, wouldn't allow them to slander the business by entering through the front door. Nema had always told Keb, "Son, ya money spend the same as the white man's money. If it don't bring the same service, spend it somewhere where it does."

Keb had walked out many businesses (but not before speaking his piece) because he, nor his money, was being properly respected. A process Keb learned growing up at the side of his own father who gained a reputation around town for "not knowing his place."

Keb knocked hard three times on the door.

"What ya'll want back ... Mr. Americus?" Saffron Jenkins said.

She startled Keb out of his own thoughts. He recognized her right away. Mr. Plafton's high-yellow girlfriend who showed out at Plafton's funeral. She was now in her late-forties and her high- cheek-boned face still had the kind of look that would make a man look again.

"How are you, Miss Jenkins?"

"Fine, how can I help you, Mr. Americus?"

Keb couldn't quite gets his thoughts together because Saffron seemed to be in the wrong place, asking the wrong question.

Saffron glanced at Set's spotty chin and nose, still visible even with the brown cloth cap pulled low. Set looked over to his father. So did Saffron.

She was embarrassed for Mr. Americus. One of the biggest Negro men in the entire town, and he couldn't even come into the front door of Jimmy's office—and couldn't come in the back because Jimmy don't treat Negroes.

Keb took a quick glance through the door. Doctor Gentry wasn't the kind of man to hire Colored servants.

"Doctors deal with people in some of their most vulnerable situations," Keb had heard Dr. Gentry tell Nema when he was a boy himself. "A white man doesn't want to be weak around nigras, I mean to say, Negroes, because it's just unnatural."

"We have an appointment," Keb said. Saffron raised her brow.

"Dr. Gentry doesn't … okay … Dr. Gentry ran to the general store, but he'll be back directly. I suppose ya'll should come on in," she said. Saffron opened the door completely and stepped back to let them in. She was wearing a very thin, white pull over dress that looked almost like a night gown, except it was more form fitting. Keb had to make himself not stare at the shadow of her pubic hair visible beneath the thin fabric. She was barefoot. "Come on and have a seat in here."

She directed them into the small laundry room that had a wooden chair and small cot against the far wall. Keb sat in the chair. Set plopped on the cot and gave it a good bounce. Keb shot him a look. The room was eight feet by eight feet and had a clothes hamper next to the cot. General Robert E. Lee kept watch from an oval picture frame.

"Saffron don't keep me waiting, unless we're going to do … ." Joey Gentry said this, before stopping one step into the small room.

The last time Keb had seen the doctor's son was about four years ago, when he ran into Dr. Gentry and Joey walking down Broadway. Then Joey looked skinny and shy. Nothing like the 16-year-old young man standing bare-chested before him now. Just under six feet, ruddy with a wild tangle of black curly hair falling around his befuddled face.

"What are you doing in Saffron's room," he said.

"They have an appointment with the doctor," Saffron snapped.

She brushed past Joey. He dropped his head, turned and left the room. Before he got two good steps out, he turned back, and leaned his bare chest through the door.

"Don't be long Saffron."

Keb's eyes shifted from Joey to Saffron. Joey left again. In the silence that enveloped the room, the three of them heard the doctor's son leisurely climb the pine stairs down the hall.

"The doctor just returned; he'll see ya'll in a few moments," Saffron said. She hesitated. Her eyes dropped from Keb.

"He'd like ya'll to wait in here."

Saffron turned and left. In the silence, Keb and Set heard her bare feet climb the pine stairs down the hall.

"Daddy, you said he was going to see me at two o'clock. What's taking so long?"

"One of his patients must have had an emergency," Keb lied.

"Daddy, isn't what I have an emergency?"

It had been over an hour and Keb the stickler for time had been fuming since 2:15 p.m. Keb knew that the emergency was any white patient who happened to drop by with a sore throat or sprained finger or a question. Dr. Gentry was not going to get to the nigras waiting in the laundry room until he serviced the needs of those who looked liked him.

If Keb had been the one in need, he would've left long ago. But the appointment was not for him; it was for his son. And Keb had learned from his own father that being a father sometimes meant taking on indignity for the son.

"That's what love is, son," Nema would say.

Keb had damn near begged Dr. Gentry to make an exception and see Set. Begged in the name of love.

It was almost 4 p.m. when Dr. Gentry walked into the laundry room. He closed the door behind him. Keb stood up.

"Mr. Americus, good to see you," he said. Dr. Gentry shook Keb's hand.

"Doctor."

"And what a strong young man Set has become," he said, giving the big-boned, 5'7" fifth-grader the once over. Intrigued by the spots on his nose, chin, and cheeks.

Dr. Gentry walked towards the cot.

"What took you so long?" Set blurted out.

"Set," Keb said.

"An emergency," the Doctor lied.

Doctor Gentry sat next to Set on the cot. He shook Set's right hand because the Cooties Hand was shoved deep into his pocket.

"Your father tells me that you're such a great young man that these nasty ol spots are trying to be your friend, but no one needs friends like that now do they?"

"No, sir," Set said.

He looked into doctor's big blue eyes.

"May I?"

The doctor patted Set on the shoulder then lightly ran his finger over the chin and cheek spots.

"Whaddaya say you let me examine the other unwanted visitors, and we'll see what we can do about sending them on their way?"

Set glanced over at his father. Keb nodded.

"Okay."

Set pulled the Cooties Hand out of his pocket. The doctor took the hand, turned it over and looked at the palm, then the back again. The white between his thumb and forefinger was now as big as a strawberry. Dr. Gentry lovingly patted the Cooties Hand a couple of times and gave it back to Set. Set turned his ear to the doctor.

"There's one here too."

The doctor leaned close and examined the white spot that seemed to be sprouting from Set's inner ear. Set stood up, pulled off his jacket and shirt. The silver dollar over his areola had grown some change. A dozen nickel and dime-sized white spots dotted his black skin.

"It's not catchy," Set said.

He looked down and watched the doctor's boney white fingers land on his chest and graze across the surface.

"Well, they're not raised. Do they hurt?" He poked around with his index finger.

"Un-unnh."

"Have they ever hurt?"

"No, sir."

"Now, did they start small and grow or have they always been this size, son?"

Hearing the doctor say "son" made Set instinctively look across the small room at his father. He saw something he had never seen before.

38

"**S**on" made Set realize that his father had never seen the Cooties Coins on his chest. The unwanted monetary lepers crowded all together. Touching and bribing each other. Passing their nasty cooties back and forth like hush money. And once they were all good and hushed and corrupted, they touched all the tiny black skin cells around them. Touched them real good so they could be on the take too. The Cooties Take. And his father saw it. Saw everything. And he hated it. And he hated Set for letting them corrupt an Americus.

It was shameful.

That's what Set thought when he saw what he had never seen on his father's face.

Shame.

It was unmistakable. Lips pursed in a lemon rind-bite aftermath. The tight scorn in the eyes. Head sliding back on the neck, retreating. The look away.

When Set opened his mouth to answer the doctor's question, it was like someone else's desperate voice came out.

"It's not my fault, Daddy."

39

"**W**hy didn't you tell me, Nut?"

"You're the map maker. You should know how to get to Set's room."

"I had no idea it had gotten that bad. Since you were treating him you should've kept me abreast of the situation, Nut. I would have taken him to a ..."

"Don't try to put this off on me. You're his father, you shoulda just told him to show you. You tell him to do everything else."

"You beg me to ... "

"I didn't beg you to do nothin. I ... "

"You beg me to let you treat him. Against my better judgment, I agree. You're treatment obviously has not been working for some time, so you should have let me know earlier to afford us a chance to take an alternative approach."

"How could I have known that the treatment wasn't working unless I gave it time to take hold?"

"I sat in that room shocked, Nut. When Set took off his shirt I could scarcely believe my eyes. I was expecting a little mark like the one on his hand. The number of them ... when he undressed I ... How long have you known?"

She was silent. "Nut?"

"It's not my fault, Keb, it's not my fault, it's ... it's my fault, it's my fault, it's my fault. It's ... "

Nut collapsed into her husband's arms. Sitting on the side of the bed, he rocked her back and forth as she mumbled through snot and tears, "It's my fault, it's my fault ... ."

Holding his wife, Keb thought that he hadn't held Set in this way. Hadn't rocked him. Hadn't even wanted to touch him. A thought that made Keb feel ashamed of himself. That's not love. His mind fluttered back to the doctor's laundry room. The sight of Set standing up from the cot to pull down his trousers. The way Set's eyes dropped when the doctor asked him to step back to get a better look at all the sores across his whole body. Looking for some pattern of infection. Trying to read the disease design. Had him turn around. Moved his privates to the side and ran his hand across the white spot on this inner thigh. Poked the spot just outside his anus. He handled Set like he was some type of defective slave. Each poke, each turn, each spot, a reason why he couldn't pay a fair price for the diseased buck in front of him.

Keb wanted Set to put his clothes back on. And do so quickly. But Dr. Gentry was too fascinated. He needed one more turn. One more poke. One more close look at that anus.

The second the doctor was finished with the examination, Keb heard his own voice snap, "Put your clothes on." Both the doctor and Set turned to look at him. Then Set dropped his eyes.

"Seems like your boy here got something wrong with his skin," Dr. Gentry had said.

All of that poking and prodding to tell us what we already knew.

"Really?"

The doctor smiled.

"Good news on two fronts. One: It doesn't seem to be causing him any pain. Two: Hell, one day he just might grow up to be a white man."

40

"It's my fault, it's my fault, it's my fault ... "

Nutilda's muffled words drifted through Set's bedroom window. Set agreed with her. He was lying on his back with his left hand stuck towards the ceiling, flipping it back and forth, trying to imagine the white sores spreading from his thumb to the rest of his hand. A white palm. Flip. A white backhand. White fingers.

"It's my fault, it's my fault, it's my fault ... "

"You promised me," Set whispered, looking up at his hand. "You promised. Crossed your heart. Hoped to die. You hoped to die, Mama."

Set removed the pillow and stuck his wide-spread fingers into the pillowcase. He clamped right hand around left wrist to make the white case snug around his fingers. Set brought his new white palm inches from his face. He flipped it over to examine the backhand. He raised it to the sky for a different perspective. Made the white- pillowcase-hand flutter like a dove above his forehead. That was when Asar stopped pretending that he wasn't watching his little brother. He turned on his side, propped on his elbow and watched Set's dove-hand flutter in the moonlight filtering through the window. Asar could still hear his mother's voice wafting through the open pane, "It's my fault, it's my fault, it's ... "

Set's been acting crazy as a June Bug since the spots started spreading, Asar thought. All secretive. Locking the bathroom door behind him like somebody's gonna bust in and yell "stick em up." Always trying to be off by himself somewhere. Don't got a whole lot to say, even to me, Asar thought, staring at the flying white hand.

It's kinda like Set is a part of the family and apart from the family at the same time. Sometimes he acts like his normal self, then he turns himself inside out, Asar thought. Different person. Sometimes it's obvious, because he just grows real quiet. He only talks to us if we ask him a question, then he shuts right back up. Stares at a bookcase. A chair. Especially a mirror. As Set stared up at his fluttering white dove, Asar stared at him trying to catalogue his brother's recent weird behavior. Trying to understand it. Wanting to help, wanting to ask Set what's going on in his mind. Sometimes he just freezes in front of the long mirror in the foyer. He's not with us but not completely alone either. It's like he has a whole different family. That's it, Asar thought. Awhole different life inside his head. When Set turns himself inside out, it seems like he's spending time with the family that lives on the other side of those hazel eyeballs.

"Set, when you go inside … "

Before Asar could completely turn his thought into a question, Set's hand-dove suddenly changed course. It had been fluttering and flipping in the space over Set's forehead. A night flying dove illuminated by the moonlight cascading through an open window. The hand-dove abruptly nosed-dived. The dove's erect index finger- beak crashed into the left eye socket's soft flesh—and dug deep.

"Ahhhhhhhh."

It was the oddest scream Asar had ever heard—and one that would visit him in his sleep for years to come. It sounded like Set was real thirsty and he had gulped down too-tart lemonade that had been on ice too long and hurt too good going down.

"Ahhhhhhhh."

Asar swung his legs off the bed and lunged past the chess board in the middle of the room to reach his little brother.

"Ahhhhhhhh" is still what he heard when he reached the side of Set's bed.

Set's plucked eyeball, ejecting out of its socket, is what Asar saw. Though it must have happened fast, Asar would always remember seeing his little brother's flying eyeball pop out slowly. Like the way things happen in dreams sometimes. Like the world in their bedroom was moving underwater.

Set's index finger in the corner of the pillowcase. Index finger in the corner of Set's eye.

Buried all the way down to the second knuckle. The slow motion jerk.

Set's slow opening mouth.

The slurred "Ahhhhhhhhhhhhhhhhhhhhhhhhhhhh."

The moonlit eyeball on a string, floating up to meet his own shocked face at the bedside.

Then slowly dropping to hang by a string below Set's chin.

Asar turned his own head towards the window to scream for help, but not before he heard, "It's my fault."

41

1927

"**I** killed my brother."

    Set had to say the words aloud to fully accept what he had done. To claim it. He still couldn't look down at Asar's face, so he brought his own hands up close to his own face. He spread the 10 fingers in front of his eye into a fan of regret. Each finger was touched by Asar's blood.

It was real.

He closed his eyes to re-trace what had happened. Eyes still closed, Set began to slowly shake his head side-to-side. He saw himself trailing behind Asar, trying to goad him into a fight. I wanted to punch Asar for defending the bohunks at the bar, he thought. Punch him for being too careful. Punch him for being born first. Punch him for being too much like Daddy. Punch him for marrying Auset. Punch him for not having skin that betrays. Punch him for not being my twin anymore. When Asar stopped and kneeled down, his head was there for the left hook. My left fist was balled. Cocked. I was just about to throw.

"Why didn't I just hit him? I should've just hit him."

Standing above his kneeling brother's head, Set had intended to let the left hook teach.

But something happened.

It felt like he was being submerged under very warm bathwater. External sound drowned out by the rhythmic opening and closing of his heart valves. Set became conscious of his entire body.

He was tingling.

Set shook his tingling left fingers out of a fist. He needed to inflict more damage than hewn knuckles could manage.

He needed to destroy something. Beyond recognition. Beyond resurrection. Because he had been damaged beyond recognition. Set Americus had faded too far from his past image, his past life, to be born again. Ressurection was a dead option. So he chose death. In his own image.

Still sitting on the log, Set opened his eyes and finally looked down at Asar's face.

"I killed myself."

❙   ❙   ❙

Set's mind drifted to their father. His skin crawled thinking about uttering words that had to be uttered. Whenever a parent would make funeral arrangements for a deceased child, Keb would say, "The parent's not supposed to bury the child; the child is supposed to bury the parent."

Set took his father's firstborn; he couldn't make Keb bury Asar too. Not under these circumstances. He looked back down at Asar's cut throat.

Set stood up from the log and stepped around Asar. He started slowly walking across the wooded-area's circular clearing. Along the way, he paused and shook his head. Then he walked back. Across. Back. Pacing to think of a way out of no way. After a dozen trips, he just stopped. There was no good answer. Only bad options on this path he'd taken the whole family. He had to choose from among the wrong answers that his wrong had wrought.

Set sat back on the log. He looked down at his brother.

"The parent's not supposed to bury the child."

He would have to do what could not be done.

❙   ❙   ❙

Set decided to start at Asar's neck. A buried treasure in pieces would be harder to find. A piecemeal secret, harder to unearth. He had to limit the possibility of accidental discovery. Limit the possibility of more parental heartbreak. He had to do what he had to do—even if it meant having to do what could not be done.

A cocktail of nerves, fear, and uncomfortable excitement made Set impulsively drop to one knee. He closed his eyes. With his right hand, Set felt for the slit across Asar's Adam's Apple. With his left hand, he brought down the sharpened, double-edged Americus Sword with enough force to cut through tendon and bone. Esophagus and vertebrae. Secret and birth order.

42

Asar's head rolled over to rest on its cheek. An unreliable witness. Set's knowing fingers moved to Asar's right leg. Just below the hip. The Americus Sword moved through flesh and femur: a butcher's cleaver through a tough leg of lamb.

Blood.

Warm on Set's large hands. He had no plan. No order. He just let his large palm move across Asar's body until it stopped at the right place. For wrong. And the sword was raised. And lowered. And blood. Separating twin from twin. Twin from self.

The left shoulder blade. Found and separated from the torso. Blood separated from the body. The left foot. Separated from the ankle. The right hand hacked from the right wrist. The blood that must be. The brother that once was. Diminished by vulgar mathematics. Subtraction by division.

Finally slowing, Set dropped his sword, closed his eye, and let his bloody palms feel their way around for a sum total.

"Thirteen," he said aloud.

Set didn't want his brother to end on an unlucky number.

His right hand found the lineal jewel. Bejeweled sword separated it from bloody torso.

"Fourteen."

43

Set buried the right hand first.

That's the hand the Asar shook with. Entered into agreements with. Confirmed his word with. It deserved to be first. He pulled the tightly rolled butcher paper from his deep coverall pocket. The sound of tearing paper vibrated through the circular clearing and bounced off the densely packed trees. Set quickly looked side-to-side. He spread the white sheet on the ground. With a knee and one hand, he held down the curling ends. With the other hand, he picked up Asar's severed hand by the index finger. Placed it in the center and nervously folded the sides as if he were a child wrapping a present. Using the Americus Sword, he dug a hole. A new home for the hand.

Then he buried the head.

The leg was next. He tore the butcher paper quieter this time. A strip long enough for the long-legged.

I I I

After almost three hours of cutting, digging, wrapping and burying, thirteen pieces of his brother were planted in the soil. Set was exhausted. But he was not done. The torso remained. The heaviest and certainly the most difficult to bury. Especially when the shovel was a sword. He was too tired to stand all the way up. He used his knees as legs and kneed his way over to the log to have a seat again.

Set's long arms were heavy. He let them dangle by his side like matching white stockings full of peeled potatoes. His eyelids were heavy too. But he couldn't seem to let them close. The one-eyed- view from the log had become too captivating to turn away.

His brother. Broken.

Cut into pieces of a man.

He only had enough paper for the map, so the torso would remain unwrapped. Set looked at the blocky rectangular hole in the earth. He had done that. Made a home-away-from-home for his brother. By the look of the grave, Set figured it was 3 x 4 feet. Three feet deep. With a three foot mound of dirt next to it. Space enough to hold the core remains of brotherhood. The vestiges of parallel lives. Set squatted down and slid his fingertips under the left side of shoulder and buttocks. Closed his eye. He flipped the slab of Asar into the grave.

44

To stretch his lower back, Set stood slowly and reached his hands toward the sooty sky. Then he raised his eye heavenward. He wished there was some help for him up there. Wished he could believe in things that weren't real. Steel, blood, and memory kept grounding him. Set returned his eye to the earth—where it belonged. He looked down at the bloody trunk. A jagged bone jutting three full inches from where the right upper thigh used to be. Surrounded by dangling tendons, tissue and stringy veins. The left chunk of thigh, a cleaner cut that would have been at home on a butcher's cutting board. To Set, the swollen nub on the pubis looked like a gory infant's fist clenched tight during a raging, crying fit. A few inches above it, the outtie belly button was the only flesh standing erect. The dark chest, with its nipples already red-crusted over, resembled a cherry pie left in the stove two hours too long.

Using his left hand as a shovel, Set scooped up one palm of mineral-rich, moist black soil from the mound next to the hole and tossed it on his brother. It sprinkled across Asar's burnt pastry chest. Then another left hand scoop. Then another. And another. And another, until the mound of earth was gone and earth had returned to earth. And brother had become history. Hidden. In the forest of memory.

Set flattened the soft top soil by leaning his full weight forward onto his side-by-side palms, until twin handprints lay across the grave like handmade hieroglyphs. He brought his open left palm up to his face. Studied its mixture of East St. Louis and blood. Brought it closer. He inhaled his palm's assemblage of damp soil, sweat and fresh death. The aroma reminded him of the sweet funk of the Mississippi waterfront. Acrid humidity laced with the scent of dead fish and disappointment.

Set pulled the remaining length of butcher paper from his overalls. He unfurled it on the grave. Gathered four rocks to hold the over 3 foot-long piece of paper in place. He stood up. Slowly turning in a complete circle, he scanned the ground, looking at the 13 other graves his twin palms had flattened. Set buried each piece of his brother by a landmark that was unlikely to move much over time. The right leg: in the tube-like hole, running along the thinner portion of a fallen pine. The penis: entombed in a boot-sized opening next to a barrel-sized boulder. Asar's head: in the watermelon-sized grave at the base of the tallest pine in the forest.

The tallest pine towered over the trees by at least 30 feet and was near the center of the woodland. It would be a good reference point. The head was a good starting place to rebuild a man. Set decided to come back and assemble Asar for a decent burial in one grave. When enough time had passed. When secrets were safe enough. This would be the completion of doing what could not be done. An honoring of the body that he had dishonored. Set didn't know when he would bring Asar back together, but he knew it might take years before it was safe. And when the time came, he knew he might be assembling only bones. Bones are more easily lost than fleshy body parts. He couldn't risk not finding a part of his brother. He needed a good map. A body map. A bone map. A loss map—to prevent buried treasures from being lost.

Set squatted. Repeatedly dipping his index finger into a gritty mixture of blood and soil, staining earth-ink, Set meticulously smeared a "T" across the top of the white butcher paper. Finger- quill never empty. Ink in abundance. Set smeared a perfect letter "A". Repeatedly dipped again. "L". It took him almost five minutes to craft "TALLEST PINE."

He refilled his index quill. Near the top of the butcher paper, Set drew a blood red "X".

He stood up and briskly walked to the Tallest Pine. Placed his back against it. Looked up. He pulled out the replacement compass that he'd bought years after his father had stomped his original birthday compass. Set found North, then positioned himself on a direct line to the largest grave. East by South East. Set placed his heel of his left foot in front of the toes of his right foot.

"One."

Right in front of left.

"Two."

Left in front of right.

"Three."

Asar's torso was twenty-seven paces from the Tallest Pine.

Set squatted, dipped his finger in the Land of Lincoln. In the far left hand corner, he carefully wrote a "2". Dipped. "7". Then "ESE" for the direction. He paused. Set didn't know what to call the core remains of a twin. He settled on "TRUNK".

Set hurried back to the Tallest Pine. Thirty-nine paces later he arrived at the next grave. Rushed back to the map to document the steps. Squatted, dipped his finger, and in the far left hand corner, directly under the "2" he wrote "3". Then "9". And "SSE". Dipped and then he had to pause. His chin dropped towards his chest. He had to make himself write "PRIVATES".

From the Tallest Pine, Set methodically paced off the remains of his brother and recorded them on a butcher's map.

He mapped the right hand last. "19 NNW".

Set lugged his tired body to each of the graves. With his big hands as rakes, he covered the plots with leaves, pinecones, twigs, dirt and pine needles. When he finished brushing the foliage over Asar's severed head at the base of the Tallest Pine, he eased his aching body down and sat with his back against the tree.

"It is finished."

He had finally moved ahead of the first-born. He wished it had not been this way. But it was. And nothing could change it now.

Set thought maybe he should feel something more than regret. Sadness. Fear. Relief. But the truth was, he just felt tired. Tired of thinking about what he had done. Tired from doing what could not be done.

45
1894

No one spoke.

Usually, the Americus Family dinner table was a combination home-classroom, battlefield-frontline, and theater-front row. A place where the family sharpened themselves for the outside world by carving into each other.

"Why waste an hour just eatin, when you can feed the mind while you feed the body," Nema would tell preteen Keb in the days when only the two of them shared the large round dinner table. At 6 p.m. sharp, they would be seated and Nema would have Keb give thanks for the food. By 6:10 p.m., Keb could hardly get his food chewed for answering his father's gruff questions about arithmetic and ceremonial incantations. About incisions and grave depth. Casket construction and the afterlife. Keb looked forward to and loathed these dinner quizzes. Most days, as 6 p.m. approached, Keb would feel the anxiety-induced butterflies start to churn. But butterflies were a small price to pay for his father's undivided attention.

Keb thought of those childhood times as his eyes left his plate, crowded with fried chicken, mashed potatoes and okra, and landed on Nema's salt-and-pepper head. Nema's face was so close to the plate that the fork-to-mouth journey was only three inches long.

Keb's eyes slid to Asar. He was sitting next to Nema. Asar also ate in silence. His eyes stared down okra as he brought a chicken wing to his lips. Keb didn't have to look to know that his wife also had her eyes buried in her plate.

It was the family's first time all sitting down together since the "accident," as Nema called it.

Immediately after the accident, they had rushed to Dr. Nathaniel Mandrake's office. The doctor's baby face seemed at odds with the brown half-moon atop his 38-year-old head. The premature hair loss and the measured way his tinny voice said words like "respectable" made the assistant county physician look like a young man growing old against his will. Especially since he favored brown suits that didn't fit his long-armed and short-legged body.

Dr. Mandrake had not been able to save the eye.

When it was finally time for the bandages to come off, the doctor had called Keb into bathroom-sized examining room. Keb stopped in the doorway. He was taken aback by the sight of his son's swollen, empty left eye socket. It had been paled by two weeks under white gauze.

"Your son has refused to wear the eyepatch."

Just minutes earlier, Set had hopped off the examining table and blurted to the doctor, "I want people to see what the eye can't see."

Keb's gaze shifted from Dr. Mandrake to his baby boy. Set stood in front of the examining table, left foot forward, arms at his side, fists balled. Keb surveyed the map of imperfection: an archipelago face of white splotches. A lone eyeball on an island of defiance.

"Hand me the eyepatch Dr. Mandrake," Keb said

The patch changed hands. Keb walked toward fists and imperfection. The father placed his arm around his favorite.

"Let's go home, son."

❙ ❙ ❙

Keb now looked at Set sitting across the round Regency dining table. This initial attempt at dinner time normalcy was not going well. Feeling his stare, Set's single eye turned and locked on his father. Their heads were the only two not buried in plates. Keb wanted to dive into that empty socket and understand Set's behavior. Set knows a man is judged by his response to a train jumping the track, Keb thought. How many times have I told him this? Refusing to wear the patch to spite me is not a proper response.

The day they had returned from Dr. Mandrake's office, Keb marched him right into the twin's room and closed the door behind them.

"Son, the doctor says you need to wear the eyepatch to heal the eye so…"

"I don't have that eye so how can a patch help?"

"Boy, don't sass me. You're going to do what the doctor says."

Keb marched towards Set. They were standing next to the chess board in the room's center.

"You just want me to wear it because … ."

Before Set could get out more sass, Keb had swung his huge right palm. The hard slap drove Set's face to the ground. He bounced, slid and cracked the back of his skull against the wooden bed frame. In three quick stalking strides, Keb stood over him with the black eyepatch extended in his slapping palm. Keb heard Nut's tiny feet running down the hall towards the room.

"I say wear it because I told you to wear it. Now, if I have to say anything else, it's going to be my closed-hand talking."

Set was whimpering. He gingerly reached up, took the patch and put it on.

"Keb!" Nut screamed from the doorway.

"Don't take it off until I tell you to take it off."

Keb turned and began to walk slowly towards the door. The wife glowered at the husband.

Keb didn't have to turn to know it was the eyepatch hitting him in the back. Nut's quick change of facial expression, from anger to fear, was all the confirmation he needed. It was in that precise moment, even before he turned around, that Keb realized the imperfection spreading across Set's body had also reached his mind. The white spots were eating away at his judgment. His home training. His concern for his life. But these realizations couldn't stop the hot rage spreading from Keb's left back shoulder blade, where the patch had landed, through his chest and up his face. The rage that sent the pumping blood through his ears that drowned out all other sound. Including Nut screaming, "Set's your favorite."

The silence heightened Keb's visual perception. Things in the room were moving fast and slow as his eyes soaked in details. Set had popped up and now was standing again by the chess board. Keb noticed the round thickness of Set's neck. The bulging vein running down its side. He saw how big his baby boy's hands were. The fists that Set held by his side were as big as a 5'7" grown man's. Set's wide stance. The tilt of his head. The slit-eyed defiance of his lone eye. That's what Keb focused on as he walked towards Set. *A black eye will teach him to appreciate the eye he's got.*

It was a blur. Keb just saw Set fall back across the chess board sending kings and queens falling to their death below. Nut, white cotton dress scrunched up to her milky thighs, was now atop Set, looking back over her shoulder. Her reckless eyeballs ablaze. She was screaming. Keb could hear her now.

"Set's your favorite, Set's your favorite, Set's your favorite!"

Keb stopped. His 6'5" frame stood over his wife and his favorite.

The husband and father looked down at his own huge hands. The fists they had become. Able to protect life. Able to take life. Nut was sobbing, her body heaving atop her son. Just from over Nut's shoulder, Keb saw Set's lone eye. Unblinking. No fear. No tears. Keb looked into the empty socket.

"That's where my son has disappeared into," he heard himself say. Keb turned around to leave the room. He saw Asar blocking the doorway with both of his palms over his ears. Tears streamed down his face. Keb walked up to him. Asar took his hands off his ears and wrapped his arms around his father's waist. Placed his wet cheek against Keb's starched white-shirt stomach. Keb rested his large hand on Asar's head. Stroked his wavy mop-like hair. Asar looked up into his father's face.

"How many eyes do I have to poke out to be your favorite?"

"Two," Set said, from beneath a fallen queen.

▌ ▌ ▌

"Two."

That's what kept running through Keb's mind as he stared at Set across the Regency dining table. Set's one eye stared back.

"Two."

That's when it sunk in that whuppin Set was not the most effective approach. Set was provoking him. Like he wanted Keb to beat him. Hurt him. Keb sat there staring at his son, thinking, I've got to think of another way to reach him. If not, this fool-boy will mess around and make me spill his blood. Or he'll grow up and spill mine.

"Pass the gravy, please," Set said, still staring at his father. Startled heads jerked up from their plates and swiveled toward Set. His were the first words spoken since they had sat down for dinner. Keb didn't have a response. His own father had not prepared him to deal with imperfection in the bloodline. Imperfection who accidentally pokes out his eye, and blames the mother and father, and wants the father to hurt him.

Keb became conscious of how hard he was breathing. His mouth was open. He heard his breath quicken like he was digging a grave by himself. He became conscious that everyone at the table now was staring at him. Nut reached in front her husband and picked up the serving bowl full of gravy. She passed it around the table towards Set. Keb watched the bowl go from hand to hand until Set's diseased hand placed it next to his plate. Keb watched the white sore between Set's thumb and index finger as he picked up the silver serving ladle. Watched dark gravy splash over mashed potatoes. This is the way it was supposed to work: dark mixing with light to make the white dark. Overcoming the white. Conquering the white.

Why couldn't Set overcome his white? He's been trained to overcome a white world, Keb thought. In his time of testing, he was failing. Wasting my efforts. Bringing shame. Shame to the Americus Family. Shame to me in front of my father. You shame Nema Americus' ancestors. You shame yourself. I hope you never have children. You would shame them too. Shame. Shame.

"Shame, shame, shame, shame," Keb heard himself say aloud. His thoughts had found their voice.

Inspired by the imperfection before him.

46

SATURDAY, JUNE 10, 1899
EAST ST. LOUIS, ILLINOIS

Six a.m. sharp. Keb closed the cover of his silver pocket watch and slipped it in his pocket. The twin's 16th and last birthday of the 19th century. And Set was late for it. What a shame, Keb thought.

Keb didn't want Asar seeing him looking towards the house. The father gave all his attention to the oldest son in front of him. He had good reason to appreciate Asar's developing body. The flawless onyx skin on his now 6'4" frame. The wiry strength they shared. They still also shared the same part down the middle of their scalps, but Asar's wavy inheritance from his half-Dakota mother hung past his ears. The father's intense stare made the son look away towards Ta Neter.

At 6:06 a.m., Set Americus came swaggering slowly out of the house. Keb put his watch back in his pocket and watched his baby boy approach. It had been years since Set and Asar had stopped dressing alike but studying Set, Keb was struck by how different his identical twins had become. Asar's 76 inches were hung on a slim, still growing frame.

The 76 inches sauntering towards Keb had a thickness about them. Set always had been a big eater, which gave his long body an imposing presence. The spotted, elephant trunk arms that swung out his white undershirt, purposely untucked, were big-boned and muscular. His shoulders: a pair of blackened Cornish hens with white polka dots. Thick neck. A swollen vein running down its side, like someone holding their breath too long underwater. Set's spotted mouth seemed stuck in a surly smirk. Keb sensed that if those discolored lips parted, slurs would begin to spew forth. But it was the pale bald skull, cocked to the left, and the eyeball missing from it, that had changed Set the most.

One day last year, Set cut off all of his hair—and kept it that way. "Just for you," Keb had told Nut. Set's head reminded Keb of an inside-out watermelon with all the red fruit scraped away. Leaving a bitter bald white rind—and a scattershot of black-seed reminders of the Negro boy he used to be.

Like most of Set's decisions in the last few years, Keb knew they were designed to shame the Americus Family name. Why not have a little modesty, Keb thought when he first saw Set's bald white head. Does everybody need to know that the sickness is all over his scalp too?

"It's spread over his whole body, why would he try to hide his head?" Nut had said, when Keb complained.

"It's not about hiding, it's about reserving some dignity."

"Set's not the one who's ashamed."

"I don't care if he turned blue. He still needs to respect and protect the Americus name and tradition."

"You're always talking about the past. I wished you talked more about Set's future. How's he gonna get a wife? A family? Some happiness? That's what you should be concerned about not your good name."

"You don't understand the value of a good name because you don't come from one."

His words unfurled and lingered in the air, stretching the distance between husband and wife.

"I see your good name, your beautiful tradition, doesn't stop you from acting ugly," Nut said. She walked past him out the room. Keb heard her slam the bathroom door down the hall.

Keb saw how Set manipulated Nutilda. Used the guilt hanging heavy around her neck, like the crosses she'd been wearing lately. She should've never promised that boy she could fix him, he thought.

"Happy Birthday to me," Set deadpanned.

Keb was momentarily lost inside the hole in Set's white face. His son had become a human sore.

"Coffin got your tongue," Set smirked. "Let me help you. It goes something like this, 'Happy Birthday, son.'"

Asar looked away from his father and Set. Instead, he focused his hard stare on the rose bushes along the 10-foot-high pine fence. Asar wished he could change the direction of his hearing the way he could his sight.

When Asar heard Set talk with his smirk-voice to their father, it embarrassed the oldest son—because it no longer embarrassed Keb. His father had given in. Which made Asar lose respect for Keb too.

Keb said nothing. He just stared at Set, almost squinting, as if he were trying to read some tiny map on his bald head.

Keb turned away from Set. He squatted down between his two

16-year-old sons and unrolled the map scroll across the bluegrass lawn. It was a map of Bloody Island.

"We already did Bloody Island," Set said, sounding irritated. "Why don't you just give us our damn presents. We're too old for these treasure hunting games, aren't we, Asar?"

Asar shot Set his death-look. Keb stood up.

"Well, if Mr. I. M. Truth won't tell it, because he doesn't want to hurt your feelings, the second son will tell you what the first- born won't say to your face," Set said. He squared off in front of Keb who was now only a inch taller. Set studied his father. The part down the middle of Keb's thick, close cropped hair, graying at the temples. The almond-shaped eyes that narrowed more when they were angry. Or disappointed. Or ashamed.

Keb just looked at his white son. He thought about the times he used to tell the twins, "The sun has found favor with us enough to dwell in us."

Now, Set has fallen out of favor. The sun has left the second son, Keb thought.

The sun is gone.

The blow caught Keb off-guard. Set's big-knuckled, upper- cutting fist felt like someone had rammed the fat end of a slugger's bat into his stomach. Keb doubled-over, making his chest parallel the ground. With both large hands, Set grabbed the back of his father's head and powerfully jerked it downward towards his own quick-rising knee. Blood squirted from Keb's nose, like red milk from a cow's teat.

The loud cracking sound of Keb's nostril bridge slamming against Set's knee is what snapped Asar into action. The punch and knee strike happened so unexpectedly that Asar instinctively recoiled. Not from fear. But from the disgusting image of the son drawing blood from the father.

The upward knee blast stood Keb vertical for an extended second. Eyes rolled to their whites. Dead to the world, he could have been an unwrapped mummy come to walk the earth again. Then he began to fall straight back. Asar lunged for his father. He was unable to catch him in time. Keb's wide back slammed on the ground, followed closely by the muffled crack of his skull snapping against the bluegrass-covered earth. Set quickly squatted, snatched up the map scroll, and ran out of the side gate.

47

Set ran north up 10th street, arms pumping, carrying the map scroll like a baton. The groggy city barely noticed. Not yet 7:00 a.m. and already the Mississippi River humidity was creeping into the molecules that brushed past Set's pale white skin. The heavy and intensifying stench of National Stock Yards death breezing by his nostril's hair follicles.

Set slowed up and came to a stop at the corner of 10th and St. Clair. His white undershirt completely soaked through. As he switched the scroll from his left to right hand, Set noticed that his sweaty palm left a wet hand print on the back side of East St. Louis. It won't be my first, he thought to himself. He turned left and started walking home to Bloody Island.

48

"**M**aa-ma!"

The fear in Asar's voice sent such a strong tingling sensation through Nut's body that her fingers released the silver hand mirror. As she started her first running step, the mirror crashed to the floor. Nut held her breath to suppress the scream that wanted to burst with her through the kitchen door that led out to the backyard. Keb's long body was spread out on his back. The only thing moving was the blood streaming out of his nose. Asar, hovering over Keb, had an expression that she hadn't seen in a long time on her 16-year-old son: the look of a scared boy. He had his ear just about Keb's blood-covered lips.

Nut dropped down to her knees facing Asar.

"What happened, baby?" she asked, still breathing hard. "Daddy fell back and landed on his head."

"You sent Set to fetch Dr. Mandrake?"

Asar's hesitation made her look up from Keb to her first-born. The pained look in her first-born's eyes told her that her second-born had done this.

She was not surprised. "Where's Set?"

"I dunno; he kneed Daddy's face and ran off," Asar mumbled.

"Why didn't you help your father?"

"This is not *my* fault."

"Boy, don't sass me. Go run and get Dr. Mandrake." Asar jumped to his feet and ran towards the side gate.

Keb lay unconscious on the ground. Nut brought the bottom of her white cotton night gown to her mouth and made a small tear. She ripped a two-feet-wide swath from around the gown's lower perimeter. Then tore it in half. Nut quickly folded one strip and pressed it again Keb's bleeding nose. The other, she folded into a make-shift pillow and placed it under his skull. Nut's gentle kiss on Keb's mouth left blood on her full lips.

"What did ya do to him?" Nema yelled, limping out the kitchen back door. His stiff knee joints showed the age that his mouth and mind didn't.

Nut tried to ignore her father-in-law but in a way she knew it was her fault that Keb was lying unconscious on his back. In her mind, she helped create the son who would do this to the father. So when the father-in-law hobbled over and pushed her to the side, she let herself give way.

Nema placed his ear near his only child's mouth. Then he slapped Keb hard across the cheek.

"Wake up, boy!"

Keb slowly raised his hand towards his face like a fallen-down drunk trying to shoo away a fly.

Nema slapped him hard again.

"That's enough, you see he's coming to," Nut said.

"Shut up. What do ya know bout anythin but lyin on ya back?"

"I know enough to know your son likes it, and I know enough to know this is not the time for this type of foolishness."

Nema averted his eyes from his son's biggest mistake and rested them again on his only child.

"Ya awright, boy?" Nema gruffly said, as he softly caressed Keb's left hand.

Keb didn't answer. Instead, he kept opening his eyes wide and shutting them tight. Keb tried to sit up. Nema squeezed his first-born's hand and placed his other hand on his chest to hold Keb down. "Ain't no need to be in a rush to get up. That's ya problem. Runnin round every damn where, fallin out and carryin on, lay ya ass down and wait for the doctor. Grown man shouldn't just be fallin out for no reason. Ya don't know what could be wrong so just let the doctor earn his money when he gets here." Nema turned to Nutilda.

"What's takin those boys so long," he said. "Why don't ya run along after them?"

"Why don't you … "

"Through this gate doctor," Asar said.

Nut and Nema turned to see a harried looking Asar leading Dr. Mandrake. The doctor dropped to one brown-suited knee, placing his black bag next to Keb. Asar noticed the doctor's half-moon baldness was heading towards a full moon.

"What happened?" Dr. Mandrake asked Nema while opening his bag to retrieve his stethoscope.

"I guess my do-everything-all-at-once-till-he-can't-go-no-more son done gone and fallen out, after I been tellin him since when his backbone was still gristle, 'Ya can't do everything,' I … "

"Our son jumped on him," Nut interrupted. "Tell the doctor what you saw, Asar."

As Nema listened to Asar telling the doctor, the Americus Family patriarch kept glancing over at Nut. This woman had ruined my grandsons to the point where one of them would strike Keb, he thought. Another reason, in a list longer than an Indian Summer, why marrying this heifer was the worst mistake Keb ever made. Nema had told his son over and over again, "When ya take on a wife ya take her for life and the life of ya children." But as Nema liked to tell Jethro Jamison when he was alive, "That boy can't see past that yella girl's bosom."

Now, look at em, Nema thought, glancing down at his son. Lyin on his back with a doctor leanin over him cause he let some titties get in the way of his good judgment.

Nema looked again at Nutilda. She returned his smirk with her own Nutty Eyed Nutilda Stare Down. Perfected during a childhood combating rude girls and curious boys. But Nema wouldn't look away. He kept his stare fixed on Nut's left eyeball which was strained so far back towards her left ear that it seemed it could slide from her socket, travel beneath her skin and magically reappear in her earlobe.

Keb slowly sat up. Nema and Nut shifted their stares to Keb.

"Set no longer lives here," Keb said.

49

"**H**e's already gone."

Nut stood looking down into the empty drawers of the pine dresser on Set's side of the room. Nema, Keb, and Asar stood just inside the bedroom doorway looking at her back. Asar began to scan the room. He looked at the end of Set's bed. It was gone. The leather suitcase that Nema had given each of them for Christmas several years ago was not in its place.

Asar quickly walked towards the closet near Set's bed. Nema's, Nut's, and Keb's eyes followed. Asar snatched the door open. They watched the back of his head quickly swivel left, right, left. They could tell that whatever he was looking for was also gone, because he grew still. Then Asar's lanky frame, that his father had trained him to carry with erect pride, curved into a pronounced slump. They watched him step into the closet and close the door behind himself.

50

Set stood the map scroll next to the suitcase in the tiny closet. He closed the closet door and looked around. Not much to see. Last night, in his rush to get back home before anyone grew suspicious, he had dropped his suitcase in the closet and left.

In the day, the room seemed a lot smaller. The last roomer had painted the bare walls red. The color sucked the light from the room. Made the center of each wall pull towards its opposite, shrinking the room before his eyes. The 12 by 12 foot box had only one window, which was next to the door leading down the stairs into the alley.

Set's new home was the backroom above Aunt Kate's Honky Tonk.

I I I

The wooden sign that hung over Aunt Kate's entrance, 'Something Doing Every Hour,' helped catch the eye of the hard working men who came to Bloody Island. It was Aunt Kate's Hungarian hospitality that kept them coming back. When customers first walked through the French Doors and into the parlor, one of the girls escorted them to one of the 20 padded chairs with the small stools in front. Another girl would immediately sit gap-legged on the stool, hike her skirt up, take the men's shoes off, then proceed to wash their feet. Free of charge—including the free peek.

Kate often joked with her girls, "If a good foot washing got the disciples to give up everything and follow Jesus, it might make these light-wallets give up a little something."

Aunt Kate fired her ovens around the clock. She found that the smell of warm fresh bread made the men relax and brought a sense of home to The Honky Tonk. As customers got their feet washed, another girl would come by with a tray of steaming dough and warm butter. Katerina Slovein liked to imagine herself as the flirty Aunt who got up early in the morning and surprised her nephew with breakfast in bed. Smiled and called him naughty when he looked down her gown as she bent leaned over to serve him.

When Set talked to Aunt Kate the day before to ask about the room, she reminded Set of a taller, whiter, version of his mother. Except Aunt

Kate seemed smarter, running a thriving business. Probably was a better herbal doctor and didn't have crazy eyes, Set thought. Same big bosom. But Aunt Kate's eyes were blue as those feathers on a blue jay and they seemed to be constantly on the verge of offering a knowing wink. Aunt Kate's hair was also black but cut short, not even reaching her shoulders. She kept it pulled back behind her ears so she could show up off two huge dimples on her pale, cheeky face with laugh lines showing the way to her eyes.

She appeared to be about 40, but it was hard for Set to tell. She was a lot to decipher. Six feet and big-boned, she had a kind of manly way to her—even in a long blue dress. But there was nothing manly about her flirty smile and the design of the rhinestone covered blue dress (from the waist up, the dress was sheer with a few rhinestones spoiling the fun). When she finally came out to meet Set in the waiting area, he put his warm bread roll down and explained that he had not come for services but to inquire about the room she had. Aunt Kate let out a girlish laugh that seemed out of place coming from such a big, grown-up woman. Kate usually didn't have to look up to a man.

"Young, long thing like you, Aunt Kate might have to give you some herself."

She threw her head back and let that laugh fly again.

"Let you nurse on these till it's time to turn you over and burp you."

Set tried to hide his slight embarrassment by looking through her blue dress. Then he slowly raised his thumb and stuck it in his mouth. Aunt Kate and Set burst out into laughter. When she was able to compose herself, Katerina Slovein looked up into his eye and simply said, "You're going to like living here, son."

Since the accident Set had grown accustomed to seeing revulsion reflected on the face of those who encountered his face. He had made it into a game. He would chart how much their brow would furrow. The distance that the mouth would travel as it turned down. The number of involuntary quick blinks, as someone tried to take in the sight of the translucent Negro boy with tracks of blue veins running all through his black-spotted crystal ball head. The children who didn't have the skills to disguise their disgust ran behind their parents and held tight to their legs.

Set preferred these real expressions of revulsion rather than the fake people who looked at the fading one-eyed boy and tried to pretend that everything was normal. That there was nothing out of the ordinary with a white Negro boy with a gaping sore, the size of a silver dollar, where is other eye should be. Some twitch or brow movement or lip quiver would give them away, and Set would hate them. Over the years, he had become an expert at detecting facial liars. That's why he liked Aunt Kate. She looked into his white, one-eyed face like she wanted to lick it. For real.

Set hadn't noticed the square 5 x 7 mirror in the room yesterday. It hung by thin wire just to the left of the door that led out into the hallway. An odd place for a mirror, Set thought. It was like a Last Chance Mirror. A looking glass to make sure that your mask was on straight before you had to go fake it for the world. Set walked towards the mirror and stopped in front of it. He had to squat down his 6'4" body to look directly at himself.

When the white spots first appeared near his privates, Set's left fingers reached for hand mirrors like they were hard candy with handles. Hoping against hope that his lying eyes were at it again. Hoping that the white spot on his inner thigh was not growing into a little stinky inky white onion. He had come to know so much about his reflected self in the presence of mirrors. Watching his skin on a march of betrayal across his body.

Witnessing the gradual change through a mirror gave him temporary distance. Space enough to make-believe it was someone else disappearing in front of him. But distance disappeared once he reached down to touch his thigh. He knew that his eyes weren't playing make-believe. It was hope that was make-believing. It didn't exist. Especially when Set reached up and saw his fingers touch his own pale, watermeon-rind face.

Set was perfectly still. His face filled the small mirror in his new home. From upper forehead to lower chin, translucent cheek to translucent cheek. His white ears were just out of the picture. But he didn't need to see them. He had spent plenty of time examining the appendage that Asar had looked into and made his disease public. That had started the process of making him the person who was staring back at him.

In some ways, it was the still the same face. The same broad nose whose nostrils flared when he was mad at his brother. The same high cheek bones that looked like walnuts hidden beneath his skin. The same fleshy lips that his mother joked had grown so full because of Set's relentless breast-feeding approach. The same square jaw that had survived many a wild punch by his older brother.

"I am the same," he lied. "Except for the eyes."

The left eye was now a human telescope into his brain. His right eye had an exaggerated blink. Like it was trying to keep itself awake. Tired after a day of doing the work of two eyes. He reached his pale, veiny, left hand up and saw it come into view in the mirror.

He extended his white index finger brushing lightly against his fluttering, blinking right eyelid. He saw that same finger move over and gently enter his left socket. Watched his fingernail curiously disappear into his skull. As it had before.

Looking into his face, Set really knew that it wasn't just his eye that was different. The world that he saw was different too. A vision shaped by absence.

Set stood there looking at his face and wondered what Asar really thought. Did his big brother really believe they were still twins, if that's not what Asar saw when they were face-to-face?

We used to be mirrors, Set thought, brushing his fingertips across the mirror in front of him. He closed his eye and head-butted the mirror, making fissures spread like a reflecting spider web. He blinked open his eye to find what he already knew: he was still caught.

51

Asar ignored his mother's persistent knocking on the closet door. He was sitting Dakota-style facing the door. He'd been sitting in the dark now for over an hour. He'd heard his father and grandfather's footsteps leave the room long ago. He knew his mother would not be so easily deterred.

He was alone now so, he wanted to stay alone. See how it felt to have what he thought about so often when lying awake in bed. He used to be grumpy about another day of being the big brother who was second to the little brother—in his father's eyes. In his mother's love. In his grandfather's respect.

He knew his family loved him, but Asar wanted to be desired. Growing up he had watched Set bound into a room and watched his father's life change. The height of his father's smile. How he spoke with his hands as if his fingertips were tossing tiny words through the air at Set. Words that only those two could understand.

Sitting in the closet with Set gone, Asar wondered would his father's words now smile in his direction, would those fingers find their voice? Asar winced at his own selfishness. He reached across his body and pinched himself hard on the left arm. He hated when he acted like Set. But he couldn't help it right now: Asar wanted to be his father's favorite.

He had shared Keb with his little brother for all of their lives. Even though he was the oldest, Set had snuck in under his father's vest and taken up residence in the place that was supposed to be reserved for the first-born. Asar was tired of his knuckle-headed brother. He knew Set was big and bad enough to take care of himself.

"I'm glad he's gone," Asar lied.

Then he said it again. With conviction. Wrong and strong—and loud enough for his mother to hear on the other side of the door.

52

The knock was so soft, Set barely heard it. An individual index finger tapping lightly on the door. As Set stared at the red door, he figured it was Aunt Kate. He knew that the "Mistress Suite," as she called it, was right next door. His was the only other room on his side of the hallway. Tucked in the alley-adjacent, back corner, he figured his boxy new home had once been a storage area.

He hoped it was Aunt Kate. Set liked the way she looked at him: like he was a barbecue rib with some extra meat on it.

Set didn't want to appear too anxious, so he waited for that finger to tap again. It did. Set reached for the knob and made himself turn it extra slow.

She stood there with her index finger still extended. Around it was a single red ribbon tied into a perfect bow.

Set was both disappointed and excited to see this girl and not Aunt Kate standing outside his door. He noticed that she was barefoot. Looked about his age, maybe a little older. She was fresh scrubbed. No face paint. Instead of lipstick, a secret was pursed on her full lips. Her mid-back-long, light-brown hair was wet. It dampened the white silk robe with random red roses as large as her buttermilk face. A red silk belt loosely tied the robe at the waist. A creamy sternum lay exposed. Set brought his eyes back up to the bow on her extended forefinger. The girl's green eyes had yet to leave his single hazel one.

"Pull the string," she whispered. When she spoke, he could see the coffin nail-sized gap between her front teeth. The gap gave her voice a breezy, lilting quality.

Set reached up, the tips of forefinger and thumb gently pinched the red string like it was a broken butterfly wing. He paused, shifting his eyes from the bow to meet her stare.

He pulled the tiny ribbon, the girl shimmied, and the already loose belt lost its conviction. The robe fell open revealing a curlier, lighter and finer grade of pubic hair.

"I'm Nephthys. Welcome to the neighborhood," she said evenly.

Set didn't know what to do. Or say. He dropped his head like the embarrassed 16-year-old boy he was. With his head still lowered, he said, "I don't have any money."

"Only gift cost you money is love and that's not what this is. Invite me in," she said sharply, stepping past Set before he could offer.

Set stepped in after Nephthys but could not make himself raise his head.

Snap, snap.

"Don't you get it, I'm your house warming gift. You don't have to pay, free-bee, freee-beee," she said, again snapping her fingers near his chin. Set was still silent. His bowed head resistant.

"I don't know how."

It was Nephthys' turn to be embarrassed. She prided herself on her ability to learn a man. A skill that made her the most popular girl of all of Aunt Kate's. The other girls thought her popularity was "because she's got the plantation pussy that these Weekend Massas dream about."

Nephthys knew that being the only Colored girl helped her some, but what kept her regulars coming back was learning them like that's what she got paid for—because it was. Figuring how to make them feel significant. Sufficient. Knowledgeable. Even though she had more knowledge in grown-folk intimacies than almost all of her customers. Since she'd learned her own body first, she got paid to teach men how to pleasure her. So unlike the other stupid girls, she didn't play act or make pretend noises. She taught her men how to make her body shudder and shake like it was full of that old-time religion. How to make her scream from a place so deep inside her gut, you'd a-swore she was being cut. It was just after these moments that most of her learning took place. In that space of heavy-breathing. The look on the men's faces that said, "Look at what I did."

Reading the quality and intensity of that look taught Nephthys about the marriage bed of the married men. Taught her about the experience of the bachelor men. Four years of reading fuck-faces, as she jokingly called them, had also taught her an awful lot about men with their britches still on. That's why she was surprised at herself for not pegging the one-eyed, see-through white Negro in front of her as a first-timer. When he walked in yesterday to talk to Aunt Kate, he carried himself like such a man.

Nephthys didn't get a chance to be with too many Colored men. The few who came in wanted to be with the white gals. Surprise, surprise, she smiled to herself, looking over Set's long body. Truth is, there was nothing she liked more than when the fathers brought their teenage sons for their first time. She knew it was a chance to create a new steady customer. But more importantly, it was a chance to live forever in a young boy's memory as his first.

Nephthys took a step towards Set. She gently grabbed his large white palm and moved it inside her robe. Smeared her wetness across his fingers.

"When it gets like that, it means I really like you." Set looked up.

"I'mma show you how to make me like you even more," she said.

I I I

Aunt Kate looked on through the missing bolt hole in the lamp fixture. She was standing on a chair rubbing herself. Wearing the exact same rose-covered robe that she'd given Nephthys for being her top girl again. Aunt Kate's robe was bigger, but just as wide open. All of their lips parted when Nephthys freed Set from his trousers.

53

A unt Kate loved by watching. In-person or through a hole in the wall. The distance offered an opportunity for intimacy that she couldn't afford face-to-face. Once a man finally got what he'd been wanting, he wished he hadn't. Kate Slovein knew having is never quite as sweet as longing. Longing was good for business.

Aunt Kate liked to make dresses just sheer enough so that in the right light, and with enough close study, you could get a mighty powerful glimpse. When she greeted men in the lounge, she would go around giving them all a big hug. She liked to whisper in their ears, "Some rascal done stole all my undergarments again." By the time she made her way around the room, those men would be investigating her like she stole something. Aunt Kate knew the power of curiosity. She often told the girls, "Your real customer is the customer's imagination." No one understood that more than Nephthys. She knew how to color the customer's imagination.

Aunt Kate's white silk robe was wide open now. She stood on the straight-back wooden chair with her eye pressed against the penny-sized hole. Her hungry hand between her legs. She could see Set standing right in front of Nephthys, his trousers around his knees. Nephthys was sitting gapped-leg on the floor, leaning back on one palm, the other hand causing the slight parting of her lips.

Set didn't know what to do with his hands. He just let them hang by his side. Dropped his eyes when he could manage to look away from Nephthys. He felt shame-faced sticking out and up like that right in front of a girl. She was leaning back, staring up at his 45-degree-angled manhood like she was trying to see the blood coursing along the shaft's thickest vein. No one had ever looked at him that way before. And she wouldn't stop. Staring and rubbing herself between thighs open like her robe and lips. She was so close to him that if she leaned forward, he would be in her mouth. She hadn't even touched him yet.

"Pay attention … to how I'm moving my fingers." Set paid attention. So did Aunt Kate.

54

The idea came soon after Aunt Kate did. She was sprawled on the floor in her rose-covered white robe, breathing hard and laughing at herself for falling off the chair. Aunt Kate was sure Set heard her, but did it really matter? It'll be a good story to tell him when I present the idea, she thought. It'll help him see its knock-you-off-your-feet potential. She giggled again.

55

The knock on the door was heavy-handed. It jolted Set's eye open. From a fetal position, he uncurled his naked six-foot-four frame from a rickety bed, not much wider than a fat man's coffin.

He sat on the bed's edge. Nephthys was all over the room. In his head: snippets of her husky voice escaping a throat that seemed too long and delicate to produce such a timbre. In his nostrils: her jasmine body oil rising from the sheets. On the wall: the faint outlines of Nephthys' sweaty handprints against the red wall in front of him. Set glanced down at his morning erection. She was there too. The crusted white remains of her—on the only black remains of him.

The heavy hand landed again.

"One second," he said pulling his trousers on.

In his 12 by 12 box, he could've broad jumped from his standing position on the side of the bed to the red painted door. Instead, he made the trip in four long strides.

"Well, good morning, Set," Aunt Kate said, talking straight to his bare abdomen and the morning erection tenting his trousers.

Set gave her a curious look when he saw same the white silk robe that Nephthys had been wearing. Kate was smiling, those dimples sucking everything in the room in her direction.

"Come in."

"Thank you, darling. I know it's early, but I wanted to catch you before you got good and gone. Could you come by my office downstairs sometime this afternoon? I have a business proposition for you."

"A proposition or another gift?" Aunt Kate chuckled.

"Well, maybe it can serve as both," she said. "But I'd rather talk business, proper-like, in the place where I talks my business. How bout 2 p.m.?"

"Two sounds good, ma'am."

"Don't ma'am me. If you gotta call me something sides Aunt Kate, call me Mama," she said, smiling hard. She took a quick glance at his trousers before stepping out the door.

"Thank you for coming down to meet with me, Mr. Set."

Aunt Kate placed her glasses in the open ledger book and settled into her thick-padded, black leather arm chair.

"When I was a little girl, my mother would sit me on her knee and sing to me as she mended Daddy's trousers and shirts. By the time I was ten, I was making most of the clothes I wore. And have ever since. Something make you kinda feel like God. Creating with your own hand, turning some plain fabric and some thread and some imagination into the clothes you walk around the world in. I made this one right here," she said proudly, as she gazed down at the teal cotton dress that ruffled up her neck.

"I thought I'd always have a dress shop, but as life would have it, I fell into another type of business. That's how life goes sometimes. Now, I ain't complaining because this business has done right by me, right enough to where now I can open up that dress shop that I dreamed about opening when I was a child."

Set nodded towards Aunt Kate, because he didn't know what else to do. He didn't know anything about no dresses.

"Actually, it wouldn't quite be like the dress shop I had in mind all those years ago. The thing about working in this business is that you come into contact with all sorts of people. And those people all have different sorts of needs. Not good or bad, just different."

She paused.

"Mr. Set, why do you think the men come to Aunt Kate's?"

"I guess, because you have the prettiest girls."

"Okay, yes, but why do you think that men come to any of the houses here on Bloody Island?"

"Because they're looking for a good time?"

"Men come because they want to be desired. Now, they know the girls here ask a price for desire, but it's desire just the same. See, most men love a challenge. They think, 'If I can please a woman who's seen and done it all, I must be some kind of rascal.' So they pay a fair and reasonable sum of their hard-earned money to create desire in one of my girls so she can turn it right back on them."

Set nodded.

"The thing is Mr. Set, the men are not the only ones who are looking for desire. They're just ones who have a place to go and get a taste of it. As long as I've owned my place, I've always had a handful of steady women-folk customers. Respectable women who have the good sense to get a little piece of good loving from time to time. The problem has always been the riga-mo-ro we all have to go through to set things up in a proper and respectable manner. Delivery boy disguises. Arranging safe homes. Finding reliable men with enough gumption to take the risk, because, as you may not know, most my women-folk clients want the biggest blackest Negro they can get. Something goes wrong, my customer gets scared and says my boy forced himself on her and a Negro man could lose his life quicker than you can say, 'String em up.' I don't want that on my conscience."

Set nodded.

"Well, Mr. Set, it came to me that if I could find a way to cut all that risky business, Aunt Kate might be able to expand the business. I plan to acquire one of those nice-sized, empty storefronts just outside the Valley. I'll offer the ladies of East St. Louis a well-appointed dress store where they can browse and shop in comfort. The kind of place where they can feel free to take their time, try on a few things, have some tea as they make up their minds. Absolutely no pressure. And while I have them in the store, I'll offer them some other services to make their shopping experience as pleasant as possible."

56

Asar just wanted to blurt out Set's name to see what his father would do. It struck Asar: that's just what Set would have done—if things had been reversed. If he had punched Daddy and fled. If his name had been banished from the dinner table—and the rest of the house.

After Keb had been helped to his feet following the punch, he ordered Asar and Nephthys not to speak of Set. And he had asked Nema not to speak of Set.

Staring into his plate, Asar imagined how his brother would have broken the dinner table silence. Asar imagined Set standing up, holding his dinner knife thrust to the heavens and shouting, "Asar Lives!"

The thought made Asar smile to himself. It wasn't just Set's white skin that stopped them from being twins. That made them different. It was the fact that Set would have never accepted a rule that banished his brother. If roles were reversed, Asar knew that Set would have fought everyone in the house before he would have stopped speaking his own twin brother's name.

Asar raised his eyes and looked at Keb, Nut and Nema. All their eyes were glued to their plates as they brought silent forks to their mouths.

"Set Lives!" Asar said, wrong and strong.

"I ... shut up boy," Keb said.

Asar scooted his chair back and stood.

"Set lives!"

Keb stood and started stalking around the table.

"You gonna hit me the way you hit Set or the way he hit you?"

Keb stopped in front of his only son. Both breathing hard.

"Set lives!"

57

The last ruler-sized slot slid open. Set picked up the two suitcases and waited for his next cue.

The rectangular room was dressed up as a three-fourth-sized version of a luxury Pullman Car. Aunt Kate personally picked out the burgundy brocade fabric that carpeted the walls. A wine-colored Queen Anne chair sat between two shoulder-high bookcases on the opposite end of the car from where Set stood. Along each long parallel wall was a 10-foot cherry-wood-stained handrail, attached to the wall with faux-gold moldings. On the floor, near Set, was a five-foot black vase with fresh cut red roses perfuming the room. Polished so shiny, Set could see the reflection of Nephthys velvet shoes.

Unlike most Pullman Cars, the bed wasn't against the wall. It resembled a wooden rectangular dining room table, with a burgundy bedspread-covered mattress on top. The four sturdy legs were four feet long, giving it an elevated stage feel. Three wooden steps were pushed up to the side of the bed closest to the vase. These were the steps that Nephthys used to climb up and take a seat. Her velvet shoes dangled out from beneath her long white dress. Their reflection on the black vase helping to give Set something to focus on beside the 12 pairs of eyeballs focused on him.

All 12 of the brocade-outlined, ruler-sized slots (five against each long wall and two against the far wall, over the Queen Anne chair) were full of blinking eyelids. Some eyes were wide as cow eyes. Others were hungry slits.

It was as if the Pullman car was alive. The brocade fabric stretched tight against the walls like textured skin on a giant face. A face with 24 eyes that followed Set when he moved.

"Put those bags over here, boy."

Nephthys' sharp tone startled Set. He almost dropped the two bags where he was standing.

"Yess'um."

He was wearing a bluish-gray Pullman Porter uniform. A spare that Aunt Kate bought from one of her few Negro clients. Set had the Porter cap pulled tight over his pale bald head. The jacket, buttoned up to the top, was broad enough, but the sleeves were a little short. The pants were too short, barely covering the top of his ankle-boots. He knew that the seeing walls were not concerned with his ill-fitting uniform. As he stepped towards Nephthys, he knew the eyes were focused on the baseball-sized hole that Aunt Kate had cut into the uniform's crotch.

Set bumped Nephthys' dangling foot as he placed the bags down in front of her. Her white sleeved right arm shot out from her side to slap his face like she meant it.

"Watch what you're doing you dumb, clumsy Negro! Don't expect a tip."

The script called for a realistic-looking slap, but Nephthys went too far. On a reflex, his left hand was around her throat before she could close her mouth good. Nephthys' glistening green eyes were wide with a mixture of excitement and fear. She loved feeling of power she got from provoking Set. Though she was only three years older, she thought of him as a very big boy. A muscular child to play with.

As Set struggled to wrestle her long, skinny body over onto her stomach, she kicked then clawed toward his remaining eye. Following the script, he grabbed her by the waist, jerked Nephthys up onto her hands and knees, and shoved the white dress up and onto her back. No undergarments. Nephthys' buttermilk behind had a thin film of perspiration caused by the struggle. Set kicked aside the wooden block of three stairs.

"Clumsy Negro!" she yelled over her shoulder. His long meaty fingers, wrapped completely around her tiny waist: his 10 fingers touched to complete the circle of desire. He entered her. Nephthys' mouth opened as if to gasp but no sound came out. Instead, the walls gasped for her. Something like a collective breath rose up and escaped from the 12 slots around the room.

"Don't expect ... a tip."

Nephthys was barely able to get the words out as Set pumped his Pullman Porter-uniformed body into her. Set momentarily looked up and looked into the eyes directly in the slot in front of them. The person was pushing their face so hard against the slot, trying to get just a little bit closer, that their eyeballs seemed to be bulging through the hole. He returned his attention to Nephthys. Her torso was still U-turned towards him. Aunt Kate had told her to act like Set was beneath her. A Negro. A servant. A clumsy porter.

"Don't approach me afterwards ... with your hand stuck out,"

Nephthys said, mustering as much derision as possible.

"Yess'um," Set grunted.

Nephthys was surprised by her own excitement. Being with Set was so unlike those days when she didn't want no man touching on her. Times when she had to do what a lot of Kate's girls did: leave the home of her own body to let a renter in. Standing on the outside of herself to keep a roof over her head. Convincing herself that the price of the roof was worth the cost.

But it wasn't that way with Set. Even when they were putting on a show for a bunch of women who would cross the street rather than have to pass them on the sidewalk. She liked that Set was really just a big boy, and being with him made her remember that really she was just a big girl. Both playing "grown-up." And trying to survive it.

Nephthys felt an incredible urge to hold on. But clutching the hard-rocking bed frame with her wide-stretched hands wasn't enough. Nephthys knew that if she didn't say, right then, what Aunt Kate had told her, she soon wouldn't be able to get the words out her mouth. And Aunt Kate got upset when they didn't follow the script. She turned away from the eyes to her left and looked over her shoulder at Set.

"Don't ... tell."

"Yess'um."

58

When the twins were napping as toddlers, sometimes Nut would slip away to the Americus Fountain and place her bare feet in the water. She would cry so hard that if Keb saw her, he'd try to approach, but she'd wave him off. He often misunderstood her tears. Joy, sorrow or healing, it was all water and weakness to him. She knew the power of saltwater purification. Especially tears of joy. Nut was amazed that those sleeping babies had actually come through her body.

Nut didn't ever want to stop acknowledging the wonder of her children. She didn't want the wonder to be disturbed by her husband's comforting words when she was crying. Only the language of salt and water was appropriate. She would go to Keb later and pour herself over him. That was their way. Communication seeping through pores in the skin. Vulnerability in the obtuse angles of thighs. Confessions offered on a bed of rose petals. Apologies scrawled on a muscular back.

Neither was shy about speaking their mind, but the body's tone of voice had a passion and clarity that their vocal chords couldn't always match.

But the screeching vocal chords of Set and Asar could compete. The sound of their needy screams easily drew Nut from under Keb's long body. At times, she pushed him off her. Like the time when the boys were seven and their pirate play involved Asar walking a plank into the Americus Fountain. Their seven-year-old engineering skills didn't include counter-balancing the long piece of wood on the fountain's rim. Before he could fall forward to his imaginary watery grave, the wooden plank flipped up, sending Asar falling straight back to the ground on his head. It was Set's panicked cry at seeing Asar knocked out cold before him that caused Nut to push Keb's sweaty body off her own and run completely naked into the backyard. Abruptly, Set stopped screaming when he saw all her nakedness rambling towards him.

59

The last Christmas season of the century and the Warm Bread Boutique was crowded with holiday shoppers. Many doing the most enjoyable kind of shopping: shopping for the self. A brunette with bangs hanging under a wide-brimmed green hat offered a polite "excuse me" as she reached over the shoulder of a petite blonde to grab a red scarf. Two women next to them reached for the same blue dress at the same time. They both chuckled and insisted the other take the first look. That was the thing that Kate loved about the dress shop. She had been able to bring the good-natured spirit of the Honky Tonk near City Hall where East St. Louis' movers and shakers did their moving and shaking.

Business had been increasing steadily the weeks she'd been open. As was her custom, Kate poured these early proceeds back into the business. Purchasing, straight from England, four Queen Anne sitting chairs for the main shopping room. Oriental rugs for each changing room. Special dresses ordered from Milan. Of course, she served lemonade and warm bread, but it was the occasional uncorking of a wine bottle that brought a friendly buzz to the ladies looking for dresses—and discrete afternoon excitement for those in the know.

Nephthys opened the secret door of the elegant, oak-wood paneled dressing room that Kate had especially made for the stars of the show. From inside the ¾-sized Pullman Luxury Car, the disguised door was a bookcase filled with books from Kate's personal library. Heavy on Shakespeare.

"Seem like ol William knew more whores than me," she had joked with Nephthys while they watched Tommy Jennings finish up the bookcase/hidden door.

Nephthys liked to watch Set come through the bookcase door. His still-growing body tightening the Pullman Porter uniform across chest and biceps. On many of the afternoons over the last three months, Nephthys found herself examining Set. Wondering what this body, that she knew so well, would eventually become.

She quickly surveyed the Pullman car to make sure all the slots were closed. They were. Nephthys didn't like the clients watching her when she first walked into the room. It seemed like such a small thing, given how much they would see once the show actually started—a fact that Set usually mentioned when he teased her about it. She liked those few moments to get prepared to block out all those eyes and just focus on Set.

Nephthys placed her purple hand bag down on the Chaise and looked in the mirror above it. She turned to the left, to the right, to check her profile. She wore a long purple dress whose fringe brushed across the hardwood floor. It poofed around the shoulders and the ran snuggly down her long arms, before ruffling out around her purple glove-covered hands. The long satin purple gloves reached up past her wrist and forearms to her elbow. She watched how the dress gathered tightly around her flat midsection then flared out at her waist as it made its way to the ground.

She was ready.

Nephthys sat down next to her purse. There was a circular plate-sized wooden table at the end of the Chaise, nearest the bookcase. On it sat a frosted crystal dinner bell. Nephthys picked up the dinner bell and rang it once. Then listened.

Just after the bell's vibrating glass tone lapsed into silence, Nephthys heard the first ruler-sized slot slide open behind her. Set had told her that the opening slots sounded like Sunday shoes shuffling across the saw dust in his father's work shed. Nephthys just stared at him. In the months that she had known him, and known him, it was the only time that he had mentioned anyone or anything about his family.

The Sawdust Shuffle began to happen in rapid succession all around the room. No matter how often she prepared herself, Nephthys was usually jolted at the first pair of blinking eyes. Nephthys always made herself stare for a moment so the eyes wouldn't sense her discomfort. This time, the first eyes were blue. Lashes long. Look, excited. The eyes were always excited. And would grow more so. Widened by seeing a Negro ravish a woman whose skin was pale as theirs. So pale, it could have been them.

As she sat with legs crossed, waiting, Nephthys made their curious desire her own. To keep things fresh, Set took pride in having each session in the Pullman be a litttle different from the last. Once, he walked through that bookcase door, leaned to put Nephthys' bag down, then took her shoe off and put her toes right in his mouth.

Another time, he sat down next to her on the Chaise and asked who were some the favorite characters from the books she had read. They went on like that for 15 good minutes. Another time, he walked in and practically threw her bags down and pushed her off the Chaise. The whole time he took her there on the floor, she never stopped scratching and hitting him.

When he tried to apologize afterward in the changing room, she'd spit in his face and stormed out. Another time, he just kissed her softly all over her whole body for the whole show. He never even tried to enter her. That was his favorite time. Hers too. And judging by the tips that slid through the slots, and fell into the peach baskets positioned on the floor directly beneath the horizontal slits, the clients liked it too.

So Nephthys never knew what to expect when that bookcase door opened.

"Yes?" Nephthys said, in response to the two soft knocks on the door.

"Porter, ma'am. Got your bags for you, ma'am."

"Well, they aren't doing me any good out there. Bring them in boy," she shouted.

The bookcase slowly opened. Nephthys felt air rush through her nostrils expanding her chest, making the S-curve of her lower back more pronounced. She briefly caught the quick-shifting eyes in the slot in front of her. They were the green leaf ones with the long lashes. They had gone from nervous to erratic. The fast moving, jumpy eyes were bouncing from the bookcase to Nephthys' torso to the bookcase to the Chaise to the bookcase.

"Where should I place these bags, ma'am?"

Set's nervous and unsure voice sounded odd given its bass tone. The tips had talked and told him that the better he played his role, the heavier the peach baskets were at the end of the show.

In the months since he had left Americus & Son, he'd added a full inch to his now six-foot-five frame. His entire body had filled out. Not fat just a huskiness that was the result of Aunt Kate giving him run of the kitchen. He usually took one of his meals with some of the girls and Nephthys was always baking him buttery pound cakes.

"Sit the bags here next to me."

❘ ❘ ❘

As the performance unfolded, Set could scarcely stay in character. His right hand raised Nephthys' dress, exposing her pale backside, as his left hand freed himself.

"My God," said the breathless eyewitness wall to Set's right.

The husky voice was so ardent that it made Set involuntarily glance up towards the ruler-sized slot to his right. Wide-opened, reckless eyeballs were lodged in opposite corners watching Set with peripheral vision. Then they closed.

60

Nutilda didn't know how long she stood in that closet-sized viewing room with her eyes closed. She just knew that she couldn't make herself move. Couldn't take one step away to pull her face from the ruler-sized slot sucking her face into that fake Pullman Car room. Squeezing her eyes tighter seemed to be her only option. I should have never come here, she thought. Nut was determined not to peek again. So she stood there in the dark listening: Set's rhythmic grunts in unison with the consistent smack of his naked pelvis hitting a sweaty bare behind. Muffled moans seeping through the booth on the right. The creaking Chaise under that girl's rocking body.

Nut's tight-eyed defense was foiled by her imagination. She could still see the girl's demanding mouth trying to catch its breath. The purple vein bulging along the side of her pale throat. Nut could still see the glint of recognition on Set's face when he first saw her reckless eyes. How quickly he had turned away.

Nut squeezed her eyes tighter hoping it would blind her inner vision. Erase the sights and rhythmic sounds that had the base of her cotton under garments soaked through.

Nutilda kept her sweaty palms pressed forward against the wall. She was afraid to drop them below her waist. Nut had enough to forgive herself for.

I I I

On a pre-dawn Sunday morning, Nut had been sipping coffee at the circular kitchen table looking through the backyard facing window. She was wearing the wool tan robe she favored when August mornings began to cool. Nut turned away from the yard to confirm that the footsteps she knew by heart were Set's. Ever since the spots had really began to multiply, he had stopped coming down to the kitchen to join her these early Sunday mornings; he had barely been speaking to her. So she was excited when she heard the footsteps. Then she heard *him*. Nut placed her coffee cup down. Set was crying.

He had stopped in the middle of the kitchen in his white long underwear and long sleeve undershirt. It was long after the herb jars had stopped flying and very clear that she had failed to keep her promise to fix him. He was then fifteen, one-eyed and fully surly.

Besides the one or two word answers that he would offer to her attempts to communicate, they had said next nothing for weeks.

Nut felt Set's judgment. Not only from the silent treatment he had learned too well from his father but also from his averted gaze. Their collective three eyes, which defined them outside their house, rarely made contact inside the Americus home. Set offered his one word answers looking over his mother's head. He used to come into this kitchen on early Sunday mornings to sit at the table and look into the yard with her, their eyes occasionally speaking in their shared solitude. Now, the few times he did come down Sunday mornings, he averted his eyes as he continued past her and went straight into the backyard for his own solitude.

That's why, on this morning, Nut immediately put down her coffee cup. His blinking, crying eye was looking right at her. Nut's eyes started to well up. For Set to come to her like this, she knew he was really hurting.

Nut was afraid to make any sudden movements. She slowly extended her open arms towards Set. Almost against his will, Set's 15-year-old resistant body, sat on his mother's lap and folded into her arms. His teary face buried into her chest. He was crying so hard that both of their bodies shook.

Nut always imagined Set would forgive her by the Americus Fountain. She had seen it so many times in her mind. She'd be dropping rose petals in the water and Set would walk up and place his feet in the fountain next to hers. Nut would hand her baby boy a rose petal. Set would smile. They'd each drop their rose petals at the exact same time and watch them submerge under the fountain's down pour. Then watch the petals resurface together, in a new place, just like their relationship.

Looking down on Set's bald, white head, still shuddering against her wool robe, Nut was just happy it had finally happened. And sad, because Set's curled armistice was carved from pain. As was his forgiveness. But it was a forgiveness Nut needed, so she took it how it came.

She knew this gesture wasn't going to make everything okay. Far from it. But she knew Set's presence in her lap would bring a measure of renewal. And renewal meant hope. That's why Nut's own tears fell from a smiling face.

She reached down in that instinctive way women do when they feel their breasts about to fall from a robe. Her hand ran into Set's lips. She quickly drew her hand back a few inches above his head. It hung there. She glanced down to find him weeping and suckling her fully exposed right breast.

It had happened so suddenly. Did Set nuzzle inside my robe? she thought. No, no it must have been how hard he was crying, and when he saw the nipple he just had a natural reaction, the way babies do when they're crying and a breast comforts them, quiets them, like Set was quieting now. His weeping becoming a whimper, his shuddering becoming a gentle rock. So her hand stayed suspended above his head. Even when the feeling of his mouth on her firm nipple began to change. From a mouth looking to be pacified to a mouth looking to be satisfied.

He's just needy and confused; this means nothing, she thought. Though Set's hungry nibbling and licking alarmed her, Nut's hand did not move. Stuck in her need for his forgiveness. Even after a full minute. Her breathing deep as the sleep of her husband upstairs. Nut still did not drop her hanging hand to stop Set. It was only when Nut's peripheral vision caught her father-in-law standing witness in the kitchen doorway that she slapped Set's lips away and closed her robe.

I I I

Standing in the Warm Bread Boutique's backroom with her eyes squeezed tight, listening to Set grunt surfaced this memory that Nut kept buried. She had enough to forgive herself for. But like that pre- dawn Sunday morning in the kitchen, she was stuck again. Trapped in a place where she, her son and shame met.

61

Nut didn't feel worthy to enter through the Americus & Son front door after leaving the Warm Bread Boutique. She passed the stairs. Kept walking towards the side gate. She kicked off her shoes and stepped across the cold grass, heading towards the Americus Fountain.

Nut sat on the ledge. Placed her feet in the frigid water. Why didn't I just leave the viewing room, she thought. Nut used to pride herself on her decisive nature. But under pressure, it had happened again. She had been afraid to act. Closing her eyes was the best she could do. Nut dropped rationalizations into the water beneath her.

At first you weren't sure if it was him.

What could you have said through that hole in the wall? No one was hurt by it.

The thing about dropping rationalizations into water is, unlike rose petals, they don't float. They sink to the bottom and drown. Nut knew all she had to do was walk out of that viewing room and say she wanted to give the boy in the porter costume his tip in person. Anything to try to talk to Set. Anything to convince him to come back home.

But the shame that had brought them together had kept them apart.

62

1927

Set stood on the wooded-bank of Cahokia Creek. He stepped out of his coveralls and hung them over his arm. Swayed his white body down into the deepening water like it was an open-air baptismal. Set washed his clothes with two stones and conviction. The cleansing of his body would be a long-term project.

He walked back up the bank, scooped mud in his meaty left hand and smeared it over the coverall's blood stains. He hung the overalls from a low lying limb so they could dry a little. It was after 5 p.m., but the July heat was still sweltering. He grabbed his knife and the two butcher-paper-wrapped rifles that were leaning against the same tree. Set walked back into the creek until he was waist-deep.

He hurled his Winchester like an arcing spear and watched it splash near the middle of the creek. Next, he threw Asar's Winchester. Watched it splash and sink. He cleaned his bloody knife. Then Set stood still. His opaque chest, arms, and bald-head sticking out of the murky water. He kept looking at the surface where the guns had entered. It was calm again. No trace of the killers of men. Or killed men.

Set had heard during That Mess that the bohunks tossed many murdered Negroes into the Cahokia Creek. There were dozens of places where someone could toss a dark American. And the calm Cahokia surface would keep the secret.

Set remembered the newspapers saying that the Washington commission investigating That Mess, reported only 39 Negroes killed. Set knew this was a lie because Americus & Son alone handled 42 bodies. Besides, it seemed like everyone he talked to knew someone, who knew someone, who had been killed or turned up missing. Set and his friends figured the number of dead was closer to 300. All those bodies had to be somewhere.

Set rotated his body in a complete circle to examine the calm surface. There could be some dead Negroes all around me right now, he thought. Set hurried out of the water and put his damp coveralls back on. He glanced again at the calm creek. Not a trace, he thought. Set headed home with the only piece of butcher paper he had left. It was rolled in a scroll, folded in his coveralls' inner leg pocket and filled with directions, blood, and secrets.

Set walked east in the shadow of the Free Bridge trying to get his lie straight. He'd always been a good liar because he'd always practiced lying by saying the lie aloud to see if it hit the ear right.

"We were walking under the Free Bridge when I felt something heavy hit me in the back of the head, and I remember falling, and when I woke up Asar was gone."

Wasn't sounding very convincing to his ear. He had to think of something quick. And convincing.

63

Set stood at the bottom the Americus & Son stairs. Looking up at the wooden sign hanging on the porch: AMERICUS & SON. He had always imagined himself to be the true inheritor of that name. The son who was the "SON". He'd always been the one who loved working with the dead. Seeing taut skin separate under his steady scalpel. Feeling the weight of their livers in his large palms. Giving a heart a good squeeze if his father wasn't around. He was the son who loved his hands in cold blood. Or warm.

He began walking up the stairs.

Even before Set reached the porch Nephthys had burst through the front door, screaming, "Set!"

With his left foot on the porch, and his right foot still on the step below, Set had to brace himself so Neph's running hug wouldn't knock them back down the 33 stairs.

"We've been going crazy," she shouted. Neph wouldn't release her long arms from up around his neck. She was sobbing so hard that Set could feel her convulsions, convulsing through his own body.

"We've been going crazy, we've been going crazy."

"Thank God," Nut shouted, as she ran out of the door towards them. Auset was right behind her. But Auset stopped in her tracks in the middle of the porch, as Nut threw her arms around Set's waist.

"Is Asar back yet?" Set said—just as he had practiced.

"Why's he not with you, Set?" Auset said.

Her voice was calm. Steady. Her eyes locked on Set's eye. Looking over his wife's shoulder, Set returned his brother's wife's questioning stare. Grandpa Nema appeared in the porch doorway. Keb by his side. As if waking from a cat nap, Nutilda blinked her eyes open, pulled her chest from around Set's waist and looked up into her son's face.

"Where's Asar at, Set?" Nut said.

Nephthys just kept holding on tight and sobbing, "We've been going crazy."

Without breaking his stare with Auset, Set reached up and peeled Neph's arms from around his neck. He gently pushed Nutilda's shoulder to the side and stepped fully onto the porch. He took a silent step towards Auset. She bent at the waist and released one, long screeching wail. Hand on doorframe, Keb slid to one knee. He squinted in the sun setting over the Eads Bridge.

"Stand up, boy," Grandpa Nema firmly said.

Keb pulled himself up. He leaned against the door frame. Nut looked at Keb's jigsaw puzzle face and awkwardly plopped down on the porch with her right knee bent beneath her. But Set didn't start speaking until little frog-eyed Heru squeezed through the doorframe, between Big Grandpa Nema and Grandpa Keb.

"Where's my Daddy?"

Set looked down at Heru, who was wearing his white nightshirt, then back up at Keb.

"We had to see if there was something to those bohunks who were parading down the middle of the street," Set said, slow, deliberate, convincing.

Just as he had practiced.

"When we got down to Bloody Island things seemed about the same as always, but Asar really wanted to make sure—because of what happened last time."

Set paused at this point. He looked away from Keb and down at Auset. She was still bent at the waist. Palms clutching her knees. A spent marathon runner at the 25th mile. Silent. Staring down at the porch.

"He wanted to go up and down a few of the bars and see the kind of rise we got out of the people. See if something was brewing. We went to the Bucket O' Blood and Hank's down on C Street. Ordered at the bar. We got the usual looks but nothing really out of the ordinary."

Set turned his eye toward Grandpa Nema and continued.

"At the bar, some bohunk turned to me and said something about raising a drink to toast the 10th anniversary of That Mess. And I told him wasn't nothing to be celebrating. And before I could get my words out good, the gibberish talker had a pistol pressed right on my forehead. I'd given the Winchesters that we'd wrapped in butcher paper to Asar, so I could order our drinks, and I was sure he was gonna raise one up, but he hesitated, like he was scared or something, and that was no time to be scared, but he hesitated. Another bohunk had a gun at Asar's temple before he had time to come out of his hesitation. He told Asar, 'Whatever you holding just drop it.' When butcher paper hit floor, they knew right away what they were. 'These Negroes got rifles', the bartender said. He raised his shotgun from behind the bar and started screaming, 'Take that outta my place, take that outta my place!' Those bohunks rushed us towards the door. Asar was in front and soon as we got outside, he threw an elbow and broke free. The bohunk raised a pistol but didn't shoot. He and another one took off after Asar."

Set paused, trying to gauge how his story was coming across to Grandpa Nema. But Grandpa Nema was hard to read. He found Keb's eyes.

"That bohunk stood real close to me, right out there on the street with his pistol in my lower back for must've been 20 minutes waiting for the other bohunks to come back with Asar. Kept muttering to me real-low like, 'You better not move, better not say one peep.' Two of his buddies stood on either side of me joshing like us four was the best of friends."

Set paused again and looked down at Auset who was still bent at the waist.

"They never came back," Set deliberately said. "I could tell the bohunks were starting to get agitated. Stopped all that joshing. Finally, the one with the gun on me, stepped by and kicked me in the rear. 'Stay outta our bars.' I didn't want the bohunks seeing me going off in the direction that Asar went so I turned and circled around."

Set paused again. Looked at his father leaning in the doorway. "I've been looking for him ever since. Been over eight hours. All over Bloody Island. I asked around in every single bar. Every cathouse. Went up and down the waterfront. Walked through the wooded-areas."

He paused.

"Nothing."

Set let the word waft over the porch towards Keb.

"Nothing."

The word faded. Into that silence, a train whistle screeched like a freshly widowed Screech Owl. Then Heru said, "Why didn't you use your knife?"

Unprepared for a question he had not practiced an answer for, Set stood there for two long seconds looking down at his frog-eyed nephew—as Heru looked up at him.

"What?" came out of Set's mouth in such a nervous, nasally alto, that Auset lifted her bent body straight again and looked right into Set's mouth.

"Why didn't you help my Daddy with your knife when those men had you in the bar?"

"I wanted to the whole time but a gun in the back beats a knife in the pocket every time."

Recovering, Set said the words with such smooth conviction that even Grandpa Nema slowly nodded with a resigned sense of agreement.

"Did you even try, Uncle Set?"

The pleading in Heru's voice, the tenderness, silenced Set. Disabled his quick mind from delivering a lie to his tongue. Or was it love silencing me? That's the odd thought that crossed Set's mind in the face of his nephew's frog-eyed earnestness. This slight boy who he had taught to pull catfish out of Cahokia Creek. Taught how to use his compass. The boy who was nephew and son. The nephew and son who he loved—and hurt. Damaged. Forever. Looking into Heru's hurt eyes, genuine emotion began to well up through Set's body. He clenched his molars together and began to breathe heavily through his nose, but he couldn't make it stop. I'm not going to to cry in front of my father, he thought. Then his water broke. A snotty gush of emotion scrunched Set's pale, now pinking face. A weeping watermelon rind.

He quickly brought his baseball-mitt-hands to his face then dropped them quickly back down to his side. He didn't know what to do with his hands. Or his body. Set's torso convulsed up and down like a broken-winged stork trying to fly. The encroaching dusk gave him the look of an enormous shadow puppet. A carnival freak. Part stork, part shuddering silhouette. Part twin, part only child. Part victim, part victimizer.

Set's quivering collapse transformed everyone on the porch into carnival spectators. Fixated on a Midway spectacle. Grandpa Nema's normally tight jaw, now slack enough for his lips to unconsciously part. Still sitting along the top step, Nutilda was motionless. Auset was an erect statue. Nephthys was standing in front of Set with both arms extended, palms up, preparing to stop him from falling forward.

Heru knew this was all his fault.

I should have never asked those questions, he thought. I'm always doing something wrong. I am wrong. That's why he couldn't take two more steps forward and hold one of his Uncle Set's huge shaking hands. He didn't want to mess up. Somehow make things worse than they already were.

It was Keb who first moved towards Set. He'd only taken a single step before Grandpa Nema reached out and grabbed tight Keb's wrist.

"He's a grown man so don't go over there huggin him and carryin on. He'll work it out," Grandpa Nema said to the back of Keb's head.

Keb snatched his wrist away and gingerly continued towards his convulsing son. He had the caution of a man approaching a would-be suicide victim on a building ledge. The side of Keb's thigh brushed past Heru's shoulder, then he stopped one step short of Set. Set's convulsions seemed to shake loose more snot. Mucous was flowing from his garlic bulb-nose, over his full lips, into his mouth.

Through his blinking eye, Set scanned his father's face for a hint of shame. The father who passed down shame-like genes when the genes didn't measure up. A tradition passed down from Grandpa Nema. Kept alive by Asar.

"This is all your fault, Dad," Set said through snot to Keb. His hoarse voice accused like a pointed index finger.

Keb took it.

"It's your fault I'm this way, it's your fault Asar's gone, it's your fault Heru's the way he is. If you would've been your own goddamn man, done things your own way. Your own way, Dad. Everything would've been different. You wouldn't have to see me like this."

Keb nodded his head in slow, rhythmic affirmation. Then closed his eyes. He extended his arms and open palms towards Set like a blind man trying to find a door. Instead, his long fingers found Set's snotty nose and lips. Felt their fullness tremble beneath his touch. Keb allowed his blind fingers to find their way around Set's face onto both sides of his warm cheeks.

Set let him.

To Keb's blind fingers, Set's wet puffy cheeks felt like the puffy wet bottom he used to bathe in the bathroom sink. When the twins were just a couple weeks old, Keb would stand at their bathroom sink cleaning Set's tiny black butt, as Nutilda washed Asar in the bathtub. Above that sink, in the mirror, Keb would occasionally catch a glimpse of a toothy smile. It seemed foreign on his solemn undertaker's face. The smile lines around his eyes, out of place. The gleam in his eyes, a mistake. Wrong for him to be that joyful. That free.

Now, standing there with his eyes closed, holding the cheeks of his full grown baby, he saw that freedom in the mirror in his mind.

Keb held that image in the darkness behind his eyelids. Held the possibility that it could be him again.

Keb opened his eyes to find Set staring at him. With the curious look of a front-row-child before a magician. At a snail's pace, Keb's face leaned towards Set's left ear. Set's head was still, but his only eye followed his father. Keb's lips were out of view when they landed on Set's humid cheek.

64

Set didn't have a plan for leaving Aunt Kate's. The Warm Bread Boutique arrangement had its benefits. Getting paid to lay up with Nephthys was money that was hard to walk away from.

It was like they were a married couple who worked together, except they weren't even boyfriend and girlfriend. They weren't anything. And they were everything. A confusing mix especially since Set was starting to catch feelings for Neph. Feelings that made him increasingly uncomfortable about sharing their private intimacies in the full view of strangers.

That's why Set was so relieved when Bogdan made the offer.

I I I

After all these years, Bogdan still didn't know exactly how Set made his money. He'd asked once and Set evil-eyed him so hard that Bogdan never brought it up again. In some ways, he didn't want to know—because Bogdan knew the options for a Negro who looked like Set had to be limited to things he didn't want to know about his friend. At Mabel's Kitchen, the late January riverfront wind was blowing hard through the lean-to-shack; they might as well have been outside. Especially since Bogdan glanced around and saw white frosted air escape from the mouths of patrons when they spoke. Of the two dozen people huddled over steaming plates of chicken, Bogdan was the only white person. The occasional hard stares he caught reminded him of this fact as he nibbled on his chicken wings.

He was grateful when Set walked in.

"Thanks for the wings. Looked around but couldn't pick you out," Set joked.

"I'm picking the spot next time."

"There still aren't that many places we can eat at together so be grateful of ol Mabel's."

"I'm picking the spot next time."

"All bullshit aside, I know it's the 27th. I … how you doing?"

"Just trying to stay busy today."

"Man." Set shook his head.

"I know, it's crazy."

"Eight?"

"Nine."

"Still hard to believe."

"I figured this was the year to finally go on out there."

"This morning?"

"Yeah. I laid a Kielbasa on the grave." Bogdan chuckled.

"I bet he got a kick out of that. He … "

"I didn't cook it."

"Okay, Bogdan," Set said, turning serious again."

"No fire this time."

"Don't, Bogdan."

"I burn people up. That's what I do."

"Stop."

Bogdan dropped his eyes to his plate. Set looked down too.

"So what's this proposition Boggy?" Set said, without looking up.

"Well, I'm getting along well over at Armour," Bogdan started, slowly raising his eyes. "The Assistant Superintendent is a Polish fellow who used to be a regular at … you know. He let me know that if I knew a hardworking man in need of job, he could have some influence in the situation. I thought about you."

Set looked up at Bogdan then back down at his plate. Bogdan glanced at his opaque bald skull. A faint design of blue-purplish veins wound across it like a rural road map.

"I didn't know Mr. Armour was big on hiring Negroes."

"We have a few, so one more won't be a problem. Besides, Mr. Armour's not the one doing the hiring. I floated it to Jaworski; he gave me a little look, but said he would keep his word. Of course, you'd have to start on the killing floor, but that's where I started too, and Jaworski himself told me that when he moves back to Chicago next year, he's gonna recommend me for his position. This is only my 9th year. When I become the Assistant Superintendent, I can help you slide right on up the ranks."

Set looked up. Bogdan wished Set had worn his eye patch.

"Slide right on up past some of those white boys?"

"You let me worry about that when the time comes. Besides you as white as … Listen, Set, the bottom line is that I've got some action on a job for you, if you want it."

Set looked back down and grabbed a chicken wing.

"I already got a job."

"I know Set. But wouldn't it be fun if we could work in the same place? Take the job as a favor to me."

Set liked the idea of working at Armour. Many of the white workers scoffed at the low pay. And the smell. The eyes. The screams. The blood. Set saw an opportunity in the blood.

Over the years, Set, and most other Negroes, knew that there were never more than a couple hundred Colored meatpackers at one time in all of East St. Louis. They knew because word travelled fast about which companies were willing to give a Negro a chance. Those chances grew when Polocks, Slavs, and other white workers, tired of low wages and lost fingers, began to agitate for better conditions back in '12. The more the workers agitated the more ads began to be placed in the Negro papers across the South—the more chances Negroes like Set Americus received.

"Friday, January 29, 1915," Set said aloud. I need to write this date down, he thought. Then Set said the date again. It felt good to be excited about something. He was on his way to meet Assistant Superintendent Jaworski. Set got giddy butterflies walking past the same holding pens where, during his childhood, a Polish sheep lost an eye.

Vlade Jaworski met him at Armour's main gate. As Bogdan had told Set, Assistant Superintendent Jaworski would be easy to spot. Set couldn't remember the last time he had to look up at a bohunk. Over 6'9", Jaworski had the perpetually raised eyebrow of a man who was accustomed to looking down at people or questioning people's actions—or both at the same time. He was pale and still a shade darker than 9/10th of Set's body.

"Americus?"

"Jaworski?"

The Assistant Superintendent didn't extend a greeting palm.

As they arrived at the top floor, Set remembered the twin's childhood slaughterhouse adventure when they were escorted along this same floor by the nice gap-toothed Negro. Set could barely believe he was back. But the sounds made it real. The bleating of sheep and squealing of pigs was much louder upstairs. More desperate. The death was closer.

As they walked along the corridor, they approached a series of white walls on their left with playful, bloody handprints. Individual thumbprints were used as eyes of blood-drawn smiley faces. Passing each wall, Set glanced to his right into what looked like boxcars with their doors wide open. Inside, hundreds of pigs and sheep and cows. Waiting. Behind the last wall was a room three times as large as the others. It was full of nothing but bleating sheep. The sheep, which had already been sheared, seemed to Set like naked pinkish children on all fours in a church nursery. Children who watched the pinkish children ahead of them get pulled to the front for punishment.

They had a seat in Jaworski's office, which was lined with leather-bound ledger books on the wall behind his desk. Set could feel the examination; he knew he was a curiosity. The carnival freak starring in a carnival that magically appeared wherever he showed up. A distinction that made the tips talk for years at the Warm Bread Boutique.

Now at 31, his broad carnival face had filled out, making his high, sharp cheekbones less noticeable. The pale veined skin that covered those cheek bones was a faded, almost translucent white. The color of the veined underbelly of a just-born dove popping out of an egg. A color that made Set seem fragile. Easily broken. And he was. Which made him dangerous. Especially at 6'5" with a neck as thick as a maypole. Each meaty hand, experience had shown, big enough to wrap completely around a man's throat. Set's hurt lay just beneath that translucent skin. You could see it if you looked close enough. A cry just behind those fleshy lips. Maybe that's why people, including the Assistant Superintendent Jaworski, stared so. Trying to look inside and understand what must life be like for a White Nigger. With a hole in his head. What goes through a mind like that? Questions people didn't mind taking a little time to figure out. Time to work out their curiosity. Something for workers to discuss at lunch. After work, over a beer, along the Whisky Chute. Keeping a carnival freak on the payroll could have its benefits, is what Jaworski thought looking across his desk at Set.

"It's the eyes," Jaworski said.

He was explaining to Set why some workers preferred not to have to kill the sheep. The human-like eyes made some uncomfortable. Slowed down work. Unlike the Swift and Morris packinghouses, Armour liked to have their killers work the same animals.

"Better for efficiency. What it takes to kill a pig is not what it takes to kill a cow or a sheep. Repetition of motion on the same animal makes for repetition of consistent results," Jaworkski said.

Set pointed up to his eye patch.

"Eyes don't make me squeamish," Set said.

From his very first day, Set got the attention of other workers at Armour & Co. In early January, the same month he was hired, the strike was finally crushed, after four months, over at Swift's packinghouse. Swift had brought in hundreds of scabs who needed to feed their families too.

Bogdan had told him that the Armour boys had been closely watching the Swift strike. Like at Swift, Mr. Armour made things so hard for employees that he almost forced you to have to stand up for yourself, for your family. There was talk that if the Swift strike worked, they might give it a go at Armour. It was no surprise to Set that Bogdan was at the center of it—even though he had a promotion into management in the works.

Bogdan was the kind of fellow who men wanted to pal around with and women wanted to smile at. He still had the same intense brown eyes from when they were kids. Eyes that were still curious about the world. The floppy ears jutting from under his oiled-back black hair still loved to hear the world's stories. People enjoyed talking to Bogdan because his desire to know their stories added meaning to the lives from which the stories came. Being a good listener had taught Bogdan that most men just wanted to work for their keep at a fair wage. Take care of their families. Be respected. Those were things Bogdan figured were worth fighting for even if it could get him in a little trouble. Or a lot.

Since Set and he had been kids, Bogdan had usually sided with the underdog, against his own best interests, because his family came to this country as the underdog. Just like he'd sided with a spotty, one-eyed Negro boy when it promised to do nothing but make his life more complicated.

Before his first day, Bogdan had told Set to always watch his back because, "When the scabs came to Swift they came in mostly white, but the few Negro scabs who crossed that line got an awful lot of attention, and as you know, word travels fast in this town."

Set knew it was easy for white workers to blame Negro scabs because more and more Negroes seemed to be arriving at the Relay Depot each week. The rumor taken as truth was that the factory owners had been importing Negroes to weaken unions. It wasn't just in the meatpacking houses. Bogdan had said that after workers struck back in June '14, and won a 2 1/2 cent an hour raise at Aluminum Ore, the company hired 190

Negroes by December of that year.

"The Protective Association over at Aluminum was upset. Wasn't letting no Colored folk through those gates before 1913. All the sudden, it's more Negroes than a cake walk convention," Bogdan teased Set on the eve of his first day on the job. "So true enough, some of the Armour boys may not like you too much, but I'll be looking out for you."

Set was appreciative of how Bogdan was preparing him for Armour, but he could also tell that Bogdan was sore about Negroes being imported as scabs. He wouldn't shut up about it.

"It was a two-for-one deal, you see. Most of those big boys, Armour, Morris, Swift, they're all Republicans. Give a Negro a job and it don't take too much more to get him to vote the way they see best. Congressman Rodenberger was the best friend these packers had in a long time. Think they want to see him go anywhere? Hell no. I know Negroes, personally, myself, who was selling their vote for five dollars. That was the going rate. These parts are called Rodenberger's Black Belt for a reason," Bogdan chuckled.

Set could feel the edge in his childhood buddy's laugh. He understood. Bogdan was trying to help his other friends organize themselves so they could better take care of their families, and a bunch of out-of-towners were coming in to threaten the very jobs they're trying to improve upon. But like Bogdan said himself, most of the scabs were white. It's just easier to hate Negroes, especially if you've already got a reason to hate Negroes.

Even on Bloody Island, where Set still lived, he'd noticed the change. Negroes had never been welcomed; they had been tolerated at best. But the last couple of years, the stares had gotten harder and longer. The sharp comments more frequent. Especially when he walked by groups of bohunks, bunched together, gibbering in their own language. He knew, and they knew, Set was too big for their talk to cross the line into action. But he'd overheard conversations by less-big Negroes to know that bohunks were increasingly replacing talk with action.

So Set did intend to watch his back.

Soon after he got started on that last Friday in January, Set had plenty of opportunity to watch his back, because there were always a lot of people behind him. True to form, Set Americus was a curiosity. If he had a silver dollar for every time he heard, "Geta loada the white nigger," Set Americus could've changed his name to J.P. Morgan.

Workers taking a piss break or pausing for a cigarette would slow to a stop as they passed his station.

Set was partly to blame. He neglected Bogdan's good advice to just do his job and not bring attention to himself. Set usually arrived at 6:30 a.m. for his 7:00 a.m. shift then promptly took off his eye patch. Followed by his shirt. He sat on the crate he kept by his station and started sharpening his knife. He never used the knives that Armour & Company made available. Instead, he brought his Americus Sword. The gold-handled, single-ruby-encrusted, double-edged knife was great for killing in style and bad for blending in at work.

As each sheep came before Set, his right fingertips gave a quick caress on the cheek. A busy lover saying goodbye. Then with one vicious slash, his left hand brought the Americus Sword across the throat. Warm oxygenated blood spurting from the sheep's jugular onto his own canvas-colored chest. At the end of some shifts, his naked torso would be red as the killing floor. If other men on the floor lingered too long behind him, Set looked over his shoulder, bloody knife raised above his head, and snarled, "Cost you a quarter to watch, a dollar for service."

A couple times, even before Set could get his words out, Bogdan appeared and said to the crowd, "You're looking at this Negro gentleman like he's your type. Don't think he swings that way boys." Despite the mutual aggressions, Set derived some conflicted pleasure from the attention. He enjoyed the power of being something people had to see. Even if that something was a Midway Freak Show on a slaughterhouse floor.

Set understood that it wasn't just his looks that made him of interest to Armour employees. These Irish and German and Slovak and Russian and Polish workers were not usually book-learned, but they were not dumb. They knew that from Armour to Aluminum Ore, management was using the Colored boys to knock down wages. Just as the newly-arrived Irish did against the Germans and the newly-arrived Slovaks did against the Irish and the newly-arrived Lithuanians did against the Slovaks. They knew the experience well because many of them had experienced it from both sides. But it seemed to Set that losing out to a Negro made it worse for them.

After a little more than three months on the killing bed, Assistant Superintendent Jaworski walked towards Set.

"Wanna talk to you, Americus."

"About what?"

Set yelled above the bleating sheep. But the Assistant Superintendent was already walking back to his office.

In three months, Set had seen several nervous working men walk into Jaworski's office, and walk out more nervous with less work. It wasn't an office he wanted to land in. To cover his anxiety, Set stomped over to the wooden crate by the far wall, where he kept his belongings, and wiped his bloody hands on the rag. When he got to the office, he stopped in the doorway.

"Have a seat, Americus," Jaworski said, still looking down at paperwork on his desk.

"Rather stand if that's alright with you. Got more blood on me than a slaver's conscience."

The Assistant Superintendent looked up. Gave Set that raised eyebrow.

"I've been watching you, Americus. Like how you handle that shiny knife of yours. And how you don't got a whole lot to say because you're too busy doing your job. A lot of these men could learn a piece about work from you. So here's what I'm proposing to do. I wanna make you a Pace Man and bring you up to 25 cent."

"What about Ragan?"

"What about em? You think he cares a rat's piss about you? You think if you was the Pace Man and you had slowed down a touch, and I offered the job to him, because I thought he could better help this company in its drive to be the best damn packing house in the U S of A, he wouldn't take it faster than he could call you a white ni … a white Colored man?"

"Well, he's not going to be too happy about someone new as me, Colored man especially, coming and taking his place, but truth be told, I ain't worried about Ragan none. It's all the other Slovaks who seem to like Ragan an awful lot that I'm thinking about."

"Now, if 25 cent an hour ain't worth a few bad feelings, maybe I just need to find me a Pace Man who ain't so sensitive."

"Maybe you do—or maybe you don't. Give me a day to think on it."

"You got till the first thing tomorrow morning." After work, Set talked to Bogdan about the offer.

"It's gonna cause you more trouble than it's worth. These Armour boys still talking about the Negro scabs that helped break that Swift strike. And we're still thinking about organizing and striking ourselves. I'd pass on it, Set."

"If you all make this union, are you gonna allow Negroes to join?"

"I'd be in favor of it if … ."

"Yes or no Bogdan?"

"If … ."

"Yes or no?"

"No."

| | |

The next morning Set Americus became a Pace Man at Armour & Company. In the same way Jaworski used to occasionally stop by Ragan's station to egg him on, Jaworski began dropping in on Set to loudly push his Pace Man.

"Show these boys how it's done, Americus! Make that shiny knife fly. Show em why we just had to pay you that Pace Man money! Show em why you bring home more for yourself than they bring home for their whole family!"

Set immediately noticed the impact of a Negro replacing a popular bohunk. The Armour men knew Ragan was there to keep the pace up, to make them all work harder, to grind them faster into the dust from which they came. But because he was one of their own, they forgave him. They knew Ragan was a hard working man with a family to feed. They knew Ragan had accepted the few-cents-an-hour-more to help feed his family because if he didn't take it, another co-worker would to feed his own family. They teased Ragan. Called him Jackrabbit. Hummingbird Harry. But it was good-natured. An expression of love that these hardened slaughterhouse men felt comfortable with.

In the five months that followed Set's promotion, there was no love in the bohunks' teasing of Set, because there was no teasing.

Only threats.

Set saw it as he walked towards his station. He knew the men near him must have seen it too. Or put it there. It was hanging from a nail above his crate. The cord was still glistening. Fresh. A stick pin positioned the eyeball so it appeared to be looking out across the killing floor. An eyewitness to the last terrified bleat and testament. As Set approached his crate, he could see and feel the eyes of the men on him. He could also see that there was something attached to the bottom of the eye. With a sudden motion, Set whipped his knife from the small of his back and slashed the optical cord, catching the eye in his bear claw-like right hand.

It was a neatly folded piece of paper, the size of a thumbnail, stuck to the bottom of the eye.

Set looked around. On most early mornings, Bogdan would stop by Set's crate to check-in with him.

"Making sure the boys haven't run you out of here yet," he'd joke. But Bogdan was nowhere around. Set would have to handle this situation by himself. The early-bird bohunks who had come to prepare for work, or watch his response, all stopped sharpening their knives and making small talk.

Most men in the area were staring right at Set.

Set turned his head slowly, scanning the room, holding gaze on one bohunk then the next. Methodically moving from face-to-face. Some scarred from knives made slippery by blood. Some with bloodshot eyes made red by surrendering to degrading work. Some just tired. All grim. All staring right back at Set.

Set detached the little paper square without looking down.

"What does it say?" Set shouted at all of them and no one in particular.

Aiming for a cluster of grim faces to his right, Set hurled the eyeball in his palm like a pitcher. The startled men flinched and ducked. Set slid the folded note into his pants' pocket.

He was itching to pull out the little note all day, but Set didn't want them thinking he was too anxious to know.

After work, he was about to read it while walking down St. Clair Avenue, when he saw Bogdan stepping towards him. Smiling.

Set smiled and put the folded square back in his pants' pocket.

"Take a day off?" Set said, before shaking his friend's hand.

"No. I'm taking every day off. Armour let me go. Seems like someone mentioned to management our interest in organizing ourselves to improve working conditions and wages so bohunks can better care for our families."

Bogdan stopped smiling.

Before Set could say anything, Bogdan had turned around and was walking back down St. Clair Avenue. At the corner, Bogdan met up with three other men. All bohunks. None smiling.

65

TUESDAY, MAY 29, 1917
EAST ST. LOUIS, ILLINOIS

Just after 5:30 p.m., Bogdan Dabrowski and a group of employed—and unemployed—workers started amassing on the streets outside City Hall. Their flesh and blood-stained coveralls, heavy boots and heavier faces mixed with the smell of musty underarm sweat and pieces of fatty-animal-tissue baking in the late May humidity. Bogdan ran his fingers back through his oiled black hair and started the first chant.

"1916 WAS LAST YEAR ... 1917's HERE NOW ... THIS YEAR'S GONNA BE DIFFERENT ... WE'RE GONNA SHOW YOU HOW."

Men kept chanting as members of the Waitress and Laundry Workers Union walked up together. Following Bogdan's lead, the men made a special show of tipping their caps at the W.L.W.U. women and moving aside to let them up front. The men stood behind their female counterparts with an air of deference and protection that their own wives would have appreciated. Bogdan wanted Mayor Mollman and the councilmen to glance out the second floor boardroom window and get a strong visual reminder that The White Woman was also at risk with all these pick-pocketing, leering, Negroes running the streets, trying to take jobs—and other things of great value—from The White Man.

By 6 p.m., hundreds of East St. Louis' hard-working and out of work white men and women had gathered. Bogdan was on the City Hall steps, facing the workers, leading a thunderous chant.

"IM-PORT NE-GROES ... WHITE-MAN-JOB-GO! ... IM- PORT NE-GROES ... WHITE-MAN-JOB-GO ... IM-PORT... ."

With such a ruckus from hundreds of voters making a normal meeting impossible, Mayor Mollman came down himself and stood on the City Hall steps next to Bogdan. Bogdan raised both his arms skyward to settle down the crowd.

"We've decided that the people's voices must be heard, so we're going to move the meeting next door into the auditorium," the Mayor said, resulting in a hearty cheer from the masses. They parted to let the

Mayor lead them next door.

Inside the auditorium, the blarney stone-influenced crowd was even more boisterous. A lone man started a slurred chant from the back of the auditorium and the men in his section picked it up.

"IM-PORT NE-GROES ... WHITE-MAN-JOB-GO! ... IM- PORT NE-GROES ... WHITE-MAN-JOB-GO!"

Mayor Mollman repeatedly smacked his gavel on the 8-foot table that they'd placed on the stage. Just as the chant died down. A woman from the W.L.W.U., sitting in the front row, picked it up in her high pitch voice.

"IM-PORT NE-GROES ... WHITE-MAN-JOB-GO!... IM- PORT NE-GROES ... WHITE-MAN-JOB-GO!"

Soon a chorus of women's voices joined her.

The Mayor and councilmen looked at each other along the table, nodded with little exasperated smiles and silently agreed to scrap the agenda.

Mayor Mollman rose from his chair, walked around the table and stood at the edge of the wooden platform. The crowd grew silent. His handsome face suggested a stage actor who heard the Lord's call and went into the ministry. Rosy cheeks and a slight build made him seem boyish. Innocent. In a way, he was. Mollman wanted to do the right thing. The problem was that he wanted to do the right thing for everybody.

Mayor Fred Mollman had been a Episcopalian minister before democratic party boss C. Locke Tarlton said, "A town like East St. Louis needs a good, honest man like you Fred to help it become the next Great City of America."

It wasn't hard for Fred to see the city's potential. Twenty-six rail lines met in East St. Louis. Goods that ended up all over this great country passed through a city just waiting for someone to lead it in the right direction. Important men like Swift and Armour founded their important companies in town. People flocked to East St. Louis, because they could see that it was a city on the move. Sure there were problems, but every city's got problems. But every city doesn't have potential and that's exactly why Fred Mollman said, "Yes," to C. Locke Tarlton, and, "Yes," to the people of East St. Louis, and why he wanted to say, "Yes," to the stinking and restless people sitting in front of him now.

"When the great citizens of a great city come to express them- selves, to the leaders who represent them, that's when democracy is having its finest hour."

Mayor Mollman's measured, soprano voice sounded like a nervous Episcopalian minister trying too hard to hide his nervousness.

"Our finest hour is not the time for hot-headedness, ladies and gentlemen. No, this is the time for well-reasoned, level heads to prevail. Attacking the Negroes is not the answer. Let us follow the example of the well-reasoned, level heads that built this great nation. The well-reasoned, level heads that foresaw this very moment, to give us an example to follow."

A single-voice rose from the back of the auditorium.

"IM-PORT NE-GROES ... WHITE-MAN-JOB-GO!"

"Now, now, hold on, hold on. We live in this great city too and we're also concerned about these mostly republican business owners importing Negroes. We've also written directly to Southern governors, including the governor of Mississippi himself, requesting that they tell their Negroes that, despite those Negro newspapers' false advertisements, there are no more jobs for them in the fair city of East St. Louis."

"It's not just the jobs!" shouted Bogdan.

He was standing in the second row with his index finger above his head.

"Once these Negroes steal the white man's jobs, they want to take that money and move into our neighborhoods and spit watermelon seeds in our front yards while they make googlie eyes at our white women. Now, that's just not right, Mr. Mayor. The good people of East St. Louis expect the mayor who they cast their votes for to do more than send notes down to Dixie. No, sir! That simply will not do. The people who took the action to elect you, sir, expect you to take action in a situation that demands action!" he said, jabbing his index finger towards the 30-foot ceilings.

A spontaneous cheer arose from the crowd.

"East St. Louis must remain a white man's town!" a worker cried from the middle of the auditorium.

His voice steely with righteous conviction, Bogdan shouted, "There is no law against mob violence."

"Now, now ... ," Mayor Mollman started.

But it was as if he had become a pantomime, because no one could hear him. The roar and stomping of feet shook the auditorium's wooden floor boards. These workers in their sweaty uniforms and boots were on their feet shouting. Not slogans. The intensity of their emotional reaction didn't allow for the forming of coherent slogans. The wall of sound that filled the auditorium was pre-verbal. Bogdan's comments rang so true with them, spoke so much to the wrong being done to white men by those job-stealing, ogling Negroes, that it hit a primal nerve. Undecipherable hollers, snorts and yelps blasted up from their guts into their lungs and through their wide- open mouths. Like when a swinging hammer hits a thumb: guttural emotion and sound overwhelmed thought.

That's exactly what Mayor Mollman thought looking out into the deafening sea of yelling faces. It reminded him of an event years ago. On a trip to Georgia with his father to look at 120 acres in Savannah. A man had come running up to the porch of their host Mr. Swanson, and said, "Trapped a coon up by Foster's place."

There had been no more than twenty men that night and three or four boys near his own pre-teen age. He would never forget the wild hollers, yelps, screeches and cries that went up when, by throwing rocks, they had made the Negro fall to the ground from his tree-top hiding place. That collective wall of sound had first made young Fred Mollman turn away. A wall of sound that he was surprised to see his own father lending his voice to. Similar to the ear-splitting sound he now heard standing on the stage watching hollering union men and women.

The last thing a city on the rise like East St. Louis needed was for a mob, like the one screaming in front of him, to get a hold of some Negro and hang him from a tree.

"This is not some damn backwater Dixie town, this is the next Chicago," he said angrily to himself, because no one could hear him anyway.

He was not going to let a bunch of Polocks and I-Tals ruin all the good work he'd done—even if they were the ones who elected him to office. East St. Louis was well on its way to finally fulfilling its potential, because the right man was at the helm. Every Great City needs a Great Mayor and every Great Mayor needs a Great City. This was his time and these gibberish speakers were not going to ruin it for him.

The workers started to stream out of the building on to the street. It was approaching dusk. There was a palpable sense of excitement as the men milled around slapping each other on the back. They had stood up for their rights. Their voices had been heard. These very men who were disrespected, as a matter of course on a daily basis. Their opinions and feelings considered as much as the sheep who they sent to Sheep-Jesus. Men whose livelihoods hung on the whim of an ornery superintendent or a greedy Negro. White men who risked limb and livelihood when all they asked for was dignity from the companies they labored for. In the sweltering auditorium, these men had remembered what it felt like to be men. Even the women.

Hundreds of them milled around in the street congratulating themselves on their manliness. Drunk on their gumption. Wallowing in testosterone. How they wanted to hold on to this feeling before dawn brought them back through the gates of Morris and Aluminum Ore and Swift and Armour & Co.

Unconsciously, men kept looking up into the sooty sky. One man looked up, then another as they slapped each other's back. This was a day that no one wanted to end. Bogdan walked out of the double doors of the auditorium.

"DABROWSKI FOR MAYOR!" someone shouted "YES, DABROWSKI FOR MAYOR!"

"NO, FOR GOVERNOR!"

"WHERE?" an alarmed voice bellowed above the crowd.

Men crowded the tall man in coveralls and began shouting before he could finish. The words jumped from spiting lips to the half-hearing edges of sweaty ears, along the crowded street. As heads swiftly turned to relay the information to the next man and the next, the rumor slid out, semi-formed, from the sides of mouths. Changing form from person to person like black coal to steam to motion to action.

"ROBBED? BROADWAY. PISTOL. TWO TIMES. NIGGER. DEAD. TWICE? TWO. TWO WHITE GIRLS. INSULTED. BROADWAY? PISTOL? TWO WHITE GIRLS. SHOT! DEAD!"

Bogdan was the mob's point as it started moving in mass down Collinsville and turned on Broadway. He megaphoned his hands and shouted, "CLOSE THE PAWNSHOHPS! TAKE THE GUNS AWAY FROM THE NEGROES."

Mayor Mollman got outside just in time to hear someone at the back of the mob yell, "GET A ROPE!" The crowd had quickly swelled by scores as people rushed out of storefronts and pedestrians stepped off the curb to join the movement.

"Everyone go home!" the Mayor shouted through his cupped hands but not loud enough to get over the wall of sound made by the chant, "GET-A-ROPE ... GET-A-ROPE ... GET-A-ROPE."

The mob moved down Broadway like a coverall-clad amoeba.

Initially, Bogdan was at the front, but he had no control of it now. Like the men around him, he just surrendered to the emotional release of hurting people. Who were hurting him. God's will: Punishing Negroes for taking away his God-given right to be able to support a family—even though he didn't have a family to support. The amoeba mob enveloped every Negro it came across. A walnut-colored man, with a glistening bald head, pushing a cart full of watermelons for sale down Broadway. Suddenly, dozens of fists and boots from every angle, driving his bloody face to the ground. From a fetal position, watching through his fingers as his blood mixed with the sticky red fruit.

Two Negro men in dark suits coming out of Ike's Bar: both going down wildly swinging in that way that whiskey can make even the worst fighting odds seem beatable.

And so it went. All the way down Broadway. No Negro man exempt from hitting the ground. Bones breaking like the Eucharist. Blood spilling like a sacrament.

The blood of Negro women flowed too. The ladies of the W.L.W.U. made sure of it. Laundry girls know their way around dresses which is why they were so adept at quickly tearing them off Negro women. Forcing victims to use their hands to maintain some modesty, exposing their faces to fingernails—with bad intentions.

Each attack seemed to embolden the crowd which had swelled to over a 1000. The coveralls and boots had been joined by suits and ties. And dresses. The wheels of street cars were pulled from overhead wires. Negro men were dragged from the cars. Their blood creating their own tracks.

On 4th Street near Broadway, Bogdan led a splinter-group of mostly-fired union boys into Sammy's, a barbershop catering to the city's Negroes, and began to beat the men right there in the barber chairs. Scissors grabbed from a barber's hands were not used on hair. When exhausted from the beatings, the gang rested a spell and proceeded to break and smash everything that could be broken and smashed. Mirrors. Combs. Bottles of oil. Bottles of rubbing alcohol. Ash trays. Waiting-chairs. Tables. Bones. Until Sammy's was simply a moaning heap of broken furniture and bodies. Including Sammy's 64-year-old body. He lie face down at the foot of a barber chair. Unmoving.

After nightfall, Bogdan led a dozen men down 4th Street, down Railroad, down Walnut, down Trendley, searching for Negroes even though they knew they had little chance of finding them given the frightening size and volume of the commotion. But they searched anyway.

As midnight approached, Bogdan's group was one of a few roaming gangs of male workers. The suits and ties and dresses had long returned home to share victory stories with their families. But the coverall-clad workers couldn't let it go. Especially Bogdan. He couldn't let the night end. Not yet. He had trusted a Negro. Been his friend. Got em a job. And been stabbed in the back for his efforts.

Lost his job in the process. No this night was not going to end. Not yet. Not until some more justice had been served on these greedy, ungrateful Negroes.

Bogdan led the boys back to St. Clair. Up and back down Broadway. Down and back up Collinsville. When it became clear that there simply were no more Negroes, Bogdan decided to set ablaze any structure that looked like it belonged to a Negro. Which wasn't hard to tell, because most of the Negroes downtown were crowded into the raggediest little over-priced shacks.

Bogdan's ad hoc gang converged on several shacks near Third and Missouri. Just as one of the men was returning with the gasoline, plainclothes detectives Samuel Coppedge and Frank Wodley walked up and drew their pistols.

Throwing a box of matches at the feet of Bogdan, Det. Coppedge said with conviction, "First man light a match, first man catch a bullet."

There was a pause. Tired faces looked from side-to-side.

"Let's call it a night, boys," Bogdan said. "These nigger lovers probably got nigger loving to get to." Bogdan smirked at Det. Sam Coppedge then spat on the ground.

Frank shot a quick look at Sam. He was relieved to see that his partner, who the other officers called, "Oops," wouldn't have to live up to his well-worn nickname.

The crowd left down Missouri Ave. slapping each other hard on the back. Their rough hands trying to pound this feeling of manhood deep into their muscle memory. Into their back bone. Into their spinal fluid. Hoping that when they walked under the gates of Aluminum Ore and Armour & Co. in the morning, they would not forget who they really were. Or when they woke up in the morning with no job to go to, they would not forget who was really at fault.

66

Samuel J. Coppedge was no damn nigger lover. Fact was, he'd officially killed more Negroes—in the line of duty of course—than any other man in the department. Seven to be exact. Each of whom he was proud of because each was exactly the type of Negro who brought down the quality of life of the good, and not-so-good folk, of East St. Louis. Now, not all seven had been directly involved in committing a crime at the time of their demise, but they were sure going to get around to it eventually. Which was why he had emptied his revolver into their black asses without an ounce of remorse. A remorselessness that allowed him to say, "Oops" just after the sixth bullet had left his gun.

Since Frank had been witness to each of the seven baggers, over their 11 years together, he was the one who let the other boys in the department know about the "Oops" tradition. It quickly went from tradition, to tradition and nickname. It wasn't that Sam hated all Negroes, he just didn't love any. He didn't even know a Negro good enough to love one. If by chance a crazy notion like that were to attempt to enter his mind, he'd stop it before it got past his skull. Yet, Sam wasn't going to stand by and let someone burn a man's house down—even if the house was a Negro's lowdown shack. Sam had built his house with his own hands. Of course, he hired a coupla Negroes to dig the foundation and ol Frank lent a helping hand when it came time to lay the bricks. But whenever visitors laid eyes on the six bedroom brick number up there on Pennsylvania Ave., they always remarked what a beautiful house it was. Everyone especially loved the huge front porch and the picket-fence-enclosed balcony directly above it on the second floor. The balcony was connected to the master bedroom with French Doors Sam had "rescued" from the Greek Orthodox Church that mysteriously caught ablaze four years ago.

After Sam let his visitors finish marveling at his house, he was quick to say, "Built it myself."

Sam loved to recline on the Chaise lounge. He called it his Thinking Chaise. That's where he was lounging waiting for Frank. Sam was still troubled by the sight of union fellas stirring up citizens to the point where they were just beating any Negro. Didn't care if it was a bad Negro or not. Even women folk. Now, he understood how they felt. Negroes coming here taking jobs. If his own job was in jeopardy, he probably wouldn't let it go without a fight. But beating up women? That's one thing that Samuel J. Coppedge couldn't stand for. He'd seen his pappy knock down his mum enough times, right in front of him, that he wasn't gonna watch another man do it to another woman. Even a Colored one.

It wasn't just attacking Negro women that bothered Sam. It was how quickly the ruckus grew out of control. By the time word came from Mayor Mollman to get to City Hall on the double, the boys had already set off down Broadway, picking up steam and agitators along the way. Sitting in his Thinking Chaise, Sam thought there must have been over a thousand people rampaging the streets.

The officers couldn't do much more than watch. Grab a few stragglers who broke off from the mob. Hell, what were they supposed to do? Shoot white men and women? "Oops" don't work on them, he chuckled to himself.

The only time Det. Coppedge physically threw himself into the fray was when he caught some of the men jumping on the Negro women who were being pummeled by groups of rioters. He just dived in swinging his club, screaming, "Not here, boys!"

Some of the fellas were so riled up, so excited, it was like ol Heinrich the Hypnotist himself had sic'd them on those knocked- down Colored girls. Punching them with one hand, while other hand was jammed up under their dresses. The whole mess just gave Sam a real bad feeling. One that he hadn't been able to shake the rest of the week. That's why he had called Frank over.

Sam jumped at the three quick fist-pounds on the door. "POLICE, OPEN UP!"

Sam watched his friend walk right over to the Thinking Chaise and plop himself down.

"What's on your mind, detective?" Frank said, leaning back with his hands clasped behind his head, eyes closed.

Sam just looked at him. This time, he'd let him have the Thinking Chaise. He walked into the hallway leading to the downstairs guest room, and came back with a straight-back chair. Frank had already lit his cigar.

To Sam, Frank looked like a skinny walrus. His walrus mustache hung down so low over his lip that he was constantly spitting it out of the corners of his mouth. Then there was The Nose, which was kind of shaped like miniature flesh-colored walrus. A nose so prominent that it somehow overshadowed a mustache that actually flopped up and down when he walked fast. When Det. Frank Wodley was in hot pursuit of a running suspect, the mustache came alive.

Sam placed the straight-back chair down in front of the Thinking Chaise he should have been sitting in, turned the chair backward and sat down gap-legged. He pulled a cigar from his right breast pocket. Lit it and leaned forward over the chair-back. Sam looked at his best friend, who was still reclining walrus-style, and thought about the best way to start this conversation. Still thinking, Sam blew a perfect cigar smoke ring towards Frank's head. The thick white ring wafted perfectly over Frank's cigar then framed his face just before losing form.

"You think these Negroes got souls?"

Frank's eyes blinked open. Cigar still in his mouth, he exhaled and looked through the smoke at his partner.

"I mean, do you think that they really got souls like us, the way a white man's got a soul."

Frank took the cigar from his mouth.

"Can't say I've ever thought about nothing like that. Souls? What … what kind of question … what make you ask me a thing like that?"

"Aw, I don't know, Frank," an embarrassed Sam said.

He leaned back and turned his head to look at the towering poplar tree posing in his huge bay window. Sam took a long drag on the cigar. Frank leaned forward on the Thinking Chaise.

"They're about as different from your regular person as anyone could possibly be. The very color of mud. The best of em, the color of dirt. Sheep wool hair. Head big as an African go-rilla. Can barely understand a damn word they say when they open those mumbling, mush-mouth lips. Those imported Mississippi Negroes might as well be speaking Latin with a jungle accent. So I don't know. They do have two arms, two legs, and I'm sure most of em got two of everything else they're supposed to have. A Soul? It's hard to say, Sam. I guess if we could see it. Like you can see the soul in the eyes of any regular new born baby. That tiny sparkle, that gleam, that lets you know this new creation is so full of light, so full of the spirit of Jesus himself. But, Sam, I ain't never seen no such light in no Negro … have you?"

Sam was still looking at the poplar tree through the bay window.

Blowing perfectly round cigar smoke circles that he knew would disappoint him before they reached the window.

"On that Skillings thing a few years back where the Colored woman drowned over in Cahokia Creek," Sam started, still looking toward the window.

"Sounds familiar."

"Remember the woman came in and said Deacon Skillings' wife wasn't no accident?"

"Yeah, yeah," Frank said.

"Well, I went down to that Calvary Church around noon because the witness gal said they finished up around one," Sam said. "I figured ol Deacon would be too shame-faced to try anything funny right there at church. Calvary ain't like some of these fancy Negro churches over there on Bond. It's just a wooden clapboard number in a cleared-out wooded-area off a little road where Missouri Ave. ends. I parked the car on Missouri, because I didn't want to get stuck on that narrow road. Nothing more than a trail. Frank, I got to walking up that trail, and I don't think I've ever heard nothing quite like it. Those Negroes were singing a song that said something about, 'Jesus got a mansion with a room just for me.' I mean that's what they kept repeating in between some moaning, hooting and hollering. I'll be damned Frank if they weren't singing with such Holy Ghost feeling that they made the hair on my neck stand up straight."

"Give me a little taste of it, Sam." Sam turned to Frank and continued.

"Like everyone else, I had come across some Negroes singing from time to time, because that's what those Negroes do when they cook and clean and such, but I'd never really paid much attention, like you don't pay much attention to birds singing outside the window. Just back background noise, know-what-i-mean? Anyway, the closer I got, the more ..."

"C'mon, detective, just a quick sample," Frank said. His bushy brow was arched like a cathedral doorway, and a wry smile was carved on his face. Frank was barely able to contain himself.

"Let's see if the Negroes can work through you to make my neck hairs stand on up."

Sam ignored his friend's teasing and pushed on with the same earnestness that was causing the teasing.

"Frank, when I got to the clearing, it was if the sound was just exploding out of that shack of a church, bouncing off the trees that was all around it. I could see the Negroes through the windows, Frank, just pouring their hearts into that song. Eyes closed, hands all raised in the air, crying, I mean tears were streaming down these Negroes faces, Frank. Crying to Jesus. 'Jee-sus got a man-sion ... with a room ... just for mee.' They just kept repeating it over and over. About the longest song I ever heard. And ... shit, Frank, I got to crying myself."

Sam fixed such a serious stare on him that Frank couldn't laugh.

Nor did he want to.

"Frank, it was like my emotions snuck up on me from behind, climbed through my back and poured out my eyes. I couldn't wipe them away fast enough. It got so bad, Frank ... I had to hurry back to the trail. I ... I was walking back to the car and ... I fell to my knees, Frank, and cried, snotty tears, chest all sore from heaving for ten full minutes. Ten minutes, Frank. Ten."

Sam turned away and looked back at the poplar tree. Frank looked out the bay window too. They were silent. Long enough for fat ashes to fall from both of their unsmoked cigars onto Sam's immaculate hard pinewood floors.

Sam turned to Frank.

"After my daddy died, we had to move in the little basement room in my grandmother's house. Wasn't big as a damn closet. Boy shouldn't have to live that close with his mama. I hated that room, Frank. When I really got down about Daddy, that damn closet, everything, Mama would read to me out of the Bible. She liked to read me the part that said God had a mansion with many rooms. Not to worry about this little ol room right now, because one day I was going to live in a big ol mansion, Frank. God had a room just for me. Just for me."

Frank just stared at his friend. Not sure what to say or do.

"Far as I know, Frank, ain't but one mansion. Once those Negroes die, if they got souls, where else can their souls go but to the same mansion that our own souls are going to go?"

Frank continued to stare. His lips slightly apart. Ashes falling from his cigar.

"If Negroes souls going to be in the same place as ours, right next door, Frank ... we ... we got to start thinking about how we treat them while they're down here with us. I mean, I just don't want some angry Negro soul, right next door to my room in the mansion, know-what-i-mean? Ain't no telling what an angry soul will do. Especially, when it's sleeping right next door. With bullet holes in em."

67

Le Roy Bundy went over his notes for the meeting. As he always did. He liked to give the impression that he was just speaking off the cuff, but almost everything he did was planned. And during times like these, it was good somebody had a plan. A plan that was going to work.

Their Wednesday meeting with Mayor Mollman had been a joke. And the joke had been on them. That clown said he thought relations with the Negroes had actually improved during June. When Dr. Mandrake, the assistant county physician, started listing the Negroes he had personally treated who had been attacked by the Aluminum Ore strikers, Mollman turned red as a bottle of soda pop. "The blood flowing to your face will not be the only blood flowing in this town if you don't do something, Mr. Mayor," Bundy snapped. Dr. Mandrake, Asar, and Mr. Sims, another dentist, all turned and glared at Le Roy. The mouth that allowed their friend to do good for The Race could undermine that work by getting them thrown out of an office before the good got done. It had happened last month in C. Locke Tarlton's office when they'd all met to discuss building the fire house down on Bond. Sure that same mouth would go back and smooth things over, as it had with Tarlton, but why go through all that? Why not just be smart and keep your mouth shut?

"You're right, your right," Bundy, head down like a bad boy forced to stand in a corner, would usually say.

The stakes were simply too high for his temper to get in the way. Tensions had been rising along with the temperature all June. Le Roy didn't think they would get through the month without the lid coming completely off. Those Aluminum Ore boys, joined by some of the fired union organizers from Armour & Co., had gotten in the habit of getting liquidy up at the Whiskey Chute, then coming out all of the bars around 5 p.m. to jump Colored workers leaving Armour and other shops on St. Clair Avenue.

Just like Mr. Sims had told Mayor Mollman, it was only a matter of time before one of these white mobs ran up on the wrong Colored man and caught some gunfire. Self-defense or not, a couple of white men get killed by a Negro man, and all hell would certainly break loose. Mr. Sims really got Mollman's attention when he said, "And hell ain't good for business, Mr. Mayor."

Le Roy had just plunked down all of his savings on the service station next to his house, and he'd be damned if he'd let someone burn it down. Not to mention his house. Unlike some of these scary Negroes fleeing across the Free Bridge to relatives in St. Louis and Ferguson, these bohunks weren't going to run him out of town.

Mr. Sims showed up first. As always. Not that Asar and Dr. Mandrake weren't prompt, it was that Mr. Sims was always a few minutes early to the meetings. Trying to control one of the few things he could in an almost uncontrollable situation.

Le Roy had been trying, for months, to get Mr. Sims to move his dental practice from tiny Alton to East St. Louis. There was more than enough work for another Negro dentist in the city.

"There's a vacant office in my building. I've already got more business than I can handle. I can just slide those folks down the hall to you. First year, until you get nice and going, I won't charge you any referral fee. After you get a good group of regulars, we can work out a deal on the referrals. You keep your name on the door, separate practices but we can buy supplies together and split the savings."

I I I

Absalom Sims was a solid 5'7", with forearms resembling drumsticks from a County Fair-winning turkey. Knotty, big-knuckled hands looked like they'd been removing teeth in a boxing ring, not a chair.

Le Roy broke the staring contest by sticking out his hand and smiling. Mr. Sims extended his own hand but not his smile.

The men walked down the foyer with pictures of Le Roy's father, Rev. Charles Bundy peering down from both sides of the wall. One, in his purple pastoral robes after being appointed a presiding elder. Another, on the steps of First AME in Cleveland with the rest of the grim-looking ministerial staff. Another with him sitting behind his big oak desk in his study. There he was shaking hands with Frederick Douglass in front of the Haytian Pavilion at the Columbian Exposition in Chicago. This foyer gallery helped remind Le Roy, each time he came home—and left—who was the real competition.

It was only quarter till 7 p.m., so no one else had arrived. Le Roy had filled his small hotel lobby-sized living room with 75 wooden folding chairs, neatly arranged auditorium-style. Mr. Sims sat in the last row against the back wall. Le Roy went directly to the bar against far wall next to the upright piano. As he poured the scotch into two glasses, embossed with a large "B" on the bottom, he glanced at Mr. Sims. Mr. Sims was sitting, left leg crossed over right, chin resting on his knuckles, looking like he was in the stands waiting for the first pitch at a baseball game. Calm. Bundy appreciated Mr. Sims' steady hand.

They were all going to need it.

Just as Le Roy was handing Mr. Sims his drink, the door bell rang. He returned to the bar. The bell rang again. Asar and Dr. Mandrake stood at the door doing a poorer job than Mr. Sims at hiding their nerves. Le Roy brought his hands from behind his back, handing each a glass of scotch.

"A little Holy Water for the Wise Men," Le Roy said, smiling.

Le Roy made his case. He wanted to help arm every Negro man in East St. Louis. Alert Chief Payne that Colored men are going to be walking patrol in their own neighborhoods, because the police haven't been able to stop the attacks on their families.

"As it is now, first thing Payne's boys do is take a Colored man's pistol from him—even when they bleeding from some white man's bullet."

"I don't see Payne going for that Le Roy," Dr. Mandrake said.

"Don't worry about Payne. He got a boss, and his boss got a boss. It's all about having something that the bosses need," Bundy said.

"Even if Governor Lowden, himself, came down here, and he probably wouldn't because that's why he sent the National Guard down, but let's just say he comes down personally and gives you the A-Okay, most of these Negroes have become so scared of their shadows, they've become shadows themselves. A gun will slip right through a shadow's hand," Asar said.

"Just because a man isn't in a big home like yours, doesn't mean he won't fight for his home. Even a raggedy house. That raggedy house is his raggedy house. We aren't the only Negro men in this city willing to fight for what's theirs," Dr. Mandrake said.

"What happens when some of these white boys open fire on these shadowy Negro patrols? These jumpy Negroes fire back. Then what? I'll tell you what: the real bohunk plan gets jump-started. They want Negroes to start shooting. That's exactly what they're hoping for, because they got 10 times more fire power—and the white man's law behind that fire power. They can massacre us in the name of self-defense," Asar said.

"What do you think, Mr. Sims," Le Roy said.

Mr. Sims hadn't said anything the whole meeting.

"Seem to me, we should wait for the other men to get here and ask them. I wouldn't risk my life on a plan I had no say so in."

"Hell, what's the point of us meeting if we don't have a plan?" Le Roy said.

"I thought the idea was to discuss ideas. Not make decisions. What if some of these fellows tonight come in and say, 'We been thinkin. Here's the plan we all gonna follow?' First thing you'd do is look at the men you came with and say, 'Who these rascals think they are?' Now, you may not say that to them, or maybe you would, being the kind of man you are, but most men, wouldn't mention it with they mouths, their actions would do all the talking."

I   I   I

About five minutes to 7 p.m., Set adjusted his eye patch and continued walking up 11th Street thinking about Bogdan Dabrowski. He couldn't shake the memory of their conversation outside of Armour. The way Bogdan looked at him like other white men did. The accusation in his voice made it sound like it was my fault Armour fired him, Set thought. *Seems like someone mentioned our interest in organizing ourselves to get better working conditions and better wages to help good white men better be able to take care of their families.*

Set hadn't seen him since, but could still hear the cutting way in which Bogdan said, "bohunks." It hurt Set. He knew his friend—his only friend—was drawing a line—and he was on the wrong side. With the rest of the job-stealing Negroes.

Thinking about Bogdan so much had helped Set decide to head over to the Bundy meeting. Even though he knew Asar would be there. Even though he wasn't ready to do a whole bunch of talking with Asar. Or with any of those other Negroes who loved to meet and talk, then stuttered when it came to action. But there was a rumor that Bundy had gotten a hold of a load of guns. True or not, Set figured it was good sign that Negroes were at least rumoring about guns, because the bohunks had been firing theirs a lot lately. Maybe it's time that I draw my own line like

Bogdan drew his, Set thought. Then he walked around to the back of Le Roy Bundy's house and knocked on the door.

"How can I ..."

"It's Set, Roy-Lee."

Le Roy couldn't quite get any words out. The years, the bald opaque skull, the veins, the eye patch.

"I'm here for the meeting. Is Asar inside?"

"Yes."

"Listen, this is not the time or place for family business, so I don't wanna deal with that now. Don't tell Asar I'm here, I'll talk to him later. I just came to hear what ya'll gonna do about bohunks jumping on Negroes all over this goddamn town. Let me sit in one of your back rooms until the meeting starts, then I'll come up front once everyone arrives."

"Alright, Set, sure, sure."

When the rest of the men began to file in, Le Roy could feel the heavinessinthe bags undertheireyes. But their voices and theupward angles of their heads did not betray it. East St. Louis is a town where hardship shapes pride. A pride that can only be earned by surviving a life not meant to be survived. A town where the exacting work eventually grinds down a man, especially a Negro man. Grinds him down like those big circular machines at Aluminum Ore, preparing him for his return to dust. The soft surfaces go first. The hard edges come next. Until only a steely smooth façade remains, similar to the ones covering these men. Cool as a long barrel of shotgun before it's fired.

"Some would have us believe that the Negro is to blame for a summer day that's too hot. Some point a finger at the Negro when the cold winter wind off the river is too cold. They say it's our fault that the small servings on their dinner tables are small servings," Bundy began.

"Ain't that the truth ... That's right."

All 75 chairs were taken and men were standing in every available space in the large living room. Leaning against the walls. Listening from the hallways, raising their voices from the back to acknowledge the times when Bundy got it right.

"Now, every man in this room is like every other man in East St. Louis. Raise your hand if you work hard on your job. Okay. Keep em up if you got to pay taxes out of your hard-earned money. Alright. Keep those hands up if all you want to do is just take care of your family and be left the hell alone. Now look around. Go ahead and put your hands down.

That's why we're here tonight. I sure don't have to tell anyone the state of things in this city. A city that keeps running, in part, because of the hard work we put in. The city some have been trying to convince us that we're not welcome in, even though many of us were here before some of these folks ever heard of a place called America."

"Say that, say that!"

"Now, I got some ideas about how we can go about working together to make sure we don't get run out of our own town, but I want to hear what you all think we should do."

"Jump those bohunks on street cars!"

"Wait for em with pipes, outside they jobs, when they've done worked all day."

"Shoot all up in they house when they're having dinner with they wives and babies!"

"Oh, ya'll don't wanna just crawl across the Free Bridge with the tails, they're sure you got, tucked between your legs?" Bundy shouted above the shouters.

"Nooo!"

"Ya'll don't wanna tell your wives, 'Pack up the kids, white man say this is his town. Don't worry baby, God's gotta a mansion waiting for us in heaven?'"

"Nooo!"

"Now, I must say that all those good ideas have certainly crossed my mind, and may in fact be the way to go, but first let me tell you what I was thinking."

Le Roy went on to tell the men (and Nutilda, the only woman in the room who insisted on coming and when Keb said, "no," threatened to walk to the meeting alone after he left) his plan which consisted of the men walking armed patrols with Chief Payne's full-knowledge. He explained that he had already arranged for the guns. "How you gonna get ol Chief Payne to let us walk around with guns when first thing these police men do is take a Negro's gun right from him," Nema Americus said, from his front row chair.

"That was the second thought that crossed my mind when …" "What was the first?" Nema interrupted.

"How to convince the people in this room that I could definitely make Chief Payne go for this. My third thought," Le Roy said, then paused, taking his eyes off of Nema and scanning the room. "My third thought, was given all the odds against us, how many of the Negro men in this town are going to be willing to take up arms against white men, to defend the homes that they pay for by allowing foremen to trample their dignity 10 hours a day? I thought, how many men will take up arms to defend their wives' right to ride the damn street car without white men pulling them off by their hair and tearing their dresses off in the street? I wondered how many men, who would shoot another Negro over a five-dollar poker pot, would raise a pistol at a white man who was trying to run his black ass straight out of town?"

Then with dramatic flair, Le Roy raised both his arms wide and high above his head. An East St. Boogie Moses. There was a commotion in the long, crowded hallway that led to the back of the house. The attention of the room shifted from Le Roy to the hallway. A man in a black suit, black shirt, and black tie emerged straining under a baby coffin-shaped pine box raised in both hands over his head. Directly behind him was another identically dressed man with a matching pine box high above his head. Then another. And another. There were eight in all.

Chairs and bodies slid to the side so the first pallbearer could get through the crowded room. He gently placed the baby coffin in front of Le Roy who still had his arms up high and wide. The next man gently placed his box along side the other coffin. The third stacked his atop. This continued, in silence, until only Le Roy's head and up-raised arms were visible behind the coffins.

Le Roy slowly rested his hands on the pine box closest to him. He undid the small latch, yanked open the coffin lid and snatched a rifle high above his head. He undid the latch on the other casket and pulled out a brick-sized box of bullets. He held them both skyward. From that position, he slowly scanned the men's silent faces for a full minute. He knew most of the men had their own guns but, being a preacher's kid, he also knew the power of collective ritual to spread collective responsibility.

"What man in this room is ready to have their wife look at them with that same respect she had on their wedding night?" Le Roy started, just above a whisper. "What man in this room is ready to stop telling his son empty lessons about what a man is, and ready to start showing his son what a man is?"

Sitting in the first row, Nema stood up his creaking body. He took two steps toward Le Roy. In silence, they locked eyes. Le Roy handed him the rifle and box of bullets. Nema turned to face the room. He carefully raised the rifle over his head. Then he lowered his tired body back into his seat.

Le Roy Bundy then reached inside the baby casket and grabbed a rifle. Before he could fully raise it above his head another man had stepped up. A spontaneous line formed. Silently. As if the gravity of arming themselves had forced their mouths shut.

"Give me two," Nutilda said, breaking the quiet.

Le Roy smiled at his best friend's wife. He grabbed two rifles and two boxes of bullets. Laid them across her open arms like a sleeping child.

It took almost an hour for the crowd of over a hundred men and one woman to whittle down to Mr. Tuppan. Le Roy handed him the gun and ammunition. When Jake turned to sit down, that's when Le Roy saw Set had joined them by standing at the mouth of the back hallway. His pale, bald skull looking like the frosted glass around a street light. Asar followed his friend's eyes to the back hallway. So did Nutilda. She fought the urge to run toward Set. Keb looked away. But he had to look back again. Set avoided all of his family's stares. Everyone just kept their distance.

"Glad you could join us, Set," Le Roy shouted. "Got something for you." Bundy reached into the pine box.

"Got plenty," Set shouted back.

The men and Nutilda spent the next couple hours huddled around several maps of East St. Louis. Trying to figure out which of them lived close to each other and what their work schedules were so they could set up joint patrols in the Negro parts of town.

Le Roy wasn't going answer the ringing telephone. But it was past 10 o'clock at night and it rarely rang this late. The men were still spread across the living room in neighborhood-based huddles, crouched around the maps. Le Roy stood up and walked to the nightstand, picked up the phone. It was Mrs. Jackson, Sam Jackson's wife. Mr. Jackson was huddled over a map across the room. The Jacksons were Le Roy's dental patients; they lived down on 10th Street. She was screaming into her receiver so loud that her high-pitched voice screeched through Le Roy's receiver into the living room.

"They're shooting, they're shooting! They're riding down the street shooting! They shot up the Americus place."

The Jacksons lived four doors from Americus & Son. "Sam! Asar!" Bundy yelled across the room.

There had never been a sight like it in East St. Louis: Over a hundred rifle-toting Negro men (and one Negro woman) running down Bond Ave. When Sam, Le Roy, and Asar rounded the corner onto 10th Street they could feel the shards of glass beneath their feet. The Americus & Son picture window facing Bond Ave. had been completely shattered. Asar rushed inside to check on Auset. Across the street. Jimmy Townsend's windows had also been shot out. Sam Jackson kept running right to his house. The two foot by two foot glass window on his door had been shot out. Asar, Nutilda, Keb and the three men who lived on 10th and the surrounding area rushed to their homes. Le Roy ran to the top of the 33 Americus & Son stairs. He made a megaphone of his pudgy hands.

"For now, let's all spread out down 10th in case they make another pass."

The men began to fan out in both directions down 10th. Sam came running back through the men. He bounded up the steps.

"Mary was sitting on the porch trying to cool off when she saw em driving up the street real slow. Praise God, she had good sense nough to get inside. Said it looked like one of those Ford models."

As the men were still fanning out, Le Roy megaphoned his hands again, "Look for a Ford car."

Inside Americus & Son, a breathless Asar pushed open their bedroom door and found Auset sound asleep. Lying on her back, looking like the moon itself was rising beneath her maternity night gown.

Their bedroom was upstairs, in the back of the house. If it had been on the porch, the ruckus wouldn't have woken her, Asar thought. Auset slept like a railroad spike. Getting out of bed one night, he had knocked over the lamp on the night stand, smashing it on the hardwood floor. Auset didn't even roll over. It had been worse since she'd been pregnant. Carrying that big ol baby tuckered her out.

So all Asar could do was smile and watch his wife's big belly rise and fall with each breath. Like his mother Nutilda, she would want to be in the middle of the action (he had to invoke their unborn child's safety to make her stay home and not come to the meeting). She was safer asleep. He locked the door from the inside and stepped out.

Outside, the men lined both sides of 10th Street near Bond Ave. They stood about 15 feet apart. Some with the barrels of their rifles leaning back against their shoulders. Others with their rifles raised shoulder-level. Many shifting their weight from right foot to left foot with nervous energy. Preparing for what could not be prepared for.

Le Roy stood at the base of the Americus & Son steps. His rifle leaning back on his shoulder. He had just returned from walking back and forth along 10th Street talking to the men. Asar and Set stood in silence on the porch, watching. There was no talk about the past. That could come later. The present was too pressing.

For all the bustle of the last hour, Asar was struck by the quiet. Only the trains spoke and they didn't count because trains don't fire guns. Their rumblings and occasional whistles were just a part of the humid, July night air.

Two identical twins who were no longer identical stood side-by-side looking out towards trains that didn't count and a future they couldn't see.

Sam and Frank sat at the small card table playing blackjack with wooden matches for greenbacks. This is how they usually passed time in the station when the nights were slow. But the nights had not been slow for weeks. Since the troubles back in May, it seemed like they ran around East St. Louis either pulling white men off Negroes or pulling pearl-handled pistols from Negroes' coats—before they went and shot one of those fool white men.

That was the part of the job that Sam hated. Now, every man had a right to protect himself. Especially in a town like East St. Louis. But he'd be damned if he'd let Negroes go around shooting up white men on his watch. Negroes uppity enough as is. There were already seven Negroes on the 70-man force. Although the Negroes were just officers, they had to work plainclothes because the sight of the Negro in a police uniform in East St. Louis was not going to fly. Uniform or not, the very idea of a Negro policeman irked Sam. Even if Chief Payne did limit their police work to Negro parts of town.

But what if one of these Negroes got full of himself and started talking about his rights as an officer? What if a Negro started patting down white women? Arresting white men. That was the plum craziest thing Sgt. Detective Sam Coppedge had ever heard. It was also dangerous as hell. First time a nigger even move like he's going to think about arresting a white man, the good white citizens of the town would take to the streets—with ropes in their hands.

"Well, Sam, have you made up your mind if you wanna another card or do you need the clock to strike midnight to move you into action?"

"Sorry there, yeah, give me another ... Frank, would you just quit if the Chief started letting Negroes arrest white men?"

"You're busted, and you've just been a regular newsman lately with all the questions."

"Well, would you?"

"Just kindly push my match sticks over here. I like when you play reporter, because it helps confirm that I'm the best blackjack player in the department and hell no, I wouldn't quit. I'd just do my civic duty to make sure that no Negro could stick around long enough to arrest a single solitary white man."

Frank started dealing the next hand.

"But say the Negro's got a good nose for crime, and he well could being a Negro and all. Say he can help identify some of these bad Negroes around here that go around robbing people, robbing stores, trying to take what the white man has before he even got time to enjoy it good. Now, that's a Negro with some usefulness wouldn't you say?"

"Sam Coppedge," Frank said, leaning back in his chair looking hard at his best friend. "Are you sitting here telling me that it would be okay for a Negro to be arresting white women?"

Sam was silent.

"A nigger, Sam? Give a Negro a gun when you know, you know, first time no one's looking he'll be the one doing the robbing. It's in their blood, Sam. You know it and I know it. Now stop all this foolish talk and look at your cards and tell me if you ..."

The ringing phone cut Frank off.

"Your turn, Frank."

Frank got up and walked to the phone sitting on the desk against the far wall.

"Police. Detective Wodley ... You saw em with you own eyes? ... Still there? ... About how many of them? ... You sure they were guns?"

That's when Sam reached for his jacket.

Even though Frank was sure the reporter riding on the running board could hear, Frank started teasing Sam from the moment he started the car.

"Maybe they're just practicing their police maneuvers, Sam."

In the passenger seat, Sam just kept looking straight ahead. Widow Jenkins probably called the department more than in other single person in East St. Louis. An old woman living by herself, she could be a little jumpy.

Tenth Street had added some color over the past few years, especially down near Bond. Hell, she probably had a right to be a little jumpy, Frank thought as they drove. But then again, the numerous visits over the years had shown her to have more than a little problem with exaggeration. Frank and Sam still laugh about the time she called completely out of breath, barely able to get out that, "The nigras are gathering outside. They … they're about to make a rush on my house!"

When Frank and Sam arrived, the attacking nigras were four or five hungry Negroes huddled around ol Witherspoon's sweet potato cart.

But still, tonight on the phone, she had told Frank there were hundreds of Negroes walking along 10th Street armed with rifles. Even if she is exaggerating, what if there were only 25? Twenty- five armed Negroes is 24 too many, Frank thought as they passed 9th Street.

"Maybe you can deputize them on the spot to join the other seven darkies on the force," Frank teased on. "Maybe the Chief will promote you to captain so you can run your own special division. Call it 'Darkie Division'. Or 'Colored Copper Division'. What about 'Purple Patroller Divis—'"

The first bullet whizzed right under Frank's walrus-shaped nose, blasted into Sam's left cheek, exiting out the right cheek, and through the passenger window, taking the lower part of Sam's jaw with it. Frank didn't really hear that first rifle blast until he saw the passenger window sucking his buddy's jaw out into the humid air. If he had been thinking or if there had been time to think, Frank would have immediately sped away, because the car was only going 20 miles per hour. Or maybe, if there was time to think, his brain would have directed him to slam the brakes, throw the car in reverse and speed away backwards. Frank did none of these things. Because it wasn't his mind that was leading him.

When the window began to suck his best friend's face into the night, Frank's hands instinctively left the wheel and reached for Sam's face. As if he could have been quick enough to save a molar. A bit of jaw bone. A piece of flesh. The car angled towards the sidewalk. He couldn't even pull his loose-neck friend's head from hanging limply out the window, because a hot bullet struck Frank Wodley in the palm, making him snatch his hand back and come to his senses. He had to get out of there.

"Gooo!"

Frank thought it was his on voice screaming, but it was the reporter, crouching on the running board, yelling over and over again, "Go! … Go!

... Go! ..." The gun shots started as muted whispers, then grew louder and faster with each half-second. By the time Frank was able to get his left hand on the wheel and mash the accelerator, jerking the car away from the curb, so many bullets were hitting the Ford police car that it sounded, from the inside, like a dozen frantic blacksmiths hammering away on the vehicle. Pure adrenaline allowed Frank to straighten the hard-to-turn steering wheel and hit the first right turn onto Bond Avenue.

Tenth Street was full with so much gun smoke that you could hear the sound of men coughing up and down the street. Then there was just post-gunshot silence.

Asar lowered his rifle. Set, his pistol. The twins inhaling the gun-powdered-air on the porch, where they used to take flight. They were still. Silent. They didn't have to look at each other to know that they were thinking the same thing: this is not going to turn out good.

68

1927
EAST ST. LOUIS, ILLINOIS

It was Keb's second kiss that did it. Set stumbled to his left knee. Seeing her husband stumble broke Nephthys from her stupor. She rushed to Set's shoulder. She felt his muscular body tremble under her fingers. Father and wife eased Set down onto his back. Before he was completely stretched out, the family was kneeling around him—except for Grandpa Nema who stood his ground in the doorway.

"Now, now, get back some goddamnit, get back, he'll be awright, if ya give him room to catch his damn breath."

In a rare family moment, everyone ignored Nema Americus.

Set lay there on the porch with his one eye looking up at his family. It seemed like he was spying on them from some secret place. Behind a horizontal trap door with a keyhole. Through it, he could see Nephthys leaning over him, her milky skin stretched and tense like a sheep-skin drum. Next to her, Keb, his usually serious face was misty and soft. In that way a father looks down at his newborn for the first time.

Set saw the his family reshuffle above him and the next thing he knew he was flying. Floating off the ground.

Am I dead? he thought.

Or was he speaking aloud? He wasn't sure. But he was sure that his body was cold and wet. He was shivering. His head felt somehow both heavy and light. As his face rose slowly through the air towards the porch ceiling, the back of his head began to throb. It felt like sharp prongs were stuck into his bald scalp. He tilted his neck back a little and saw the underside of Heru's chin. Set was confused. But he was moving now. Floating through the porch door in the hands of Americus Family pallbearers. No casket. He watched the white sky moving above him. His legs tilted up and he started rising at an angle. Was there really a heaven? How can you go to heaven when you don't believe in it?

He wanted to make the flying stop. But he couldn't.

Set landed on his bed. His eye still looking straight up at a new white sky. As he felt his boots being unlaced, he heard footsteps leave the room.

"I'm in my bedroom."

He wanted to turn and look to see exactly what was happening.

He couldn't turn his head.

"Something's wrong with me," he thought. But he felt his lips moving. "Am I talking?"

Everyone seemed to be ignoring him.

Set felt his socks come off. His coveralls sliding off his shoulder. No one was speaking. Occasionally, a hand or elbow or chin would come into his field of view. His coveralls slid down his torso, past his bare feet, leaving him in his undershirt and underpants. He saw Keb take the bejeweled knife out his pocket.

"Heru, toss these in the laundry room," he heard Keb say. Heru was distracted by the gold handle's glimmering ruby.

"What good is a shiny knife if it couldn't help my daddy," Heru said.

"Gone, boy," Grandpa Keb said.

Heru squatted down and began to gather the long-legged muddy denim. As he stood up and began walking towards the door, he noticed that the right pant leg, hanging over his arm, was stiffened with dried mud. Carrying the unruly bundle, he could barely see his feet stepping down the steep, curving staircase. At the bottom, he saw Grandma Nutilda and his mother Auset huddled on the couch, arms over shoulders.

❚ ❚ ❚

Heru used his left foot to kick open the laundry room's swinging door. When he dumped the dirty coveralls into the wicker hamper, the right pant leg hung stiff over the rim.

Heru went to knock it back in the hamper and immediately knew it wasn't the dried mud making it stiff. He stuck his boney arm up the leg. Felt the long pocket sewn inside. Heru took the coveralls out and reached down through the waist. His fingers grazed the small horizontal zipper. He unzipped it and pulled out the folded scroll of white butcher paper.

He knew it was a map before he unfolded it and unrolled it on the pine floor. Being raised in a house full of map makers, he knew that if the treasure was valuable sometimes you buried the map. Hid the guide. In the earth. In an earthen jar. Inside a secret pocket in a muddy pair of coveralls.

On his knees, he leaned forward and placed his nose near the word, "TALLEST PINE."

He knew it was blood.

"Whose blood made you?" he whispered to the map.

There wasn't much of a smell, but he smelled it again anyway. The way he loved to smell the ink on one of Grandpa Keb's freshly finished maps. When Grandpa Keb was about to complete a map, he would call Heru into his office. On his tippy toes, Heru would look over his grandfather's shoulder watching his meticulous hand go from ink jar to map, from ink jar to map. When the last mark was made, Keb would look at Heru.

"A light to travel by."

"Can I smell the light?"

Grandfather and grandson would share a good chuckle. A laugh that comes from the joy of completion. From the sharing of passions. The passing down of tradition.

Heru would walk from behind his grandfather's chair to the side of his wagon-bed-sized desk and carefully bring his onyx nose, a nostril hair's length from the wet map.

"Smells like treasure."

This was their way. Their private ritual.

I I I

Heru liked to imagine that his relationship with his father could be like it was with his Uncle Set or Grandpa Keb. So when he leaned down to smell the "TALLEST PINE" again, he imagined it was his father's map.

"Smells like treasure."

Like many treasure maps, this one had secret code words like "TRUNK" and "HEAD". Heru liked these maps the best because the mysterious codes made the treasure hunting more exciting.

But Heru was most excited to see "TOR" neatly written at the bottom of the map. He knew the area well. On his fifth birthday, Heru had been excited when Uncle Set and his father Asar decided to include him on their decision to honor Dr. Mandrake with an annual ceremony. His father told him it was a secret—with its own secret code word "TOR." It was the only private thing that he, his father and his Uncle Set shared together.

They had cut the tree down themselves in the small in wooded-area where the totem now stands. They blackened the outer bark by laying it horizontal on five saw horses and setting small fires. Turning it occasionally like they were roasting the longest pig in he world.

When the 30-foot-log cooled, Asar chiseled DR. MANDRAKE down the pole. The well-spaced letters were the size of a grown man's head. They painted the carved out letters in bright white paint. At night, it looked like the name—and memory—of DR. MANDRAKE was haunting the forest.

Heru figured that the map, with all the different coordinates, must have been a map for different parts of a Winchester. Winchester rifles were Uncle Set's hobby. He had over two dozen. He was especially fond of those new Winchesters he'd just bought at Rayton's down on Broadway. As soon as they'd returned home, Uncle Set had started disassembling the rifle to see if Heru could put it back together again. That was one of the things they did together. Uncle Set would often say beforehand, "A Winchester rifle's a powerful thing, son. Learning how to take apart power and rebuild power, learning how power works, will teach you a lot about life."

Last year, Uncle Set made a pirate game of it by burying the parts of a disassembled Winchester in the backyard, then gave Heru a map.

"If you can find the pieces of the rifle and put it together in an hour, I'll give you a silver dollar," Uncle Set said.

It took Heru almost two hours, because there were so many pieces to find, clean, and put back together. Heru didn't get the silver dollar, but he'd had fun anyway combining his map-reading-skills with his power-making-skills. The map Uncle Set gave him that day resembled the map he was looking at now. He thought maybe "TRUNK" was code for stock and "HEAD" was code for buttplate.

Heru just couldn't believe Uncle Set would leave Bloody Island without his Winchester. He figured Uncle Set had found the man who took his rifle—and used it on him—and used the man's blood to create the map. Uncle Set didn't want to get in trouble, so he took the power apart and buried it.

"That's how the map got written in blood," Heru whispered.

He was barely able to contain his pirate-mystery-solving-skills pride.

Maybe I could get the Winchester for Uncle Set, Heru thought. Do something good to help him feel better—and stay out of trouble. Maybe I could find Daddy too. Just because Uncle Set couldn't find him didn't mean that Daddy was … maybe he's just hiding.

"Maybe, he's just scared," Heru said. "I've been scared plenty of times."

Heru carefully folded the map. Put it in his pocket. Took a deep breath. He pushed open the laundry room door and headed back upstairs, thinking about how he was gonna sneak out the house— and make things better—and keep Uncle Set of trouble.

Heru stopped in the doorway of Uncle Set's & Auntie Nephthys' bedroom. Grandma Nut was pulling the covers up to Uncle Set's neck. Although July humidity was thick in the bedroom, Heru watched his Uncle Set tremble beneath covers. Grandpa Keb stood next to the bed with his hands on his hips.

I   I   I

Heru stood there watching in the doorway for almost a full minute. No one noticed he had returned. He backed out the door frame.

Heru walked down the hall to his own bedroom. From the top drawer of his dresser, he pulled out the wooden DO NOT ENTER sign that he had painted himself. It had pirate's skulls before DO and crossbones after ENTER. He hung it on the outside doorknob by an old shoestring. Then closed the door. One benefit of being a boy who's wrong: family knows to leave you alone when you want to be wrong by yourself.

Heru went to his closet and got his leather treasure hunter bag, which had skulls and crossbones etched on each side. He put in Seker, his compass. Heru liked to name his birthday gifts. Seker was his own spelling of seeker. It was the perfect name, because the compass helped him seek out treasures buried in the earth. Helped him bring the dead above ground.

He also put in Tehuti, his hand-shovel. Named after Mr. Tehuti, his fourth grade teacher who Heru thought was the wisest man in all of East St. Louis. Seemed like he could answer any question, uncover anything, unearth any mystery. Heru imagined his hand- shovel unearthing mysteries too.

Along with Seker and Tehuti, Heru placed Uncle Set's map in the treasure hunter bag and hid it in the back of the closet. He went to his dresser and picked out his clothes for his adventure: brown knee pants, tan shirt and brown boots. And his version of a disguise: brown apple cap which he planned to pull low. He laid the clothes on top of his toy box then changed into his night shirt.

Heru climbed in bed. Turned on his side, making a pillow out of his hands. He lay on his side and made himself close his eyes. But just like on every night before Christmas, Heru knew he wouldn't be going to sleep anytime soon. Behind his closed eyes, he imagined finding his father hiding somewhere and letting him know that everything was going to be alright. That it was okay to be scared. That he'd been scared himself many times. That it was okay to come home. Heru imagined bringing the pieces of Uncle Set's Winchester back to him. Maybe they could put it back together as a whole family.

Everyone talking. Everyone working together. Behind his closed eyes, Heru imagined that he could do something good. Something so right that it could stop him from being so wrong.

"That would be like Christmas-time in the summer," he whispered.

❙ ❙ ❙

There was just a hint of daylight when Heru awoke. He hadn't even remembered falling asleep. He swung his legs on to the floor and raced over to the closet. Grabbed his treasure hunter bag. Placed it next to his clothes to make doubly-sure he wouldn't forget it.

After he got dressed, Heru cracked the door and stuck his head out. Tip-toed down the hallway in the direction of Bloody Island.

When he got outside, he was relieved no one in the family had noticed him. And disappointed for the same reason.

With his treasure hunter bag over his shoulder, Heru headed down 10th Street with his brown apple cap pulled low. Not much reason for it yet, since it was still early dawn. Tenth Street near Bond Avenue was quiet except for a gray-bearded, Colored man stacking steaming sweet potatoes in his push cart. He didn't even look up when Heru walked past.

Since Heru had joined his father and Uncle Set five times on their annual pilgrimage to the Tomb of Remembrance, he felt confident that he'd be able to find the area again. They had always taken a route that went along the Free Bridge. He remembered how afraid he had been walking in the shadow of the huge structure. Thinking if it tipped over, it would land on him and break him into tiny, tiny pieces. On Heru's first trip, he had begun to cry. He wrapped both his arms around Asar's leg.

"I'm scared, Daddy." Uncle Set chuckled.

"Like father, like son."

Asar slapped Heru's arms off his leg.

"Stop crying."

❙ ❙ ❙

There would be no crying this time.

Heru felt like a big boy as he walked towards the Free Bridge. His first time striking out alone into East St. Louis. He didn't feel like a 10-year-old, froggy-eyed, sissy boy. With his cap pulled deep over his brow, no one could even see his eyes, even with his chin up. He knew that a big boy walked with his head held high. Especially a big boy in the Americus Family.

"I'm gonna make my family have a big smile every time they look at me," Heru confidently said out to the Free Bridge.

"I'm gonna find my Daddy and make him wanna give me a big hug when he sees that I found Uncle Set's Winchester all by myself. Then we're gonna walk into the house with our heads held high and the whole family is gonna put that Winchester together. You just wait and see, Mr. Bridge."

Heru passed the ramp of the Free Bridge and began walking along side it. The farther he walked, the more the Free Bridge seemed to become the Monster Bridge. Its massive steel legs held the bridge 219 feet above the Mississippi River on its way to Missouri. Heru stopped and stared up into the bridge's underbelly. It looked to Heru like it could gobble him up and no one would ever know where he'd disappeared to. Swallowed by a steel monster with no mouth. The thought made him walk faster.

"This ain't no time to be scared," he said aloud to calm his nerves.

Just the kind of thing his father would have said to him. He slowed his pace.

Heru veered from the bridge's shadow and began walking across the marshy wetlands.

It was almost 7 a.m. when Heru approached a thicket of trees that looked like a small forest. He immediately recognized the location. He knew the Totem of Remembrance was just about 25 yards within the perimeter of the wooded-area.

He thought about the first time that his father and Uncle Set brought him. How in silence they had walked around this pole seven times. The moist look in his father's eyes. Heru had tried not to stare but couldn't help repeatedly looking up at him.

Heru remembered feeling jealous. The way a son does when a father shows another little boy too much attention.

Heru wanted to moisten his father's eyes.

Maybe I should die like Dr. Mandrake, he'd thought then. Living in Americus & Son had taught him that the deceased became more dearly after they'd departed.

69

The Americus Family finally came together in the living room after 2 a.m. early Monday morning. They needed to think through what their next move should be. Keb barely looked at Set during the conversation. Neither did Nutilda. They decided that Keb and Grandpa Nema should accompany Nutilda on the 9:30 train to Chicago in the morning. Since Auset could go into labor any hour now, she couldn't travel. Set, who had returned to Bloody Island to check on his place, would return in the morning to watch over Auset and Americus & Son with Asar. Both Nut and Grandpa Nema initially fought the plan because they wanted to stay too. Keb finally convinced them.

When Asar trudged up to their bedroom, Auset was still sleeping atop the covers. Asar silently undressed and lay next to her. She didn't even stir. He turned to his side and looked at the only girl he had ever loved.

He was exhausted but another hour passed and he still couldn't sleep. Asar was proud that East St. Louis Negroes had stood together and defended the neighborhood. Yet, he was uneasy, because he didn't know if those men in the black Ford would come back the next night. Or during the day. He needed to talk to Set before the rest of the family left in the morning. He figured Set was tossing and turning in bed too. Asar slipped out of bed, dressed quietly and walked into the East St. Louis night, heading towards Bloody Island.

I I I

Chief Payne had several of the officers push the police car onto the lawn in front of the station. Concerned that Sam's mother would see the car, Jonesy and Leftwich volunteered to clean the blood splattered across the seats, dashboard, and windows. Chief Payne wouldn't let them. He wanted everyone to see what these Negroes had done. Wanted them see the blood and count the 54 bullet holes on the car's frame. To run their index fingers around the rim of each hole as they counted. Like he had done himself. Chief Ransom Payne wanted the good white citizens of East St. Louis to become intimate with these holes and who had caused them.

He wanted them know that bloodletting demanded bloodletting, like liberty demanded bloodletting. He wanted them to patriotically praise the blood. Pledge allegiance to the blood in Jesus' name.

The car seemed magnetized. As if the 54 bullet holes were really black holes, each with its own gravitational pull. Each with a specialty in attracting different types of people. There were the groups of ladies who worked as secretaries in the City Hall building. The ones who arrived just after dawn, before the early-bird men who ran the city. The women with keys who opened the doors and prepared the office for the decision-makers. These women, with their floppy, wide-brimmed hats and high-neck dresses, gathered in a semi-circle around the car. But careful not to get too close. Chief Payne had stationed Jonesy out front to tell the story of those 54 bullet holes.

"Went to help some Negroes up there on Bond and they told em, 'We don't need your help white man. Got our own guns'. Then, I guess to show us all whose city this really is, who's boss here, those Negroes just started opening fire on white men sworn to protect them. Killed two good men," Jonesy told the secretaries.

"My word," said the brunette secretary, bringing palm to mouth. The bullet holes quieted boisterous school children on their way to school. Jonsey, who himself had three rambunctious boys, was struck at how quiet the passing kids would get. None of the ooohing and ahhhing that he was so familiar with. Each group of playful school children who approached stopped playing at the sight of the Stigmata Ford.

There was one group that was the most magnetically drawn to the car. It was the group that Chief Payne had in mind when had the boys push the car onto the lawn in front of the station. These men were not quiet when they walked up in groups of five. Groups of seven. Nor did they keep moving along because they had nowhere to go. These were out-of-work Aluminum Ore men. Their strike broken. Their jobs under the hands of another.

Word spread fast among them. They went knocking on each other's doors. Passing the word that had been passed to them. Some came with their pistols already stuffed in their pockets.

It wasn't just the men from Aluminum Ore. These Aluminum Ore men lived right next to former Swift meatpacking men. Former Armour men. Men, four to a room, who couldn't find work, because they'd been blacklisted for standing up for their human dignity. Because owners were importing these Negroes. Because Negroes would do the work at half the wage. These were the men who showed up around the Holy Ford, right around the time they should've been showing up for work somewhere. These white men with more vowels in their names than dollars in their pockets. Men who gathered around the car now by the dozens shouted at each other with nickel shot-breath.

"Negroes shooting policemen now!"

"Come up here, start smelling themselves real good till they just got no respect for the law!"

"Taking white man's livelihood wasn't enough for these Negroes."

"Wasn't satisfied till they took some white lives too!"

"I'm not gonna wait around here and let these Negroes take what's rightfully mine, no, sir!"

70

Just after 10 a.m., over a hundred armed white men gathered on 4th Street and Collinsville to wait for the street car. Since it was two days before the 4th of July, Independence Day bunting hung from the doors of businesses along Collinsville. The red, white and blue bunting also hung from the front of each streetcar.

The sight of a growing armed crowd caused people to come out of the businesses lining Collinsville. Merchants were concerned about violence affecting their shops. There had been skirmishes but nothing big like the troubles back at the end of May. In June, talk of the Negro problem had dominated the Collinsville Avenue Merchants Association meeting. After two hours of heated argument, the only thing they could agree on was that they wished the Negro problem would go away. So when Norm McKay stepped out of McKay's Pharmacy, there on the corner of 4th and Collinsville, he was alarmed and hopeful. He wished the Negroes would just leave, but he certainly didn't want any more people to get hurt. Besides all that hollering and shooting was horrible for business. One of those fires in May could have jumped onto his pharmacy, he thought standing on the crowded sidewalk watching the gunmen joke and jostle. Bad enough, in May, a rock had busted his picture window. Who had to pay for it? Norman K. McKay that's who? Mr. McKay wanted to shout to the men who were now gathering on the street in front of his pharmacy, "Take it somewhere else." But as he struggled to find just the right thing to say, a hearty cheer went up from the still growing band of armed citizens in the street. The Collinsville Avenue street car was rumbling down the track in their direction.

As the street car began to slowly began to approach, the men began to tightly cluster around the place where it would eventually come to a stop. In their excitement, many jostled for a closer position.

Mr. McKay had hoped there would be no Negroes on the car when he first saw it coming down the line, but that sure was wishful thinking with these Mississippi Negroes arriving at the Relay Station by the dozens. On some days, when he looked out the pharmacy window, it seemed that 1/3 of the street car riders on Collinsville were Negroes. The street car coming to a slow stop was no exception.

Dr. Mandrake had jumped off the street car just as it started to slow down. "Very fortunate," he said aloud as he walked briskly back up Collinsville. Usually, on the street car he liked to close his eyes and feel the air brushing across his face. He liked to imagine he was in a private motor car with his own driver. The assistant county physician should have his own private car. A man who saves lives on the county's behalf should have a car provided to him by the county. Or at the very least be paid a salary whereby he could purchase a motor car befitting a man of his stature, Dr. Mandrake would often think aboard the street car. Then, as was his custom, he would sit with his eyes closed, imagining he was being driven to see a patient in the roomy seat of a well-appointed vehicle. Maybe a Hupmobile. He'd offer respectful nods to Negroes as they'd smile and wave when his motor car passed.

Dr. Mandrake would get so caught up in these day dreams, sometimes he would miss his street car stop and have to hurriedly jump off and double-back on foot. But on this day, he was not in his imagined Hupmobile. With the whites making things so hard on Negroes of late, the street cars had become increasingly testy, and he didn't feel so comfortable slipping so deeply into his mind. Good thing, because as the train was beginning to approach the 4th Street stop, he could see a boisterous crowd of men right there in the middle of the street. It just gave him a bad feeling. Especially with the shooting on 10th and Bond last night. So he just jumped right off the street car and headed up Collinsville in the other direction.

❙ ❙ ❙

"I should have stayed my ass in bed last night," Asar said aloud, thinking about his wife. After arriving at Set's and talking until dawn, they had started back towards Americus & Son. The twins didn't get far before they ran into another set of twins—mayhem and chaos. They fled into the wooded-area just outside of Bloody Island. Asar looked at the back of his brother's bald head as they made their way through the pines, oaks and spruces. Smoke and gun fire filled the air above them. They were trapped. Again.

"What the hell?" Set said, stopping and turning around face to his brother.

"Hyena probably."

"Don't think so. Sound …"

The sound that ricocheted through the dense forest made them both quiet. Even the stoutest man could get a little spooked in these types of thickets. Reverberating and echoing off trees, forest sounds were amplified and could seem to be coming from several directions at once.

It was a very high-pitched, long, warbling kind of wild animal cry. It felt familiar. That was it. The recognition that silenced them both: It was human.

I   I   I

Dr. Mandrake didn't pass out. Instead, he felt his spirit pass up and out of his body. It was like he was back in medical school observing an operation. Detached. Studious. Calm. That's what made him such a good doctor. Being able to step back and get a better perspective. Step back and think for the patient who was in no condition to think for himself.

The other interns teased him. The Stiff. A nickname born out of jealousy, he always thought, because he was at the top of his class. Besides, a patient is always more concerned about the skill of the doctor than the flair of his personality.

Detachment works. It allows the physician to be led by his training not his emotions. If he had a nickel for every time a fellow student flinched when an artery was hit and blood started shooting and flying everywhere he'd be as rich as Mr. Armour. That's not even mentioning the three fainters he'd witnessed with his own eyes. Imagine! Fainting during surgery. Now would a patient want to have charm by the bedside or equilibrium? Besides, detachment just works. That fellow down there with blood gushing out his ear cavity should try it, he thought. Just pull back. Pull back until you're so far inside yourself that the person outside is someone else.

I   I   I

Set and Asar were both lying flat on their stomachs. The front of their shirts and pants covered with moist soil and crushed leaves from shimmying along the damp ground for the last twenty yards it took to reach the thicket's eastern outer-rim. The lightly vibrating earth below their chests let them know that a distant train was coming.

Set was stiff as a Americus & Son client. A rigor mortis that did not extend to his good eye lid. It was blinking rapidly. Trying to blink away the sight of Bogdan standing over Dr. Mandrake.

Hidden behind bushes and trees, Set's blinking eye was starting to water, but he couldn't dislodge the vision of Dr. Mandrake. He was naked from the waist up, hands tied behind his back, puffy left eye swollen completely shut, blood pouring out his right ear hole, his gaze fixed on the ground before him—where his right ear lay.

Like Dr. Mandrake, Set was transfixed by the ear. An extremity separated by the body received a new life in death. Resurrected from the ordinary, the overlooked, it was now irresistible to a stare. Possessing the power to draw all men to it. Like the gaggle of out of work Armour & Co. and Aluminum Ore men posing in a half moon around Dr. Mandrake—as a photographer prepared to capture their picnic grins and index fingers pointing down to the born-again ear.

"Wait a minute now, boys," Bogdan Dabrowski said, breaking from his finger-pointing pose.

Bogdan had a minute to wait, because former Armour & Co. union organizers had lots of time on their hands.

Warren T. Markesian stood up from behind the black blocky camera throwing frustrated hands into the humid sky.

"Damnit, I'm just about ready, get back over there!"

Warren had gone to grade school with Bogdan and lived a few doors down from him on Market Ave. As soon as the boys started dragging Dr. Mandrake out to the clearing, Bogdan had the idea of creating a souvenir. He sent one of the fellas to tell Warren to bring his camera.

"Hold your horses, hold your horses," Bogdan said, raising an open palm to Markesian.

Bogdan Dabrowski stepped towards Dr. Mandrake.

"I don't think it's right for all us to be smiling and posing for this picture and this boy here isn't participating hardly at all. He isn't even smiling. Now, Warren doesn't everybody have to smile including one-eared Negroes too?"

The boys chuckled.

Asar felt his abdomen tighten against the moist ground.

"Last time I checked, everybody did mean everybody," an exasperated Warren said.

The smile disappeared from Bogdan's face.

"Smile nigger."

Dr. Mandrake looked down from his position hovering in the sky, just above the kneeling Negro with the closed, puffy eye and missing ear. He shouted down to the Negro.

"Come up here and detach yourself."

But the Negro didn't seem to hear. Nor did the men around him. Maybe the Negro was too busy trying to twist his pained expression into a smile since the white gentleman held a knife to his remaining ear.

Asar felt he had to do something. In one smooth, quiet motion, Asar did a push up, brought both his feet beneath him, momentarily resting in a crouching, pre-pouncing position.

A startled Set reached out with his meaty slaughterhouse-hand and aggressively grabbed the back of his big brother's shirt. Asar whipped his head around at Set. It was what Asar saw that gave his anger and body pause.

Asar stared at Set's mix of wide-eyed desperation and concern. It was so ardent that it held him with more force than Set's clutched hand around his shirt. Asar froze in his crouch studying the fraternal love etched on his little brother's pallid face.

Asar quietly eased his long body back down on his stomach.

To watch.

Set knew it wasn't the time. Much as he wanted to get his hands around Bogdan's throat. Shake some sense into him.

Set could barely believe that Bogdan was involved in some mess like this, not to mention leading it. It wasn't the kind of man Bogdan was. Wasn't how his father raised him. But there he was with that black hair oiled back and a knife at Dr. Mandrake's ear. What can I do? he thought. There must be twenty men out there. Far as he could tell, most of them had rifles or pistols. All he had on him was his knife. Running out there without a pot to piss in wasn't gonna help Dr. Mandrake. It was just gonna get all of them killed. Best they could hope for was that one of those bohunks would come to the bushes to relieve himself and lay his rifle down in the process. And there wasn't much chance of that. Their only real option was watching and waiting.

"You call that a smile, boy!" Bogdan yelled. He slapped the back of Dr. Mandrake's head.

"Now, everyone else can smile like they been told, so we can make this picture just right and look at you. Either you think you too good because you one of those yellow educated Coloreds or you just lazy like the rest or both. Goes to show you boys, these bucks all the same," he said looking back over his shoulder.

Dr. Mandrake looked down at the one-eared Negro. "It will not kill you to smile for these gentleman."

To his surprise, Dr. Mandrake heard the one-eared Negro repeat those exact same words, faster and louder.

"It will not kill you to smile for these gentlemen It will not kill you to smile for these gentlemen It will not kill you to smile for these gentlemen."

Dr. Mandrake began to feel dizzy like he was falling, because he was falling. Right atop the Negro. Right into danger.

"Well, alright then, that's what I like to hear, now let's see those teeth."

"Oh my God!"

Dr. Mandrake screamed in a high-pitched voice that was so full of terror and alarm that, on a reflex, Bogdan, took quick step back. The other men laughed at him. The worst possible response for Dr. Mandrake.

Embarrassed in front of his friends, Bogdan picked up a jagged rock, the size of a healthy cantaloupe. Like some country pitcher, he reared back and smashed the rock into back of Dr. Mandrake's skull. The cracking sound echoed off nearby trees like a home run hitter's bat connecting with a fast ball. Except this ball splattered blood all over Bogdan's coveralls before it knocked Dr. Mandrake's face into the dirt.

"You had one more time to mess with me you black sumbitch and now you got no more times. Get your dirty ass up and smile before I change my mind."

When they had first grabbed Dr. Mandrake, while he was briskly walking along 2nd Street, Bogdan had told him that if he acted like a good Negro—and not like one of these agitating uppity Negroes who have the unpatriotic gumption to think he's the same as any white man—they would let him go, after they finished having a little fun with him.

"When we're done, go on and tell other Negroes that East St. Louis isn't the town for them anymore," had said.

When they finally got Dr. Mandrake out near the woods, Bogdan leaned down and whispered reassuringly into Dr. Mandrake's ear.

"These boys a-tell you, I'm a man of my word. We just wanna have a little fun with you and keep a souvenir for the memories."

The rock to the back of Dr. Mandrake's head hit with such a force that it completely knocked off his equilibrium. With his arms tied behind his back and his throbbing forehead resting in the forehead-sized depression in the moist dirt, Dr. Mandrake was having a hard time raising his head. He was disoriented. His sense of direction failing him. But Dr. Mandrake knew that he had to separate his forehead from the ground—so they could see him smile. He knew that his life depended on his forehead leaving earth. Survivor's impulse had been triggered. Instinct. The primal process of producing what will deny death. He had to show them his smile that was slowly imprinting on moist soil.

On his knees, arms tied behind his back, Dr. Mandrake began to incrementally lift his face off the ground.

To Asar, it was like watching an arm wrestling contest between two evenly-matched men. Two evenly-matched forces: Dr. Mandrake's heavy head and gravity. Straining with his eyes closed and nose still pointing towards the earth, Dr. Mandrake was able to get a little more than two inches off the ground. Then he was stuck. Again. A stalemate with gravity. Then another two inches up. And stuck again. That's when he shot his unswollen eye open. Wide. As if looking at the ground would push him away from it. Deny death. Because of their prone position, Set and Asar were able to see Dr. Mandrake's face first.

Asar opened his mouth to speak but only a puff of air escaped.

Set's one-eyed squint became more pronounced.

A film of dark-brown soil covered Dr. Mandrake's light-brown forehead. A physical reminder that his light-brown skin had not been able to save him from the plight of so many of his darker kinsmen. A matching dark-brown reminder spotted the tip of his aquiline nose.

It was the way that Dr. Mandrake had his teeth bared. His upper and lower gums, and incisors, and molars all showing like a wounded German Shepherd cornered in an alley. Lips tightly upturned. His bruised cheeks, taut and trembling in their straining effort to hold a grotesque type of cheer. The one eye, that was not blackened and swelled completely shut, was wide-open and aglow like a child's excited eyes on Christmas morning in front of a present-laden fir.

When Dr. Mandrake had straightened his kneeling body, spine erect, with his arms still tied behind, he tossed his head back and released a loud throaty laugh. Then without a trace of his Howard Medical School education, he spoke.

"I sholl is ready for dat picture now, suh!" Deny death.

"That's more like it, boy," Bogdan said.

He gave Dr. Mandrake a friendly slap on the back.

"Okay, gentlemen, let's huddle in close around our darkie friend here before he starts putting on airs again."

The camera's flash made Dr. Mandrake squint a little. So the photo that would eventually hang over Bogdan's fireplace mantel for over three decades, doesn't completely capture the wide-eyed exuberance of the Dr. Mandrake's smile. But the smile would be big enough to elicit dozens of sly comments from visitors to the Dabrowski household.

"Those Negroes sure know how to have a good time."

Bogdan's stock reply would always draw a laugh.

"Yep, give a Negro a lemon and I'll be damned if he don't make some lemonade."

❙ ❙ ❙

The more Set watched, the more his odd mix of emotions continued to swirl. He was both disgusted and weirdly excited by the strange spectacle. He was angered by Bogdan's viciousness and angry with himself for not being able to intervene. Set felt sorry for Dr. Mandrake and was ashamed of him for letting these bohunks have their way. Then Bogdan pulled his knife out again.

Dr. Mandrake's scream immediately reminded Asar of the sound that sheep make when their eyes are plucked out. Asar placed both of his hands to his ears. And closed his own eyes.

Set turned and watched Asar cover his ears. Hide behind his closed eyes. He'd always been irked by Asar's squeamishness. Embarrassed by it. He felt an odd urge to dig his fingers into Asar's sockets and pry his eyes open. Make him stop running from life. When life was uncomfortable. Ugly. Set knew you couldn't appreciate the beautiful without knowing the ugly.

71

Auset woke up screaming, "Make my baby bleed!"

Starting around the beginning of her final trimester, the dreams had become more consistent. Before, they had happened about once a month. But she'd already counted five in her last trimester.

The Mississippi River-inspired humidity increased the sweat that the dream extracted. The sheets were soaked beneath her pregnant body. Auset's breathing was still rapid. Her milk-filled breasts were heaving up and down.

"Just worries," she said.

She tried to calm herself down by rubbing slow circles into her bulging naked belly.

The dream was almost always the same.

She's lying on her back in a casket with her right ankle of her V-parted legs hanging over one side, and her left ankle hanging over the other side. Mr. Keb, dressed in his mortician black, is at the end of the casket, leaning down between her legs speaking in that African talk that he uses sometimes during special services. His huge baseball-mitt-hands stretch forward between her thighs, sweaty fingers wiggling like slimy night crawlers. Mr. Grandpa Nema is on the other side of the casket, leaning down and whispering something in Mr. Keb's ear. The quick coming contractions make her entire body pulse. Auset opens her mouth to say, "Let my baby be," but each time the words came out, "Make my baby bleed."

The contractions intensify and she can feel the baby coming. She tries to bring her legs down. She can't let her baby be born in a casket. But it's like her legs are tied. Then she looks down and sees a little foot slide out of her. It's always a breach birth. Then another little foot.

Mr. Grandpa Nema whispers something in Mr. Keb's ear, and Mr. Keb reaches in with his slimy fingers, grabs both of the baby's tiny ankles and starts to pull. Auset fights by bucking up and down.

"Make my baby bleed!"

But Mr. Keb just keeps slowly pulling the baby towards him. The knees coming into view. The private parts. It's always a boy. The shoulders. The head always gets stuck. Because she is squeezing her vaginal walls with all her might trying to hold on to her baby.

But Mr. Grandpa Nema whispers something in Mr. Keb's ear, and Mr. Keb says some words in that African language. The baby begins to move slowly out of her again. She feels like her insides are ripping apart. She squeezes her eyes tight and squeezes her vaginal walls tight trying to hold on. She opens her eyes to see her baby's tiny body—with a grown-man head—in Mr. Keb's baseball-mitt- palms. The spitting-image of Mr. Keb himself. Right down to the inch-wide part down the center of his scalp. The umbilical cord is wrapped around the baby's throat. Mr. Grandpa Nema reaches into his pocket and hands Mr. Keb the knife. That's when she wakes up. Screaming.

"Make my baby bleed!"

72

Dr. Mandrake's scream and the echoing gunshots in the distance made Asar reach for his little brother's hand. Without looking, he found it and squeezed it tight. Set squeezed back.

Asar turned and placed his lips close to his brother's left ear and whispered.

"Auset."

Since Grandpa Nema, Keb and Nut had planned to leave early for the train to Chicago, Auset was now home by herself. Asar had figured Set and he would be back at Americus & Son well before Auset even woke up. She was already such a heavy sleeper, but since the start of her third trimester, she'd been sleeping past 11 a.m. some mornings.

Like an alligator navigating a wooded-island full of fellow predators, Asar slowly short-armed his long body around in the opposite direction. Once Asar had completed his turn, Set did the same. The former twins quietly made their way on their stomachs towards the other side of the tiny forest.

Visible from this opposite end of the wooded-area, there were more than a dozen bohunks, carousing with the excitement of a turkey shoot. Two separate flasks were making a way around the men. All seemed to be armed. The tipsy man wearing a bowler and a black bow-tie shot his pistol in the air. The other men cheered.

"Let's go!" someone shouted.

"No, let's wait for a few more."

Asar and Set could see the stragglers coming towards the group. Two men with their arms over each other's shoulder, each free hand carrying a pistol. A few yards behind them, a stumbling man slurring, "Wait-for-mee." The twins could see that there were others behind him. Apparently, all coming from Bloody Island.

Set tapped Asar on the shoulder and motioned with an index fingers to his mouth for them to slide back so they could talk.

After dragging their bodies about 20 yards from the perimeter, Set whispered in his big brother's ear.

"If word has spread to The Island, these bohunks are probably all over town treating Negroes like they're treating Dr. Mandrake. If I pull my cap down low, these drunks won't be able to tell me from President Woodrow Wilson himself. But you go out there, they'll shoot you up right quick, way before you can get to Auset."

Asar turned his head to look at is brother.

"She's not your wife," he whispered.

Asar turned away, trying to figure out the best way to exit the tiny forest. Set grabbed his wrist.

"Use your head, Asar, If ..."

"I'm going, Set."

Asar snatched away and turned to look for the best exit.

Set reached from behind and cupped one of his big hands around Asar's mouth. He brought him to the ground. With his free hand, Set grabbed a baseball-sized rock and slammed it against the back of Asar's head. Asar's body gave way. He was out cold.

There was no way Set was going to let his brother go out there and get killed by these bohunks.

Set quickly scanned the area, then dragged Asar between a bunch of bushes to his left.

He stood up and brushed some of the dirt off the chest and knees of his coveralls. He grabbed his blue cloth cap out of pocket and pulled the brim down tight over his bald head. As he adjusted his cap, Set glanced down at Asar. He wanted his identical twin to be his identical twin again.

One.

But Set knew that was impossible. No matter how much Set could try to explain to Asar, Asar couldn't understand what it was like to be betrayed by skin. For all the training their father gave them, for all the problem-solving skills, for all the chess board strategies, for all the riddles resolved, Asar didn't know what it was like to have a problem he couldn't solve.

Set did.

He lived with a problem he couldn't solve.

Set knew it was the difference that separated them as much as their different skin tones.

73

The scream was familiar. Not that Auset recognized the screamer. It wasn't that type of familiar. It was a familiarity of feeling. A knowing. Like knowing when a man with a smile does not have good intentions.

Auset had been lying there trying to decide upon a name for the little girl growing in her stomach. Listening to how the names rolled off her tongue. Naming her baby girl had become Auset's most effective way to calm her breathing, her anxiety. Especially after hollering herself awake from a bad dream. She had convinced herself that she was going to have a daughter. A reflection of her. A reminder of her own power to shape the world in her image. Thinking of names for a female child also gave her some distance from the baby boy in her reoccurring nightmare.

She liked Mary. Simple. Resolute. Pronounceable. Auset had cringed at "A-use-t" enough times, had heard enough childhood jokes beginning with, "Ah-used-ta …" that she was firmly committed to a name that was butcher-free.

Mary-Ann … Anne-Marie … Mary-Jane … Mary-Jo.

That's when Auset heard it. On *Mary-Jo.* She froze. Captured atop a canvas of bed covers. Lips parted, stuck on the syllable, "Jo." Brow furrowed. The only motion was the concern in her eye expanding to fear. Auset instinctively yelled for her husband, "A-sarrr," the way a child calls out, "Maa-Maaa" when being chased by a dog.

Auset sat up on the bed. She pulled the damp sheet around her naked, copper body. She placed her left palm over the daughter in her medicine ball belly. She wobbled over and opened the window that overlooked the backyard.

A row of leafy oak trees towered over the rose bushes that ran along the 10-foot wall's perimeter, so Auset couldn't see out onto the street. Couldn't see the woman's face that housed the mouth, that released the scream—that could have been her own. What she could see, and now smell through the open window, was smoke. Not the familiar black cloud of smoke wafting up from engine trains on the Alton & Southern, Cotton Belt, St. Louis Iron Mountain & Southern, and the other rail lines that overlapped at the Valley Junction a mile south of Americus & Son. Nor was it smoke from a single train on the Vandalia line which ran right up 8th Street past Bond Ave.

This black smoke was closer. And more full.

Wood burning, not coal.

Auset could smell it strong now. She could feel her eyes beginning to water as the black cloud drifted towards the window.

She moved to close the window when she heard the shotgun blast. Then the same woman's scream. Then the second shotgun blast. Then silence. Auset quietly closed the window and backed away towards the bed. She lay down. Placed both hands over her belly. In her advanced condition, she knew it was important to stay relaxed. Asar will be home soon, she thought. He'll have a plan.

"Daddy will have a plan," she said gently patting her palm on her belly.

Auset began to calmly rub circles into her medicine ball stomach, trying to still her kicking daughter.

"Daddy will have a plan."

74

Set walked out of the wooded-area and started strolling towards the Free Bridge ramp—as a white man. He didn't adopt a special walk. He just captured the earth with his feet. Like it belonged to him. Captured the distant black smoke with his eyes. The sound of occasional gunshots with his ears.

It was just after high noon The riverfront humidity was thick. By the time Set had walked beneath the bridge's ramp and reached 10th Street, the humid air had perspiration beading on his bald head. Sweat was escaping from the sides of his blue cloth cap pulled extra low and rolling down his cheeks.

As he approached Piggott Avenue, Set could see a small crowd up ahead on the next block. The Piggott Avenue Street Car was pulling up to 10th and Piggott. Set's body involuntarily shook.

Before the trolley car had come to a complete stop, several of the burly bohunks in he the crowd had snatched a Negro from the train onto the ground. Set broke into a trot until he was at the melee's perimeter. The frenzied bohunks were swinging and snarling and stomping and kicking with such abandon that wild punches were landing on each other's shins and elbows and thighs. One well- aimed kick connected squarely with the bridge of the Negro's nose, splattering blood onto Set's black shoes and the black ankle-boots of the white man next to him.

I I I

Asar blinked open his eyes. The trees immediately disoriented him. He lay there for a moment, staring up into their branches. At first, he couldn't figure out why there were trees over his hurting head or why his head was hurting. A throbbing, pulsing pain in the back of his skull.

"Auset."

Asar jumped to his feet. Too fast. He placed his hands out horizontally to steady himself, but all those hands could do was poorly break his fall. Asar got to his knees. Then slowly to his feet. He took a breath and started stumbling towards his wife.

The smell hit him before he could reach the perimeter of the wooded-area. Asar stopped. He was completely still. A deer drinking at the brook who catches a hunter's scent. Or the scent of the hunted.

Asar stood there. Inhaling. Letting the stench caress the hair follicles in his flared nostrils. He kneeled behind a bush.

Dr. Mandrake was lying on his back, tied atop what looked like a make-shift wooden bed frame. His head and neck hung back over the top rung. His arms, at his sides, were tied at the forearm. His back was arched. Bowed-out like his chest was trying to reach for the sun. The frame holding Dr. Mandrake lay on a three-foot-high, smoldering heap of blackened wood.

Asar could hear shouts and gunfire in the distance. He stood up from behind the bush and leaned his body out between two close growing trees. He quickly looked side-to-side as if he were a kid again, about to cross busy Collinsville Avenue.

Asar stepped quickly out into the clearing. He would be seen if any Bloody Island bohunks passed by. It was dangerous but he had to bear witness as a sign of respect.

The smell was nauseating. Like a whole side of rancid beef ribs left in the kitchen for week, then set ablaze. Asar let his quick blinking, watering eyes scan the Dr. Mandrake's body. The man who'd ushered his own body into the world.

Dr. Mandrake's chest was a black and flakey as his neck. Crispy. His charred head was smoking the most. It was leaning back with his neck extended, mouth wide-opened as if he was in the middle of a vicious scream. A ribbon of gray smoke was rising up between his lips. A Colored chimney stack.

Burnt to a crisp.

Asar hadn't noticed it at first. But that's the way it was with the missing. Absence doesn't make itself immediately known. Absence unfolds slowly before you until the absence itself becomes present. Just like the absence of Dr. Mandrake's private parts unfolded right before Asar.

Asar shook with a quick involuntary shudder. A chill. In humid July. He stepped closer and bent down at the waist. He looked around the ground. It was gone. The slightest hint of a nub remained. He wanted to believe that maybe it had just burned off. A victim of fire and depravity.

Asar leaned closer until he was just a few inches from the smoldering crotch. The rising heat wafted warmly across his face, as it did when he leaned inside the fireplace to rearrange crackling pine.

Asar didn't want to touch it. He had to. He had to know it. Know that it was real. Know that a human would take the time and effort to do such a thing to another human being. Asar extended the tip of his index finger. He paused just an inch from the nub.

Hesitated.

Then he pressed his finger into the crisp hot flesh. He grit his teeth as Dr. Mandrake got the chance to burn someone back.

75

Asar didn't know how long he'd been standing there looking at his singed index finger. He just came to and there he was. Someone could have walked up on me and I wouldn't have known, he thought. My God. He looked over his shoulder. Then hurriedly turned his body completely around. Then again. No one there. He glanced down at all that was missing from the smoldering physician.

Asar felt a fear rising in him that was as raw as the childhood fear he'd felt when he and Set had been chased by packs of dogs. The kind of irrational fear that made them scream "Maaa-maaa" when they knew Mama was nowhere around. Asar fought to hold down the desire to release a scream that was trying to expel itself from his gut. Not a "Maa-maaa" scream. Something too primal for actual words. He grinded his molars to staunch his urge to shout. Grunt. Chant. Holler. Scream. A sound to relieve the absence of sound in that clearing. A scream to silence the voice repeating in his head.

"When they catch you, they'll burn you and cut you too."

Asar knew he had to protect his wife. Their unborn daughter. He knew he had to head towards the house, through the city, to save them. He knew it wasn't Set's responsibility—even if Set had a better chance of passing through the city because of his white skin. Asar knew he had to risk the fire. Risk the absence of his manhood. He turned completely around again. He knew he had to overcome the fear that had seized him.

But he couldn't.

He turned completely around again.

Then he ran fast as he could back into the tiny forest.

76

On 10th Street, a street lamp stopped Set. Each of the pinkie toes had bunions the size of a small acorn. Working intimately with human and animals bodies since he was a child had given Set a curious attention to detail. Right before slitting the throat of a sheep, he once noticed a mole on its nose. The mole made him still his knife. He had never seen a mole on a sheep nose before. With the sharp point of his knife, he sliced it off. Brought it close to his one eye. Put it in his trouser pocket. Then cut the sheep's throat. So bunions on the feet of a dead Negro, hanging from a street lamp, was the kind of thing Set Americus would pay attention to.

He let his eye travel up the man's brown trousers, brown vest and brown suit jacket. His alabaster neck snapped at an unnatural obtuse angle inside a tan rope. His unbruised freckled face held eyes still open and wide with shock. A look that seemed to be saying, "I can't believe you're doing this to *me*."

Set continued walking. There was chaos within sight of almost every intersection he reached. Set found it impossible to look away. Negro women being pulled off street cars and stomped by face-painted street walkers. Negro men pulled out of stores and shot dead up and down Broadway. Negro shacks on 4th set ablaze with Negro residents inside, forcing them to make a choice between being burned alive or shot to death by awaiting mob of fire-starters.

On Piggott, he saw a Colored man, in blue denim pants and white undershirt, make a run for it out a side door, pistol in hand. Immediately some 20 or so rifles were firing. A wild turkey shoot. When the first bullet hit him in the buttocks, he did a little kangaroo hop, then went down to both knees. The next bullet blasted through his forehead, speckling blood on his undershirt, before he fell to his side.

Set wasn't sure what to expect when he saw Americus & Son still standing on 10th and Bond. Except for the shot-out picture window, which Asar boarded up last night, it seemed oddly untouched. The fires he'd seen had been on the side streets off 10th. The few Negro families who lived on the street, were clustered around Bond and there was nothing shack-y about them. Since fire sees no color when it starts to spread, he figured the bohunk mobs didn't take a chance on blazing the few Negro homes when they were in primarily white neighborhoods.

Now he stood at the bottom of the stairs. How many times had we taken flight over these wooden steps? he thought. He could see himself next to Asar. Arms windmilling. Smiles as open as the wind. Sometimes, they would in mid-air, turn and look at each in mid-flight. Each twin, in matching clothes, looking at his brother to see how their own bodies looked while flying.

He took the stairs two at a time, noticing the glass shards beneath his feet. Set walked over to the large wooden swing in the porch's far corner. He ran his hand along the back until he felt the tiny lever. Slid the compartment's door back. Reached in and grabbed the key. Smiled. That key had been there for as long as he could remember and he was sure it was there when his own father was a boy. That was the Americus way. Tradition. Consistency. A back-up plan.

Set entered the house and closed the heavy door behind him. Most of his childhood memories were accompanied by noise. He and Asar arguing over chess. Grandpa Nema yelling at them for their poor chess skills. He and Asar punching each other over chess. Mama yelling at them to be quiet. Mama crying. Mama yelling at Daddy because he wouldn't talk. Mourners crying in the sanctuary. Mourners yelling in the sanctuary. Grandpa Nema yelling at mourners to have some goddamn dignity and stop acting like a bunch of sad-face clowns. He and Asar laughing at Grandpa Nema's cussing. Mama yelling at him and Asar for laughing in the sanctuary.

So standing in the foyer, absent of sound made him feel like a stranger that he had become. An interloper. A thief.

That feeling made him walk quietly up the stairs and directly to the door of the room that he used to share with his twin brother. The room that Asar now shared with Auset. He just stood there. Listening. To the absence.

❙ ❙ ❙

When Auset's water broke, it seemed to break something else inside of her too. Being alone with those contractions hitting her so hard made her brain freeze up. She couldn't think straight.

Unlike her.

Auset prided herself on her straight-thinking, her quick mind. She had no anwers now. She didn't know where Asar was. Didn't know how stop the fires outside. Or the smoke. Or the bullets. Or the pain from her contractions. She couldn't think, but she could push. Auset felt her baby girl moving down through her body. It felt like the head had crowned. She wanted to lean up and see, but she felt so light-headed. So dizzy. So drowsy. Where was Asar? She wanted to scream for help, but with all the shooting and fires and screaming right outside, she didn't want to bring any attention to herself. Even if she wanted to scream, she didn't think she could get more than a hoarse whimper out of her sore throat and chest.

So she was stuck. Her mind.

Throat.

Her eyes, which she couldn't seem to keep open for more than a few seconds at a time. Her mouth. Her baby. She couldn't push her baby no more. She didn't even know how long she had been lying in her water and blood. She had just enough energy to lean up and see her bloody baby's head sticking out of her.

Stuck.

❙ ❙ ❙

Set slid the key into his old bedroom door. He knew it would open because the front door, back door and all the bedroom doors, except for Grandpa Nema's, had always had the same lock.

"A-sar?"

Set let the door swing open.

He was caught off guard by the blood. By the sight of his naked childhood crush with her legs as wide as his wonder. The head of the child that could have been his.

Auset's puffy eyes were pregnant slits. The crying. The exhaustion. She had lost so much blood that she was afraid that if she gave in to her desire to keep them closed, she would never wake up again. Her baby would never wake.

"A-sar?"

The tall blurry figure at the door had to be Asar. Hadn't the door been locked? Why isn't he coming to help me. Am I dreaming, Auset thought. Her heavy lids closed again and she struggled to re-open them. He was here. She was not dreaming.

"Help-me."

Set could see Auset's lips moving, but she wasn't saying anything.

Being in his old room. Seeing Auset like this. He couldn't help but think about what might have been. Wonder if she still thought about him—in the way he sometimes still thought about her. She was having an Americus baby. In his old room. And they were together. It was a dream and a nightmare at the same time. With blood. A baby's head. Lips that moved but did not speak. His senses were overwhelmed.

He was stuck.

Except for his one eye. He clenched his molars tight, trying stop the welling emotion. Too late. His own water broke.

"Help ... me."

The energy it took to move her lips, closed her eyes again. She wanted to open them again but she couldn't. Tired ... tired, she kept thinking to herself. Tired.

Set cautiously stepped towards his pantomiming sister-in-law. His first love.

Auset thought she heard Asar walking towards her. She felt herself smile but it was only in her mind. Her puffy eyes and copper-penny-face were still impassive. But Auset was smiling inside. Hand resting on her stomach. Daddy's here, she told her daughter with her thoughts.

"Help ... us."

Set saw Auset's lips move again, but she said nothing.

He walked to the end of the bed, and slowly dropped to his knees, one knee at time, as if preparing to pray between her thighs. A thank offering to the semi-born.

He extended both of his long muscular arms forward, fingers outstretched. Ten digits hovering over a tiny head. Set watched all 10 of them tremble.

"Push Auset," Set gently said.

"Tired," Auset said, but her moving lips made no sound.

"Push," Set said resting his large hands on the grapefruit-sized head.

"Tired."

Set tugged as if he was using two hands to pull a maple leaf off a tree.

"Push," he said, more firmly. "You've got to push harder." Nothing.

Set could see she was barely conscious. Her eyes, which had been partially open when he first walked in, were now completely closed. She wasn't responding. Set wasn't sure what to do.

He carefully released the infant's head, rolled his pants up, pulled his Americus Sword from his leg strap.

"Push," Set said, as he gently poked Auset's lower inner thigh with the point of the knife. On reflex, she jumped.

"Push."

He softly jabbed the opposite thigh. Her whole lower torso jumped.

"Push, Auset, push," he said jabbing the other thigh.

Her whole body jolted. Set dropped the knife on the bed and began to pull again on the infant's skull. Auset began to push. The baby began to move. Excited by seeing her straining, trying, Set spoke again.

"That's it. Push. Don't make me poke you again. Push Auset, push."

And when Auset pushed Set could feel the slippery infant sliding until the shoulders emerged.

"Push."

Auset pushed. The baby moved. And moved again. The chest was showing. Set tugged harder. The umbilical chord. Then a bloody baby boy slid right out of his first love's body into his bear claw palms. Set glanced excitedly up at Auset. But she was barely there in the room. Her sweaty head was completely back.

Eyes still closed.

Set grabbed the corner of the bed sheet and wiped his little nephew's face. A wrinkled, chubby face as black as his used to be. He could see his brother within those wrinkles. He could see himself in his nephew.

Except for the color.

Set felt the emotion rising up through his own chest. He leaned his face close to the newest Americus. Set was crying hard now. He saw the opportunity before him. There was a way that he and Asar could be twins again. There was a way that Asar could once again share the same human experience. A shared experience that could bond them. Allowing each of them to once again understand the other without need for verbal language. Without need for explanation. Articulation. Common pain would be communication enough. For the two to be one again.

One.

Set knew that in order for he and Asar to truly be one again, Asar needed to have a problem that he could not solve.

To share in the knowledge of the unsolvable problem. To bond through costly mathematics.

It was the only way.

Set knew he had to do what could not be done. He reached for the Americus Sword.

77

Is it dark enough? Asar had been looking up through the forest trees, asking himself that question ever since the sun had started to set. It was the witching hour. That time when the remnants of the fallen sun could make beautiful a sky full of brownish-gray grime. The magic of dusk turned Armour smoke stacks into giant brushes creating mood light. Soot into sienna. Burnt-orange mixed with magenta overtones. Copper highlights. Twilight in East St. Louis provided bloodletting with an attractive backdrop.

But in Asar's mind, dusk was not dark enough to leave the tiny forest and check on his wife.

"Not dark enough," he whispered up into the trees.

He shook his head. This is the most reasonable way, he thought. If I would have tried during the day, I would have never made it. If I'm dead, how does that help Auset? When our baby is born, she'd be without a father. Set understood. That's why he stopped me from going. He knew he could make it through. And he did. I know he did. He's there looking over her until I get there. I made the most reasonable choice, Asar lied to himself.

"Father wouldn't have waited until darkness. Nor Set," he said aloud to the dirt around his feet.

They would've made the brave choice. In the Americus Family protecting family trumps all.

Asar had conquered fear many times. Being chased by wild dogs through the streets. Confronting his father during dinner table arguments. Deciding to marry Auset. Standing on the porch last night defending his family with gunfire.

But this time, fear was conquering his mind. His limbs. He was undone by witnessing Dr. Mandrake's dismembering. The fallen ear. Severed manhood. Crispy body. Asar couldn't make himself leave the forest until it was dark enough. Couldn't yet risk his life ending like the doctor who was there for him at his beginning. Even if it meant risking his wife's safety for a couple more hours. That's what shamed Asar most. Asar loved Auset. But how much?

He thought of their times snuggling in bed. Looking at the mole resting inside her cheek's right dimple. Gazing into Auset's bedroom-eyes.

"I love you more than life itself."

Asar wanted to believe those words. Words that now were being tested.

He looked up into the darkening sky. "I love you more than life itself."

Asar needed to remind himself. Convince himself.

He doubted if Set would need such convincing—because he wondered if his brother still had feelings for Auset. After all these years? From the time Set and Auset were childhood sweethearts, until this very day? Even when Set was pushing her away? Even when she finally gave way to his pushing and ended up in the twin brother's arms? The twin brother's bed?

Asar wondered, as he had so often, did Auset really love her second choice? Could he really believe her many assurances? He thought back.

"I'm asking for your hand in marriage, but not if your hand is itching for someone else."

"I love you Asar Americus. And the only thing my hand is itching for is your ring on my finger. Now stop being silly and kiss me before I kiss you first."

Auset had seemed so genuine, Set thought. She was so moved by my insecure proposal. So in love with me. But she was also so sweet on Set when we were were young. All those times in church, finding ways to be around him—as he found ways to be around her. They were just kids, but maybe some of those feelings are still there.

Asar lay on his back, looking up into the trees, doubting himself. Night fell.

Asar stood up.

He brushed off his back. Dusting off his fear wasn't so easy. He still felt unsteady. Unsure. But it was time. He had to go. He wanted to go.

I   I   I

Asar gingerly walked to the edge of the tiny forest and peered towards the clearing. It was dark as him. He could be invisible out there. Yet, he knew once the roads became paved, there would be street lamps that could help set him afire. Street lamps that could help him swing.

Asar stepped into the night knowing light could be death of him.

"I love you more than life itself."

78

Set rocked his nephew in his arms. And looked at Auset. He had washed his sister-in-law's body down with cool water and covered her with a clean linen sheet he got from the laundry room.

Auset kept dozing in and out. She still looked ashen. Eyes puffy. She had opened her mouth to speak a few times. Lips moving but not a peep. Then she'd fall out again.

Set looked down into the tiny black face immersed in a pink wool blanket. He opened the lower part of the blanket. He'd already changed the bandages twice. The bleeding had completely stopped.

He gently ran his hand over the wrinkled bald scalp.

Looking into his new nephew's beautiful blackberry face, Set thought about Asar. He knew this beautiful baby could bring his brother a necessary pain. A necessary pain that could reconnect twins. A reconnection made possible through a connnection of absence.

When the spots finally started to rapidly increase all over his body, Set would lock himself in the upstairs bathroom to figure and measure which spot would push him over the 50% threshold into whiteness. The bohunk tipping point. The white spot that would slip him across the color line. Make him a racial fugitive. A criminal to himself. For a crime, for a problem, that can't be solved.

Set looked down at his beautiful nephew.

"Now, Asar has a problem he can't solve."

79

Low-running, Asar shot across 10th street, heading for the wagon. He dived head first and came to a rolling stop beneath the broad wooden underbelly. The street's dark emptiness made it feel like an open-air casket.

It was after 11 p.m. Most of the street lamps had been smashed. Though Asar knew the lights were destroyed to protect the guilty, Asar was thankful for the increase in shadows. Even if they were shrouded in blood.

He had been taking the backstreets and alleys. His already fast-beating heart accelerating while escaping each temporary hiding space to get to the next. The shadows cast by wagons and doorways offering insufficient cover for his 77-inch body.

Each time Asar would dive beneath a wagon bed or throw his back against a dark wall or duck behind a Model A, the comfort provided never lasted more than a few breathless moments. It would take just one white man to glimpse a moving shadow.

Asar couldn't shake the nerves. He tried by keeping his mind focused on Auset's sweet copper-penny-face, the perfectly round mole lodged in the dimple of her right cheek. The perfection inside her round belly.

But the image of his wife and unborn child were in competition with the image of his own body dangling from a poplar tree. A fire simmering beneath. A knife raised at his retreating manhood.

These are the images that had kept his body shaking since he'd left the little forest. Three hours of cautious cowering. Seeking respite in nightfall. An hour before, he had been in an alley. Back pressed against the rough brick wall. He heard the hinge creak. If the two coverall-clad bohunks who came out of the back door had simply turned right, and not left, they would have ran right into him. Forcing him to run into the open.

The time it took for the sound of a rusty door hinge to reach Asar's ear was time enough for fear to shoot up from the arch of his feet, through his calves and thighs, past his bladder on its way to the rest of his body. The warm urine had started to stream down his leg into his black shoes before the second bohunk was completely out of the door.

Now, curled beneath this wagon bed, the pissy stench of that close call was an olfactory reminder of his cowardice.

Asar quickly poked his head from under the wagon bed, looked both ways, and quickly pulled his whole body back beneath.

It looked clear, he thought to himself. Gotta be sure.

Asar took a deep breath. Head out. Looked both ways. Head in. Back out again. Another deep breath. With a burst, Asar rolled from under the wagon and came to his feet in a running crouch. He low- ran the final three blocks to Americus & Son. Straight up the front stairs, three at a time, onto the porch. Asar could see that there was furniture stacked up against the door, which he could see had been forced open. He figured that Set had forgotten about the spare key on the porch swing. He pressed his dry-cracked lips in the space where the double-doors met.

"Auset."

His voice, controlled. Forceful. Commanding. A verbal veil for his wife's benefit. He was too embarrassed to call Set's name. He paused. Listened. Again. More insistent.

"Auset, it's me. Come and unblock the door."

Asar pressed his ear, hard, against the door, splinters scratching his cheek. When he heard the hesitant foot steps, the first thing he thought was that Auset was going to smell his pissy fear. Discover him.

Asar took a step back so the urine wouldn't talk to her through the doors' junction, before he could explain himself. Explain why it had taken him so long to get there. Explain the time it took to cower under those wagons. To shrink his tall frame behind those motor cars. Explain the surprising amount of time it took to completely empty his bladder down his thigh, pass the side of his knee, over his calf and into his black shoes. Asar was ashamed of how he got to this door, but love had made his arrival possible. Auset had pulled him past fear. Pulled a shaky courage through Asar that pulled him through the crossroads. Through a bloody city. Up 33 stairs to a door of the dead that held the living.

His living.

His old life and new life. Flesh of his flesh.

Asar heard the furniture being moved behind the door. "I love you more than life itself," he whispered.

He dropped his eyes. Glanced down his body. He was glad it was dark. The right side of the double doors opened. Standing inside, back lit by a lamp on a table in the foyer, Set was cradling a pink bundle in one arm, clutching a Winchester with the other hand.

Asar walked towards the flesh of his flesh. He stopped a couple of steps from Set.

The brothers stood there. Face-to-face.

In the silence.

In the stench of strong urine.

Set handed the bundle to Asar and stepped around him to close the door. He leaned the Winchester against the wall and began re-stacking the chairs and endtables against it.

With his arms extended forward from his body, Asar held the bundle in his baseball-mitt-hands like a ball player catching a shallow fly ball. He felt dirty. He was. And smelly. Strong piss and July riverfront-town humidity fouled the foyer air. He didn't want to desecrate this fresh life. His fresh life. But he had to see. Had to see the baby girl that he had made. The child that would make him anew. Fresh again. He brought the pink bundle close to his body, then up towards his face. Balancing the child in one of his arms, he used the other grimy hand to peek into the pink folds.

The plump face was the color of dark chocolate cake. Asar's favorite. Big almond-shaped eyes so brown they were almost black. And that face. That face was his face. Asar had grown up seeing his face in his brother's face, but this was different. He hadn't made his brother. He had made this face staring back at him.

Nothing could befoul this beauty. Not piss.

Not dirt. Not shame.

He brought the blanket to his filthy chest. Leaned in and kissed those chocolate cake cheeks with his dry, dirty lips. He turned around and found his brother staring at him. Smiling. It had been so long since he'd seen that smile which used to be his own. Asar smiled back. He needed to see his wife. Share this smile, this joy with her. Together, they had made new life. Asar turned away from his brother and headed for the stairway.

Despite his mother's frequent threats, Asar had spent his childhood recklessly running and jumping up and down these stairs. Now, with his child in hand, he climbed them like they were made of hollow blocks of ice.

Asar paused at their bedroom door. It had been kicked open too. He entered with a smile so radiant, so bright, that they could have turned off the lamp on the night stand next to the bed—where another Winchester leaned. Auset was lying there with a clean white sheet pulled up to her neck. Her eyes, still puffy, were closed. Her copper face looked strained, stressed, as if she had been running for hours from a wild pack of dogs. Asar knew that giving birth to the perfectly-shaped perfection in his hands had to take a lot of work. Especially on a day when the bohunks had lost their minds. But it's going to be okay, he thought.

I'm here now. Auset is safe. Our child is safe.

Asar sat down on the side of the bed. He exhaled deeply. Looked at Auset. Looked at their baby. Back at Auset. Even exhausted, his wife looked beautiful. Asar could not make himself stop smiling. So focused on his joy, he couldn't even smell the stench of strong piss saturating the room's humid air.

"Auset," he whispered.

She did not respond. He leaned close, examined the mole in her right dimple.

"Auset."

Her eyelids slowly opened to a slit.

"A-sar," she said in a voice barely audible.

"Yes, I'm here, it's going to be okay."

"A-sar."

"It's okay, I'm right here, I'm right here. Our little baby is right here."

Auset's eyes slowly closed.

"Sleep, Auset, sleep, everything is fine."

Ever since she was more than a few months pregnant, Auset had been saying that she knew the baby was a girl.

"Our little girl's is going to be the smartest and prettiest little girl that this city has ever known … look at her parents," she'd say to Asar in her playful way.

That playfulness, that openness, was what made Asar love her so. A love that seemed to be almost separate from him. Separate and in charge of him. He was intrigued by the intense feelings Auset created in him. Feelings that pulled him through blood. The feelings that had led to the little girl in his arms.

Asar peeked his dirty face into the folds of the pink blanket. That's when he saw just a sliver of the bandage. He opened the bottom half of the blanket. Saw the bandages around his baby girl's pubic area.

Set appeared in the doorframe.

"He must have heard me," Set solemnly said. Just as he had practiced.

"When I got on the porch, the door was kicked open, so I rushed for the stairs. When I noticed this here door had been kicked open too, I half-way didn't want to walk in Asar. I came on in and saw Auset on the bed. A noise spooked me and I turned around to see him make a run for it. Must've been hiding behind the closet door. Didn't get much of a look at him, but I know he was a damn bohunk. Filthy foreigner. They come here and get treated better than Negroes born in this country. Talking gibberish. Acting like we got a tail. Hunting us in our own town. I ain't got no tail," Set said, slapping his palm hard against the doorframe. Set began to cry.

"I ain't got no tail."

Asar stared at his brother as if Set were a partially-finished jig-saw puzzle. He could feel his own eyes rapidly blinking. Each closing and re-opening an attempt to decipher the picture with the missing pieces. Asar's brow was dirty and deeply furrowed. He was staring at Set so hard, Asar was squinting.

"What?" Asar mumbled.

Asar's mind was moving fast. Constructing. He glanced over at Auset. Her puffy eyes slit open, looking towards Set. Set's leaking eye looking towards heaven. Asar glanced down between the blanket's pink folds at the almost fresh bandage.

A single blood spot.

Asar tenderly loosened the white gauze. Pulled it back.

Leaned his grimy face close.

That's when he heard Auset's weak whisper.

"Is it a girl?"

80

1927
EAST ST. LOUIS, ILLINOIS

The smell of pine filled Heru's nostrils. The pine trees were nestled next to poplars, which leaned into spruces and crowded against more pines. All reaching to the sky and eating sunlight. He looked down to see where his brown boots stood. The ground was a soft bed of leaves, pine needles, decomposing pinecones, wild flowers and grass. He looked back up through the tangle of limbs and branches. The outer perimeter of the woodland was more dense than the center but he could still see the Tallest Pine towering above the tree line.

Heru secured his treasure hunter bag's strap over his head and opposite shoulder. He began maneuvering towards the center of the forest. His left hand clutching the map. The right alternating between pushing aside branches and securing his brown apple cap, as he ducked under low-hanging limbs. He'd stop and look up every few feet to make sure he was still in line with the Tallest Pine.

The closer he got to his destination, the less dense the terrain. Until he was able to walk without worrying about his cap. Heru finally came into the center of the forest. It reminded him of his own circular backyard. Except there were not 33 circular headstones. No Americus Fountain to sit on. But there was a fallen tree that seemed like a perfect resting place. And across from it, the tallest tree in the forest.

Heru walked to the base of the tree. He squatted down. Unfolded and unrolled his map. He gathered four pinecones to keep the corners from rolling up. He closed his eyes, and let his index finger fall onto blood.

"27 ESE TRUNK."

He would start there.

From his treasure hunter bag, he pulled out Seker, his compass. Heru stood up and placed his back on bark. Looked at Seker and moved it left until the needle hit "ESE." He put his left forward, then his right heel almost touching his left toes. He paused. Stepped back to the tree. Uncle Set's feet are longer, he thought.

He put his left foot forward again.

Then, cautiously, his right foot about four inches in front of his left. "Two."

Left foot forward four inches.

"Three."

With his eyes carefully calculating the foliage beneath his feet, Heru counted off 26 Uncle Set steps. Then took one more. He returned Seker to the treasure hunter bag. He squatted and began to use his hands to brush off pine needles, leaves and pinecones all around him. Then he leaned forward with all his weight on this palms. Searching for soft earth. Nothing. Heru moved a foot to his right. Brushed the ground. Leaned forward on palms and he felt the earth give a little.

Heru kept pressing his palms into the earth to the left and right, forward and back to see how wide and long was the rectangular hole.

Heru opened his treasure hunter bag and pulled out Tehuti. The hand-shovel's blade looked like an elongated ace of spades that narrowed into a 3-inch-double-edged point for unlodging treasure from rocks. Uncle Set had showed him how to keep it extra-sharp using a grinding stone.

Heru jabbed Tehuti's long pointy blade into the ground. Watched it disappear. Then he started flinging dirt over his left shoulder. What if it's not just a Winchester, he thought. He kept earth flying. Maybe Uncle Set buried the pieces of the Winchester, and some money, and some diamonds from those bohunks. Maybe he didn't want to bury all the money and diamonds in the same place in case someone stumbled upon it. Maybe the map is a real treasure map, he thought.

"Maybe Uncle Set wanted me to find it."

Heru's left arm began to fling dirt faster. When he began to tire, he switched to his right hand. After 15 minutes, he was able to climb into the 4 foot long hole, kneel down and dig at one end for awhile. Then turn around and dig until the other end was about the same level. Heru returned again to the other end and kept flinging dirt out of the hole. Then Tehuti struck something. But it wasn't a box. Every birthday present his father ever buried for him, began with a map and ended with a shovel eventually hitting a box. Seker was the result of a shovel striking a cantaloupe-sized hexagon pine box. The hollow "CLUCK" sound of a tongue clucking the roof of a mouth.

There in the tiny forest Tehuti hit something so soft, it made him snatch the shovel back into the air and hold it there. No "CLUCK." Just soft silence. And the hint of stink. Mixed with fresh soil and pine, rising with the East St. Louis humidity.

Heru leap-frogged out of the hole and stood beside it. Tehuti hung from his left hand along his side. His frog eyes peered down at the thin layer of black soil covering something much too soft to be a gift box. Wasn't no Winchester part this soft. He took a step back. His thumping heart propelled a rising urge to run. Even though running was not what he wanted to do. He wanted keep digging, but he didn't want to find out what could be in a hole as long as the toy chest at the end of his bed. And as solidly soft as Big Grandpa Nema's leather medicine ball.

Heru dropped to his right knee. Laid Tehuti down.

Dropped to his other knee and stealthily crawled to the ledge like a cat creeping up on a sleeping field mouse. He peered over the edge. From that vantage point, he could begin to make out part of the outline that shaped the dirt around it.

The two by three foot form resembled the rectangular pitcher's mound that the big boys played on at Lincoln High. He twisted the treasure hunter bag onto his back. Lay on his stomach. Like an alligator, he short-armed his body forward until his head, shoulders and upper part of his chest were learning over the hole. The intensifying smell, rising into his face reminded Heru of the time the whole family had gone to Chicago, only to return a week later to find out that Grandma Nut had left the pork roast on the kitchen counter. He reached down with his left hand and began to brush away the top layer of dirt from the mound beneath him.

Despite the moist dirt sticking to it pretty good, Heru cleared a surface about 8 by 8 inches. The sooty dirt still made it hard to figure out what he was looking at. He hung over the hole and stared. The smell and size told him it was some type of dead animal. He pressed his index finger into the supple flesh. Probably a fat pig buried on its side, he thought. Except it didn't make sense that Uncle Set would bury a pig and make a map.

Unless there was something under the pig. Or in the pig.

That's just the type of smart thing that Uncle Set would do, Heru thought. But Heru couldn't figure out the thimble-sized bump on the pig's side. It was blackened with dirt.

Smooth. Round.

He gently poked his finger into it. He squeezed it between his thumb and forefinger. It was both soft and firm in that way that a very ripe cumquat is soft and firm.

Heru knew he couldn't lean much farther in without losing his balance and falling in head first. He scooted forward just an inch and started clearing dirt away from a wider area. Getting more perspective. And more fun. It had become the type of pirate adventure that Uncle Set, during their fishing trips to the Cahokia River, would tell him about during his own childhood: twin pirate treasure hunting. Heru smiled and playfully squeezed the soft and firm cumquat again. The feeling between thumb and finger, and the recognition that context provides, and the expansion of frog eyes, and the expansion of quick breath, and the feeling of falling into the grave released Heru's high-pitched scream, "Maaa-maaa!"

The cumquat was a belly button. An outtie.

Heru knew it was his father's. Asar's pronounced outtie.

He was still screaming when he slid right on top of it. His legs turning to taffy as he screamed for his mother. From a shimmying prostrate position, he tried to scramble off a piece of his father. Heru only stopped screaming because he began to hyperventilate.

Couldn't catch his breath. Couldn't get to his feet.

Legs kicking like a shimmying swimmer. Treasure hunter bag flopping on his back. Through his dirty tan shirt, Heru could feel his own belly button against his father's soft and firm belly button.

Outtie-to-outtie.

Inhaling, exhaling, deep and quick atop a chunk of his father, Heru kicked and flopped in silence. A panicking mute frog with broken legs.

▌ ▌ ▌

Heru didn't know how long he'd been flopping and kicking, but he was starting to get very tired. The exhaustion made him calm down enough to catch his breath. He did a push up off his father's chest and climbed out of the grave. Rolled over onto his back. He felt his bird-chest slowly expand and contract. Expand and contract. With each inhale he could hear the crackle of the dried leaves his back was lying on.

The backyard-sized clearing in the center of the woodland only had a few spruces and pines. Heru looked up into the hole in the sky that the clearing created. Clouds slowly passed in and out of view. In one, he saw a white elephant with its long nose curling up. Another passing cloud was a huge bottle of milk. Like the thick glass bottles the milkman left on the porch on Monday and Thursday mornings.

In the round cloud with a hole towards the top, now slowly coming into view, Heru saw the face of Uncle Set.

It was almost 10:00 a.m. The warming day and rising humidity was starting to intensify and spread the smell of spoiled pork roast.

He had to do something.

But he couldn't seem to pull his skinny back off the magnetic leaves. Couldn't turn on his side to face, to confront, what he could hardly comprehend.

The possibilities. The implications.

The living clouds had turned from distraction to destruction. From elephants to uncles. Heru tried to corral his mind. Control the thoughts that started to stray towards Uncle Set. And his father. Funnel them like the sheep Uncle Set showed him at Armour & Co. But the shape-shifting cumulus wouldn't cooperate. Lying there on his back, he saw a cloudy knife.

A cloudy belly button.

A cloudy piece of white butcher paper. A cloudy map.

Uncle Set's cloudy face.

It made him have to turn over on his stomach. Heru rested there for minutes and minutes, looking at the earth beneath him. Feeling the earth beneath him. Knowing what lay in the earth beneath him. Heru closed his eyes.

He knew what he had to do.

He had to do what could not be done.

Heru slowly pressed his body away from the earth and climbed to his hands and knees. Stood up. Looked into the hole. At the piece of his father. He turned around and slowly walked towards the Tallest Pine. And the bloody map that was spread out in front of it. He squatted. Heru couldn't make himself just go down the coordinates like it was some laundry list. He closed his eyes and let his index finger drop: NNW 19.

Heru stood with his back to the Tallest Pine. From the treasure hunter bag, he pulled out Seker, the compass that his father gave him—would now find his father. A piece at a time. Heru slid his back around the tree until Seker read NNW. Using Uncle Set strides, Heru started counting off paces towards a barrel-sized boulder straight ahead.

On his 19th step, he was a couple of feet from the boulder. He returned Seker to the treasurehunter bag, kneeled and began to brush away the spruce leaves and pine needles. He pressed his palms flat searching for soft ground. The earth gave. The rectangular shallow grave was only the size of one of Uncle Set's boots. Heru pulled Tehuti from the treasure hunter bag. Carefully, he began to shovel loose soil, afraid of what Tehuti might hit. He knew there would be no "CLUCK" sound of steel hitting a hollow box. He knew Tehuti would find something soft. That's why Heru's left hand was shaking each time it brought Tehuti back into the earth. Again. That's when he felt it. The shock of contact made his already trembling hand drop Tehuti into the boot-length rectangular hole. It was about two feet deep. Heru just squatted there for a few moments. Still. Silent.

Using the tips of his left index finger and left thumb, he reached into the hole and grabbed Tehuti by its handle, trying his best not to let any parts of his hand touch the grave. He peered inside. Couldn't see what Tehuti had hit. But he knew it was just beneath the surface of loose soil. An arm length away. A finger tip away. A bloodline away.

Heru lay down on this stomach to help control his shaking hands. He looked down his nose into the hole. Closed his eyes. His left arm warily moved downward towards the treasure he didn't want to find. His chary fingertips towards a door of no return. Into adulthood. At 10-years-old. His middle finger reached the cool soil first. He paused in that position. Stiff. His forearm hanging down into the grave. Heru started to wiggle and walk his fingers, barely brushing across the top of the soil.

Then Heru did it. Let those fingers begin to move into the dirt. Tentative. He touched softness. Flesh. It made his stomach tighten. His breath hold. He let his index finger and thumb find the end of it. Slowly, he began to retrieve his arm from the grave.

Heru's wide eyes watched his own rising, black skinny forearm. Shaking wrists connected to a shaking forefinger and thumb, connected to a shaking and slippery piece of flesh. Tendon and veins sticking out of one end. A burnt blood sausage, Blutwurst, bursting out of its casing. The Blutwurst trembled and slipped free from thumb and forefinger back into the grave.

He would have to pick it up again. And hold it tighter.

Feel it more. Know it more.

Again, Heru dropped his hand over the ledge of the grave. His left palm knew exactly where it was going. Heru felt his slender fingers clutch around the cool, veiny flesh, heavy as an overstuffed Blutwurst. He pulled his arm out the grave, rolled on his back, and extended his father's phallus high above his forehead. He raised his right hand too and grabbed the severed penis between his thumb and index finger. Heru slowly began to spin the flesh like a butcher inspecting a sausage-packing job gone wrong. The jumble of exposed veins and tendons on the severed end. The uncircumcised head at the other.

The penis fascinated Heru. The absence of his own had made a wall between him and his father. A wall porous enough for shame to seep through.

Looking up at the flesh in his hands made him think about the problems that privates had caused him.

The day he saw his Uncle's privates made Uncle Set treat him like he was a bad boy. Made bad things happen in Uncle Set and Auntie Neph's marriage. Made everyone mad at Heru Americus.

"I'm not even a real Americus. I'm too wrong," he said to the silent flesh in his hands.

Heru continued to slowly spin his father's privates between his fingers.

"Now, look at what I've done." He shook his head side-to-side.

"I made Uncle Set so mad that he did wrong. Maybe I'm catchy. The only contagious Americus."

Heru brought the penis down close to his face. Turned the head towards his eyes. It looked like a bullet. With two small holes at the top. Deadly, Heru thought.

He made his way to his feet. Walked back towards the tallest tree, still slowly spinning his father's privates in the outstretched fingers before him. Heru thought he should be crying. But tears are not what he felt. He was a big boy now. His father wouldn't have approved of no crying at a time like this. He knew what he had to do and he planned to do it like a big boy should.

When he arrived at the tallest tree, Heru gently placed his father's privates into his treasure hunter bag and squatted down in front of the map.

"SSW 24."

Set pulled out Seker and placed his back against the tallest tree. He inched his back around the tree until Seker read, "SSW."

He took a first step.

Heru consulted Seker and stepped and dug and consulted and stepped and dug and consulted and stepped and dug until there were 13 uncovered graves of various sizes in the tiny forest. A grave the length of a tall man's leg, containing his father's leg. A grave the size of a grown man's boot, containing his father's foot. A grave the size of a grave digger's arm, containing his father's arm.

At each discovery, Heru stood above the rim of the grave and stared down into his wrong treasure. Slow shaking his head at what his wrongness had caused. But he did not cry. He was a big boy now. Heru placed his back to the tree and retrieved Seker from his treasure hunter bag. He inched his back around the tree until Seker read, "ESE 1." Heru placed one foot in front of the other and said aloud, "One." He squatted and brushed away the leaves and twigs and pinecones. Placed his delicate palms on the ground until he felt the earth give. He knew what was in the grave even before he started digging. It was the only missing piece in the jigsaw puzzle that used to be his father.

Heru pulled Tehuti out of his treasure hunter bag and began cautiously digging into the earth. Careful not to allow the pointy- three-inch blade to go too deep with each scoop. The deeper the hole the more attention Heru gave to the depth of the blade. When the grave got around a foot deep, Heru would allow Tehuti to enter the soil no more than three inches to remove the dirt. After the hole passed a foot and a half in depth, Heru put Tehuti aside. He began hand-scooping the soil. A delicate palm-full at a time. After five minutes of using his small left hand as a shovel, he scooped his palm in again and his knuckles grazed something. The shock of the contact made his thin fingers separate wide like his eyelids. His eyes watched the black soil slide between those fingers fall back into the grave.

He started to clear away the dirt where his knuckles had been. His fingertips dancing atop of his father's wavy hair. He could see the faint outline of the wide part running down the center of his father's scalp. He lowered his index finger and ran it along the soil strewn scalp on his father's head.

Using his pinkie, Heru began cautiously clearing dirt from the hair line. He felt a strange need to be careful not to get dirt in his father's eyes. He dug around the ears and back of the neck. The brow. Picked particles from the folds of his father's eyelids. Out the left nostril. The right. Fingered black soil out the mouth.

Heru moved dirt away from the chin until the throat was visible. The prominent Adam's Apple now deflated. Like his father. Deflated like Heru was beginning to feel. His resolve to be a big boy began to slowly seep out the irises of his big eyes. Pin-pricked by the jagged city. Its serrated woodland.

"Big boys don't cry."

He took a deep breath and continued.

Heru placed both his shaking hands under his father's cheeks. Gently lifted like he was lifting the black crystal vase in the living room that Grandma Nut told him not to touch. Heru raised the dead who gave him life.

Face-to-face.

One smooth black face covered with a veil of dirt. The half-lidded eyes, opposite of Heru's wide-open ones. Absent of blink and light and life. Vertebrae and trachea jutting from a mass of blood and soil-stained throat muscles and veins. Slightly parted lips, thick as orange wedges. The dirty lips before him made Heru think of all the times he had looked up into his father's mouth.

Wanting these lips to curve into a soft smile towards him. Laugh his way.

Say how proud he was of him.

Palming Asar's cheeks three inches from his own face, Heru was sure these lips must have smiled and said how proud he was of him.

But he couldn't remember when.

Couldn't recall these lips forming into kindness. Couldn't hear softness tumbling over them. They were silent in death, as they had been silent in life.

"I'm proud of you, son."

Heru whispered the words to fill the few inches between them. A hollow space between father and son. To hear how the words would have sounded at close range. Ventriloquist love.

Face-to-face.

"Say it again, Daddy."

Heru could feel the emotion welling up inside his chest. He was not going to cry and bring more shame to his father—especially after hearing those words.

Heru could barely get the words out of his mouth. His tightening chest restricted his breathing.

"I'm proud of you, son."

Heru kneeled down and delicately placed his father's head back into the grave. He stood up. Tearless. Turned in a slow circle looking at 14 mounds of dirt, 14 uncovered graves, 14 treasures he didn't want to find.

Heru was intimate with wrong, so he knew it was wrong for his father to be buried piecemeal. Like some divided dirty secret. Even as at ten-year-old, he knew that wasn't the Americus Family Way. Especially for one of their own. He had to make it right.

He had to put his father back together.

Make him whole again. Then place him in the ground whole.

Bury him with honor.

That was the Americus Family Way.

That's what Mama would do, he thought. Make Daddy whole again. She would put him together so he could return to the earth with honor.

Heru would have to become Auset.

Doing the work of his mother: making things right.

"Where would Mama start?" he said aloud.

He turned his body in a complete circle, scanning the 14 plots around him.

"In the beginning. Mama would begin at the top."

Heru lay back down on his stomach and watched his hands slowly disappear inside the watermelon-sized hole at the base of The tallest Pine. Retrieved his father's ventriloquist head. He would start at the top.

He knew he would have to hurry because the "DO NOT ENTER" sign that he'd left on his bedroom door would only keep his family at bay for so long. It was approaching 3 p.m. They would eventually discover that he was gone and start to worry.

A few feet in front of the tallest tree, Heru squatted down and placed his father's head on the ground with the care his mother would have placed an infant in a crib. When he stood up, the head rolled over on its ear.

Heru raced around the clearing until he found two large pinecones. He screwed the pointy cones into the ground, just below both ears, so his father could keep his head to the sky.

Heru ran over to the largest plot. He stood over the grave looking at the size of his father's torso. He could tell he was not going to be able to lift it. He started walking around and looking for a strong stick. In the more densely wooded-area behind the Tallest Pine, he found a fallen limb as long as two baseball bats and thick as a bat's home run end.

He returned and jabbed the limb into the ground underneath the upper torso. Using the rim of the grave as a leverage point, Heru raised upright his father's trunk. He balanced this piece of a man on severed upper thighs. It looked like a soil-covered, muscular midget who'd lost his head and arms in some carnival trick gone horribly wrong. The sight made Heru's thin body shudder hard.

Still using the stick to balance the torso, Heru climbed into the grave. He grabbed the shoulder and let the stick fall. Heru stood beside his father. The top of Asar's severed neck came up to Heru's upper chest. For the first time, Heru looked down on his father. A bloody piece of meat who couldn't even stand up by himself. Heru wished he hadn't seen him like this. Wished he wasn't in this grave.

Wished he didn't have to be a big boy. The idea was much better than the reality.

Yet, he felt a guilty satisfaction towering over the man he never could measure up to. Heru leaned the piece of a man against the long side of the grave. From behind, he lodged one end of the stick between the severed thighs. While the other end angled up, resting on the opposite long side of the grave. Heru climbed out. He grabbed the end of the angled stick and pulled down hard, raising his father and flopping him graveside.

Heru walked around to the other side of the plot. Stood over his father. He squatted down and tried to pick him up, even though he knew couldn't. Grunting, he got him a couple inches off the ground, and grunting put him back down. Heru looked over to where his father's head was looking skyward with the help of pine cones.

He thought about bringing the head over to the torso and doing the rest of the work there beside the biggest grave. But he didn't think Auset would do things that way. She would start at the head, at the beginning, and work her way down, so that's what he would do too. He glanced at his father's trunk. Then back over to his father's head.

He was going to have to roll him.

Flip him over, back to front to back to front, through the dirt, until body embraced head.

Heru was disgusted by the idea. But he knew if he was going to do things like his mother, it was the only way.

He squatted down and placed his left hand under his father's shoulder and his right hand under his naked buttocks.

Flipped him.

As his front landed with a *phlatpt,* leaves, dirt, and pine needles blew out from underneath the torso on all sides. Heru flipped his father again.

Phlatpt.

And again.

Phlatpt.

Heru flipped a piece of his father across East St. Louis until he reached his head. He lined up lower severed neck with upper severed neck. Like Christ and the church, the head and body became one.

He looked up a the sun and figured it was around 3:30 p.m. They must know I'm not in my room by now, he thought.

He had to hurry. He raced across the clearing and picked up his father's right arm from its grave. Rushed back and stuck the tangle of tendon, bone and veins in the torso's shoulder socket.

Then the right hand to severed wrist. Upper arm to shoulder socket.

Lower arm to upper arm. Left hand to wrist.

Heru connected the upper leg to the upper left thigh. Lower left leg to the upper left leg.

Left foot to left leg.

Upper right leg, to the right thigh. Lower right leg to the upper right leg. Right foot.

Heru stood, resting his back against the Tallest Pine. Breathing hard. Looking down at the work of his hands.

The worst kind of jigsaw.

The kind that came from the puzzle company, but the pieces didn't quite fit right.

To Heru, his father looked like a naked Negro laid to rest inside a kaleidoscope.

Now, he had to lay him to rest in the ground. Again. At least the unfitting pieces can rest together, he thought.

That's when Heru noticed it. He had forgotten a piece. He reached inside his treasure hunter bag and carefully pulled out his father's most private part. He held it across both open palms, eye-level. As if he were about offer it up to the Jigsaw God. The uncircumcised phallus was moist and sticky. The severed end hung over the edge of his left palm. And from the severed end, with its mixture of ruptured skin, gristle and shame, hung a two-inch vein with no torso to pass blood to.

Heru brought the contents of his open palms close to his nose. The pungent musky smell reminded him of the kitchen while his mother was cooking chitterlings on New Year's Day. Heru angled his palms side ways. Looked at the two tiny holes on the black head of the penis. He couldn't figure out why there was a need for more than one hole. Heru lowered his open palms from his face down past his waist. He paused there. Looking at the thing that had helped make him. And unmake him.

He took the phallus in his petite, boney left hand. With his hand positioned in the middle, he squeezed it tight. Both ends, on either side of his fist, expanded a little: a long balloon filled with sand. Heru felt the cool, stinky flesh, giving beneath his fingers. Relaxed his grip, then squeezed it again. He paused and stared at the flesh of his flesh.

Heru slowly moved the severed end towards the crotch area of his muddy knee-pants. Until tendons touched brown cotton. Heru stared down at it. Hanging from his clothes, the penis looked like a carnival prop. Heru wanted to see how the phallus looked connected to his black skin.

With his right hand, Heru unbuttoned his trousers. Let them fall to his ankles. He looked down at his smooth white underwear. Saw the ouline of absence.

With his free hand, Heru pulled down his drawers and shimmied them down to his ankles. Gazed at the round nub on his pubis.

He was disgusted by his wrongness.

Heru placed the severed end of his father's phallus against the rounded nub of his pubis. Felt the cold, slimy vascular tissue and veins against his own skin. Saw a vision of himself as he should have been. And embraced it. Flesh of his flesh. An ugly inheritance made beautiful because it made him right.

Whole.

Capable of being loved.

Heru couldn't take his eyes off it. He imagined it attached. A union made in longing. In that way the eye can long to see something in a passing cloud. And that longed-for-thing can appear in that passing cloud. Can become what the eye wants it to become.

"I capable of being loved now."

Speaking those words aloud sent a tingling, prickly feeling through Heru's exposed body. Like stepping into a cold bath. Except the shudder was longer. An elongated vibration.

He was a black piano wire with the sustain pedal depressed.

Heru pressed the exposed vascular tissue against his pubis with more pressure. Enough to start a thin trickle of fluid down his narrow inner thigh.

The tickle of the liquid dripping down his inner thigh was just enough stimulus to make him aware of his surroundings again.

That's when he dropped his father's penis. At the sight of Uncle Set.

His uncle was staring at him from across the forest. Heru abruptly bent down and snatched up his drawers and knee pants. Keeping his eyes on Uncle Set, he buttoned quickly. Bent down again and picked up his father's penis.

Uncle Set didn't move. Just stared.

Heru's mind was jumping from one direction to the next. Uncle Set must have discovered that the map was gone when the family saw that I was gone.

How long had he been standing there? Did he see me squeezing Daddy's privates? See me looking into the tiny holes?

Or was he here even earlier?

Did he see me rolling Daddy through the dirt?

Uncle Set started walking across the thicket towards Heru.

Heru watched the ginger way his uncle stepped across the land. As if he were walking barefoot through a burr patch. As if Uncle Set had not fully recovered from yesterday when Heru saw him break like a dry twig. Break like a promise. Break like a family.

Uncle Set was dressed in white pants and a white undershirt. From a distance, he now looked like a lean polar bear learning to walk upright. Except slimmer than the ones Heru had seen in picture books.

Watching his uncle get closer and bigger made the sound in Heru's chest pound louder and faster. His emotions were switching and mixing just as fast. He was excited and relieved that his Uncle Set was up and walking. He was embarrassed and afraid that he thought his uncle could have done this terrible thing to Daddy.

But why did Uncle Set have the map? Did Uncle Set just find Daddy this way?

Maybe he buried him because he didn't want the family to have to see Daddy like this?

Heru's mind was spinning. He felt a barely controllable urge to run towards and away from his uncle. It made him tap his left foot up and down at a speed near his heart rate. Heru looked down at his foot. It was as if someone else was making it bounce. He looked back up and saw Uncle Set's polar bear-shuffle 30 yards away. Ten yards from the biggest empty grave.

Heru wondered what his uncle was thinking as he approached the grave. He was still too far away to clearly see his face. To read his one-eyed expression.

Was he mad? Coming to get me?

Wanting me to explain what happened? Does he think I did this?

Is he coming to make me explain how his twin went to pieces?

Or coming to help me bury Daddy the way he came into the world: whole?

Give me a spanking?

Heru fought the urge to cry. No matter what happened, he had decided he was going to be a big boy. He was going to make his father proud—even if it was after his father was dead.

He saw Uncle Set pause at the biggest grave. Look inside at absence. Then look up directly at his Jigsaw Twin. And continue walking. Towards him.

Was he gonna tell Grandpa and Big Grandpa what I'd done? What he'd done?

But could Uncle Set really have done this?

But who else? The map was Uncle Set's. The more questions Heru's mind asked, the more unsure his mind became.

Heru's mind raced on as Uncle Set shuffled forward. His head swiveling left and right, looking at the mounds of moist dirt, next to holes in the earth. And back to the Jigsaw Americus lying above ground.

At 15 yards, Heru could make out his uncle's facial expression: amusement. Lips pursed. Playful like those of a father catching his son playing house with a neighborhood girl. Lips pursed because they want to curl themselves into righteous anger, but got stuck half-way. Caught on reluctant admiration for the gumption. Indignation softened into amusement. On lips pale as the flesh of a grapefruit.

Heru glanced down at his hyper-active tapping foot. That's when he noticed that he still had his father's penis in his hand. He looked back up at his approaching uncle. Ten yards away.

Too late to hide it now. Too late to drop it.

Too late to think of anything to say.

There was only time for shame and frustration and fear to well up inside him. Only time to cry. And as much as he tried to stop the tears from breaking the levy, he could not. As much as he wanted to be a big boy for his father, he could not. He was just a ten-year-old frog-eyed sissy-boy who squatted when he pee-peed. An embarrassment to the Americus Family. An embarrassment to his father. Who was simply wrong. All wrong.

So Heru stood there crying snotty-tears with his father's penis in his left hand. As Uncle Set towered directly above and in front of him. Looking amused.

"What you got there?" Uncle Set said.

His hands were clasped behind his back like an inquisitive philosopher.

Heru wiped some snot off his upper lip with the back of his right hand, then looked down at his left hand. The same place Uncle Set had fixed his one-eyed stare.

Uncle Set was standing so close, and staring so hard, that he made Heru nervous enough to start squeezing his father's penis. He didn't want to but he couldn't help himself. His anxiety made him need to hold on to something, and hold on to something tight. His vise grip began a small trickle of body fluid from the severed end. He looked up into Uncle Set's wide nostrils, a forest of follicles, then back at his own hands. Squeezed harder. Watched the flesh of his flesh give way under his tiny fist. But the giving flesh could not stop the tears that no big boy should cave to. Could not stop the clogging snot that forced him to breathe through his open mouth. Could not stop the heaving motion of his bird-chest as he struggled to catch his breath. Could not stop the shame pulsing up his straining neck and across his liquid face. Could not stop his Uncle Set from staring at him, waiting for an answer they both already knew.

"Boy, you hear me talking to you. I say what you got there?"

"My daddy's privates."

"Now, why you go and do a thing like that, son?"

"I didn't do ... I was just trying ... ."

"Boy, don't stand there and lie to me, I saw you playing with it, putting it all next to your own privates like you got some kind of a sickness, like something is wrong with you."

Wrong with you made Heru drop his head. He knew it was the truth.

"That's not how Americus Men act, son. You weren't raised up to be perverted. No matter how mad you are at your daddy, it's still no reason to cut your father all up, and you know you gonna have to be punished for it."

"I didn't do it! I ... ." Heru shouted, through tears, towards the ground.

"I'm not even sure what the law says about punishing this type of behavior, it's so wrong."

Heru looked up with pleading eyes.

"They'll do something to me even though I didn't do nothing?"

"Son, ain't no telling what a bohunk will do."

"You gonna let em, Uncle Set?"

Set's eyes had curdled from amusement to disgust. The stare's weight crumpled a weeping boy to the ground. A cheap accordion fallen from an organ grinder's hand. He awkwardly sat atop his bent left leg, while his right leg was straight as his uncle's stare.

Heru let his own stare fall to the blood sausage in his left hand. It's foreskin and head and two holes and tendons and veins. In that moment, he hated everything about it like he hated everything about himself. It angered him that such a small thing could cause so many problems. Enraged, Heru squeezed his father's phallus with all his fist's strength. He wanted to hurt it. Hurt his father for having one and for not protecting him, so he could have one too.

He wanted to destroy it. Decapitate it.

Heru had barely gotten the head clenched between his molars, when he saw his uncle's upper-cutting, right palm emerge from behind Set's broad back and smash underneath his 10-year-old chin. His father's penis flew up and out of his open mouth. Soaring like a trapeze man flipping towards the sooty sky. The force of the upper-cut lifted Heru at a 45-degree-angle up into the air. For a suspended second, remains of the father and remains of the son became The Flying Americuses. A daring carnival act without a net.

Heru's back hit the ground first. Seker and Tehuti tumbled out of his treasure hunter bag beside him. He didn't see his father's penis land.

"What the hell is wrong with your sick ass, boy?" Set shouted, leaning down inches from Heru's face.

Heru felt Uncle Set's spittle spray across his forehead. His frog eyes bugged open wide to witness all the danger before him.

Heru's nervous left hand quickly swept the ground by his side, feeling for a rock to get Uncle Set's angry face away. Girly fingers brushed then squeezed Tehuti's handle. He thrust upwards with all his might. Heru watched the 3-inch steel-tip immediately disappear deep into the empty eye socket. The way a skeleton key disappears into keyhole. Uncle Set's right hand moved towards his own face then paused in mid-air. The barrel-chest and left wrist fell atop Heru. The nephew felt air rushing out his own bird-chest as he watched the Americus Sword plop from the uncle's palm.

The left one.

Heru couldn't catch his breath or move his bird-chest. Spraying blood had sprinkled both.

A Bloody Island baptism.

Heru was being blessed by dead-weight.

Only his eyes could move. From his uncle's face to his uncle's knife. A ruby-handled pirate sword that knew its away around a body.

Uncle Set's neck hung over Heru's still-heaving rib cage. Bald skull facing the ground, chin to earth. His vision hemorrhaging.

Heru wanted to both scoot from under his uncle and stay there and watch blood ooze from Uncle Set's eye socket. Watch the warm thickness pool on the ground before being absorbed into the earth. He wanted to watch the work of his hands. The hands that had defended his own life. Saved his own life. The hands that had killed the killer of his father. That had crafted a make-up gift to the daddy who deserved a son who wasn't wrong.

Hands that had proven Heru could do right. Could be right.

Hands that had proven that Heru Americus was capable of love. He let himself cry.

Cry open and hard until his bird-chest shook Uncle Set atop him. Heru closed his own trembling eyes.

"I'm proud of you, son."

81

Heru slid from underneath Uncle Set and stood up. He looked down at the back of Uncle Set's bald skull. He slowly turned in a circle looking at the empty graves. He stopped on his Jigsaw Father. Heru took a deep breath, then another. He wanted to make himself stop crying. There was still work to do.

Heru wiped his snotty nose on the back of his left hand. With that same hand, he reached down and picked up his father's phallus. With his right hand, he picked up Tehuti. Heru walked over to Asar's puzzle body, kneeled down and attached the final piece.

He came to his feet. His tears had stopped flowing. Heru looked down at his father. Gazed upon the flesh of his flesh. For minutes and minutes. Until he began to feel his emotions welling again. Once the tears began to fall, Heru bent down directly over his father's face, so they could share the same tears. Heru knew Asar needed to cry too. His well empty and full, Heru began to dig a new well, a new home for his father. When the grave was finished, Heru placed Tehuti aside, and began to reassemble Asar in the tomb. Starting at the beginning, with the head first.

Once his father was whole again, Heru climbed out of the grave. He was exhausted. He grabbed a palm of soil from the mound next to the gave. He extended his arm and hand above the hole in the earth. Spread his fingers and watched earth fall to earth. This is how Heru covered Asar. This is how Heru completed his father's journey.

By hand. The left one.

It was almost nightfull when Heru finished. He put Seker, Tehuti and the map into his treasure hunter bag and slung it over his shoulder. He squeezed the Americus Sword handle in his left hand as he looked over at Uncle Set.

Heru walked across the clearing until the trees became dense again. He stopped in front of the Totem of Remembrance.

Dr. Mandrake's name was inscribed vertically down the tree- length pole and painted in white letters—but the bottom three feet were untouched. Using the Americus Sword, Heru kneeled down and carved a three-inch high "A". Then an "S" next to it. An "A".

He carved his father's name, horizontally, around the of Remembrance—until the "A" of "ASAR" touched the "S" of AMERICUS."

The circle complete.

Heru wanted to remember his father complete. Whole.

Right beneath his Father's name, Heru carved an "H". Then next to it an "E". An "R". Using the Americus Sword, Heru carved his own name, horizontally, around the Totem of Remembrance—until the "H" of "HERU" touched the "S" of AMERICUS."

The circle complete.

Heru wanted to document his role in this place. In this family.

He wanted to remember.

And be remembered.

He had done what could not be done.

Heru stood up. Turned his body in a slow circle. Night had fallen but he was not afraid. Heru let the Americus Sword fall from hand to earth.

"I'm proud of me."

ACKNOWLEDGMENTS

Dedicated to Author & Professor Eugene B. Redmond,
Poet Laureate of East St. Louis, Illinois

This novel is made possible through the One Spirit and the invaluable support of many individuals. I am deeply grateful. My daughters Eyerusalem Coleman-Kitch and Harlem Auset Anita Coleman-Datcher for reminding me life is to be lived. My mother Gladys Steen for her love and courage. My sister Alex Datcher for inspiring me to follow my dreams. My brother Elgin Datcher for showing me how to win. My cousin William Belcher for being a fellow dreamer and my favorite road-dog. My stepfather Norman Avery for passing down a love of history and for being a father to the fatherless. Dr. Haki Madhubuti for his belief in black folk and our literature. Dr. Pauline A. Bigby for her encouragement. Maxine Bigby Cunningham for her creative support. Author Jenoyne Adams for her insightful agenting and editing work. Kamau Daáood and The World Stage Anansi Writer's Workshop for developing my craft. Jazz Lions Dwight Trible and Bobby West for exhibiting and demanding artistic excellence. Poet A.K. Toney for his genius soul. Quincy Troupe for literary-leading by example. publisher Dr. William Banks Sutton for originally believing in *AMERICUS*. Agent James Levine for his early support of my work, including this book. Jordan Elgrably of the Levantine Cultural Center, The Staff of The Truth About The Fact, and the Beautiful Struggle Collective for doing the ground-level work of promoting intercultural dialogue. A special nod goes to writer and activist Carmen Bordas for leading by example and loving me well.

I am thankful for the people who read, commented and/or assisted on one of the novel's 19 drafts, including Drs. P. Gabrielle Foreman, David Killoran, Vorris L. Nunley, and Rob Latham, and authors Eugene B. Redmond, Dolen Perkins-Valdez and Eric Jerome Dickey. This book was made more beautiful because of Francisco Letelier's powerful cover art and Denise Billups' elegant layout design. Thank you both. Among numerous research sources the following were essential: *Metu Neter, Vols. 1—3* by Ra Un Nefer Amen, *The Gods of the Egyptians* by E.A. Wallis

Budge, *Never Been A Time: The 1917 Race Riot that Sparked the Civil Rights Movement* by Harper Barnes, *The Official Patient's Sourcebook on Vitiligo* by Drs. James N. Parker and Phillip M. Parker, *Made in the USA: East St. Louis* by Andrew J. Theising (thanks for the map), *Race Riot at East St. Louis: July 2, 1917* by Elliott M. Rudwick, *All the World is Here!: The Black Presence at White City* by Christopher Robert Reed.

Lastly, I would like to thank East St. Louis home-boy Miles Davis for his album *Kind of Blue*, which served as my looped-writing music for each of *AMERICUS'* 19 drafts.